THE FEEDING

In the stillness the girl could feel his hot tongue licking the sweat from her breasts. Each time he drew blood, she shuddered.

"Again," she breathed. His hard face came again to her throat, which was aglow with sweat. His breath was hot, and when she reached out and took hold of him he began to tremble.

Teeth bit, drew blood, then a hot licking tongue smeared it across her neck. She sank back onto the bed and closed her eyes. Dimly, she felt his tongue again, one last time, traveling down the length of her body.

Then she fell away from the world, into a deep sleep filled with the odd sensation of being submerged in water.

She would drown there.

A TOM DOHERTY ASSOCIATES BOOK

This is a work of fiction. All the characters and events portrayed in this book are fictional, and any resemblance to real people or incidents is purely coincidental.

THE HOUSE OF CAINE

First edition: April 1988

A TOR Book

Published by Tom Doherty Associates, Inc.
49 West 24th Street
New York, NY 10010

ISBN: 0-812-51773-3
Can No.: 0-812-51774-1

Printed in the United States of America

0 9 8 7 6 5 4 3 2 1

FOR KEN BLUME
—King of the Road

But first on earth, as Vampyre sent,
Thy corpse shall from its tomb be rent;
Then ghastly haunt thy native place,
And suck the blood of all thy race.

—Lord Byron, *The Giaour*

The devil is a tricky bastard. I should know, he brought my rotting remains back from the grave as proof.

—Anonymous

CONTENTS

Prologue

People would say later that a good case could be made for the proposition that 1966 was the year the world began to go mad. It was the year the United States mislaid a hydrogen bomb; the Chinese cut off one another's pigtails in a parody of *1984*; the Russians banned *Hello, Dolly!* and the Arabs banned Coca-Cola. In the United States it was the year young civil rights activists demanded "Black power," and the year young theologians exclaimed, "God is dead."

—Charles Kuralt

Rachel Knolls thought: He bit me. *The son of a bitch actually bit me*!

She was a tall girl—personally she thought of herself as lanky—and when she moved, it was with gawky, long strides that seemed to her a God-given curse. Tonight, however, she was glad for her long legs. The longer the better.

Unnerved, she moved between the broken slats of the fence and started to make her way through the cemetery. She knew the shortcut, all the people of Millhouse did. Anxiety kept drawing her gaze over her shoulder, because one of the men, the thinner of the two, had come after her.

"Serves you right," she muttered as she stumbled through the dark. "Next time you'll know better than to go messing around with strangers."

Abruptly she stepped to her right, thanking God for the moonlight as she spotted an open grave ahead. She had nearly plunged in. She moved carefully around the grave and started running again, a fast-paced walk, actually, through the low-cut grass, past the large elms, white pine, and birch.

The gloom intensified. The moon disappeared suddenly behind dark clouds.

She slowed. It was terribly hard to see. A new density of trees sprang up around her. Was the man still following her? she wondered. She paused to listen. She could hear or see nothing. Where the caretaker's house ought to have been was merely a dense gloom. If only she could see a lighted window, or even a passing car. *Anything* to run toward for help.

She took a deep breath and for the hundredth time cursed herself for offering them a lift, for playing the fool. But when he had approached her at the bar and said his car had broken down, could she give him and his friend a lift, and those eyes of his had flashed, she had felt the excitement, the adventure in the moment, and hadn't been able to resist.

Until now her infrequent flirtations had always proven to be exhilarating experiences—picking up a man gave her life a sense of excitement missing since her college days. Not only excitement, they were a relief from her tediously long engagement; he the procrastinator, not she.

"I'll drive," the thinner one had said. And she hadn't worried.

"He'll be our chauffeur," the other said, smiling, guiding her into the backseat of her car.

A few minutes later the car stopped alongside a deserted road and the driver got out. She glanced around. They had stopped by the cemetery. Suddenly she was afraid. She screamed at them, telling them they'd better leave her alone, knowing they would not.

"Let me out of the car!" she yelled, feeling his hand on her thigh, an experienced hand with long, well-manicured fingernails that teased her flesh. She shuddered. She knew then that they meant to play with her, like a toy.

The thinner one shoved a tree branch through the opened window, probed with it between her breasts. "Let me spank her first," he said. "Let me beat her."

"No," the other said. Then he fanged his teeth and went for her neck.

From that point on it was pure reflex. She didn't know from which man the sounds were coming, those uncanny sounds that separated themselves from all other night sounds, the laughter, the chuffing yelps of frenzied excitement. Not that she had the leisure for contemplation. His teeth sank into her neck. Together they fell back against the door. And then she was throwing him off, getting out of the car as both men leaped at her, getting in each other's way, snarling at each other for their inefficiency. In the next instant she was off, running.

Now everything grew quiet. Her eyes darted ahead of her, looking for someplace to run, to hide. She saw something move to her right. A shadowy figure, fleeting through the trees. Oh, Christ, he's gotten ahead of me. The car, she told herself. Go back to the car. She turned, started to make her way back through the trees, her breath coming short and hard. She stopped suddenly when she saw the figure of a man silhouetted in front of her. *Oh, God, please don't let them hurt me*, she thought, oh please don't.

A wet and slimy fear took hold of her as she spun in a new direction, started to run, not knowing what lay ahead, only knowing she had to run. Soon someone was running beside her. A woman, moving fast. A woman? Was it possible . . . they were on all sides now, closing in, the woman the closest, her face drawn tight in a grotesque grimace of hunger.

Still the girl ran, past the dark trees into the underbrush. The foliage was thick, matted, overgrown with tangled thorns and spiked berry bushes that tore at her cotton dress and snagged her hair. She burst into the open, saw a light; hope flared brightly, briefly. An instant later the woman leapt into the air, and brought the girl first to her knees, then to her stomach. The girl tried kicking at her, tried to fling her off, but the woman had already sunk her teeth into her throat. The others began howling like dogs, their maddening red eyes ablaze in the dark.

In blind panic, the girl rose, slammed her elbow into the woman's rib cage. The woman went down, her face full of frustration and rage.

Never stay in the open, the girl's brother had once told her. She took off running again, heading for the trees. All too soon she heard them galloping behind her; whining filled the air. She'd never heard people wail that way before. She began to cry, still running with a speed that surprised her.

Laughter now, faces grinning. Their sounds grew louder. Closer. The car was very near, she thought. Somewhere just beyond the fence.

She felt a stab of pain in her chest as she lunged forward, then a stinging sensation as a tree branch was smacked across her buttocks. Then across her back. She could see her car just ahead; they had left the door open.

Once more hope filled her. Once more it died as the woman's face appeared out of the gloom.

The girl went down inches from the fence. She reached out, grasping for safety. A pair of cold hands took hold of her ankles and began dragging her back into the underbrush.

"Oh, God, noooo," she moaned. "No," she pleaded, her arms stretched out before her, fingers digging into the ground. A car appeared suddenly at the top of a hill, its headlights fracturing the darkness. The girl yanked herself forward, screamed. But the car, sleek and orange, went whizzing by, its tires smacking asphalt, its radio blaring.

Then they dragged her back into the woods, where hot licking tongues, long fingernails, and fanged teeth had at her, even as she curled herself into a helpless ball, transformed herself into a stillborn fetus being devoured by animals. Maybe she heard human voices, maybe dogs yelping, she wasn't sure. She closed her eyes, succumbed to the awaiting darkness.

She lay there, her blood flowing.

Draining away.

Until she lost consciousness.

Of the three, the woman was the hungriest. After drinking more than her fair share, she reluctantly let the others have what was left.

Before leaving the woods, they ditched the girl's body and searched the car. Except for an automobile club packet, registration, and a bottle of CB Fuel Saver, the glove compartment was empty. As the two men checked the trunk of the car, the woman continued to search the interior. In the backseat were an evening gown wrapped in plastic, a pair of high heels, and a cosmetics bag.

The woman took a small mirror from the bag and glanced at her image. Hissing, she flung the mirror aside. Then she took out a bottle of perfume and applied a dab to her neck. The heavy, lush scent caused her to swoon. She rolled her head back and closed her eyes. Then she spread her legs, slid her hand under her dress, and pressed it to her vulva.

She remained still for a long time, imagining.

Later, on the way back to the house, a different sort of hunger rose up in her. But she would have to satisfy herself with the heady scent of perfume, the taste of blood still fresh in her mouth, and memories.

Perhaps, in the future, things might be different.

Perhaps.

The thought sent her rushing and reeling into the night. The others were too exhausted to keep up with her.

PART ONE

BEFORE THE BEGINNING

Do you imagine that we see the
hundred thousandth part of what
exists? Consider, for example,
the wind. The wind whistles, groans,
bellows, sometimes it even kills.
Have you seen it?

—Guy de Maupassant, *The Horla*

1

ROB MARTIN

Fairground, church, water tower, and graveyard, it was all still there, written across the mercilessly hot face of the Connecticut landscape. Add to this the five o'clock express train to New York ripping through the junction and a factory whistle blowing and you have Millhouse, Connecticut. Not the greatest place in the world. Rob Martin knew that. Still, for him it was unfinished business. A place where parts of him were buried. The parts that counted.

He was two days into a grueling drive up from Miami when the fairground caught his eye. He didn't stop. At least not at first. The church and water tower came next, then the graveyard. Just past the last tombstone he made a quick

U-turn and pulled the vintage Jaguar, an old X150, to the side of the road and shut off the engine. His friend, Larry, was seated beside him drinking beer.

It was quiet except for the radio. Rob leaned over and switched stations, from Donovan Leitch to the Mamas and the Papas to the news, where he stopped.

"5,500 National Guardsmen were sent into the area. Twelve persons injured, 122 persons were arrested."

They were still covering the race riot that had erupted in Omaha, Nebraska, over the Fourth of July weekend. Rob clicked off the radio and mumbled, "Damned if we haven't got another Vietnam right here in the States."

"Look at them!" Larry Campbell cried out suddenly. "Holy shit! They're all over the place. What are those damned things, anyway?"

"What things?" Rob asked. Larry's eyes were bulging as he peered out over the hood of the car; he had smacked one hand against his forehead, and his back could have been used for a ski slope as he leaned forward.

"Fucking bats, that's what they are!" Larry stared straight ahead in dumb amazement.

"What are you—"

"Look at them—they're smiling. Smiling bats!"

Suddenly Rob understood. "Oh, hell," he said. "I warned you about that crap, didn't I? Bats, for God's sake."

"Can't you see them?" Larry was almost

screaming. "They're swarming all over the friggin' place."

"No, Larry, I can't see them." Rob dropped his sunglasses on the dash and pushed open the car door.

Because they had been in a hurry to leave Florida, because the editors hadn't given them much notice, Larry Campbell had rushed about in a frenzy, picking up everything he could lay his hands on in the way of drugs. Not that he would use it all, but he was hooked on the high of collecting the stuff. The glove compartment of the car looked like a miniature narcotics lab. Six bags of grass, twenty pellets of mescaline, an aspirin tin full of cocaine, bottles of uppers, downers, laughers, criers, some LSD, and three sheets of high-powered blotter acid. In the trunk of the car was a cooler full of beer, two quarts of Jim Beam, and a 16-gauge shotgun.

It was the 16-gauge that worried Rob the most. There wasn't anyone more unpredictable than Larry Campbell once he took that one toke over the line. That had happened in North Carolina at a place called South of the Border, and Rob felt apprehensive now about having Larry along with him. In fact he felt jittery—even *scared*.

"Hey, why the hell is it so quiet?" Larry stretched his long vulturine neck, and peered out over the car door. "Hey, we've stopped. Why'd we stop?"

Rob pointed. "The town's just the other side of those trees."

"No kidding? We in Connecticut?"

"Yeah."

"What happened to North Carolina?"

Rob laughed nervously. "That was yesterday. Today we're in Connecticut."

"Now that's the way to travel," Larry said and slouched deeper into tufted black leather. Large oily gobs of sweat covered his forehead, hung from his drooping mustache. He didn't notice. Beer had spilled on his denim shirt and Levi's. He didn't notice that, either.

Rob leaned against the car, trying to collect his thoughts. It was still hard for him to believe that Larry Campbell had just turned twenty-four and was writing a twice-a-week column for the *Miami Herald.* He was probably the youngest person in the country to be writing a regular column for a major newspaper. He had been doing it for a year, and already it bored the crap out of him. "I want adventure!" he'd scream between pounding his typewriter and pacing his small office on the third floor of the *Miami Herald* building. "Adventure!"

So naturally, when he'd heard that Rob had landed an interview with Robert Kennedy, he went ape shit.

He pleaded with Rob, cajoled, he'd do anything, even help Rob write the piece. No credit, he just wanted to meet the man. He'd even pay the expenses, *all* the expenses! On and on he went until finally Rob agreed.

Rob was scheduled to interview Kennedy at his summer home in Cape Cod on the eleventh.

He had planned to fly into Boston on Saturday and meet with Kennedy on Monday, but Larry had insisted they drive.

"He'll love the Jag! He's crazy about women and cars. Any asshole can fly, Rob. Think of it. You and me talking to *Bobby Kennedy*! In *my* Jag!"

Rob turned away now and stared off at the tree line. Heavy oak and chestnuts loomed like sentinels against a thin blue sac, and under the lush spread of green leaves, graves. Only a few headstones were visible from where Rob stood.

"I'll be right back," he said, moving away from the car.

"Where you going?" Larry asked without looking at him. The heavy aroma of beer hung in the air.

"To take a pee," Rob said.

"Over there?" Larry sat up abruptly and peered off in the distance. "Over there!" he cried.

Rob took another step away from the car. "Sure, why not?"

"Why not? It's a fucking cemetery, that's why not."

"Do you think they'll mind?" Rob asked and kept walking. At the edge of the shoulder, where the gravel quit and the weeds took over, a narrow path had been worn into existence by the years of trampling feet. It wound down the embankment, curved around a dilapidated fence, then disappeared from view through the thickest clump of trees.

"I thought you were in a hurry to get home to Millhouse?" Larry hollered.

Rob did not answer him aloud, although in his mind he replied: *I am home, buddy boy. I am home.*

"Hey, Rob!" came the voice over his shoulder. "Watch out for those fucking bats!"

Rob pushed on for a while, following the path that widened in some places, and in other places almost disappeared altogether. At the second row of trees the path split in two; he went to the right and made his way deeper into the wooded area. The sun disappeared suddenly and the hush thickened as he made the final turn. Off in the distance he could still hear the low hum of an occasional car whizzing by, and as he walked he heard Larry singing:

"Oh, my, my, ain't I nobody's baby?
Oh, my, my, I ain't nobody's baby."

But now Larry had apparently given up making noise, because it was quiet, exceedingly quiet. Perhaps he's fallen asleep, Rob thought. Or perhaps he's passed out. Whatever the case, there was no longer any sound coming from the car.

Rob turned aside from the path and climbed the high bank. The light grew thinner and the trees thickened into a fat stretch of timberland. It was a steep climb, and he paused to catch his breath at the top. Here no sun shone at all; an intangible pall reigned over the face of things. Rob knew this to be the heart of the cemetery.

For years it had been this way, graves placed around the outer perimeter, leaving the center thick with trees. A secret playground, where kids went at night to fool around. Rob himself had gone there as a boy. The Miller kid had insisted they do battle, so off to Crestwood Lawn they went, and Rob kicked the living hell out of him right next to Mary Bennett's grave.

Rob squinted into the gloom. *Mary Louise Bennett, that you? Sure that's you. And*—he shifted his gaze left—*and that's you too, isn't it, my grotesque friend. All these years and you're still hanging around.*

He moved in the direction of his gaze until he stood in front of an old tree stump, its heart rotted out, a hole dead center, twice the length of his arm. At the bottom, he was sure, was a murky pool of rain water—and years of leaves turned to slime.

But don't put your hand down there, Rob, because . . .

He stared at the hole in the stump, tempted to do just that. After all these years, he was ready to see what was down there, instead of letting Elizabeth and Tony scare the crap out of him like they had when they were kids.

"There's a monster down there, Rob!" Tony would say. "No kidding."

Elizabeth added, "I saw him once, Rob. Honest to God, I did."

From the beginning it had been Elizabeth's

idea to fool around in the cemetery, despite Rob's reluctance. He had told her the usual weird stories about what goes on at night in cemeteries, but he had always seen by her face that it made not the slightest difference. The cemetery seemed to excite her, though not the danger, for she had never accepted that there was any. She was like a woman possessed.

Rob guessed that for her it was a chance to do something that one ought not to do, something forbidden, like stealing apples from Lady Johnson's tree. In a sense, it was an act of defiance, the boys against the girls sort of stuff, and why Rob went along with it through most of his teen years was still a mystery.

He hesitated now, caught by a great urge to confront that stump once and for all. He took a step forward and then stopped, flinging a look back along the path he had come.

The highway lay off in the distance, almost hidden by the trees. He could make out the hood of the Jag as it sat glimmering outside the cemetery, steel-gray and elegant. North and south, as far as his eyes could see, were empty woods, except for the dark outline of an old farmhouse to the south, and a fence that curved and twisted away to the north before it vanished behind another clump of trees. The fence ran along Old Post Road, which led farther north to Millhouse, then on to Peabody, Ramsey, and Clarksville, until finally it crossed over the state line into Massachusetts.

Tony and Rob used to make beer runs on

that road in Tony's old Chevy. Go across to New Castle in Massachusetts where nobody knew them. Sometimes Tony'd let Rob drive the car, despite the fact that Rob was fifteen at the time, and a lousy driver.

Look, Tony—no hands! he'd hoop and holler.

Hey, retard—watch what the hell you're doing.

We should have brought Elizabeth along. She'd have loved this. Zoom, zoom!

Hey, watch it, slow down—there's a cop up ahead!

Rob had been car crazy since his eighth year. He'd sit behind the wheel of his father's green Plymouth and pretend he was driving it. A few times he even thought about starting the thing up. Once he did, and wound up plowing down the fence in the front yard. His father just stood there shaking his head and saying to his mother: "The boy won't live to be twenty."

Maybe, Rob thought, his father was right. Maybe he had died back there before he was twenty. Maybe he'd wake up on his soon-to-be thirtieth birthday and find that he was still sitting in his father's Plymouth. A kid. Just a kid with sandy-colored hair and blue eyes whose father took him hunting on weekends. The memory rose in his mind with startling vividness—creeks, sunlight, rabbits scurrying through the underbrush, crisp cold air, the sky ice-blue, like the walls of his parents' bedroom.

Rob shook his head. Strange what a person

could take for logical and natural, if the poison was administered in subtle enough doses, over a long period of time. He hated guns now, as much as he hated the taking of drugs. His irrational fear of both annoyed him somewhat, but all too often he'd heard of men too moody to be trusted with a bag of grass or a rifle in the house, and perhaps he knew himself to be such a man at times, moody and dark-spirited.

He laughed. *Hey, you're a nice guy, you know that. Think about your sweet side*!

Sure, okay—I dig. In the meantime, Larry is waiting.

He turned again, lost for a moment. Far away, drifting on the dull air, he could hear the familiar church bells. The Protestants of Millhouse always gathered on Thursday evenings for a special prayer meeting. He knew where he was all right, and things hadn't changed.

He faced the stump, spit speculatively. The oddness of his coming back to Millhouse after all these years was beginning to bother him. He had a feeling that perhaps it wasn't such a hot idea.

He threw a glance at the waist-high stump, waited a minute longer, then stepped closer and looked down, into its murky depths.

Fuck it, he thought. You came back to find yourself, didn't you? Isn't that why you're here? To put the pieces together, to settle an old question?

Go ahead, then.

Start by getting rid of some of those childish fears . . .

He plunged his arm into the cavity of the stump.

"You see, nothing's . . ." he began to say to himself. But a stablike realization stopped the words in his throat, just as if someone had hissed in his ear: "Wrong, idiot!"

Something was down there, he realized, feeling the slimy warmth of water swirl around his arm. Something soft. He tried jerking his hand out but it was caught, something had wrapped around it, and as he pulled he felt . . . what?

A spongelike ball with . . . hair? His hand was wrapped in hair! He pulled harder, heard a sucking sound, like a washing machine gone crazy. The murky water surged and stank. Jesus! That smell!

Panicked, he shoved his other hand in, grabbed his own wrist, and pulled. Something was jamming his arm against the inside of the stump. Scared shitless, with all his strength, he yanked his hand up and out; a face came with it. A woman's face, eyes bulging, flesh turned green —her head appeared, then part of her body, and then she started to sink.

Stumbling back Rob screamed. A wild, demented scream that caught in his throat. Then he took off, running, away from the stump, away from the car. Crazed, bug-eyed, his body dripping sweat, he ran deeper, much deeper, into the woods.

2

Clarksville *Gazette*, July 5, 1966 (Page 3)

THE GHOULISH VANDALS
Cops mount guard against
grave robbers

Clarksville, CT—Police will keep a round-the-clock vigil at St. Agnes's Cemetery because of the desecration that took place there during the July Fourth weekend.

"We're giving it extra special attention," said Capt. Walsh. "We'll have a patrol around there at all times from now on."

Reese Long, St. Agnes's caretaker, told

police that six coffins had been emptied during the weekend. Bones from four of the bodies were found scattered around a mausoleum and two underground vaults. The remains of two recently interred bodies have yet to be located.

"Whoever did it went through a lot of effort to get into the coffins," Capt. Walsh said. However, he stated that no jewelry or other valuables were taken, so theft as a motive has been ruled out.

Cemetery officials noted that a similar desecration of St. Agnes's took place ten years ago to the day. All names are being withheld until families are notified.

3

ELIZABETH ARBOR

The night after the newspaper article, Elizabeth Arbor had a dream. Not feeling well, she had gone to bed early. For a time she lay in bed, listening to her mother and father chat on the front porch. It was a quiet night, still. A few stars flickered off in the distance; the moon hung up in the sky like a bent spoon.

There was an expectancy in her as she looked from her window out into the night. She could feel it, feel something tangible moving toward her; feel also the heat . . . the heavy dead air that enticed her to sleep in nothing more than a pair of panties.

Her breasts felt swollen and heavier than

usual, so she turned over to lie on her stomach. Droplets of sweat rolled from her temple and she wiped them away. The sound of a fly buzzing about in the room drew her attention. Or was it a mosquito?

She raised herself on her elbows and peered at the ceiling. The sound came closer, then moved away, toward the window. Clouds had begun smudging the moon, causing shifting shadows, first light, then dark. Now the familiar sound of the front door as it opened and closed, and the sound of her father throwing the two safety bolts into place came echoing up the staircase.

A few minutes later: "Are you still awake, Elizabeth?" her father asked through the closed door.

"Yes, Dad," she said to the man who had once, a long time ago, carried her up those echoing stairs and lovingly put her to bed. He was tall and still strikingly handsome and always wore work overalls. His dark-brown eyes still made secret signals that only she could understand.

"Good night then," he said.

"Good night."

"Good night, Elizabeth," came another voice, the voice of a woman who stopped saying much of anything as long ago as her husband had stopped carrying his little girl up the stairs.

"Good night, Mother."

Elizabeth listened as the door at the far end

of the hallway closed. She could hear their voices raised in conversation for some time, until finally the house was still. As still as the girl with soft red hair and pale-blue eyes, and pale, pale skin beneath freckles who lay atop the sheets, sweating.

Not the same girl as the little girl who'd talked nonstop about New York City and about someday being a model and how she'd even like to be an actress maybe. And played practical jokes on people because she always liked to see the surprised look in their eyes. And appeared in the kitchen one night dressed only in a big red cardboard heart she had made, saying: "I'm a valentine, love me."

No, something had gone out of Elizabeth Arbor over the years. It was hard for anyone, including herself, to say just why.

Tonight, however, her lack of enthusiasm for living was not bothering her, although it did nettle some. No, it was that damn fly. That damn buzzing sound that she could hear again just above her head.

She flung her hand out to swat it away.

The sound continued, but in a different way. It seemed to be coming from outside her window, as if the fly had somehow gotten outside and could not get back in again, because the sound grew more furious, mixing with tiny taps against the windowpane . . .

TAP-buzz-buzz-TAP-TAP-TAP.

She rolled over on her side. Sweat began

forming on her eyelids and between her breasts as she stared off into the darkness. In her mind she could see the black woods behind her house, the darkened houses the other side of it, now and then a lighted window, especially at old Doc Tanner's house, where lights blazed all night, a patrol car moving slowly up Main Street. All else was still. Millhouse had shut down for the night, leaving in the wake of activity a solitude as still and deep as a grave.

Millhouse, Elizabeth thought vaguely, known throughout the country as the proud home of Caine Furniture. Known also as a town of scenic charm, or so they say. She could see perfectly the sign that hung from its gold chains on Fairmont Avenue as you entered the town.

MILLHOUSE
VILLAGE INCORPORATED 1874
WELCOME

Elizabeth knew the "welcome" was in smaller letters than the words preceding it because, if truth be known, the people of Millhouse really didn't take too well to outsiders. Tourists, maybe. But the people in Millhouse enjoyed their solitude, though what was so God-all special about boredom was beyond her.

Perhaps that's why Rob got out, Elizabeth old girl. Did you ever think of that?

Sure, I thought of that. But Tony's still here,

isn't he? And all the others. What about them?

Who?

Them! Them!

God, how she hated these nights. Hated the endless wait for sleep to overtake her, the disconnected thoughts that would run rampant through her mind, the thought that tomorrow was Thursday, and that Tony would most likely stop by the shop and ask her out for Saturday night. The last time she had pleaded illness. The time before that the excuse had been: "Mother's having guests over. I'll have to help her with dinner."

It was unfair of her, she knew. Unfair and selfish and . . .

TAP, TAP, buzz, TAP, buzz.

Will you go away! she screamed inwardly. Please, God—make the damn thing just go away!

She turned angrily on the bed, reached for a second pillow, tried to find a position that would allow sleep. Images came instead. Images she hadn't seen in years.

She saw Tony and Rob Martin standing together by the ambulance and heard someone in the shop say that Rob's mother had just died.

So she had joined them, half meeting, half avoiding Rob's watery blue eyes, and watched as he sagged against Tony, while off to the side Frank Martin, Rob's father, kept saying over and over, God, why? Oh, why, why, why, why? The stretcher bearing Celia Martin was wheeled from the house. The sheet covering the body was lifted and tossed to one side by the wind that cut across Elm Street. People gawked at the partially exposed corpse. By noon, it was all over, Elm Street had returned to normal except for—

Rob, standing alone, crying.

Elizabeth turned again, hugged the pillow, tried to force sleep. Suddenly she felt profoundly tired. Felt the years toppling in on her, pinning her to the bed. She turned toward the window, slowly, every movement requiring great effort. Somehow she had been compelled to turn, to gaze out of the window.

And focus.

Focus hard on what was about to come her way.

As if from a long way off, she saw an unfamiliar deserted road. Above was a turbulent gray sky, with dark clouds. A small black figure suddenly appeared at the top of the road, and began moving downhill. Only a shadowy figure, though. Not the recognizable featured substance of a man.

Elizabeth watched as the figure grew larger, as a second layer of blackness formed around it, a billowing blackness that made no sense. The shape moved, faster, rushing toward her, suddenly in focus. It was a man dressed entirely in black, his coat blowing wildly about him to form the wider blackness.

She heard the wind now, almost felt it as it became a whirlwind of sound that blended with the buzzing of the fly. The wind whipped and tore at the man's clothing, and still he kept his head thrust forward, in a kind of insatiable, even predatory contempt for the elements. He walked on, coming closer, faster.

His face appeared. Deep-set eyes, a wide sensual mouth tightened into denial, skin stretched tight and pale. So pale—those eyes—those—

He stopped, looked in at Elizabeth's window.

Now, through his eyes, she could see herself lying atop the bed, the sweat covering her partially naked body, her legs open and waiting.

He tapped once on the windowpane. And Elizabeth Arbor, feeling a sudden gush of warmth, let him come in.

Let him come in . . .

Oh, yes, Elizabeth Arbor . . .

. . . let him come in.

4

TONY RIZZO

There were two lawyers doing business in Millhouse, and as far as Tony Rizzo was concerned, that was one lawyer too many. Especially when Jamerson & Sons (the sons were still in law school) was getting most of the business. In other words, Duke Jamerson was the more prominent of the two.

But on July 7, Tony thought that maybe, just maybe, the tide was about to turn.

He sat back and for a minute stared at the man who towered over his desk. The man was sweating heavily through his lightweight summer suit and a drop of his perspiration plunked down on Tony's new satin-smooth blotter.

Tony noted it, saying: "I'm sorry. It's hot in here, I know. My air conditioner quit me yesterday."

The man turned his head, seeming to speak under his breath. After patting his cheeks dry with his handkerchief, he said, "I really would like to get this arrangement cleared up and be on my way."

"I understand," Tony said and flashed a warm, businesslike smile. "Just give me a minute to get this straight."

He reached for the stack of legal documents that the man had laid rather ceremoniously on his desk not half an hour earlier. Ignoring the man's heavy sigh of impatience, Tony began to read carefully.

It was all quite simple, really.

Julia Caine, the last of the Caine bloodline who had controlled Caine Furniture Enterprises for the past ten years, and who had died on the morning of July 5, had been specific about her own funeral arrangements. She was to be buried at Crestwood Lawn Cemetery outside the city limits of Millhouse, CT. There was to be no stone to mark her grave.

Nor was there to be any funeral service. Other than the three men she had hired to bury her, no one was to be allowed at the grave site. A judge rather than a priest had been asked to deliver the last minutes of rite and prayer, which were to be given at the front gate to the cemetery. Friends who wished to show their respects were to send an empty limousine in their place.

Her last request, perhaps the oddest of all—at least to Tony's mind—was that under no circumstances was she to be buried on a Saturday or Sunday, and that the burial was to take place at sunset. Not before, not after.

Tony had just begun to read the second document when the man said, "Will you accept the position?"

"You want me to administer her estate."

The man looked suddenly angry. "Not at all. The Caine estate will be handled by a Mr. Dragffy in Boston. It will be your job to take care of whatever legal matters arise here in Millhouse, as per his instructions."

Saying this, the man finally sat and folded his thin bony hands over the edge of his attaché case, and pursed his mouth. At that moment he bore an astonishing resemblance to an undertaker, his gaunt face nodding in communion with himself, his lanky body hunched in thought. When Tony did not speak, he filled in the gap by brushing aside a lock of his pitch-black hair, the action emphasizing his pale receding forehead.

Tony said, "This Mr., ah—"

"Dragffy. Thomas Walker Dragffy."

"Yes, well . . . is Mr. Dragffy a lawyer?"

"More or less. He is retired now."

"Then he's not legally practicing at this time?"

Subtley yet unmistakably, the man studied Tony in amusement. "Does that present a problem for you?"

Tony shrugged. "No, not at all. It's just that there is the factory to think of. The clinic, the house—I mean practically the whole town."

"All that will be taken care of by Mr. Dragffy, under your watchful eye, of course. Mr. Striker will continue as plant supervisor and run the factory. The house is to remain closed for the time being. Mr. Thomas, your local veterinarian, has agreed to look after the upkeep and health of the dogs."

Tony looked up from the papers strewn across his desk. "Dogs?" he asked.

The man nodded glumly. "Yes. Julia Caine's dogs are to be left on the premises."

Oh, those dogs, Tony thought to himself. Those three vicious-looking Dobermans she was so fond of calling her pets. Others in Millhouse were much more fond of calling them all sorts of other names, "killers" being the most popular among the young folks, "demons" and "pains in the asses" the two favorites of the older generation.

"Oh, those dogs," Tony said with a dumb grin.

The man moved ahead quickly. "As the groundskeeper has been let go, the dogs, at least until the disposition of the Caine belongings, will be necessary. So you see, Mr. Rizzo, everything has been arranged, all matters of importance covered."

"Yes, I understand," Tony said, but he really didn't. What exactly was he being asked to do.

Spy? If Mr. Dragffy was handling it all from Boston, and the factory, house, and all other matters had been taken care of, what was left for him to do?

"Then you accept?" the man asked.

Tony hesitated. "The funeral takes place—"

"Tomorrow at sunset," the man filled in smoothly. "The sheriff has already been apprised of the arrangements, the judge selected. Friends have been notified of her wishes."

"Well," Tony said almost in spite of himself, "what's left for me to do?"

The man took a long time before answering, as if to weigh his words carefully.

"You are to coordinate," he said at last. "If you accept, you will be a coordinator for the Caine estate."

"Coordinator?"

"Precisely. Mr. Dragffy will need your assistance in handling certain matters. Perhaps you'll be asked to meet with a client, or you'll be called upon to draw up legal papers pertaining to the factory or the clinic. Naturally, the doctors on staff there will continue to run things, with Dr. Walker in charge."

There was a sudden loud honk, the sound of a motor revving up, and Tony glanced out the window to see a red Ford convertible speed past his window. A real beauty.

The man cleared his throat. "To continue. You will not be held legally responsible should something go wrong. Document four is a disclaimer stating your position. Your salary has been set at twenty thousand dollars a year. You will receive a check today for five thousand dollars. A similar check will arrive every third month."

Goddamn, Tony thought. *It keeps on getting better and better.*

He waited for the man to continue. However crazy it all sounded, Tony was sure that it was all on the up and up, and suddenly all he wanted was for the man opposite him—who looked as though he were ready to pass out from the heat—to keep filling in the details until there was nothing left for him to do but hand over the check.

Slowly the man opened his attaché case and Tony held his breath. A fresh handkerchief—damn! The man wiped his jowls, behind his ears, and across his forehead before saying: "Naturally, we would not want to rush you into anything. If you feel you need more time to think it over—"

"Well, it is rushing things a bit," Tony said and felt like kicking himself.

Something is bothering you, Tony, isn't it?

It was like another voice speaking to him from inside his head. *Yes,* he said to himself. He had answered instinctively, without thinking. If someone asked him why he was hesitating, he would not have known what to reply.

He leaned back in his chair and glanced out the window again. Just north of Maple Street, atop Mountainview Road, stood the Caine house. Tony couldn't see it from where he sat, but he held a clear picture of it in his mind.

Actually, the house really wasn't all that impressive. The Caines weren't the kind of people to build a shrine in their honor. In fact there was a time when Norris Caine, Julia's older brother, had worked in the factory right alongside the other workers, taking his turn at odd jobs, including clearing away the massive amounts of sawdust that would accumulate over long and tedious nine-and-a-half-hour shifts.

Norris proved to be a good worker, industrious, first on the job, and the last to leave at night. So it was only natural that he take over the Caine estate, which included the factory, a dozen warehouses, three motels, two restaurants, and the recently built medical building, soon after his father, Landon Caine, died, during the late summer of 1939. To be precise, Norris Caine took control on September 1, the day Hitler's army attacked Poland.

Like his father before him, Norris had brought the people of Millhouse through some pretty tough times. While the rest of the world was gearing up to nix the Fuhrer, Norris and the people of Millhouse were building furniture.

"But no one is interested in buying furniture today," the foreman had said.

Norris Caine, a man with a quick mind for business, had replied: "The war can't last forever, Sam. You keep building furniture and I'll keep paying you."

The next morning he went out and hired anyone in town who was willing to work, and started at once building warehouses. In a time when it was tough to find work, unless it was in a defense plant building aircraft or tanks, Norris Caine put an entire town on the payroll.

Landon Caine had accomplished the same thing during the years following the '29 depression. A town that was on the brink of picking over the garbage dump for scraps of food or salvageable clothing suddenly found itself employed by Caine Furniture. First they literally built the factory, then they began working in various departments within the company.

The Caines—who were always willing to create jobs, build buildings, and form companies—had inherited their large wealth from Edgar P. Millhouse, the founder of Millhouse, CT. Bored with traveling abroad, tired of living in New York City, Edgar P. Millhouse came to Connecticut and started a town. That he had no sons for heirs was something he would regret until his dying day. A day that came sooner than expected.

Edgar P. Millhouse was not there to see Norris and Julia Caine born. He was not there to see his only daughter, Emma, take an overdose of laudanum, and to see his son-in-law die from convulsions on a hot summer night, alone in bed, or at least some people said he was alone;

others, well—they knew otherwise. And he was not there to see Norris and Julia Caine living as brother and sister in their fourteen-room house atop Mountainview Road. Norris with his pale skin, his awesome body, his terrifying temper. Julia with her soft purple eyes, her anemic ways, her thin frame that looked as though it would break if touched.

No, Edgar P. Millhouse was not there to see the way his grandchildren would choose to live in quiet seclusion, shunning marriage, preferring each other's company to that of anyone else's, until on a spring night, a night rich with fragrance, a quiet night—calm—someone would come to Norris Caine's bedroom and . . . *Bang*!

No, Edgar P. Millhouse was not there to see that someone had put a bullet neatly into his grandson's head.

Norris and Julia Caine . . .

The end.

Tony sighed. Things were coming apart.

The last of the Caines. The last of the Millhouses, as well.

Until this moment Julia Caine's death hadn't quite reached him. Until this moment it had been just another regrettable passing. But his instincts now told him that her death was more than that. Much more.

"Mr. Rizzo? Please, Mr. Rizzo!"

Tony swung his chair around, peered at the

apparition before him. For it was an apparition, wasn't it? Because the man seated before him no longer resembled the man who had been seated there a moment ago.

For one thing, he was no longer sweating. For another, he looked more like an actor than an undertaker. Even his skin seemed to be less fleshy, more . . . tight? Was that it? That he looked younger? Damn it, what the hell was going on?

The man sighed as if he were being asked to deal with a slow learner, a child who just couldn't get it right. "Then you *do* want more time to consider the offer, is that right? Am I understanding you correctly?"

"Just a minute," Tony said quickly, more to buy time than to actually read the last page of the agreement he held. He could sense that the man sitting across from his desk was growing increasingly irritated, and wondered why the man didn't withdraw his offer. Just say, "Forget it, Mr. Rizzo. On second thought, I believe the job is not for you."

And that—precisely—was what was bothering Tony. Had been bothering him all along. Why not Jamerson & Sons, or some big-shot lawyer from New York or Boston?

Tony struggled with the question while he read the rest of the letter of agreement. Everything was in order. Tony would not be held legally responsible should anything go amiss.

He looked up suddenly, caught the man

(Mr. Hannock he'd said his name was) pinching closed his gold pocket watch. Mr. Hannock himself looked up and smiled crookedly.

"Well, have you reached a decision?" he asked.

Oh, what the hell, Tony thought. "Yes. Yes, I'd like very much to work for the Caines."

"Mr. Dragffy. You'll be working for Mr. Dragffy. The Caines, I'm afraid, are no longer—"

"Of course," Tony interrupted, feeling kind of stupid. "Of course." He glanced down at the agreement. "Is this the only paper that I need sign?"

"That's all," the man said hurriedly, and Tony could tell that a great flood of relief had gushed through him. So much so that he was now on his feet, nodding, exuberantly opening his attaché case and producing a check.

Tony quickly dated and signed the agreement which had already been signed by Mr. Dragffy.

Mr. Hannock arched his neck. "There are two copies," he said.

"Oh, yes." Tony hurriedly signed the second copy, handed the original across the desk, at the same time accepting the check. Hannock wasted no time in closing the signed copy away in his attaché case and preparing to leave.

"Well," he said, "I'm sure you'll find that you've come to the right decision. Mr. Dragffy is a considerate and mild-mannered man. I'm sure you'll find it easy to work with him. Now, if you'll excuse me—"

At the door, Tony said, "Now that we're working together, would you mind answering one question for me?"

The man shrugged. The urgency had disappeared from his manner. "Not at all," he said. "What is it you wish to know?"

Tony studied him a minute longer before speaking. Sure enough, his features—his face—had changed. How that was possible, or why it was so still eluded Tony, but there had been a transformation of sorts, no mistake about it.

"Well," Tony said, "I was wondering why Mr. Dragffy chose me for the job. I mean, why not—"

"Jamerson was considered," the man said. Then he cast a glance back over Tony's shoulder, as if he could see, through the window and around the corner, to number Seventy-two Main Street, where an ornate door and a gold-engraved plaque bespoke of the law firm within. "Jamerson was not born in Millhouse," he said coldly. "He is an outsider, really. An opportunist. It was important to Mr. Dragffy that he employ someone who was born and raised here, someone who knows the people intimately. Who knows what it is like to be part of a community."

Tony nearly beamed. "Then Mr. Dragffy knows of my work? Knows me?"

"You might say that, yes."

"Oh," said Tony, looking at Hannock curiously. "Well, I'm looking forward to meeting him."

The man smiled wryly. "And he you. I'm sure he'll be in touch soon." He hesitated a minute longer, then: "Now if you'll excuse me, I'll say good-bye." He never put his hand out to shake Tony's. Instead he turned, opened the door, and disappeared down the hallway, leaving Tony with his hand still extended, tiny beads of sweat flowing freely down his temples and chest.

Shortly before seven o'clock that evening, just as Tony was about to leave the office, he happened to glance through the window and think again of Julia Caine. He felt the strain of the day in his shoulders and across his chest.

The sun was low in the sky, casting heavy shadows along Maple Street. There were few people on the streets. Wearily, he went back to his desk, where he poured himself a drink, but after one sip realized that his stomach was in no mood to put up with it and put the glass aside. His mind was still off center, trying to cope with the idea that Julia Caine was dead, and that he was working for some anonymous gentleman from Boston. Who was this Mr. Dragffy, anyway? A friend of the family? One of the Board of Directors? Did Caine Furniture Enterprises even have a Board of Directors?

Again, suddenly, so vividly that he might have been dreaming it, Tony saw the Caine house looming on the hill, its massive gray facade backlit by the sun, the iron fence waltzing around its perimeter, the one prominent tree to the side casting a giant shadow over the west wing of the house where the shutters were always kept shut, some said nailed permanently shut, because Norris and Julia Caine hated the sunlight. Especially during the summer months.

Tony could never remember seeing either of them without sunglasses, or without heavy clothing. He also could not remember having ever seen them together. In fact, he probably had only seen Julia Caine once in the past few years. But the image was still fresh in his mind.

She was standing in front of Sue's Cafe, talking with Mr. Striker, the factory supervisor, and Tony had gone up to them and said hello. She smiled and talked for a while, even made a joke. Then, for no apparent reason, her behavior became odd, and she scarcely seemed to know Tony. Completely disregarding his presence, she made several vague gestures, said something nasty to Mr. Striker, then angrily walked away.

Mr. Striker told Tony a few months later that she hadn't been out of the house since. He called these periods "meditations" and said that she "wasn't feeling herself." Whatever they represented, these manifestations of her malaise seemed to Tony rude and unnecessary; but then it was not he, but Julia Caine, who had spent months at a time living alone in her fourteen-room house on Mountainview Road.

Tony sighed, locked the office door, and went home. It was a longer ride than usual.

5

The next day Rob Martin stood with the setting sun to his back, his face molded with concern, and told an old friend what had happened to him the day before. To his surprise it was much worse than he'd imagined.

"*. . . I don't know why, but I started crying. I was . . . I mean, it was frigging scary. To put my hand in a stump like that and then to have . . . At first I thought I was imagining it. What am I, crazy? I thought. Am I seeing things? Dreaming? So I looked closer, hoping it was a put-on, a practical joke. And then I realized that it wasn't a joke. It really was a woman's head. Jesus Christ, I couldn't figure out what to do. The next thing I know, I'm* *running. I didn't go back to the car. Larry was there, stoned out of his mind and acting crazy. And he had a gun. The gun was bothering me a lot, so I ran like hell because I didn't want to go back to the car and I couldn't stay there, so I just ran and then walked because my leg was killing me. I must've strained it or something when I first started running. Finally the sun went down and I headed back to the car, but Larry wasn't there. He was gone—vanished! He took everything, his clothes, the gun, and everything in the glove compartment. So I waited. But he never showed. I started driving around, looking for him. I almost went to the sheriff, but with the drugs and all I figured it would be trouble.*

"I don't even remember how I got to the motel. I meant to come see you. But I was exhausted and, well . . . anyway, Larry's still wandering around somewhere with that damned shotgun.

"Christ, I don't know what to do."

Rob ran his fingers through his hair; he was too confused to go on. From time to time he heard the low hum of a car winding down the back road and then continuing toward the cemetery.

Other than that it was dead quiet.

And for the second time in less than a day, he wasn't sure where he was or by whose side he stood.

PART TWO

THE HOMECOMING

He who makes a beast of himself
gets rid of the pain of being
a man.

—Dr. Johnson

The mind will kill you quicker than
anything.

—Dr. William Yates

1

JULIA CAINE'S FUNERAL: GRAY BEGINNINGS

". . . yea, the night-monster shall settle there, and shall find her a place of rest."—Isaiah, 34,14. (Revised Version)

The march in review of the empty limousines started at precisely eight o'clock, as the sun was setting, and as the coffin was being taken from the hearse and placed on the flatbed trailer that was attached to the tractor. The judge seemed annoyed that the procession had started down the long narrow road earlier than anticipated; they were supposed to pass as he delivered the last rites. Quickly he glanced at the sky, then opened his prayer book and began to make holy gestures, trying to get in step with the passing cars.

Other secret mourners were hidden, singly or in groups, throughout the woods, gawking and praying and telling Julia Caine good-bye. It was just Rob's luck to be watching this the first day back in Millhouse. He thought he'd throw up.

About then Tony Rizzo's elbow nudged into his ribs. "That's quite a story, Rob. No kidding. I like the part about the head coming up out of the stump."

Rob kept his eyes on the judge, who bent over and kissed Julia Caine's casket. Part of the job, Rob guessed. He waited before saying, "It isn't any story, Tony. It happened. Just as I told you."

Tony didn't say anything for a while, but rather seemed intent on watching the goings on at the front gate to the cemetery. Both men watched as one of the three attendants—grave diggers to some, caretakers to others—placed a wreath over the coffin with meticulous care, fastening it down to prevent it from sliding or bouncing on the roughly paved road. Off to the right, just outside the gate, the sheriff of Millhouse sat inside the patrol car smoking as the attendant pushed and adjusted. Every now and again static would come from inside the patrol car, then garbled voices; the sheriff finally leaned over and lowered the volume on his radio. The car was running, a bluish-gray exhaust rising lazily and steadily on the thin, lifeless air.

"You don't believe me, then?" Rob asked.

"Believe you? Of course I believe you," Tony said.

"Oh, from what you just said I thought . . . Hell, it happened, that's all!"

"Okay, don't go blowing a gasket for God's sake." Tony's eyes glinted with affectionate good humor. "We haven't seen each other in ten years, and already you're looking to pick a fight with me. Relax, you'll live longer."

"What do you think I should do, report it?"

"Like you said, there's drugs involved. The sheriff might think . . ." He broke off and looked at Rob with a half frown. "Jesus, you're putting me on, right? Still the clown after all these years. Well, I'll be goddamned."

Rob didn't bother to reply. No one was going to believe him. He could see that. Not unless the woman's body was still there, in which case he'd have some explaining to do, like: "What were you doing in the cemetery in the first place?" or "This missing friend of yours, he wasn't drinking, was he? Smoking grass?"

For a moment Tony's eyes narrowed, then he broke into a shit-eating grin.

"Look, why don't we stop by the Holiday Inn after this," he said. "I saw Reese and I think he'll be there. Marty'll be there. Maybe one or two of the others. Have you stopped by to see Elizabeth yet?"

Rob shook his head. "No, no, I haven't."

"You mean she doesn't know you're in town yet?"

"No, I overslept, then spent the rest of the afternoon looking for Larry. I was just going by to see her when you popped up."

Tony smiled and nodded with that good friendly gesture of his. "It's good to see you, Rob. It really is. You haven't changed one goddamn bit. No weight, no older. Ten years and you still look like you."

Rob looked down, abruptly formal. "Thanks," he said.

"Thanks? Thanks! You shithead. You're supposed to tell me how good I look now."

Rob pretended to study him, weigh things carefully, nodding, frowning, until finally he said, "You look okay."

"O-kay! Well, how about that!"

"All right, you look good," Rob said, grinning, remembering that when Tony was a kid he used to dream about Noah and the Ark, and how on the night before Rob left town, what with Tony having six beers and umpteen shots of bourbon, he wanted Rob to build an ark with him, because he was sure the world, his world, was coming to an end. Rob leaving town was the worst thing that ever happened to him.

But Rob could see that Tony had survived all right, because he stood there grinning with a face shaped like a beach, thick brown hair, and still those farmboy shoulders he had inherited from his father. Wherever the sun touched him he was bronze. Dressed in an expensive silk suit, tailored shirt, and brown leather shoes, it was obvious that Tony Rizzo's star was definitely on the rise.

And Rob felt a stab of jealousy. Not so much for his success, but because Tony had done it right there in Millhouse. Tony's father had been a farmer; as a kid Tony had sworn that he would one day become someone important in town. Someone as important as Norris Caine.

Rob supposed he had to admire that too, Tony's blind ambition. He himself had never been that success-oriented. If he had been, he sure as hell wouldn't have spent two years in the army, then wandered off to Los Angeles after his discharge, then on to New York, Chicago, and then Miami. For a while it pleased him, being a gypsy. Now, looking at Tony, he supposed his drifting around had been a mistake. Still, he knew his continual anxiety over losing two parents within six months would never allow him to stay too long in any one place. Especially if that place was Millhouse.

"It's strange, isn't it?" Tony said, and Rob looked up as though he'd only caught sight of him a second ago.

"What is?" he asked.

"All those years we spent in this damned cemetery, and all those years you being away, and where do we end up?" Tony broke out laughing. "Funny the way it still spooks you. No kidding. And then *sloooowly* a giant head appeared . . ."

"Do you think that's what it was?" Rob asked.

"Hell, yeah. Elizabeth and I always knew you were afraid of cemeteries. Especially this one . . ." His voice trailed off, and Rob knew he was remembering that Frank and Celia Martin were buried here, and that it had to be uncomfortable as hell for Rob to be standing there watching yet another funeral.

"I just thought of something," Tony rushed on. "The hell with the Holiday Inn. Let's go right over to Elizabeth's house. Surprise her. What do you say?"

Rob hesitated. "No, I don't think so. Not just yet."

"Oh," Tony said, and Rob thought he could detect a certain relief in him. A kind of "thank God for that." Elizabeth and Tony? Was that it? Were they, after all these years, finally getting it on together?

Both men turned to gaze down the hill. There were still a number of black limousines passing the gate, their headlights turned on and looking strange in the dull gray light of dusk. It was odd to watch empty limos snake their way up Nickle Road, their back windows devoid of grief-stricken faces, empty glass observing the dead. It was strange to see the sleek black casket with gold handles and fancy gold trim lying on a flatbed trailer; stranger still, Rob supposed, for him to be so close to his parents' graves, yet he had not stopped by to pay his respects.

He would have done so yesterday if things hadn't turned so damn weird. That's where he had been going. To say "Hello," and "How are you?" and "Good-bye, see you next time," to two people he had deeply loved.

Rob glanced into the trees at the center of

the cemetery, scanned first right, then left. *Larry, you son of a bitch! Where are you? Probably asleep on Old Man Harris's grave, that it? Or passed out next to Norris Caine. Larry, you horse's ass, where are you?*

Church bells now, the Protestants heralding Julia Caine home. The light was fading fast. Figures moved around below, blurred and ghoullike, two people getting up on the tractor, the third moving to stand beside the judge, who then looked over his shoulder at the sheriff. A slight nod, and then the sheriff closed his car door. The attendant waited for the judge to get into the patrol car before shutting and locking the cemetery gate.

Rob heard a sigh escape Tony's lips as the patrol car joined the rear of the procession where it grew steadily smaller until it disappeared from view.

Silence.

The lone attendant glanced around, then motioned to the driver of the tractor. The sudden belch of the engine starting up sounded like a gun going off. An ugly cloud of black smoke shrouded the coffin.

"Where do you think they'll bury her?" Rob asked, and the sound of his own voice startled him.

"I don't know," Tony whispered. "No one does. Except for them, of course."

In a similarly low voice, Rob muttered, "Strange. Really weird."

Tony nodded. "Yeah, I thought that myself." And then as an afterthought, "Maybe by the creek. Some say she liked the sound of water."

Probably so, Rob thought absently. His mother was the same way. The creek sings, she used to say. Calm even in the frenzy of your father's temper.

The tractor moved off slowly, up the incline, along the level, then started its second climb up the brown scar line that ran through the green. A tall man dressed in black walked behind the coffin, silhouetted against the trees and headstones.

The sun was almost gone, and the darkness was creeping in.

"Well, that's it," Tony said and turned to face Rob. "Let's get the fuck out of here."

"Aren't you curious?" Rob asked.

"About what?"

Rob watched the tractor move over the hill and out of sight. The coffin seemed to float for an instant, to hang suspended, as if allowing Julia Caine one last chance to sail off to heaven. "About where they're actually going to bury her?" he said.

"Not really, why?" Tony asked, but his friend did not answer at first.

Finally he said, "Just one more gone down the road forever, is that it?"

Tony shrugged. "I don't understand."

And Rob knew that he did not, that he wasn't the least bit curious. That, above all else, was what separated them. Had always separated them. *Curiosity*.

Perhaps that's why Rob had left Millhouse after all. Perhaps that's why he had tried so hard to become a reporter, instead of becoming a salesman or a shoe clerk or a furniture maker for Caine Furniture as his father had been. It was curiosity that had finally brought him back to Millhouse. Or was it suspicion?

"You about ready to go?" Tony said, and seemed a little annoyed. "We'll take my car."

Rob hesitated. "No, you go on. I'm going to look around town for a while. Maybe that crazy bastard will show up there."

"Well, hell—I'll go with you," Tony insisted.

"No, you go on, really."

Rob guessed Tony understood because he immediately said, "All right, I guess you got some catching up to do."

Rob nodded.

"Are you sure you won't reconsider staying at my place?"

"Hell, no!" Rob quipped. "With that crazy uncle of yours? You can't be serious. Besides, I've already unpacked. I'll be all right."

"Okay—but the Shady Rest Motel isn't my idea of ideal accommodations." He hesitated, and for the first time Rob noticed a slight nervousness under his otherwise relaxed manner. "Hey, how about stopping by my office in the morning?" he said. "We'll go out for breakfast."

"You're on."

Rob smiled, and Tony replied as he walked away, "28 Maple Street. Around nine. I'll see ya."

Rob watched as Tony dissolved into the shadows of the path that led down an embankment to the side road. The sound of his footsteps crunching pine needles faded, then was gone, leaving Rob behind to ponder the darkness which surrounded him. The darkness grew thicker as off in the distance, atop Nickle Road, Ned Taylor's dog began to howl. A wailing cry that rose, then fell, only to rise again.

Oh, God, Rob thought, and felt as if something were trying to slip between him and reality. As if his standing alone in the dark was absurdly and terrifyingly unreal.

"Oh, hell," he muttered. The dog's howling grew louder, making his flesh crawl. Nervously, stumbling as he went, he made his way down the embankment.

When he reached the car he stood for a moment, trembling, listening. Night had come to Millhouse, its dark hide pitted with leprous spots of light. The dog's howling had changed to a whimper, and the cemetery seemed suddenly alive . . . motionless, but alive. As though calling to him.

Now is the moment, Rob thought. If he did not move now he never would. With wrenching effort, he pulled open the car door and got in. Then he started the car and drove off, slamming the gas pedal to the floor.

2

Until you know the shape of evil, you cannot hunt it down. He was counting on that. He had always counted on that. Yet the thought gave him no pleasure. In silence he looked at the others, who had just arisen and were crouched at intervals in the gloom of the basement below the house. A remote place, alone and forgotten, lit only by candles.

He stared at the creatures without expression, knowing they feared his next move. Only the woman half smiled at him, surreptitiously.

He moved toward her, and as he moved the dense air parted. The candlelight touched his pale skin with soft, gold tones, like old burn-marks. It enveloped his body with faint gleams, and as he moved, his shadow, thrown to one side, leapt up and down the wall, as if expressing some vague restlessness.

Slowly he took the woman's hand in his; she offered no resistance. Dry blood still caked the corners of her mouth; her eyes were ablaze with confusion and delight, like those of a virgin bride being led to the marriage bed. Only she would be allowed to drink tonight, he decided. The others would have to be punished.

He was sure that the next time they would use a more prudent approach to their stalking. He would eventually teach them the right way. But for now, they would fast. An apt punishment. A punishment that only the strong of heart could endure.

He led the woman past the coffin, past the two men, to the foot of the basement stairs. The thinner of the two rose to complain, while the other reached out, grabbed hold of a water bug, and stuffed it into his mouth as if he were devouring a small plum.

Eyes met eyes, until the thinner man averted his gaze from his master to the stone floor. He knew that complaints would not be tolerated; he could ill afford further punishment.

Arm in arm the man and woman began to climb the basement stairs with a stately, unhurried cadence. Their image conveyed the perverse rich essence of dust and ash, of the deadly attar of royal corruption. Fancifully, the woman glanced back over her shoulder. The others hissed at her, their eyes full of wretched hunger.

The door at the top of the stairs was opened, then closed, leaving the others below to their own council.

The house grew still. The *Drink*, pure and delicious, was about to begin.

3

At night, Millhouse settles down from its scorching midsummer conflagrations and becomes encapsuled. The sky abandons its white-hot fierceness and mellows into splashes of red and quickly dissolves into a thick cloud of inky darkness. With night, Millhouse pauses, breathless.

To Elizabeth Arbor, the darkness outside her window was just another subtle reminder that Rob Martin had come back to town and hadn't bothered to stop by to see her.

Slowly she ran the last of the dishes under hot water, placing them in the drying rack on top of the sink. Then she glanced through the kitchen doorway to where her mother and father were seated on the front porch, keeping themselves busy by chatting the night away. As she stood there listening, a car engine coughed into life—she held her breath and waited. Soon she heard the car pass by, heading down the hill into town.

Damn him, she thought.

She could picture Rob Martin's old house clearly. Although it was across town and she hadn't seen it in months, the image was startlingly clear: the two of them sitting on his front porch, then her dragging him across the railroad tracks to Nickle Stables, where they would take the dirt path down to Nickle Road and then into the cemetery.

Even in cold weather they would sometimes go there: "What, and freeze my ass off," he would object. She never let his protests stop her, and in an odd way she sort of enjoyed her domination over him. There was no question then that she was the dominant one. It had been her conviction that this would be the best way, probably the only way, to ever land the likes of Rob Martin.

Now, however, she guessed it probably hadn't been the right approach, after all.

Elizabeth gazed distractedly around the linoleum terrain, her finger rubbing the insect bites on her neck. *Well, which is it, Rob? Are you coming to me, or am I going to have to come to you? Because I will, you know. I surely will.*

"Elizabeth?" Her mother's voice drifted through the living room.

"Yes, Mother?"

"Would you mind bringing your father a glass of ice tea, please?"

Elizabeth sighed. "Sure. How about you?"

"No, just your father. If you wouldn't mind."

No, no, why the hell should I mind? Why should I mind standing here with my hands red and raw at twenty-seven, in two months twenty-eight, shuffling like an old lady because my back is killing me while I deliver a glass of ice tea to my father? Whoopee!

She flung the dish towel on the table and threw open the refrigerator door. A minute later she stepped onto the porch with two glasses in her hands and a freshly lit cigarette in her mouth. She said, "Here you go, Dad."

"Oh, thanks," he said, accepting the glass she gave him. "It's just what I need right about now."

Elizabeth sat on the stoop, plopping her legs down one step and spreading them some. "I think it's going to rain," she said, knowing that it was the best way to enter her parents' ongoing stream of conversation.

"Oh, do you think so?" her mother said, and her father added, "We could use some rain."

"Why, have you started a garden or something?" Elizabeth asked, as though acting silly would help her get through the night.

Neither of her parents said anything, and she supposed that after twenty-seven years they were used to her shenanigans. Still, she wished there was more humor in the house, instead of the godawful dullness that seemed to grow thicker and more stifling with each turning of the moon.

Her mother finally said, "I thought you gave up smoking cigarettes, Elizabeth?"

"I've started again," she muttered and glanced at her father, whose eyes at once began signaling: Watch your manners, sweetheart. Your mother is only concerned for your well-being.

And that was the point, wasn't it, Elizabeth thought as she glanced away, searching for something interesting to focus on. She, Elizabeth Arbor, should not need the watchful eye of her mother. Should she? Should she? Hell, no, she shouldn't. She should be off in New York City in some dreamy little cafe in Greenwich Village talking about art and poetry and the Beatles, maybe. She was not too old to talk about the Beatles, was she? Not too old to get down in the streets with the younger ones and scream and holler: "Yank, get the hell out of Vietnam!"

Elizabeth winced, and tried to stop herself

from thinking such thoughts for fear that someone in Millhouse might read her mind and have her arrested for being a dissident.

She sipped from her glass, the sickening sweet taste of ice tea nearly turning her stomach. She put the glass down on the porch, reached into her pocket for her cigarettes, and lit a fresh one from the butt of the other. The trouble was, she didn't know what to do with the dead Indian. She glanced at her glass of ice tea.

And her mother said, "Don't you dare."

"What?"

"Put that cigarette in that glass."

Elizabeth made a wry face, and her father said, "There's an ashtray over there on the table."

"Oh," Elizabeth said, got up, and moved to the far end of the porch, where she crushed out the cigarette. For a minute she glanced down Standford Road and across treetops, where she could just barely see the upper half of the Caine house. Its top spire had two oval windows that to her had always looked like a pair of bloodshot eyes whenever they were lit at night.

She would sometimes stand on the front porch in the hours after midnight and wonder what they were doing up there so late at night. Sometimes the lights would be on until dawn, when suddenly—off!

Now, she supposed, with Julia Caine gone,

those lights would shine no more. At least not for a while. Word had already gotten around town that the house was not to be sold; it was not to be lived in, either.

Elizabeth shook her head. "What a waste," she said aloud.

"What is, dear?" her mother asked.

"The Caine house, letting it go empty like that." She hesitated a minute. "Who do you suppose will eventually live there?"

"I don't know, but I certainly wouldn't want to," her father answered, then swatted a mosquito with a rolled up newspaper. "Damn pests."

"Oh, why not?" Elizabeth asked.

"Why what?" her father muttered, looking around for his next victim.

"Why wouldn't you want to live in the Caine house?"

An awkward silence.

Elizabeth turned to face him fully. "Dad?"

He buried his chin in his chest, sighing and looking askew at his wife. "I wouldn't, that's all. Too big."

"Really? I thought you always wanted to live in a bigger house?" She waited for his reply. There wasn't any, and she noticed that, as always, he'd become evasive at the mention of the Caine house, as if he were being asked to discuss something that was, for him, distasteful.

"Well, anyway," he said at last, "it's still too

big for me. Now I think I'll go upstairs and shower before bed. How about you, Lucille? You feeling at all tired yet?"

"You go on," she said. "I'll join you in a little while."

"All right," he said and, without looking at his daughter, moved hurriedly through the screen door into the living room.

Elizabeth watched him through the window as he moved to the foot of the stairs and then stopped, a look of concern clouding his otherwise cheerful face. Slowly he raised his hand to his forehead where he rubbed, then rubbed harder, as if to dispel a bad thought.

Then he went slowly up the stairs.

"Elizabeth?"

Elizabeth turned to face her mother, who sat neatly in the porch swing, her thin frame having grown thinner with the years, her frail hands resting in her lap. "Yes, Mother?" she said.

"You seem restless tonight. Is something wrong?"

"Nah, just my back acting up, that's all." Elizabeth sucked in hard on her cigarette, then let out smoke like a locomotive getting up steam.

"Oh," her mother said, and "I thought perhaps it was . . ." Her voice trailed off.

"Yes?" Elizabeth said.

"Well, Mrs. Appleton stopped by today. She said she'd heard that Rob Martin was in town.

Have you heard that? Is he back?"

Elizabeth nodded, biting her lip at the same time.

"What *do* you suppose he's doing back in Millhouse?"

Elizabeth shrugged. "How should I know? He hasn't actually stopped by to tell me."

"Do you want him to? Stop by and see you, I mean?"

"God, what a question! Yes, Mother. Yes."

"Well, I for one do not. He's trouble, Elizabeth. He and his parents have always been trouble, and I wish you wouldn't see him."

"How? How was he ever trouble?" She shook her head. "I don't understand it. Frank and Celia Martin were lovely people. They always treated me like I was special. They never bothered anyone, yet I'm always hearing how bad they were. Why?"

"Never you mind. We have to live in this town, Elizabeth, long after Rob Martin has run off again. Please, dear, don't get involved with him again. He's trouble."

Elizabeth had begun hearing that same sort of remark the week after Rob had left town, two weeks after his father had died in a freak accident. Joe Joly was postmaster then, and he'd stopped by to drop off a package for Elizabeth's father. "Trouble them Martins were," he had said to Elizabeth's mother, not knowing that Elizabeth was within earshot. "I say good riddance."

But then he was an old grouch so Elizabeth hadn't thought much about it, until the phrase was repeated often enough to make her sit up and take serious notice.

Helen Jacobs was the next to spew her venom in front of Elizabeth. "My job was to try and teach the boy something," she had said. "But who could teach the Martins anything. Celia thought she knew it all. Actress, hah!"

"Has he really gone for good?" someone else had asked.

"Sure enough," smiled Helen Jacobs.

"Well, thank God for that."

On and on the remarks went, each time growing worse in tone, but quieter in voice, whispers followed by covert glances to see if there was anyone around for whom the words hadn't been intended.

Elizabeth glanced sharply at her mother.

"You're getting as bad as everyone else in Millhouse," she protested. "No, you are. Listening to all sorts of gossip. It makes me want to scream."

"Don't be melodramatic, Elizabeth. The boy is no good."

"May I ask you one more time—what has he done?"

Mrs. Arbor said unemotionally, giving her daughter a flat, even stare, "It's not what he has done, but what he might cause to happen in the future that concerns me." She rose to her feet abruptly. "You listen to me, Elizabeth—have nothing to do with Rob Martin."

She opened the screen door and closed it behind her, a small woman who seemed to be shaking, who had been more talkative and more worried than usual.

An hour later Elizabeth was watching TV and mulling over her mother's words when the telephone rang in the living room; she picked it up on the first ring. "Hello," she said.

"Elizabeth, it's Tony."

Disappointed, she said, "Oh, hi."

He paused. "I'm not calling too late, am I? I didn't wake you?"

"No, I was just sitting around watching TV."

"Oh, good. Well . . ." He hesitated. "Well, have you seen him yet?"

"Who?" she asked, playing innocent.

"Rob Martin. Haven't you heard? He's back in town. Hasn't he stopped by or called you yet? Didn't you know?"

"Yes to your last question, no to the one just prior."

"Well, I'll be damned. I was sure when I left him that he was getting ready to sneak off to see you."

"You've been with him, then? Today?"

"Yeah, he and I were at Julia Caine's funeral."

Elizabeth said, "I thought no one was supposed to attend."

"Well, Rob and I stood on the knoll just inside the cemetery and watched. Besides, I've been hired as a coordinator for the Caine estate. Can you believe it, me officially part of Caine Enterprises. I'm impressed, how about you?"

"Well, yeah. Heck, that's good news, Tony. Congratulations."

"So what do you say we celebrate tomorrow night? Run over to Peabody and have dinner, maybe take in a movie afterward?"

"I don't know. Can I call you tomorrow afternoon? There's a lot of work at the shop. We have a wedding coming up . . ."

"Sure, whatever you say. Maybe we can get Rob to come along. Would you like that?"

Elizabeth took a long time answering, and when she finally did she couldn't take the slight edge of sarcasm out of her voice. "That's alright, if Mr. Martin is interested in seeing me. Otherwise—"

"Of course, he is. Don't be silly. He's just having trouble finding a lost friend. You'll never believe it when you hear this. He stopped . . ."

Elizabeth sat back and listened to Tony talk, thinking about the first time she'd ever laid eyes on Rob Martin, a skinny, sandy-haired kid with a dirty face picking flowers in the woods for his mother. Holes in his trousers, T-shirt hanging out, he looked like an orphan, the most lovable orphan she'd ever seen, then or since.

"Well," Elizabeth broke in, "I'm sure his friend will turn up."

"Yeah, I guess he will. Listen, my uncle wants to use the phone, so—"

"Right," she said. "I'll call your office around two and let you know whether or not I'll be working late."

"I'll be there. Good night."

"Good night, Tony," she said, then added, "and congratulations—" But he had already hung up. Slowly she put the receiver back into its cradle; then, feeling agitated, she shut off the TV and went quickly upstairs to her bedroom.

Standing in front of the dresser, she slipped out of her skirt, removed her blouse, her gaze never leaving the mirror. She wasn't wearing makeup, but she didn't need any, the way her freckles jumped out during the summer months. And she did have heavy, dark eyebrows and long lashes.

She turned, sighed—images of Rob Martin came and went. No, she scolded herself, I'm not going to think about him anymore. She reached for her robe. All she wanted now was to be quiet for a while, to read a book and escape from her own thoughts. It didn't work, for in spite of herself she couldn't help wondering where Rob was, what he looked like, and what he was doing. Again and again she caught herself staring blankly at the printed page. *Damn*, she thought, and shoved the book into the nightstand.

She was just about to take a shower when something dragged her gaze to the window. For some reason, she had begun to shiver. She took a deep breath and stared into the night.

The sky was dark, with heavy clouds along the line of the horizon. Nothing unusual about that, she thought. Then she saw it. The light. Two eyelike splashes of murky light coming from the small windows atop the Caine house. And she wondered: Who could be up there this time of night? And what could they possibly be doing?

Soon the lights went out. Good, she thought. "Good," she breathed and laid back on the bed and closed her eyes, suddenly very tired.

Later, much later, with the moon about to set, Elizabeth, caught in the restless throes of sleep, would again see those lights burning—like the deep and fiery eyes of hell itself. They would continue to burn until just before dawn when a bleached-white hand would finally extinguish them.

Then her world would fly to pieces in waste and profusion, and would not reassemble for a long, long time.

4

Old memories, like syrup poured slowly over him, clinging to him, sickening sweet and sticky and oppressive. Entering Millhouse on Fairmont Avenue, Rob slowed the Jag and tried to shake off the feeling. Hesitantly he glanced through the bug-splattered windshield.

Main Street was paved but during the summer months it was so dusty that it looked the color of his hand. Its high-curbed sidewalk was always in need of repair, especially in front of the Town Hall that was the heart of Millhouse. Since it was the only building in town large enough to house more than fifty people at a time, it served as the high-school gymnasium, a lecture hall, theater, and polling place.

Rob eased the Jaguar slowly around Millhouse Square and down the street, his gaze locked on the Pepsi sign at the other end of the block. Sue's Cafe was under that sign, had been since he was a boy. It was the only place in town where you could get something to eat after eleven o'clock at night on Fridays and Saturdays. It was closed Sundays, and during the week shut up tighter than a drum at six.

Most of the other stores he remembered were still there as well, quiet and dark at this hour. The Ugly One's meat market, where Mr. Whitset always wore horn-rimmed glasses and a white apron covered with blood as he mixed up a batch of his country sausage.

Jacobs Hardware—his first name Arnold—his bulky silhouette against the glow of an open potbelly stove as he stood around chatting with the other men of Millhouse.

The Log Tavern, where another group of Millhouse men gathered, most of them employed by Caine Furniture; then the dress shop; two five and dimes, a big to do about that, the Thomases competing with Woolworths; post office; the Republican Club; the police station; the vegetable market, where the Hubberts lived on the second floor. The people of Millhouse took a dim view of living over the store, but Ronny Hubbert was a bad ass and really didn't give a crap what anyone said.

All was quiet and dark, not a soul on the street. Only weird shadows, now and then a mannequin's face peering through the gloom. Glass eyes, empty.

Rob pulled the Jag up to Sue's Cafe and stopped, letting the motor idle as he looked in. The place was deserted except for a couple sitting in one of the booths. Matt Russell was still manning the grill. Sue Woodard was behind the register counting cash.

Rob shut off the engine and got out of the car. A man appeared suddenly out of the darkness. Rob spun around. The man started toward him and then stopped. They stared at each other for a second, then the man moved on, glancing over his shoulder before disappearing into a doorway.

He had come and gone so fast that Rob hadn't time to get a good look at him. But he was sure it was Tony's uncle.

Rob waited, listening for the sound of a door being opened. Silence. Was the man just standing in the doorway?

Rob took a few steps across the street, then stopped and looked back. The doorway was empty. He started to move again, hearing only his own footsteps, listening for others.

There was no echo.

Relieved, Rob crossed the darkened street and stopped outside the cafe. To the right of the door a child's hand had drawn a scarecrow in yellow chalk on the red bricks of the building.

The tiny bell above the cafe's door announced Rob's arrival.

Sue looked up, squinted, then went back to

counting money. Abruptly she jerked her head up again, staring at Rob.

"Wait!" she wailed, edging around from behind the counter, her teased black hair bobbing on top of her head like a beehive ready to topple on its side. "Wait just a darn minute. Rob? Rob Martin?"

He nodded. "Hi, Sue."

She froze for a moment, staring at him in stunned amazement. From the corner of his eye, Rob glimpsed the woman at the nearest booth as she stared at him suspiciously, then leaned across the table and began whispering to her companion.

Then Sue was hugging him. "Oh, dear Lord, it's so good to see you, hon. So good," she whispered.

She was still a pretty woman, Rob thought, returning her embrace, and remembered how he'd gotten drunk one night and sung "Good Night, Lady" outside her window. She hadn't come out. In every small town you'll find a Sue Woodard. A woman who had married young, lost her husband young, then lived alone in a quiet way.

He guessed she still lived in the same small yellow house on Dickens Street, just around the corner and within walking distance of his old house on Elm Street. He guessed, too, that she hadn't remarried. Not that it made any difference to him now. His infatuation for her had long since mellowed into a soft memory, which he called upon only when he was going through hard times. A memory that was too distant to ever fully ignite, but when beckoned would produce a warm and cozy glow.

Still, she was a pretty woman, Rob thought. Then and now.

"You look delicious," she said and took hold of his hand. "Matt, look who it is. Rob. Rob Martin. Frank and Celia's son."

Matt looked up from the grill with those half closed eyes of his and waved his spatula. "Hi, Rob," he drawled and immediately returned his attention to the hamburgers that were sizzling on the over-greased grill.

"I just can't believe it," Sue said, still staring as though she were looking at a ghost. "It's as if you've never been away. I mean, how long has it been?"

"Ten years," Rob said, and wished she would let go of his hand.

"Ten years? That long?" She ran her free hand to her forehead, pushing aside a loose strand of hair. "I wish I'd have known you were . . . I look awful. We've been cleaning up the place all day, getting ready for a dinner party here tomorrow. The Walkers' fiftieth anniversary—you remember, of course you do. Patricia Walker, your English teacher—remember her?" She paused for breath. "Rob Martin, I—"

"You still look pretty," Rob said, unable to not say it.

"Oh, go on. I've put on weight. Twenty pounds at least. It's *his* damn cooking. Isn't it, Matt? Your cooking?"

The round pink man at the grill shrugged.

"So . . . come over here and sit down," she said and dragged Rob to the counter, where she forced him onto a stool. "What can I get you? Are you hungry? A hamburger. Matt, put—"

"No, Sue—really," Rob said. "Coffee. Just coffee."

"Are you sure, hon? You look . . . well, hungry. I can have Matt scramble you up some eggs. How'll that be?"

Rob shook his head. "Just coffee."

"Marianne, cup of coffee!" Sue yelled, and Rob watched as a young girl in sandals came shuffling out from the back room. She was a pretty thing with long blond hair, and looked lost. Or was it Rob who was feeling lost?

"Nice girl," Sue said to him in a low voice. "One of those, you know, flower children. She was ditched at Earl Plummer's gas station about a month ago. No place to go, so I gave her a job."

The girl set a cup of coffee in front of Rob, passed the cream pitcher and sugar bowl his way, then turned and, with two glasses of water in her hands, walked over to the couple in the booth.

"Kids today, right?" Sue continued in that same low voice. "I just can't figure them out. Nothing seems to make them happy."

Rob watched the girl disappear into the kitchen. "How old is she?" he asked.

"Just turned nineteen. She dropped out of college to live in a commune. Took up with one of those peace marchers. The first time she met him they were running through tear gas together, dodging police. They caught him and locked him up. She passed out pamphlets until he got out. Next thing she knows she's standing in front of Earl's gas station, wondering where her hero's gone."

Rob sighed wearily. "Jesus . . ."

"Hey, don't go getting blue on me. You're all right, aren't you? You look so *successful.*" She smiled and glanced out the window. "That your car?" she asked.

Rob said, "Yes," and wished he hadn't. But he didn't want to go into the Larry story. Not if he didn't have to. Because he could already tell that though the world was changing, Millhouse was not. Sue was wearing brown loafers and a faded yellow dress that reached down past her knees. She talked the usual Millhouse conservatism, shaking her head where the younger generation was concerned.

The country was divided, Rob knew. Right down the old middle; Marianne and her peace marcher and Larry on one side, Sue Woodard and Millhouse on the other. And Rob—well, he was caught in the middle. Too young to relate to the older generation, and too old to relate to the younger crop coming on strong. He belonged, he guessed, to the Left-Out Generation. No wars to protest, no drafts to dodge, no en masse demonstrations, just a twenty-nine-year-old guy who felt obsolete. Worse, he felt uncommitted.

"Pretty thing," Sue said, still gawking through the window. "What kind of car is it, anyway?"

"A Jaguar," Rob said, fidgeting with his spoon, pouring a little cream into his coffee.

"Expensive, I'll bet." She winked. "I always knew you'd do all right. I always had a hunch about you. You're doing really good, aren't you?"

Rob laughed nervously. "I guess."

"Where are you living now?"

"In Florida. Miami."

"Doing what?"

"Reporter. I work for the *Miami Herald.*"

"Go on! A reporter. You hear that, Matt? Rob's a reporter for a big newspaper in Miami. I just knew he'd do all right for himself."

Matt raised his spatula and waved it. "Real good," he said.

Sue said, "Well, I'll be damned. A reporter. What are you doing here in Millhouse?"

"I'm on my way to Cape Cod. I just figured I'd stop by, see how everyone was doing."

"Oh, Cape Cod," she said dreamily. "I always wanted to go there. Almost did, once. Couple of summers ago, remember, Matt? But, well . . ." She lowered her voice. "*He* got sick. I had no one to look after things, so . . ." She smiled and shifted gears without missing a beat. ". . . what's doing in Cape Cod?"

"The Martins always did have fancy ideas,"

a man's voice broke in clearly from over Rob's shoulder, and someone giggled and said, "Shhhh."

Rob didn't bother turning around; it was enough to feel them there, without turning to confront their dull gray country faces, without looking into their dumb-stupid eyes.

Sue Woodard said, "Don't pay them no mind, hon. They're just *jealous*"—she raised her voice on the word—"that's all."

But the man's remark had brought home to Rob why he'd left Millhouse in the first place. Hardly back one day and it was starting up again, the innuendos, the snide remarks he'd begun hearing just before his mother died. About how the Martins thought themselves better than the rest. How Frank Martin was causing trouble for Caine Furniture, thinking he should run things instead of Al Striker. And how Celia Martin used to be an actress in New York City, and how she'd do anything to get back in the limelight. That she was using people, important people, to get what she wanted.

And Rob used to wonder: *Are they talking about my father? My mother? Those two people I live with, who go to bed at nine o'clock, who spend little or no time going anywhere? Who never read a newspaper or talk about anything other than the weather? Those two people?*

But after a while he knew they indeed were talking about his parents. And he had recognized the subtle but nasty looks thrown his way.

At first it had bothered him, bothered him a whole lot, but in the end he just figured, what the hell—people could say what they liked.

Still, deep in the night, every once in a blue moon when he couldn't sleep, he would think of those times and it would well up in him, the hurt that came when he realized that the people of Millhouse had never liked his mother and father. He never knew why, really. But now he was sure in hell going to find out.

Sue Woodard placed a warm hand on Rob's arm, looking past him into the booth. "So, why are you going to Cape Cod, hon?" she asked, without looking at him.

Rob took a sip of his coffee, then said, "I'm going there to interview Robert Kennedy."

More snickers from the table behind Rob as Sue turned to face him in shock. Even Matt opened his eyes some and stared with interest.

"Go on," Sue breathed. "You're . . . you're putting me on, right?"

"Monday—two o'clock," Rob said. "I'm interviewing Kennedy at his summer home."

"You mean *the* Robert Kennedy? John F. Kennedy's brother?"

"You got it," Rob said as behind him a little coughing began. The man had gotten to his feet and was moving toward him, he could tell. Rob froze his face and waited.

"Is he really going to see Kennedy, Lou? Ask him," came the shrill voice of the man's female companion.

"Hush up, Joan," he said.

And Rob saw a shadow beginning to form on the counter in front of him, a large shadow, and suddenly felt the closeness of the man.

"They told me you weren't coming back no more," the man said, "that you'd quit Millhouse for good."

"Who's they?" Rob asked, swinging around to look up at the man with a day's growth of beard on his face, a crooked nose, and a thick mouth that looked as if it were set in stone. What was left of his hair was gray and oily.

"Why did you come back?" the man asked solemnly.

"I told you, I'm only passing through," Rob said.

"Some things never change, isn't that right, Sue?" the man said. "Don't see him for ten years and then up jumps the devil driving a fancy car and telling stories about meeting with that Kennedy fella."

"It's no story," Rob said. "It's the truth."

The man snickered. "That so. Why, because you say it is? Plenty of people say things that ain't true. Especially today. Everyone running around making noise just to be heard."

Rob could feel the spoon beginning to bend in his hand. Carefully he laid it down beside his cup. "The lady asked me a question," he said. "I gave her an honest answer. I don't see where that's making noise."

The man's eyes suddenly went ablaze.

"Noise ain't always loud, boy. Gossip is noise, and most of the time it's whispered. Prayers are noise, quiet though, if you get my drift. Lies, they're—"

"I don't see where I was doing any of that," Rob said, and planted his feet solid on the floor just in case.

The man's mouth, severe in repose, became mocking as he smiled. "Maybe yes. Maybe no," he said. "What do you think, Sue? He telling us the truth?"

"Just leave him alone," she said. "Please, Lou."

"I'm not bothering anybody. Am I bothering you, boy?" He moved suddenly, shoved his large body between Rob and the next stool and plunked his big scarred fists onto the counter. There was something silly but menacing about the man as he attempted to saturate each gesture with weight and importance. "How long you gonna be here in Millhouse, boy?" he asked. "As long as it takes to finish that cup of coffee?"

"Cut it out," Sue said.

"And here I was thinking we didn't have to hear no more stories," he went on. "Listen to people going on about how queer the people of Millhouse was." He turned slightly and began tapping the counter with his finger. "It was right here at this counter that your father told me how he'd gone to college. How he'd taken a degree and knew engineering. How he married an actress who was somebody. Somebody important, he said. You think you're important, now don't you, boy?"

There was a brief silence. Rob knew that Sue was furious at the man, whose chest was as big as a bear's. He tried like hell to figure out who this animal was. Lou? Lou? He couldn't remember a Lou. Yet there was something familiar about his face, about the fierce ice-blue glaze of his eyes.

"No," Rob said. "I don't think I'm important." He shrugged. "They give me a job to do and I do it. This time it happens to be Robert Kennedy, that's all. Why, does it bother you?"

"Listen, you two," Sue said.

But the man named Lou went right on. "I was just saying to someone yesterday—the world's going crazy, but not Millhouse. We're stayin' just the same. We don't have no drugs here, no sit-ins, no protests—we're stayin' the same. And that's the way we like it."

"That right?" Rob said, and laughed.

"Think it's funny, do you?" He inched forward.

"Okay, hold it right there," Sue said, her voice full of anger. "This is my place, Lou. You don't come in here and start trouble with my customers. You understand my meaning, Luke Tucker?"

And it suddenly became clear to Rob. Luke Tucker had been an old drinking buddy of his father's, until one day Frank Martin accused him of trying to put the make on Rob's mother.

They had had a fistfight in the Log Tavern; Luke Tucker had won.

"Look, I really don't want any trouble," Rob said. "I just stopped by to say hello to Sue. That's all."

For the first time a slight edge of tension had crept into his voice, and Tucker responded by lifting one hand, wiping it against his shirt, then balling it into an obvious fist.

"I don't like Robert Kennedy," he said abruptly, his voice dripping contempt. "Didn't like John Kennedy, either. Them Kennedys are what's wrong with this country. Goddamn kids with hair clear down to their asses burning their draft cards. Before them Kennedys nothing ever happened bad. All of a sudden these bad things are happening. Too much freedom, shooting off their frigging mouths. Throw them damn niggers in and whataya got—a country that ain't worth a shit."

He hesitated, staring Rob down.

"Jesus, all I'm doing is interviewing him," Rob said. "I'm not voting for him, for chrissakes."

"Hah," Tucker snorted. "You're a Democrat, sure enough. I can always tell a damn Democrat."

"So what if I am?" Rob almost shouted. "That's my business. Look, you got something to say about my family, say it. Otherwise get out of my face."

"Whataya say?"

"You heard me."

Tucker's face turned a chalky white, his teeth gritted, his eyes fixed on Rob as he muttered, "You looking to get yourself killed, boy?"

Rob didn't answer, but he didn't drop his gaze, either.

After a few seconds of eye-to-eye combat, a woman's hand reached out and took hold of Luke Tucker's arm. "Come on, Lou, let's go home," she said. "You got no right picking on him like this."

Sue came up behind Rob. "Damn it, Lou, Joan's right." He threw her such a look of anger that she backed off a little. "Jesus, Lou, all I'm saying is—"

"That's all right, Sue," Rob said. "I'm leaving." Luke Tucker looked at him, and he and the woman moved aside and let Rob rise from the stool.

At the cash register, Rob said, "By the way, Sue, you haven't seen a tall, good-looking guy with a mustache come through here, have you?" He thought it best to leave Larry's excessive flow of brown hair out of his description.

"No, no, can't say that I have," Sue answered.

"Oh, well—" Rob reached for his wallet.

"Why, is he a friend of yours?"

"Yeah. I just thought he might have stopped by."

"Well, no—but if he does, what should I tell him?"

"Tell him . . . tell him I'll be staying at the Shady Rest until Sunday. After that it's anyone's guess."

"I'll do that for you, Rob. I will. And it sure is good to see you again. Really it is. Matt, isn't it good to see Rob again?"

Matt nodded. "Real good."

For a moment longer, a cloud of bygone remembrances veiled Sue Woodard's terrific soft green eyes, a smile both happy and sad distorting her sensuous mouth. A woman lost, Rob thought vaguely. A woman who, like himself, had been born in the wrong place at the wrong time.

Abruptly she reached across the counter and took hold of Rob's hand. "In case I don't see you again, you take care."

Rob nodded. She squeezed his hand hard and then let go.

"The coffee's on me," she said.

"Thanks," Rob said, and started for the door.

"And don't come back because if—" Luke Tucker started to say, but Rob hurried away, and by the time he crossed the street all he could hear was Sue screaming and shouting and telling the man with the big fists what a complete asshole he was.

Rob got into the car, started the engine, and then drove up Main Street, a bit faster than before, heading back to the Shady Rest.

5

AN OLD TALE RETOLD

Later, much later, after Marianne had gone home, after Lou—his close friends called him Luke—Tucker had sent his gal on her way alone, after Sue Woodard had put the closed sign on the front door and drawn the curtains over the windows and pulled down the shades, Sue and Luke went into the backroom to share a bottle of bourbon. Sue was not in the habit of doing this. But she knew Luke Tucker was all wound up and heading to the Log Tavern, where he would start saying things he shouldn't. Things that were best left buried with the rest of Millhouse's past.

She guessed she was right to do this, because along about the third drink of Jack Daniels, Luke looked up with those bloodshot eyes of his, his face dripping sweat, and said: "The boy's father murdered Norris Caine. You know that, don't you? Shot him in cold blood."

Sue stared at him for a minute. After a time she said softly, "Nonsense."

"Oh, hell yeah, there's no mistakin' it," he said. "Frank Martin killed Norris Caine. You know how I know?"

Sue laughed nervously. "Come on, have another drink. Forget the Martins. Here, let me give you a refill." He moved his glass as she poured and a few drops spilt on the tablecloth and over the back of his hand. "Hold steady, will you."

He stared at the drink, then licked the back of his hand dry. His head drooped some as he snickered. "Do you know how I know? Because Frank Martin told me he'd done it a few days after his wife died. He'd been drinking and he told me, just like that, about the night Norris Caine died."

She began to tense. "You know that isn't so, Luke. You and Frank were enemies. He wouldn't even speak to you after the fight you'd had."

"No, that was just it. He came to me and apologized, said that it was really Celia's fault. That she was no damned good." He seized her by one arm. "You listen . . . listen good, because this is what Frank told me. You listen, goddamn it, because I'm only gonna tell it this one time."

With a brusque movement of her shoulder, Sue tried to free herself, but Tucker's grip tightened as he said: "I'm going to tell you how it happened in Frank's own words, the way he told it to me. It was in the spring that Norris Caine died. The spring of '56 . . ."

It was a little after one A.M. when I brought my fist down hard on the alarm clock to stop it from buzzing. I waited a second before searching the bed beside me. It was empty. Damned if I hadn't been right. I reached out and turned on the lamp. Celia's closet door stood open. I figured she didn't want to close it for fear of waking me up.

The shoes she'd kicked off earlier were gone. She never did like wearing shoes. First chance she'd get she'd kick them off.

Perhaps that's why I married her. She had this way of walking around barefooted all the time that made her sexy. You know, those delicate feet of hers and those shorts she used to wear, showing off her legs . . . real sexy. Everyone else in town thought so, too, because I'd overhear a conversation, or catch a look cast her way. Sometimes I'd pretend to be asleep on the sofa in the next room and listen to the guys talk. They always got around to Celia. Ripe, they'd say, like a piece of fruit.

Anyway, I swung my legs over the side of the bed and sat up, thinking over and over again, Who is she with tonight? The Miller boy had been nosing around, but that didn't mean much. The boy's father's a drunk, so the kid's always out hustling a dollar whenever he can. I was the first in town to give him a job . . .

Luke Tucker paused. "Do you remember that, Sue? Frank giving the Miller kid a job?"

She glanced away and looked through the partially open door. Matt was hunched over the grill, scraping grease, head bent, eyes almost closed.

"Do you remember that, Sue?" Luke dug his fingers deeper into the flesh of her arm. "Frank giving the Miller boy a job?"

She nodded.

" 'Clean up the garage,' Frank said, and 'All right,' Chris Miller said, never asking what the pay was. Frank liked the boy for that."

Liked the fact that the boy was more interested in getting the job than the amount the job paid. So I gave him an odd job every now and again. Lately I hadn't had anything for him to do, but the boy kept coming by.

I got up and stared at myself in the mirror over the dresser. Christ, I looked awful. I remember running my hand over a two days' growth of beard, thinking I'd have to shave before Celia got back. I didn't want to face her without being clean-shaven.

At first I thought she was sneaking off to meet the same man. I found out different though, because Al Striker finally told me what the rest of the town already knew. That . . . that my wife was out nights whoring around.

I remember I ran the razor over my face a few times, rinsing it under the water. Then I cleaned the razor carefully, dried it, and took it back into the bedroom, where I laid it on the dresser next to my wallet and loose change. You see, I still wasn't sure who was to blame, and who should die and how.

The funny thing was, I'd already half guessed what Al Striker told me. I found out the day after her thirty-sixth birthday. I'd been laid up with a busted nose along with two fractured ribs. You remember the accident I had? Well, anyway, I was on pretty heavy medication at the time, so Celia must have figured I'd be asleep all night.

The following morning I didn't say much, but what I did say was enough to let her know that I knew she'd been out the night before.

Things ran pretty smooth after that. A year went by, maybe two, then her nightly escapades started up again. I didn't say anything because I felt ashamed, and afraid that if I did mention it, she'd leave me. And I would never let that happen. Not then, not ever.

Things quieted down some after that, until this past January. I wasn't sure at first, but suspected. The damn thing was I'd become a heavy sleeper. Come nine o'clock and I'd be out on my feet.

But eventually, well—I knew who she was running with, and it wasn't the Miller kid. Hell, I knew better . . . knew who she was screwing around with. She was screwing around with Norris Caine. That's right, Luke. Norris Caine. And when I finally admitted it to myself that night, I knew I just couldn't sit around anymore. I'd done that for too many goddamn years.

So instead of waiting for her to come back to the house, I went out looking for her. Rob and Tony Rizzo had gone to New York City to do some celebrating . . . I don't remember why.

Luke Tucker hesitated. Sweat ran freely from his forehead, dripping on the table, into his drink. He shivered suddenly, shook himself all over, then quickly swallowed his drink and poured another.

He was having a hard time concentrating. When he heard the wet mophead hit the floor, he looked back. He watched as the little white snakes wiggled across the green and white tiles, first this way and that, Matt's rhythm slow and meticulous.

Again Luke attempted the ritual of oblivion in drinking, pouring; but the bottle was empty. He pushed it aside, and it fell to the floor but didn't break.

"Anyway," he muttered at last, too drunk to keep his head up. "Frank, he . . ."

* * *

I watched her come out of the Caine Inn that night. I didn't stop her. I just let her go on, and then I waited. A little while after that Norris came out. I would have shot him right there in the parking lot, but the night clerk came running out and gave him a set of keys he'd left in the room. And a scarf. Celia's scarf. The red one she wore most of the time.

I just stood there, sick to my stomach with hatred for that man. I'd worked like a dog for him all those years, improved his company, and what does he do? He keeps me living in poverty while he steals my wife. Can . . . can you see how it was . . .?

"Do you, Sue?" Luke Tucker asked. "Do you see why Frank killed him?"

Sue slowly shook her head, staring across the table at a man who looked ghostly white under the dim overhead light. "You don't know what you're saying, Luke," she said.

"I'm not lying to you," he said. He was on the verge of passing out. His head dropped and he jerked it up again. "Frank followed him home that night, waited until Norris went to bed, and . . . and then he went up to his room. That's what he did. And shot him. Killed him and was glad of it too."

Sue said, "You don't know what you're saying. You're drunk and stupid and don't know what in the hell you're saying. Norris Caine committed suicide, everyone knows that."

"Sheriff Blackwell, he . . . he knew otherwise, that's why he left town." Again his head started to fall over.

"Bull," she said, and he jerked his head up. "Blackwell left town because his wife was ailing, and needed to get to a warmer climate. You're so goddamn drunk you don't know what you're saying."

"But I do . . . Frank, he told me . . ." Luke's eyes rolled back in his head, then around, as if he were trying to determine where he was.

Saliva filled the corners of his mouth as he said, "Some people think . . . that, that Norris came out of his grave to get Celia. That it was him who caused her death." He looked frightened now, scared. "Did ya ever hear that? Did ya, Sue? That he came out of the grave to get her?"

Sue Woodard was now as deathly white as the man before her. She flung her arm in the air, as if ridding herself of a pest. "Stupid. You're so fucking stupid!"

"No, listen to me!" Tucker screamed wildly. "Frank, the way he died—it was no accident. I know. Norris got to him too. Norris was always . . . you know . . . that . . . Rob, he's gonna start it up again. It's all gonna start . . ."

He made one last pathetic attempt to pull himself together, but it was too late. With a shudder, he fell back in the chair, arms limp, eyes blinking shut. He passed out, saliva running down his chin from his slack lips.

"No, you don't know what you're saying," Sue said and got to her feet. The room swayed with shadows; she'd bumped her head against the overhead light and sent it swinging. "So you're going to sleep it off here, Luke Tucker. And in the morning I'm gonna tell you what you just told me, and I'm gonna make you promise not to breathe a word of that evil story ever again. You hear me, Luke Tucker? Never again. Not to anyone. Norris Caine committed suicide. Hear that? Suicide."

Abruptly the lights went out in the restaurant.

"Good night, Miss Woodard," Matt said at the front door.

"Good night, Matt."

Sue turned to look one last time at the man sprawled dead drunk and unconscious in his chair. The front door closed, and in the wake of a tiny jingle of bells, she shuddered. The chill she felt would be with her for the rest of her life.

6

Surrounded by deep shadows, the man's watery brown eyes shone as he stared longingly at the young man's body. The thick vapors of burnt wax and the pungence of blood filled the air. The man stood still, eyeing the fresh corpse. The skin sparkled in the flickering light of the candle.

Slowly, deliberately, he inched closer to the table, the thick crevices of his face made harsher by his longing, his desire. The imagined scent of fresh blood filled his nostrils, and he swooned.

The others were hidden away, watching him, he knew. That was why they had left him to guard the body. They were testing him. Shit.

They were waiting for him to make his move.

Even knowing, he could not resist. As he fanged his teeth laughter rang out behind him. He spun around, saw sharp green eyes focused on him. Cat eyes. Piercing. The man squirmed under his Master's gaze. The others stood to the side, smiling.

There was a long silence and then the Master's lips quivered into motion. "Kneel!" he commanded. The man hesitated, then obediently sank to his knees. He could feel a great power electrifying the damp air of the basement around him.

He waited. All waited as the Master, with great ceremony, moved to the table. Enraptured, the Master drew back his lips, and then, with unusual greed sank his teeth into the young man's neck.

7

A curious sucking sound, faint, yet distinguishable from all other sounds, began filling the room. It might have been the sound of the blood pumping in his own ears. Yet it seemed more than that.

Rob's body stiffened as the sound grew ever so slightly louder, invading every nuance of his being. Was he awake, asleep, he wasn't sure.

He rolled over in the small cast-iron bed as the invasion continued, and the storm of his senses grew more and more intense. First he felt a mysterious warmth, as if he were in the lustful throes of lovemaking. Then a stifling sensation, frightening, as if something were drawing the life out of him.

Perfume suddenly filled the air, intoxicating in its lushness, and he could feel himself losing control.

He began to shiver. He yanked the covers up over his body, at the same time trying to kick them off. Church bells rang out, his mother's face appeared, chalky white, lifeless, and somewhere in the distant past a great door opened.

8

The sheriff, thrice elected to the office, each time by the narrowest of margins, eased the patrol car along the back road. Smiling, he glanced around the densely wooded area. Sometimes the sordidness of his present existence, not to mention the job itself, made him clench his square yellow teeth in anger and earlier that night he had put his fist through the john door at the station house.

Now, with one hand draped loosely over the steering wheel, his overweight body angled toward the door so that his face caught whatever breeze was coming through the window, he felt none of that anger. In fact, he was glad that one of his deputies had called in sick. The night shift suited him. It had been his favorite time during his prison days at Foxworth Prison in Georgia. A mysterious time, quiet; he liked the night.

Peter Salino, the sheriff's senior deputy for the past nine years, sat beside him, fidgeting with the air conditioner and drinking a bottle of Pepsi. "Hell, Conley, I don't know what's wrong with this damn thing," he said sourly. "There's nothin' but warm air comin' out of it."

Sheriff Jones shook his head and continued scanning the wood-framed warehouses in the smutty moonlight. Or was it dawn breaking? He glanced at his watch, 5:10 A.M. Even this close to daybreak, when the last thing he wanted was to stumble onto trouble, he conscientiously made a close check of the twelve Caine warehouses that sprawled just east of the factory.

He slowed in front of the last building, checked to see that all the doors were shut and bolted, then faced his deputy. "Next time I take my own car out," he said.

"Damn, I told Jimmy to have it fixed. He took it over to Earl's only yesterday. I thought—"

"You know," Jones said, raising his voice until it boomed off the front window, "it's gettin' so everything is Jimmy's fault. Why is that, Pete?"

Salino looked at the sheriff stupidly and hit the switch on the air conditioner.

"What's that supposed to mean?" he sulked.

"Just that," Jones said. "Last week it was him who fucked up the accident report. Yesterday it was his fault those damn kids screwed up the gym floor. Am I right?"

"Shit." Salino swallowed the last of his Pepsi and tossed the empty bottle on the floor between his feet.

Slowly the sheriff cruised behind the warehouse, smiling to himself. He liked his deputies to compete with one another. The tension was good for them. As they cruised around to the front of the warehouses, he stopped the car suddenly and said, "Shine the spot over there, Pete."

"Where?"

"Beside number three."

Salino hit the switch on the large chromium spotlight and began searching the side of the building. The hot flash of light bounced off the rough wooden siding, caught the Caine Furniture sign and sent the light glaring back into their eyes.

"What?" Salino said. "I don't see anything."

"Never mind, shut it off. Must have been a shadow, I guess." He watched as his deputy swung the light into place, adjusted it, and turned it off. The sheriff hadn't really seen anything, but knew Salino was feeling better for the brief exercise. Little things meant a lot to him.

The sheriff drove on, crossing over the railroad tracks and making a quick left onto the narrow dirt road that ran behind building number nine, which was the largest and oldest of the warehouses.

Salino turned to look at him questioningly. "What are we doin' back here?"

"Change of pace never hurt no one," the sheriff answered.

The road grew narrow and pitted near the south side of the building. In the distance, the signal lights at the junction started to flash, first yellow and then red. Already the earth had begun to rumble as, from the north, the train was ripping toward Millhouse on its way to New York.

Abruptly the car took a pothole pretty badly and Salino grabbed the strap. The rancid stench of chemicals wafted into the car as they passed the chemical storage tanks and turned west. The train whistle blasted through the night.

"I don't know why they don't fix that goddamn road," Salino said.

"Because the Caines were always stingy sons of bitches, that's why," the sheriff barked.

Irritably, Jones wiped his forehead with his fists, then sat up straighter. Salino was already bent over the dash, peering intently through the windshield. He must have seen it, too—the figure of a man moving through the darkness.

In the silence which accompanied Jones's acceptance of the image, he heard the goddamndest sound—clearly, distinctly, the cry of a wounded animal. There was one final burst of agony as Salino looked at his superior for confirmation of what he had just seen and heard.

Both men turned and stared ahead of the car, where the headlight beams fell on a dozen or so furniture crates. Off to one side crouched the half-naked figure of a man. "*You*!" he screamed, and dashed into the middle of the road with a wooden club in his hand; blood stained his face and chest.

"Jesus Christ!" Salino bellowed. "What the hell—" He clicked on the spotlight as the sheriff hit the accelerator, and almost at once jammed on the brakes. The man was running straight toward them, apparently intent on throwing himself at the car.

"Fuck!" the sheriff spat, swinging the car to the left. Both men ducked as the club shattered the spotlight.

Salino leapt from the car. The sheriff threw the gears into reverse, but before he had finished turning around, Salino had his revolver out and was aiming. Blood gushed from a cut on the deputy's forehead, cut by a piece of flying glass.

"No, don't shoot him!" the sheriff ordered. "Get in—*get in*!"

Salino scrambled back into the car. "You're letting him get away," he screamed.

Both men kept their eyes on their assailant, who began running flat out for the chemical tanks. The sheriff shut off the headlights and sped in the opposite direction, trying to cut him off before he made it across the tracks.

"Son of a bitch, crazy bastard!" Salino yelled, pressing one hand to his forehead to stop the bleeding. "Did you get a look at him, recognize him? Did you?"

The sheriff swung the car over the tracks, hit the accelerator.

"Christ, I'm cut bad. Conley, I'm . . ." He held out his blood-soaked hand. "Oh, shit!"

"You'll live—now shut the fuck up," Jones scowled. Salino was breathing heavily, his chest heaving as if trying to catch his breath. "Here he comes," the sheriff said, and hit the brakes.

Salino shoved his door open. The man stood in the shadows, facing him, the club rotating in his hand. He remained silent, unflinching, his eyes piercing the dark surrounding him.

"Tell you what," Salino said, "you put down that club and we'll talk. We ain't gonna hurt you."

Still the man said nothing, just shifted the club into his other hand. Then he hissed, like a Texas rattler getting ready to strike.

"Get away!" he screamed. "Or I'll . . ." The rest of the sentence was drowned in a sudden outburst of hysterical laughter.

"Look," the sheriff said, and opened his door. Salino put one foot to the ground, then pulled back quickly, but too late. His shoulder was in the grip of something hot, like fire scorching his flesh.

Salino screamed once. An animal stench

filled his nostrils as teeth fastened onto his neck, teeth that tore away part of his flesh. Screaming, beating his fists wildly in front of him, blinded by his own blood, Salino fell back, stunned, struck his head against the dash, then collapsed to the floor of the car.

Jones was out of the car by then; he drew his revolver.

Two bullets tore open the night. The man with the club spun around, eyes rolling, mouth agape and dripping strings of saliva, yet he did not go down. For the first time Jones got a good look at his face. He was a young kid, twenty-three at most. His face seemed drained of blood —pale, all of him seemed pale and young and bloodied—and then he was off again, running.

"Shoot him!" Salino screamed, groping for the dash. "Kill that son of a bitch."

"That's what I just did," the sheriff said stupidly, watching the figure race across the tracks. A voice came over the radio, harsh with static as the train cut through the darkness. Still the sheriff did not move. He just stood there in dumb amazement, looking first at his revolver and then at the train flying by.

When he was able to move, finally, he glanced at Salino, who was moaning and rolling his head over the back of the seat. There was a raw gaping hole where the attacker had actually bitten away part of Salino's neck.

When the sheriff turned back the train was gone; so was the boy. Only hazy shadows loomed above the railroad tracks, their purple hue making his eyes blur.

Salino leaned his head out the car door. "I need a doctor, Conley. Bad, I need . . ."

"All right, all right." Still unable to understand what had happened, the sheriff climbed back into the car and sped off.

It wasn't until later, after Salino was treated and held at the clinic for observation, after the cemetery and surrounding area had been searched thoroughly, after the sheriff had told each of his deputies to keep their damn mouths shut about the incident, that he went back to where it all began. Rummaging around the furniture crates, he found what he was looking for.

The dead carcass of a mutilated dog. Its throat, like Salino's, had been ripped away.

Carefully the sheriff wrapped the dog in canvas, put the sack into the trunk of his car, then drove west, heading for Doc Tanner's house.

9

The old man suddenly found himself awake. Sleep had been snatched away and he did not know why. Today he had seen more than his usual share of patients; after turning in at his customary hour, he should have slept until well after dawn. Yet he could tell at once the sun was still down. What had awakened him?

And then the feeling came. Intense evil. A malignancy.

Grim-faced, he hurried from the bed and got dressed. Fear added a slight shakiness to his movements, and he fumbled with the buttons on his shirt.

He had hoped this moment would not

come, and had convinced himself that it would not. But things had started up again, he could tell, and he realized it had probably been inevitable.

He moved into the living room and turned on the light, then began to pace. He had rough, uneven features, and his dark brown skin clashed with his shock of white hair; his shoulders and waist were narrow. He moved about the room with an awkward shuffle, glancing at the telephone, out the window, all the while waiting for someone to call, to arrive with the news.

After a time he opened the door and stepped out into the night air, hot, sultry—moonless. Beyond the town, traffic hissed on the highway.

He knew everyone in town and everyone knew him, yet he had no close friends. None, he believed, who could actually be trusted. He probably should have spoken up years ago, but who would have believed him? Yet he had the feeling that there were others in town who knew.

Orrin Wicker and Raymond Cass, two of his cronies—they must know. Once, over a game of checkers, each had alluded to the notion, but neither actually came right out and said anything. Too afraid. Everyone afraid of everyone else. Mistrust was a way of life in Millhouse.

The old man's hands clenched and unclenched tensely at the thought of finally confronting the people of Millhouse with the truth. If it hadn't been for his ailing wife, he would have spoken out years ago. But she was gone now. He had only himself to worry about.

He moved back into the house, determined. He looked at the mantel clock. He had been up an hour. It would be light soon. He waited as the sun began to rise. He waited, without eating his breakfast, without leaving the room.

And still he waited, until at last he heard a car making the climb up the road toward his house. He moved to the window and peered out. The sun was just breaking over his front porch as the sheriff of Millhouse rounded the last bend in the road and turned into his drive.

The sheriff was not to be trusted, he knew. Instantly he felt himself retreating. He would not say anything. This was not the right time.

Moving away from the window, he waited.

10

Abruptly, the sound stopped. The slant of light that poked down on the bed was sinister simply because it was associated with the dim terror of a bad dream.

Rob lay in the enveloping darkness, feeling weak and lost. Somehow he knew there was no escaping what was about to happen.

There was a moment of silence as he tried to rise. No sound anywhere—no sound, no movement; his body refused to move as a spasm of nausea passed through him, his stomach contracting in violent tremors.

Then he felt it. A vagueness of shape and shadow that began moving toward him. His ears filled with the twining shades of howl and whisper: *You won't get away . . . there's no way out . . .*

Then it happened. A woman appeared suddenly out of the mist, flinging herself at him, kissing his mouth, sucking his tongue, pulling and kneading his flesh.

Rob tried throwing her off, but others had taken hold of his arms and pinned him to the bed. Faces leered at him as the woman fondled him; she was a thin seductive creature with long fingernails. She grabbed hold of his penis, bent to take it in her mouth.

"Stay still," she whispered, "this won't hurt."

He watched as his blood spurted against the walls, all over her hands and face. He could not move and she would not let go. He screamed, wondering where the blood was coming from, knowing that something was very wrong.

He tried desperately to rise; hands and legs smothered him, her legs, their hands; she rode atop him now. Her thighs jerked convulsively as her muscles tightened around his body, drawing him deeper inside her. She opened her mouth, hissed, then gave a long, uncontrollable cry of pleasure as orgasm engulfed her.

"Oh, yessssss!" she screamed.

Rob awoke suddenly, sat bolt upright in bed. He had awakened to birdsong, to a hazy predawn light filtering through the slits between the drapes. He sat there, shaking, doubting his senses. So vivid and erotic was the dream that he half expected to find the woman still there. But he was alone, in a disheveled bed, in a musty room.

He reached down between his legs and felt around. No wetness. He threw back the sheet, looked carefully at the mattress, searching for telltale signs of secretion.

Nothing.

"Jesus," he breathed, and got out of bed.

He took a deep breath and calmed himself. He had been prepared to run screaming from the room, but an inner rationale had kicked into play.

The dream returned with startling clarity; he looked around the room once more. Nothing; no woman, no shadowy figures lurking in the corner, except for his clothes flung over the chair, propped up, lifelike, as if supported by some invisible agency. Nothing had been disturbed.

Rob did not know that only moments earlier, just before the sun rose, a woman had stood outside his window, watching him.

Rob shuddered, still in the grip of his dream.

11

As the first light of dawn seeped into the sky, the vampire's hand reached out and closed the lid of his coffin. In his mind's eye he saw the house above him, elevated on the hill, a high, eccentric tower, a glorious Gothic crown. He settled back in the coffin and his pale, strongly lipped mouth curved into a smile of pleasure.

He was constantly aware of the tallness and rich texture of the high, narrow house that he owned; he held always in his mind a precise image of its winding stairways, its dark passages, immense rooms, high attic, its red slate roof or pinnacle.

This was the moment he loved best of all. To

lie there in the darkness and imagine the house erect above him; a house that wore its years with pride. . . . And with the taste of blood still fresh in his mouth, his tongue sliding wetly over his lips, his hand straying to his genitals, the vampire closed his eyes.

Then all was as still and black as a tomb.

PART THREE

BLOOD CONNECTION

"Let all dreams and phantoms of the
night fade away, lest our bodies
be polluted."

—Ambrosian hymn
(c.340–397)

1

It was Saturday, hot and humid. Rob took the footpath that ran alongside Fairmont Avenue, until he reached Millhouse Square. He paused under the huge oaks to look around. Then he turned south on Main Street, which was deserted except for an old man sleeping in a parked car in front of Earl Plummer's gas station.

Ah—familiar things—memories of himself as a boy doing just that. Waiting patiently with his father for the gas station to open.

Somehow, in the daylight, Millhouse looked less threatening, more as he remembered it to be. He walked faster now, trying to outpace last night's dream.

Still, something seemed to be gaining on him. It was difficult in that early-morning light and landscape to believe that anything was wrong, yet the feeling persisted. And as he crossed Maple Street, he was suddenly struck by the odd sensation of being observed. He glanced back over his shoulder and found that sure enough, he'd been right. A tan Chevy had come to a stop on the other side of Main Street. He couldn't tell who the occupants were, but knew they were watching him.

Damn, it was a weird feeling being spied on. Annoying as well, giving him a slight case of the creepy-crawlies. He turned to confront them, forcing them to make a decision.

Immediately the Chevy moved away from the curb, the driver still observing him from the sideview mirror.

So that was that. Two old farts ambled by, gabbing and walking crooked on their canes. Cars began moving in both directions, a kid passed by on his bike, and Rob could sense it was business as usual, just another quiet Saturday morning in Millhouse.

He hesitated for a minute, then began looking down Maple Street for number twenty-eight, which wasn't hard. There weren't but twelve buildings on the entire block.

The brass plate beside the heavy oak door read: Anthony Rizzo, Counselor at Law. Rob took hold of the doorknob, turned it, and stepped into the soft beige interior of the hallway. Just ahead of him was a flight of impressive wooden stairs. To his right stood a mahogany table with vase and flowers above which hung a gilded-edged mirror.

Eyes met eyes. Rob's own. He straightened his tie, turned, and then turned back to frankly stare at himself. He hated what he saw. Because of his run-in with Luke Tucker last night, he'd decided to wear a suit this morning. That Tony worked on Saturdays was impressive; that Rob had opted to discard his usual uniform of the day—corduroy sports jacket over Levi's jeans—for a sad-looking lightweight summer suit, which was at best ill-fitting, was not.

The waist of his pants cut in, damn it, making him feel the need for a diet. The cut of the jacket made him look like a farmer who had suddenly been asked to dress up for his daughter's wedding. To make it all seem worse, he'd watered down and parted his hair, a style he'd gotten rid of about the same time women began burning their bras.

And all this because of Luke Tucker! It was amazing how quickly one was forced to conform when confronted by an ape with an apelike temper.

The steps creaked as Rob started his climb.

At the top he hollered, "Tony, you here?"

"Be right out," Tony shouted. His voice came down the hallway from the right, from what Rob assumed was a bathroom.

"I'm having a little trouble with my contacts!" Tony said, confirming Rob's guess. "Make yourself comfortable. There's coffee going—help yourself."

Inside Tony's office, Rob did just that, and helped himself to a donut as well.

Nice office, he thought, munching. Not big but impressive in its antiquity. Old hand-carved desk, pictures of Millhouse as far back as 1907, copper spittoon and gilt table and chairs.

Nice. Real nice.

"Hey!" Tony said as he appeared suddenly behind Rob, who turned with a start, nearly spilling his coffee.

"You always sneak up on people like that?" he asked, checking his suit for damage. A few spots on his sleeve was all.

"Here, use this," Tony said and handed him the damp paper towel he'd been using to dry his hands. "It should rub right out."

After a few strokes Rob looked up. Tony was just standing there, staring at him. Not at the coffee stains, but directly into Rob's eyes.

"Kennedy!" he said. "You bastard, in two days you're going to interview Robert Kennedy and you never said a word."

"Oh," Rob said, and dropped the towel into the wastebasket. "How'd you find out?"

"Find out?" Tony laughed shortly, crossing to his desk. "This is Millhouse, old buddy. Not Miami. The whole town is talking about it. Kennedy. I'm impressed."

"That right?" Rob said dully.

"Oh, look at you. Mr. Cool One."

"No, not at all," Rob said. "When I first got the assignment, I couldn't sleep for days. But—"

"Well," Tony interrupted and dropped into his desk chair. "Sit down for chrissakes. I'm really eager to hear about it."

Rob hesitated, looking at the man he'd once considered his best friend—no, his *only* friend—and saw something he didn't expect. He saw a certain uneasiness, almost as if Tony were saying one thing but thinking another. As if there were something . . . Rob couldn't quite place it. But it was there all right, whatever it was.

"You didn't let me finish." Rob sat on the arm of the couch, like he used to do in the old days, when he and Tony would BS in the living room on Elm Street.

"Oh," Tony nodded. "I'm sorry. You were saying?"

"Sure, I couldn't sleep," he said. "But not because I was necessarily excited about meeting Robert Kennedy."

Tony eyed him for a minute. "What, then?"

Rob eyed him as well, not sure what he was about to say. During the last few years he had become all mixed up. He felt lost. So fucking lost that at times he wondered who he was. Who he *really* was.

Perhaps that's why he had taken Larry Campbell along. The kid seemed so alive, so full of a new kind of energy. Like the Kennedys. But, well—that was the problem, wasn't it?

He ran a hand across his forehead, squinted, then ran his hand over his eyes as if to clear his head. "Look," he said, "you hungry? I'm hungry. Why don't we talk as we walk?"

"All right. Where to?"

"The Caine Inn, I guess."

"Lousy food."

"Quiet, though. Right?"

Tony lurched out of his chair. "The Caine Inn it is."

Even as Rob and Tony joked a bit going down the stairs, and nudged each other playfully into the street like good buddies often do, at the opposite end of town, Elizabeth Arbor opened the back door of the flower shop and looked up, feeling as idiotic and ineffectual as anyone who imagined they saw things go bump in the night. But she had seen lights burning in the Caine house last night, hadn't she? Not once but twice.

Now, standing alone, her thoughts came more quickly, and she squinted until the massive gray facade of the Caine house came into focus, its high spires jetting into the sky like arrows aimed at heaven.

The house stood apart and alone, a monstrous thing with as much charm as the Greyhound bus station. But what amazed her, what completely amazed her, was the intimacy she felt toward it, as if in some odd way the house now belonged to her. But then why shouldn't she feel that way? She had always imagined herself living in a grand house on top of a hill, hadn't she? It was part of her old dream of someday becoming a famous actress.

Elizabeth should have stopped there; it was

the logical end of her musing. But something wasn't right.

Brooding, her brain in a swirl, she thought again of her mother's words: "Don't get involved with Rob Martin. He's trouble," and how her father had seemed nervous as hell at the breakfast table. And how, for the first time that she could remember, he had looked really old. Something she had preferred not thinking about until now. But there he'd sat, looking old and not saying much and acting strange.

Well, Liz old gal, the mind sometimes has a mind all its own. It sees what it wants to see.

"Hah!" Elizabeth snorted. Behind her she heard a polite but attention-getting cough, which caused her to half turn and stare into the soft gloom of the flower shop. Beyond the dark, oak-wood hallway stood rows of exotic ferns and tree flowers that wavered for an instant, like a jungle steaming with heat after rain. Through this muted array of foliage came Mrs. Dodd.

"Elizabeth, would you watch the front of the store for a moment?" the woman said. "I'm going to run over to Hadley's."

"All right," Elizabeth said, yet she did not move. Mrs. Dodd was also acting a bit strange this morning, wasn't she? Whenever Elizabeth had mentioned Rob Martin's name, she'd changed the subject. That wasn't at all like her.

Now it came to Elizabeth, full-blown—an image of Mrs. Dodd in her gray suit and too fashionable blouse, her smile fake, her fingertips tapping nervously.

Or was she, Elizabeth, the one who was feeling nervous? The floor seemed to sway beneath her.

"Elizabeth, did you hear me, dear?" Mrs. Dodd asked.

Elizabeth clutched at the door frame. The world steadied.

"Yes, yes—all right," she said, and listened as the front door to the shop opened and then closed.

Crazy, Elizabeth thought. *Why is everyone acting so crazy*? The words vibrated in the lifeless air as if she had actually spoken them aloud. She turned into the shop and felt a sudden physical heaviness, a leadenness in her limbs and a tightening of her chest. These same sensations had jerked her awake this morning near dawn. Or was that yesterday morning?

She shook her head, trying to drive away the fuzz.

But it was no use. No use at all, because instead of ridding herself of the feeling that her head was stuffed with cotton candy, the motion increased the numbness. Images came and went, swimming before her eyes—her hand went up, trembling, to her forehead—and after a minute's hesitation, she glanced again at the Caine house, which seemed to be receding, but Elizabeth knew that that couldn't be. She was receding—no, she was falling.

Caught between breaths, she panicked. Instinct made her hand reach again for the door frame. As she began her slow descent, she saw an odd-looking man standing under the elm tree across the way, looking at her. His face was pale, so pale, and those eyes, they were the eyes of a savage dog, she thought.

She made one last-ditch effort to straighten up, realizing how quiet it was. There wasn't a sound to be heard, not even the voices of the kids who at that hour usually played baseball in the park across the street. An empty white-hot scene lay spread before her. Except for *him.*

He moved suddenly, stepped from beneath the tree and began heading toward her. Now there was nothing in Elizabeth's mind but the single thought that someone—yes, someone—was walking across the street, walking inexorably in her direction.

The last thing she saw before going under was a yellow flash of heat, and then a great chasm of yawning darkness took hold of her, turning everything to black.

2

There were three coffins in all; long and sleek-looking things, resting in the dark-blue shadows of the factory's back room. The room was oppressively hot, its high narrow windows barely letting in enough light to see by. The hinges creaked as Jack Gardner closed the door.

"You want a drink, boy?" he asked as he moved forward and switched on a small overhead light.

"No, sir."

"Why not? It'll clear up those pimples of yours. Fetch the bottle out of the satchel over there."

The boy, J.D. Salinger, moved awkwardly

toward the worktable. He never knew why his father decided to name him after a famous author. And what's more, he didn't give a crap. All he knew was that he shouldn't have taken this job.

The smells of dust, woodsap, and gasoline ravaged his nostrils as he reached into the satchel and took out a bottle wrapped in a paper bag. He'd lied to his parents, telling them he was going down to the creek, swimming. He wished now he was.

He turned and glanced again at the coffins. Three coffins. Jesus!

"You afraid of death, boy?" The old man uncapped the bottle. He took a healthy swig and closed his eyes; J.D. could almost see the man's ruddy face light up. "Death came to me one night, did you know that? I told him to get stuffed. Just like that, I said: 'Get stuffed.' And do you know what he did?"

"No, sir."

"The son of a bitch laughed and said I wasn't worth taking. Now whataya think of that?"

J.D. smiled. His legs felt like rubber. He wished he'd told Frankie or one of the other guys what he was doing today, but Gardner said that was part of the deal. Twenty bucks for the day's work, and another ten if he kept his damned mouth shut.

"You didn't tell anybody, did ya, boy?" the old man suddenly asked.

"What?" J.D. looked across the dim light to where Jack Gardner now stood, beside one of the coffins; he ran his hand inside the sleek box as if caressing a woman's body.

"Tell anyone what you were doing today. You didn't, did you?"

"Heck, no!" J.D. almost shouted. "You said not to, so I didn't."

"Good, because I ain't supposed to be here. Just using the room to help out a friend. No one knows, exceptin' you. Of course, if you told a friend or something . . ."

"No one," J.D. protested. "Hell, we agreed. That's what you're paying me for."

"And the work, don't forget the work," the old guy said, his eyes glued to the inside of the coffin. "Pretty things, aren't they? I made a few of them in my day, yes sir," he ran on. "I don't know what the man does with them, and I don't much care, either. He pays well enough, but, hell—he wants these three in a hurry. Do you know how much sanding goes into one of these beauties, do you? Now that's what I'm gonna need you for. Sanding."

Jack Gardner turned suddenly and glanced at J.D. across the wide expanse of gloom. He was wearing a faded pair of overalls over a plaid shirt. His black workman's boots were laced with string. When he looked up, his long scraggy hair fell over one eye. He brushed the lock aside as he smiled.

"Here ya go, boy. Take a swallow." He held out the bottle.

J.D. hesitantly closed the space between them, took the bottle, and drank. It felt like acid was going down his throat, burning its way into his stomach.

He must have gasped or choked or something, because the old man reached out and took hold of his shoulder. "Easy, boy. Take it easy," he said. In the dim, yellowish light, the man seemed gigantic; his hands were huge and covered with soft black hairs. "You're not afraid now, are you, boy?" he asked. "Of them coffins?"

"No," J.D. said, his stomach in knots.

"Come over here and sit down."

"I'm all right."

"Sure you are. But I want you to sit anyways."

"No, really."

But the big hairy hand was gripping his shoulder and though it held him easily, J.D. knew if he refused to sit it would clamp down like a vise. As they walked over the sawdust-covered floor toward the work bench, Gardner's face kept appearing and disappearing in the shadows.

"Now, listen, boy," he said. "I want to get through with this before it gets dark. Okay?"

J.D. nodded as he sat.

"That's a lot of work for us to do. While I'll be cutting and fastening the lids, you'll be sanding." Gardner reached into his overalls and came away with a ring of keys. He moved back to the door and locked it. "Don't want nobody walking in on us unexpected, understand? If I should tell you sudden like to hush up, you do it. No questions. The watchman sometimes checks around back here."

Jack Gardner was standing in complete shadows now; only the tips of his boots showed in a small splay of light.

J.D. looked closer at the floor. Sawdust had been spread over huge orangy-brown stains on the floor; oily stains, some of them still looked fresh.

"I'm gonna start sawing now," Gardner said quietly. "You just sit there and rest for a minute, okay?"

The blade of the power saw suddenly glittered in the dark. J.D. stared at it, his jaw slack. The saw was turned on; it made a shrieking sound, then faded to a low hum.

J.D. sat transfixed, watching the blade whirl, trying to catch a glimpse of the old man's face. He began imagining the worst. He pictured Gardner drunk and coming at him with the saw. He glanced again at the coffins, at the stains on the floor.

The blade began crying out again, a harsh sound, like a person whining, and J.D. could imagine parts of himself lying in each of the coffins; he could feel the blade tearing into his flesh, hacking off his limbs.

The blade cried: J.D., J.D., J.D., J.D.

His muscles tightened, and he broke out in a cold sweat as he saw blood, his blood, splattered all over the walls and floor of the tiny room.

But none of that happened.

Soon he found himself on his feet sanding the side of a coffin. A slow circular motion.

In the dim light the saw continued to chew up wood. The old man looked up once, smiled, and then went back to work.

3

"So you didn't relate to John F. Kennedy, either," Rob said, as Tony stopped to pluck a leaf from a tree. Around them the common lay lush and green, with the soft sound of water cascading over a miniature waterfall. A few ducks glided lazily upon the pond, while a flock of pigeons ravaged the handfuls of popcorn that an old woman tossed in front of her.

"Well, did you?" Rob persisted.

"I have to be honest with you. Not really."

Rob grunted. "Yeah, well, that's my point."

Tony didn't come back with a quick response of his own, but seemed to be thinking the matter over, weighing the facts like a good lawyer should. Rob savored the silence, glad for a moment to be standing in a Norris Caine-built paradise. But his peace was short-lived. He watched a car move slowly down Fairmont Avenue, and cross the railroad tracks.

"Tony, that tan Chevy. Who owns it, do you know?"

"Where?"

"Over there, take a look."

Tony stared into the distance. As the Chevy turned onto Nickle Road, he said, "I think it's Mr. Whitset's."

"Oh." Rob hesitated. "The Ugly One?"

Tony's eyes sparkled. "Damn, you remember that? You remember him?"

"Remember him? How could I forget?"

"I'll be damned, after all these years . . ." Tony broke out laughing. "I'll never forget the night we caught him parked behind Caine Pond with Tina . . . oh, what the hell was her name?"

"Ross. Tina Ross, and he said he'd give us steaks every week for a year if we didn't tell anyone."

Tony nodded. "After what we saw him doing to her, who'd want anything he touched!"

They both fell out laughing, and the old woman looked up because they had scattered her pigeons with all the racket they were making. With a look that could freeze the blood in a person's veins, she rose to her feet, turned, and left the park.

Rob was the first to stop laughing. "Tony, I

believe we just saw a fine example of righteous indignation."

"Yeah, well . . ." Tony was sobering up fast himself. "Why were you asking about the tan Chevy?"

"Nothing, really. I just thought he was following me before. Watching me."

"Really?" Tony looked away nervously. "Whitset still owns the meat market, you know. On Main Street. He probably always will. His wife died about a year ago. His oldest son, Ramsey, you remember him. He was just elected to council . . ."

All the signs are right, Rob thought stonily. The rambling on about trivia, the tugging on his earlobe. Rob knew Tony as well as anyone—better, probably—and there was no mistaking the signs. It was obvious that Tony was suddenly feeling tense.

"You know, I still think about those times," Tony said, and began to walk. He seemed easygoing now, as if he were ambling away from a sore spot.

Rob followed after him. "What times?"

"*All* those times. You and me, and Elizabeth. The night we torched Matt Russell's garbage can because he wouldn't give us anything for Halloween. All of it."

"*You* torched his garbage can. I watched."

"Oh, bullshit. It was you that had the matches!" Tony looked at him and smiled.

It was a warm smile, the kind Rob remembered seeing during his younger and more vulnerable years, when things were less complicated. When life—odd journey that it had become—had seemed less like a tinted photograph. And Rob, seeing his smile, felt the youthful tug of affection he'd once held for the man.

An hour later the feeling was gone. Somehow Rob couldn't hold onto it. Not that he hadn't wanted to. But the more Tony talked about the good old days, the more Rob felt the distance between them, as if time had separated them forever.

Maybe that's why Rob had mentioned Kennedy again. He talked about how confused he was about interviewing Kennedy, even uncertain as to whether or not he should. Tony seemed to become instantly annoyed at the notion.

"You should be excited about meeting him," Tony said. As if to give his statement emphasis, he shoved his empty plate aside and waved to the waitress. "Check, please."

They were seated apart from the rest of the room, just to the left of the kitchen doorway. From time to time dishes rattled and doors opened, making it harder for Rob to concentrate. Still, he was determined to get his point across.

"Let me ask you something, Tony," he said. "What's Robert Kennedy's stand on Vietnam? I mean, was he for or against the recent bombings in Southeast Asia?"

"Look, Rob, all I said was—"

"It's a simple question, Tony. Was he for or against it?"

"He was for it," Tony almost shouted. He turned to face the room when he realized that his voice had carried. A few eyes looked his way.

Rob shook his head, thinking how bizarre—bizarre and scary—it was that most people in the country hardly knew anything about their top officials.

"You're mistaken, Tony," Rob said. "'Approach to revolutionary war must be political.' His words. L.B.J. is for the escalation of the war. Not Kennedy."

Tony opened his mouth to speak but closed it again when the waitress came to the table. Irritably he snatched the check from her hand. "Thanks," he said to her.

"More coffee?" she asked.

Rob made a stab for the check. "Tony, let me get that."

"Next time." He turned apologetically to the waitress. "No more coffee for me, thanks. Maybe he'd like a refill. I have to get going.

Rob shook his head, and then waited for the woman to walk away from the table before saying, "Let me take the damn check, will you?"

"No, I owe you this one." Tony nervously began frisking himself, looking for his wallet.

"Sure you do," Rob said, and then both

were silent. The silence was uncomfortable, as if they were complete strangers. Rob felt his heart growing heavier, darker by the moment, as much with sadness as confusion. It's true, he thought. There's no going back. Yet he knew he had to go back, to face the truth about his parents, himself. If he didn't, well, he might as well call it a day, because he was walking around like a corpse, thinking that the best of him had been laid to rest in Crestwood Lawn along with his mother and father.

Tony shot him a small sideways glance, followed by, "You about ready to go?"

There was only the slightest trace of annoyance in his voice, but it was enough to prompt Rob to say, "It's a bitch, isn't it? Being with someone you haven't seen for ten years."

"It is," Tony agreed.

Rob laughed. "I know I've been driving you crazy. Look," Rob said, "don't pay any attention to me. I'm just a little antsy, that's all. It's this frigging Larry business. I don't know where he is, or why the hell he ran out on me the way he did." He ran a hand over his forehead. "Jesus, I feel lousy."

"Well, if it'll make you feel any better," Tony said, "so do I."

There was a pause. Then Rob said, "You do? Why?"

"I'm not sure. I think it's one of those things you figure out a week after it happens."

Rob looked at his friend, who looked away.

He could see that Tony was telling the truth about feeling lousy, and that only made him feel worse. In that moment all he wanted was to feel close to Tony, to have a sense of shared experience. He said, "Do you know, I almost came back to Millhouse after the army—to live."

"You did?"

"Yeah, I was tempted. I came awfully close to doing it."

Tony said, "What stopped you?"

"I don't know. I guess I felt there was nothing left for me here after my folks died. And yet"—their eyes locked—"I feel there's something here that I should be doing. Something that I've left undone." Rob shrugged.

"Elizabeth, maybe?" Tony suggested.

"What do you mean?"

"Maybe you still have something going for Elizabeth."

Rob could tell that Tony was anxiously waiting for his response. "I don't think so," he said evenly.

"But you're not completely sure, are you?"

What Rob wanted to say was: "Look. Once Elizabeth was at the center of things. Everything revolved around her. She held our world in the palms of her hands and no one could touch it. Now that moment has passed. It won't be back." He also wanted to say that he had always known that Tony loved her.

He said instead, "I thought she'd be married by now."

"To who—me?"

Rob nodded. "I thought maybe—"

"You don't understand. We're just friends. There'll never be anything different between us."

Clumsily, Rob said, "I'm sorry," and Tony said, "So am I."

There fell a silence which neither man seemed able to break. Rob cursed himself for not being able to say what was really on his mind. For not being able to express how confused he was, and scared.

At length Tony was the first to speak. "Well, I gotta get back to the office. I've got some calls coming in. You want to come back with me?"

"Not now, if you don't mind."

"All right."

Tony moved, as though to rise, but Rob placed his hand on his arm. "Tony, I've got something to ask you. Something important. Right before my mother died, I . . . I started hearing things. About how she and my father were causing trouble here in Millhouse. You ever hear anything like that?"

He waited until Tony slipped his wallet into his jacket pocket, then, as if he had been guilty of an oversight, permitted him to rise.

"Is that why you finally decided to come back to Millhouse?"

The question was unexpected. "I guess so. It's tough being an orphan that young," Rob replied. "I'm looking for answers . . ."

Tony paused; he seemed to be beset with private trouble. "I never get involved with other people's personal lives." He hesitated again, studied Rob as if judging whether to impart a secret to him. "Do you understand?"

Rob didn't. For an instant he thought Tony was going to explain what he meant, but saw him change his mind.

Glancing at his watch, he said, "I gotta run."

And Rob, embarrassed and feeling juvenile, said, "Sure, you go ahead."

"What are you going to do about your friend?"

"I guess—I guess I'll report him missing," Rob said. "At least stop by the sheriff's office."

Tony nodded. "I think that's a good idea."

4

It was Doc Tanner who brought Juniper back, what was left of Juniper: a torn-to-shreds bundle of blood and dirt and fur. "I thought you'd want him back," Doc Tanner said. "Even though the sheriff told me to dispose of him. I . . . I don't know what to say, Ned."

Ned Taylor said nothing at all. He took the dog and held it to his chest against his overalls.

For a moment the Doc just stood there watching, his arms and hands limp at his sides. At last he muttered, "Hard to say how it happened, Ned. Another animal, maybe. But from the looks—" He broke off, afraid to speak what was on his mind.

Finally, with slow shuffling steps, he left the house.

At around ten A.M., Ned Taylor laid Juniper on the kitchen table and covered him with a sheet. Then he walked out to the barnyard, where he could see the sun glint from the tractor on the low hill where the oldest cucumber patch was. It was sunny and hot; the sky was clear and in the heat there was a closeness that was almost pain.

Then, as he lifted the ax—the ax that had been used only yesterday to lop off a chicken's head—he knew, with a sudden certainty, what had happened to his dog. The same thing that had happened to his cattle a few years back. Coyotes, some said. Others said a pack of wild dogs. But he knew better.

"They done it," whispered Ned Taylor. His agony was overwhelming but he fought it down.

The ax caught a splay of sunlight and glistened for a moment as he moved into the barn. Running his thumb along the edge, he wondered if Doc Tanner knew what he knew. He wondered about torn flesh, lifeless eyes, and death.

On the night of August 8, 1956, Ned Taylor had been awakened from a deep sleep by someone quietly but insistently calling his name. As he sat up in bed he was astonished to see the figure of a woman outside his window. She looked perfectly real. There was an odd smile on her face. "Don't be afraid," she said. "It's only me. Please, open the window." Instinctively he reached for his shotgun. The woman moved quickly—too quickly. When he looked back, she was gone.

The next day he was sitting in Sue's Cafe—about eight people were there having breakfast—when Doc Tanner came in. The Doc looked ill. Ned stopped to speak to him, telling him, quietly, about his dream.

Doc Tanner didn't speak but looked at him strangely, and after a few more words, Ned decided he'd better keep quiet. (Privately, he had thought the Doc had gone a bit senile.) Looking back now after some ten years, Ned Taylor realized what the man's silence had meant. That it wasn't a dream. The woman had been standing there sure enough. Looking to come in.

Ned Taylor lifted the ax to the grindstone. Sparks flew. Tiny pinpricks of life that seemed a blessing.

He watched as the edge of the ax grew sharper. "No more," he whispered. "No more . . ." The stone turned.

Being born twice is no more remarkable than being born once. But they weren't born again. Were they? "No," he sighed, and watched the wheel turn again and again and again . . . Then the words were torn from him, the right words: "Forgive me, Father, for what I'm about to do."

Sparks mixed with tears.

The ax glinted once more in the sunlight as

Ned Taylor moved back into his house. He would do it tonight.

Mrs. Walker watched Ned Taylor cross the backyard, with a fierce look in his eyes and an ax in his hand. Somehow, he looked different. He didn't look tired anymore. He walked faster than usual, and his face looked alive and, though she didn't like thinking it, crafty, like he was up to no good.

She had stopped by Lucy Morgan's house to pay her respects. Lucy's sister had passed on during the week, and everyone knew how lonely Lucy would be without her sister. Twin sister, actually. The only twins ever to be born in Millhouse.

The sad thing was that Emma Morgan had left Millhouse some years back, and although Lucy hadn't seen her sister in seven years, they wrote to each other, faithfully, once a week.

It was to Emma's last letter that Lucy now clung. She seemed lost, staring through the kitchen window at the white cat on the porch. The cat got up, walked a few feet, and then lay down again in a new patch of sunlight.

"It seems strange, doesn't it, Betty?" Lucy Morgan said, her fingers clinging tightly to the edge of the paper she held.

"What's that?"

"The way things turn out. The way everything keeps on moving. I remember the day the Caldwell boy ran his car off the road into that big elm tree yonder. It only took them an hour to take his body away, and remove his car. A few minutes after the car was gone, I looked out and nothing seemed to have changed. Ned's cows were still chewing the grass; Ned went right on plowing. It was like it never happened. Everything just went on like before."

Betty Walker sighed. "Life has a way of being like that, I guess."

"But it shouldn't be, should it? People should count for something." She paused to wipe tears from her eyes.

Betty Walker came to her side and gave her an awkward hug. "Things will work out, Lucy. I promise."

"You mean things will go on. That's the way Millhouse is, isn't it? Nothing seems to change it. Not death, not anything."

Betty Walker felt a terrible embarrassment. She knew she should say something that would comfort her friend, but she just couldn't find the words.

"It says here in Emma's letter that she was born again," Lucy Morgan said. "Odd, isn't it? Her whole life she never held with religion. And now—"

Both women stared at each other. There was no sound, but there was the feeling of things moving, growing in the shadows of the kitchen. An evil, a scourge, an obsession that would soon devour an entire town.

5

The white Cadillac stopped in front of the sheriff's office just after eleven o'clock. The chauffeur jumped from the car and opened the passenger door. A woman, dressed in a pale-blue business suit and frilly blouse, waved aside the chauffeur's extended hand and got out of the car unaided. Walking quickly, not using the silver-topped ebony walking stick she carried, she went into the building.

From the opposite side of Main Street, Rob watched the chauffeur climb back into the car. Edna Gale Hutchson, he thought. He remembered the woman from years ago, remembered all the stories that preceded her. How her father had given a party for his "little darling," converting his house into an Oriental garden for a hundred or so guests. The party cost ten thousand dollars at a time when sirloin steaks were a quarter a pound and bread cost a nickle a loaf. How she studied psychiatry in Switzerland, and helped subsidize a famous writer from New York City. Some said they were actually lovers.

Edna Gale Hutchson was an astonishingly full-breasted woman who lived on Rosco Lane—the very mecca of Millhouse—that well-cared-for street that held the privileged few.

That such a woman had come to the sheriff's office personally was surprising; that she seemed agitated was a sure sign that something wasn't quite right in Millhouse.

Rob moved closer. The barrel-chested man seated behind the wheel toyed with the lapels of his monogrammed jacket. The "E.H." monogram had always caused a stir—it wasn't often that one saw a deliberate display of splendor in Millhouse. "E.H." had always provided that rare moment.

Soon the car was started up; slowly it eased away from the curb and continued down Main Street.

Rob waited for the Cadillac to disappear from view before crossing the street. As he approached the building, he noticed that "E.H." had left the sheriff's door open. He inched forward, trying not to call attention to himself, and peered in. The outer office was empty, but he could hear voices raised in the back room. He stepped inside. The voices grew more distinct.

"Oh, come now, Sheriff. Here it is eleven o'clock and I arrive to find the front shades drawn, your deputy in the park entertaining that Cass girl, and you back here . . . *relaxing.*"

"Sleeping," the sheriff growled. "I was sleeping, Mrs. Hutchson. I haven't gone to bed since yesterday!"

"Be that as it may, you should be concerned over the dog incident last night. This isn't the first incident of its kind, you know."

"A dog gets killed, so what?"

The woman's silhouette came to an abrupt stop near the door. Rob drew back. "There was a man involved, wasn't there?"

"Look, I don't know who's been telling you things," the sheriff said with great intensity, "but two dogs had a fight and one got killed. That's all."

There came a silence, and Rob knew they were measuring each other, each calculating the other's next move.

Finally the woman said, "Sheriff, I will come directly to the point. My late husband was the one who endorsed you in the first place. I've continued to honor his commitment. But now I find that you are not living up to that endorsement." She hesitated. "Say what you will, but there was a man involved in what happened last night, and if you let the guilty party go unpunished, you will be finished as sheriff in this town. I don't intend to watch all that I've worked so hard for thrown aside because of your laziness. Am I making myself clear?"

"Now just hold on. I'll check into your story. If there was somebody responsible for killing that dog last night, I'll find out who. How's that?"

"Very well. I shall expect an update of your progress first thing in the morning."

"Yes, all right." The sheriff hesitated. "Is your car out front?"

"I prefer leaving by the back way, if you don't mind. I wouldn't want people seeing me coming out of the jail house, especially with the shades drawn."

The sound of the back door closing reached Rob's ears just as he was retracing his steps to the front door. When he turned around, he was startled to see the sheriff standing there, staring at him.

"What do you want?" the man demanded.

Rob opened his mouth, then closed it again, and said nothing.

The sheriff wasn't the sort of man Rob had expected him to be. Indeed, he had expected something very different, something along the lines of the traditional small-town constable.

Instead, he found a rugged individual—broad through the shoulders and broad through the chest—wearing an expensive purple shirt, striped yellow tie, and a gray felt hat stuck far back on his head. His trousers were black and neatly creased; his boots the color of his trousers and highly polished.

Still there was something deceptive about his appearance, Rob thought. Not even the neat cut of his clothes could hide the enormous strength of his body—his muscles seemed to be flexed even though he was standing perfectly at ease. And although he had a paunch, it was obvious that those extra pounds could be used to crush you in an instant.

"Well?" he said gruffly, and moved behind his desk.

Rob waited until he sat and propped his feet up, before explaining why he was there. As he spoke, the sheriff's face, reddened by a combination of sun, wind, and whiskey, seemed hardly to change expression. He merely scribbled a few notes in his pad.

Finally he stopped scribbling, swung his legs off the desk and said, "Nothing to do now. Gotta wait seventy-two hours."

"Seventy-two hours?" Rob wondered. "Why's that?"

The sheriff glanced at him appraisingly, his voice cool. "'Cause that's the law. This Campbell fella, he's over eighteen, right?"

"Sure, but that doesn't—"

"An adult ain't legally missing around here until after seventy-two hours. Even then . . . I mean, no sign of foul play, was there?"

"No, none that I know of."

The sheriff looked thoughtful for a moment, and his eyes assumed a trace of expression; the pupils seemed to narrow. "Hell, he could of just gotten fed up," he said, dropping the note pad meaningfully onto his desk. "People do that all the time. Happened to a girl working at Sue's place. She turned around one day and her friends were gone. Took off and left her."

"I know, I heard," Rob said.

"Well, there you go then," the man said. With the satisfied air of someone who'd just solved the mystery of the Sphinx, he got up, walked to the window, and let up the shades. A yellow haze spilled over the windowsill and across the wood floor. Both were covered with a fine layer of dirt. Millhouse dust that seemed to cover the town from one end to the other; clinging to clothes, filling the air, strewn about by the men who worked in the factory. A town, Rob thought, buried under its own preoccupation.

Abruptly the man turned and said, "Your friend wasn't drinking, was he? Fooling around with drugs?"

"No," Rob lied.

The sheriff stared at him. "What was he wearing?"

"I . . ." Rob shook his head, trying to get a clear mental picture. None came, except for Larry's rolling eyes. "I don't remember," he said. "Levi's, a denim shirt, I think."

"Think? Hell," the sheriff snorted, "that's the trouble with witnesses. They never remember what they saw." He frowned. "Your description accurate?"

Rob glanced nervously at the sheriff's pad. "Of course it's accurate. Tall, brown hair, large mustache . . ."

"How's he wearing his hair. Long, short?"

"Ah . . . sort of long."

"Shit, he ain't one of those city freaks, is he? One of them goddamn hippies?"

"I told you—he's a reporter."

"Twenty-four, you said."

"That's right."

The sheriff stared at him. His voice turned raspingly sarcastic. "Damn, what the hell does a twenty-four-year-old kid know about reporting? I got a son his age. All he can do is get drunk and chase women. Shoot, he can't even do that right."

"Look," Rob said, and took a breath of hot, stuffy air. It was like breathing inside a plastic bag. "Larry's not like that," he exhaled. "That's why I'm concerned. He's not the kind of person to do something like this."

"Like what? Disappear? People do it all the time. I just told you that."

"For what reason?"

"Hell, who knows. You might as well put all the reasons in a hat and draw one out. It would be the easiest way."

Rob drew inward, considering. Things had

sure changed in Millhouse. Sheriff Blackwell had been the law in his day. A skinny, excitable man with jutting jaw and a nose for justice. Also a nose for getting at the truth, and quickly.

"The Law Man," the kids used to call him. Once a year he would run the oldest of them through the jail house, trying to keep them in line by scaring the crap out of them. Most of the time he succeeded.

"What if something has happened to Larry Campbell?" Rob blurted out.

The sheriff said, "If it was something serious, I would have heard by now."

As this was a deliberate put off, Rob ignored it. "Maybe not. He could be lost in the woods somewhere. He could be hurt."

The sheriff grunted in exasperation.

"Okay," Rob said, "but shouldn't I at least fill out a report or something? At least get that out of the way?"

The sheriff cleared his throat, then threw open the window. Hot air rushed into the room. "Hey, Harley!" he exclaimed and leaned out the window. "I noticed you was doin' some burnin' yesterday."

Outside, the man with the toothpick in his mouth grinned. "It was a good day for it!"

"Next time get the permits!" the sheriff joked.

"Hell, no. Town gets too much of my money as it is."

The sheriff laughed. "How's your brother-in-law doin'? I hear Topeka still ain't recovered from that tornado."

"Fourteen dead. A hundred million in damages."

"That so. Now who do you suppose is gonna pay for all that mess?"

"Sure in hell ain't gonna be me!"

The man leaned over, peered at Rob for a moment through the window. Then, with a knowing nod, he moved on.

The sheriff grunted and turned back to face the room. "One of these days he'll set the whole goddamn town on fire. Just last week he . . ." He broke off, as if he'd suddenly realized he was talking to a stranger. "Well, like I said—you come back on Monday if your friend hasn't turned up."

Rob caught himself on the verge of an appropriate reply and instead said, "Is Sheriff Blackwell still living in town?"

The sheriff threw him a look, saw that Rob was all attention, then dropped into his chair. "He's dead," he said, almost in a singsong. "Committed suicide shortly after leaving town. Why, did you know him?"

"Yeah. I used to live in Millhouse."

"That so? I didn't catch your name."

"I didn't throw it," Rob said. Without meaning to, he frowned. He thought better of it in the next instant. It had occurred to him that he was going to need all the help he could get, including the sheriff's. "Rob . . . Rob Martin," he said. "I used to live on Elm Street."

"Ah," the sheriff nodded. "Before my time, I guess."

"I guess."

"Rob Martin," the man repeated, as if trying to conjure a recollection to go with the name. He was staring at Rob, his large, dark eyes still as bullet holes, and Rob had an irrational feeling that any moment he would begin snarling like an animal. Then the man moved, grudgingly, and let the matter go like a schoolteacher dismissing his class.

6

A few minutes later Rob was on the street. He could tell that Millhouse, like some magical elixir, was beginning to change the way he thought, even the way he dressed and acted.

Damn it, he hissed and ripped the tie loose from around his collar. Hot, getting hotter. He glanced down the street. *Some fucking reporter,* he thought angrily. He couldn't even handle a hick sheriff, so how in hell was he going to take on Bobby Kennedy?

He should have questioned the sheriff about that dog being killed last night. There could have been a story there. Luke Tucker, Tony—both should have been tackled head-on. What the hell was wrong with him?

I don't know nothin', Rob's father had said, *and the hell of it is, I broke my back, spent every cent I had to keep you in school, and now you don't know nothin', neither. Now ain't that somethin'?*

Yeah, Paw—it's something, all right.

As the morning progressed, turning into a typical hot, humid, miserable July day, Rob found his mood changing from anger at himself to a mild curiosity. Already vague rumors had circulated about some horrible thing that had happened last night, but no matter how hard he pried, no further details were forthcoming. A dog had been killed. "Mutilated," Mrs. Baker let slip while handing Rob his cigarettes and change. But she quickly amended this, saying, "Cut up bad by a passing train."

Across the street the DeJohn sisters watched as the young man standing in front of the ice-cream parlor opened his pack of cigarettes and removed and lit one. "Joan, dear, isn't that—"

A faint voice answered.

"Yes, Emily, that's him."

Emily DeJohn was the older of the two. She was a thin woman, bone-thin through the shoulders and chest, and her lips trembled when the young man looked her way. She turned to stare at her sister, a little fidgety, as if to say: *Come along, dear. We mustn't get involved.*

When Rob passed the large, dusty windows of the Millhouse Supermarket, Peter Appleton, of Appleton Appliances, was chewing the fat with Al Jacobs. Both men moved aside so as not to be seen. Appleton thought: *The kid's going to be trouble.*

"You're panicking, Pete, and it's not a pretty sight," Al Jacobs said to him in a half whisper. "I thought you had more spunk."

"Goddamn it, you know full well what I'm feeling. And if you had any sense, you'd feel the same way!"

"We're just wasting time," the taller man said. "We all know what has to be done."

"Al, please, this ain't ten years ago. Last night someone carved up that dog. People know that, and are making a big deal out of it. So we have to handle it like a big deal or people will suspect."

Al Jacobs straightened, drawing himself to his most impressive and domineering height, and glared down into Appleton's face. "You're a fool, Pete," he said. "We're all of us fools for listening to Whitset. Now get away from me and let me finish my shopping."

Jacob's words, usually not spoken so harshly, struck Appleton across the face like a mallet. He swallowed a few times to compose himself. Then, unable to say another word, he flew out of the market, slamming the door behind him.

* * *

The next half hour passed in a kind of a blur to Rob. The old men of his youth kept limping through his mind. Jack Gardner, Tony's uncle, who was fond of telling yarns about Indians. According to his own estimate, his grandfather had killed at least twelve with his bare hands. Old man Harris, who had gotten drunk one night and fallen into the creek. They found him the following morning in the next county, still drunk but smiling, telling how he swam the entire way holding his breath. And Ned Taylor with his bear, "F.D.R." he called him, and how he would charge a dime if a person wanted to see the bear walk the barrel blindfolded.

Rob's mind lingered over the details of that one for a moment. Then he shook his head dumbly, and stared down at the green counter of the coffee shop at the back of the pharmacy. He was trying hard not to reach for the glass of Alka Seltzer fizzing in front of him. He was trying even harder to clear his mind, to keep from wondering just how many of the old-timers were dead, when the postman dropped his empty mail sack on the floor and sat down beside him.

Rob looked up. He did not recognize the face.

"Coffee, Sally!" the postman boomed, then elbowed a little more room for himself on the counter.

"How about a donut?" the waitress asked. She was a plump thing with bobbed hair and earrings that jangled when she walked.

"Nah," the man said. "I'm not supposed to eat that crap anymore. Ulcer." He pressed the fingers of one hand into his potbelly and belched.

"I thought coffee was bad for ulcers, too. The acid or something."

"Depends," the postman said with authority. "It seems to do okay by me."

"So, what was all the commotion about?" the girl asked, passing him his coffee.

"The Arbor girl," he mumbled before he swallowed.

Rob immediately paid closer attention. So much so that the postman glanced at him before going on with the story. Hazel, the man's eyes were; eyes that looked daily into hundreds of lives. That knew all there was to know about the people of Millhouse.

"So, what happened?" the waitress asked, her face flushed with interest.

"No one knows for sure," he said. "Mrs. Dodd came back to the shop and found her lying unconscious on the floor."

"She wasn't shot or stabbed or anything?"

"No, nothing like that. They took her over to the clinic to run some tests." He fixed his eyes on the donuts. "Hell, Sally—give me one of those things, will you? But don't tell the missus!" Then, as an afterthought, he asked, "Are they fresh?"

"Fresh as they'll ever be," the waitress said,

lifting the lid on the plastic bubble.

The postman turned unexpectedly to face Rob. "You vacationing hereabouts?"

"Yes," Rob said and drank his Alka Seltzer. It was better than getting into an ongoing conversation.

But a few seconds later the man asked, "You here for the fishing?"

"No, just sightseeing." Rob hesitated. Under different circumstances he would have immediately fled the drugstore, perhaps even fled the town. But he was now beginning to consider it a challenge. The whole point was to stretch yourself as a reporter, probe the limits of your talent. Investigative journalism was like your body: Exercised, it grew firmer, more sure of itself; unused, it became droopy and uncoordinated. "Elizabeth Arbor," he said, "does she still live on Standford Road?"

The postman stared at him. "You know her?"

"Used to—years ago."

"Ah," the man said and took a bite out of his donut. "Yeah, she's still living up there. Worst street in Millhouse during the winter months. Ice and snow gets so bad you can hardly deliver sometimes." He glanced at his donut, and then turned to the waitress. "I thought you said they were fresh?"

"Fresh as they'll ever be," she repeated.

"Damn town's going to the dogs," the man mumbled, and then seemed to realize what he had just said. "Hey, Sally, did you hear about that dog getting killed last night?"

The waitress looked up nervously. "No, no—and I don't want to hear about it, neither."

"Why, you squeamish or something?"

"Forget it, Brock, all right." She shrugged one shoulder, as if to remind him of Rob's presence. "Just forget it, all right."

The postman shook his head, watching her move to the far end of the counter where she began filling salt and pepper shakers. He said, "I'll never understand it. The longer I live in this town, the more I get to wondering."

Rob sat up. "How's that?"

"Secrets. This damn town's got more secrets than people. Wasn't that way in St. Paul. People were open there. Everyone knew everyone else's business. Here everyone's got their secrets. I don't think there's any one person who knows all that's going on."

"Aren't most towns like that?" Rob asked.

"Hell, no. In St. Paul a man farts and the whole town knows what he had for dinner."

Rob laughed. "Well, maybe it would be better in that case if they didn't know."

"I'm not sure," the postman said. "It's like the government today. Secrets. It ain't healthy. No, sir. Ain't healthy. You take this Vietnam business. They ain't telling us the truth. No, sir. Hell, they ain't telling us half of what's going on over there. That's why the kids today are so mad.

I don't blame them. Who the hell wants to die for someone else's secret?"

The waitress was staring hard at the postman now, but she looked away when Rob caught her eye. The drugstore darkened briefly as a truck passed by outside, cutting off the sunlight.

Rob knew the truck by the slogan scrawled on the side: Freshly picked today—Hubbert's Vegetables. He watched Ronny Hubbert climb out of the truck. A short man, almost stunted, like an old jock gone flat. Hubbert's eyes drifted for a second. Then he crossed to the other side of Main Street and disappeared into Beck's Body & Fender Shop.

Familiar faces were beginning to show themselves, laced together with new faces, forming a jigsaw puzzle that kept Rob thinking. New relationships, even newer ideas needed considering. Remembering Elizabeth, Rob felt a pulling inside his gut. An unexpected worry seized him.

"So, where are you from?" the postman asked.

Miami," Rob said, having a difficult time concentrating. Images of Elizabeth were coming faster now, one on top of the other, but the man was talking, saying something about the Fountainbleu Hotel, honeymoon—years ago. Rob couldn't hear him.

Looking back, they had both seen that Rob's leaving was inevitable. Not just pretty, Elizabeth was also smart—smart enough to know that he wasn't going to stay in Millhouse forever. But there were moments when he could see the hope and love in her eyes. Feel it, almost, as she touched him. Hear it in her voice; sounds and images that washed over his mind, through the years, persistent—coming closer.

The reawakening of this tender closeness made Rob realize that Tony had been right. He had come back to Millhouse to be with her.

His head, as well as his stomach, began to swim. Faces and objects, the old drugstore receded from present reality.

There was a "Hey, what'd I say?" from the postman as Rob dropped a dollar on the counter and headed for the front door.

Nothing was to be explained, everything was to hang suspended, until he saw her again.

7

The man's eyes were what Elizabeth remembered as the most striking feature of his face. The eyes of severity are generally narrow ones, closely drawn; his eyes were as severe, as evil, as any she had ever seen; yet, they were not narrow but full, beautifully shaped, overwhelmingly alive, and sensual.

Those eyes . . . Elizabeth thought, and then turned away as one of the nurses passed by the partially opened door.

Embarrassed, Elizabeth put on her skirt, buttoned her blouse, and then, legs still shaking, got into her shoes. The floor wavered as she stooped.

Damn, it's moving again. She held onto the

examining table for a second. All of her ached; her stomach felt uneasy. She gazed at the wall, discovering nothing to distract her upon its oppressive whiteness.

She glanced through the window to the deserted parking lot. So this is what it's like to be inside "The Clinic," she thought.

The infamous clinic where Julia Caine had been operated on, not once but three times. Where Mrs. Dodd came each week for her arthritis shots. Where, ten years ago, the staff had worked for six hours to save Frank Martin's life. The blood bank of Millhouse. They had none of Elizabeth's blood, because she was afraid to give blood. But where the others would line up the last Friday of July and January to donate a pint or two.

Elizabeth had often wondered at how dedicated the people of Millhouse were to the routine of blood donation. It had all started when the bleachers had collapsed during a baseball game, and two people had died because there wasn't enough blood to save their lives.

"A scandal!" Julia Caine had exclaimed. "It must never happen again." And what a Caine wanted, she got. Millhouse residents had been lined up ever since.

Elizabeth took out her cigarettes, lit one. She had come out of her reverie and was staring at her hands with an intensity so great that she didn't notice the doctor stop at the door.

"Miss Arbor?" Elizabeth's head snapped up.

"What? Oh." She looked at the doctor.

He rapped a finger against his jaw. "I hardly think you should be smoking. Do you?"

Elizabeth sighed. "I guess not." Unhurriedly she looked for an ashtray. There weren't any.

The doctor continued to study her. "Dr. Walker will be along shortly," he said.

"Yes, thank you," she said impatiently.

"One must always be prepared for delays, I suppose."

Elizabeth was about to speak, but restrained herself. Without another word, the man walked away. Shaking her head, she moved into the hallway, found an ashtray, and snuffed her cigarette.

She glanced around at the emptiness of the clinic. Everything appeared natural, yet seemed unreal. Even the stoop-shouldered nurse at the admittance desk looked paper-thin, like a vaporous cloud floating above her charts. The wheelchair in the corner, the tall green plants, the magazines on the table, all seemed fake, like the rendering of some mad artist. Van Gogh, maybe.

Damn, it's moving again. The floor shifted as if someone were pulling a carpet out from under her feet. The nurse looked up. Their eyes locked for a moment. Elizabeth quickly went back into the room, closing the door behind her.

The eyes were fake too, she thought, slumping against the table. Of the dream she had had midweek, she could remember only the eyes. And they were the eyes of the man she had seen today, weren't they? Yet one was a dream and the other was not. Maybe she had only imagined that a man had been staring at her before she had fainted. It was possible.

Hell, no—it's not impossible. He was there!

A little surprised that her legs were still holding her up, Elizabeth reached for her purse. Obeying old habits, she looked at herself in her compact mirror. She didn't look half-bad.

Then she heard the voices, one raised, the other low and reproving. In the next room? She glanced up. The voices were coming from the small air duct above her head. An angry voice—no, frightened, talking about . . . what? She strained to listen.

"He knows, I tell you. We must . . ." Whisper, whisper—"Go to him, he'll listen to reason . . ." A hush now as the whispering continued, a word or two more spoken in louder tones—"You must . . . we're responsible if anything goes wrong."

The silence which followed was almost deafening, as if the whole world had abruptly gone away. Elizabeth listened a minute longer, then turned and through the window in the door saw eyes peering at her. Dull eyes this time, eyes that seemed to mean her no harm. The door opened.

Doctor Walker never impressed Elizabeth as being a giant in his field, yet everyone treated him as such. He was a heart specialist, one of the finest in the country. From looking at his eyes one would never expect it. He appeared always to be half-asleep. Even his voice was dull and listless.

Today was no exception. He did not look at Elizabeth when he spoke. His droop-lidded eyes focused only on her chart.

"That's it, then?" Elizabeth finally asked. "Blood pressure?"

"Yes," Dr. Walker murmured, his thin white hands folded one atop the other. These hands were used to holding delicately precisioned instruments. Clever hands that played around with people's hearts.

"I see," Elizabeth sighed.

"You have slightly elevated blood pressure. All of the other tests were negative."

The doctor assured her that she was in perfect health, that she need only relax and take life a bit easier. If, however, the fainting spells continued, she would be advised to see a neurologist.

Prescription in hand, more confused than cured, Elizabeth followed the doctor into the hallway. It wasn't until he had said good-bye, until he had walked half the length of the hallway, that she realized that one of the voices she'd heard coming through the air duct had belonged to him.

Abruptly she turned to gaze after him, and as she turned she had the uneasy sense that she too was being gazed at. She hesitantly glanced back over her shoulder.

Standing in the doorway of the waiting room was Rob Martin. He might have been standing there since the moment before he had left Millhouse, Elizabeth thought. Hands stuffed into his pockets, tie askew, hair parted neatly to one side, he hadn't changed a bit. Elizabeth hesitated, and then felt her heart drop.

Like Elizabeth, Rob did not move. He could not move. Thinking he would find a familiar face, he found it hard to adjust to what he saw, and at first he thought that it wasn't Elizabeth he was looking at. He was at the point of saying, "Sorry, wrong person," when he realized it was the way she wore her hair. Long and flowing over her shoulders. And the skirt she wore, its black and white stripes seeming to move, to ripple along her thin—very thin—body. He remembered a plumper girl, with freckles and short hair. What he was looking at now was a woman. An excitingly sexy woman.

When at last he did move toward her, she made no gesture of greeting. She simply said, with an almost imperceptible motion of her lips, "Hello."

"Well," he said, letting his breath out as he came to stand in front of her.

"It is you, isn't it?" Elizabeth said with a half smile. "I mean, there isn't a smidgen of doubt it's you, is there?"

"Smidgen?"

"Slightest, smallest . . ." Her eyes grew narrower, gazing deeper into his. In the past this would have pleased him, but now he felt awkward and ill at ease.

Then she moved forward and wrapped her arms around him. Immediately he felt the heat of her body pressed to his, and then felt the firmness of her. Taut through the legs. Her thin rib cage and chest were close and hot.

Squeezing her harder, he said, "You feel good, Liz. Real good."

She stepped back and held him at arm's length. "Oh, really? That's interesting."

He hesitated, not knowing what to say. He just stood there staring at her, at a loss for words, trying to decide how to break the silence.

Elizabeth took a stab at it. "How'd you know to find me here?"

"Brock, I think his name is Brock. The postman. By now half the town knows you're here."

"Figures," she said, crinkling up her nose. "A person can't even faint without the whole damn town knowing about it."

Rob looked suddenly serious. "Are you all right?"

Not answering him directly, she cast an evil eye at the nurse, who looked up momentarily and then went back to scribbling in her charts. "I will be," Elizabeth said, "as soon as I get away from here."

Rob was amused. "The clinic is supposed to be the best, or hadn't you heard?"

"Oh, sure, great. A good place for breeding snakes." She took a last hard look at Rob. He smiled, and she said, "I'm ready to go if you are."

8

A few minutes later Rob brought the Jag to a stop on Elm Street and let the engine idle. The weatherbeaten shell of his old house was to their left; the front yard was still filled with familiar things: birdhouses and birdbaths and the old swing that hung precariously from the lowest limb of Potter's elm. Jason Potter had planted the tree, so that's what they called it. Potter's elm.

Rob could still picture the inside of the house as the result of his father's endless labors: handmade shelves, book racks, and cedar chests that his father had made when he wasn't off hunting. Frank Martin was fond of two things outside of his family—killing animals and making furniture.

"Who lives here now?" Rob asked solemnly. "Do you know?"

"No one that I know of. The Talberts used to live there, but after his wife died he moved away."

"Oh. Did they have any children?"

Elizabeth leaned her head back and gave her hair a toss to one side. "No. No children." She hesitated. "Does it give you a strange feeling? Seeing it again after all these years?"

Rob said, "Sort of," and could feel the sudden godawful pain of emptiness. Set among thinly leafed trees, fronted by a parched lawn, the house was a bitter reminder of his parents, of his desolate and defeated youth.

"Rob?"

"Hummm?" He turned to look into Elizabeth's crystal blue eyes, which were at once happy and sad.

"Why did it take you so long to come see me?" she asked.

He looked thoughtfully at her for a moment. "The truth?"

"If it's something I'm not going to like hearing, then lie." She attempted a smile. "Okay?"

He nodded and asked her if she knew about Larry Campbell, and she said that she did. He said, "I could tell you it was because of him being missing. But . . . but that's not the reason.

Part of it, maybe. But not all of it."

"And the other part?" she asked reluctantly.

Unable to answer her, Rob turned to look one last time at the house, seeing and hearing images and sounds from his childhood. Buoyant, almost tripping footsteps, rushing to get through the screen door; hedges neatly sheared —gone now—and roses, yellow and faded pink, old-fashioned roses, sweetly scented. Also gone. And he felt again the haunting presence of Elm Street, and the object of his first conscious passion. Felt her stronger than ever as she sat beside him, waiting for his answer.

Suddenly agitated, he jammed his foot to the gas pedal. The word "Tony" was drowned out by the roar of the engine.

"What?" Elizabeth said and held on.

It wasn't until they had begun climbing Mountainview Road, until they could see the Caine house looming on the horizon, that he repeated the name "Tony." He gave her a brief look before adding, "I thought you and he would—"

"I see."

That was all Elizabeth said, but it was enough for Rob to realize that she was disappointed, perhaps even hurt.

He slowed the car as they rounded the bend. The road dropped sharply, like a twisting waterfall, and passed through an archway of interlocked trees; suddenly the house appeared in front of them. Cautiously he eased the car onto the shoulder and switched off the engine, not quite knowing why he had stopped.

Long blue shadows reached from the house down the cant of sloped lawn toward the car. Between the house and the side gate stood an enormous oak tree, and directly above the house, startling as a sudden explosion in the middle of the night, stood the scorching sun.

Rob slid a cigarette from the pack, tossed the pack on the dashboard, then glanced at Elizabeth. Her eyes were locked on the upper half of the house.

Everything below the roof lay in shadows. The spires had two small windows, one of which had been left slightly open at the bottom, as if someone were seeking relief from the heat within.

"Why have we stopped?" Elizabeth asked.

It was only then that Rob realized the real reason for his stopping. *Larry's inside that house,* he thought. *He's holed up in there—stoned, half-crazed, waiting.*

"I don't know," he said and moved to light his cigarette. "It's peaceful up here. Quiet."

Elizabeth gave him an odd little smile, half-friendly, half-mocking, and went back to staring at the house.

"Are you sure you don't have to get back to the shop?" he asked.

"Mrs. Dodd insisted I take the day off," she muttered without looking at him.

"Shouldn't you go home? Get some rest?"

"Why, are you thinking about doing something that will raise my blood pressure?"

There were two Elizabeths, Rob knew. There was the simpler Elizabeth, a girl who said little, preferring to let things take their course.

And then there was the unpredictable Elizabeth, the girl who would say the most outlandish things just to see what a person's reaction might be. A woman who would provoke action. One never knew when the more adventurous woman would appear, or how seriously she should be taken.

Rob leaned forward, trying to see her expression. Just a blank stare at the Caine house.

"It seems so isolated, doesn't it?" she said.

"There's a feeling of death about it." He tossed his cigarette into the ashtray.

She turned and looked at him curiously. "Or new life."

"I don't understand."

"Someday new people will move in. I was wondering who they might be."

Rob shrugged. "Does it matter, really?"

"Depends. We could use a little excitement around here. Fresh blood."

She leaned her head back and seemed to be daydreaming. Her dress lifted to her thigh as she stretched her legs. It seemed a deliberate action, as if she were insisting that Rob consider her in a new way. After a moment she turned, revealing a shy, thoughtful expression.

"Ghosts," she said, and began to smile.

"What?" He stared at her blankly.

"Don't you remember? My nieces and nephew. The night Tony brought the chicken bones to the house?"

It had been a silly thing to do, but Rob suddenly remembered how much Elizabeth had loved doing it. Three or four times a year, Mrs. Marshall, Elizabeth's aunt, would ask Elizabeth to baby-sit for her three children.

On this particular night, while Tony kept the children busy in the parlor, Elizabeth and Rob sneaked into their bedroom. Rob climbed onto a chair and threw a sheet over himself. The chicken bones were spread on the floor beneath his chair. Elizabeth, covered with a sheet and holding a leg bone, got into the closet. Soon the children were brought into the room. "My finger is touching you," Elizabeth moaned, prodding each child with the chicken bone. Rob had taken ketchup and poured it down the front of his sheet. "I'm blee-eeding," he said, raising his arms. "See, I'm covered in bloo-ood!"

The next morning the children begged their mother not to let Elizabeth baby-sit again. Not ever.

Oddly enough, it was that night, after Elizabeth had finally gotten the children to bed, after Tony had disappeared, laughing, into the night, that Elizabeth and Rob came as close as possible to making love without actually committing the act.

What stopped Rob that night was the fierceness of Elizabeth's passion, an aggressiveness he'd never experienced before.

He'd just stood there in the dark, staring down at her. Her body was fuller then, rounder; the moonlight slanting through the window shading her breasts like the crests of waves. Her hips were also highlighted; she had positioned herself in such a way as to make it impossible for him to refuse.

Finally, when she realized he intended not going through with it, she said, "Come lay beside me. That's all. Just be with me."

They lay side by side for a long time. Then Rob realized that she was crying, and knew that in some way her tears were meant to be attractive, that she was still reaching out to him.

Now she looked at him with that same desire. A raw look, naked. Without thought, he reached over and kissed her. Her hand immediately grasped the back of his neck.

"You're sweating," she said, continuing the kiss.

It didn't surprise him when she slipped her hand inside his jacket and pulled him closer. Hesitantly he let his hand run over the curve of her leg.

"Oh, Jesus, Rob—why did it take you so frigging long to come back. Why?" she murmured.

"I don't know," he said and closed his eyes, trying to block out the sun's glare, her face, the past ten years that seemed bent on crushing him.

"Do you want me?" she whispered.

When he opened his eyes he saw that she was blushing. "Very much," he said.

"Let's go somewhere." She looked at him pleadingly. "Now—right now."

As he straightened up he glanced over her shoulder and suddenly realized that he'd seen something moving beside the house. Dogs. They grew in size as they came to stand at the edge of the drive. Three vicious-looking things with muscular shoulders and maddened red eyes that peered at him through the heavy grillwork of the fence. They were like nothing he'd ever seen before.

Damn, he thought and reached for the ignition key. He imagined he could hear their snorts and the snapping of their teeth as their jaws crushed bone. Later he would even imagine he'd caught a faint odor of the dogs, and could feel their wild heartbeat. The Caines were gone, but they'd left something of themselves behind.

As Elizabeth pressed closer, Rob started the car. Gravel sprayed the underside of the Jag as he made a quick U-turn and accelerated down Mountainview Road. Through his rearview mirror he could see the dogs still standing there, backs hunched, ready to defend or attack.

9

Expressionless, eyes closed, they lay in the dark shadows beneath the house. The air was dense with the dry pungence of perfume and aged cement. The tallest of the men, lean and well muscled with a pockmarked face, seemed almost to awaken.

He had a sixth sense that warned him whenever danger was near.

Soon he could sense that the danger had passed. His lips twisted in a malicious smile born of arrogance and limitless power, then a darkness settled upon his consciousness—but not a darkness without awareness.

Never without awareness.
He returned to a peaceful sleep.
Aware.

10

Inside Rob's motel room the light was merely a soft gloom. A slight breeze lifted the curtains at the partially opened window. A still-fresh path of water droplets ran from the bathroom to the bed. The only sound was the constant drip-drip-drip from behind the bathroom door.

They had begun their lovemaking in the shower; but without pausing had moved onto the bed. They did not stop even when a group of people scurried from a car to the adjoining room, shouting and carrying on and banging luggage. She had only stopped once, to look at him, holding his face between her hands, as he continued his slow steady thrusts.

Rob also heard, or thought he heard, the faraway sound of dogs howling and it reminded him of a night not so long ago—the night of Julia Caine's funeral—yesterday. Only yesterday, Rob had thought, kissing Elizabeth's neck, her breasts.

She had put her arms back against the headboard and let him do what he liked. Everything seemed unnatural, yet he could not stop, nor could he bring himself to a climax. Suddenly she had tensed and begun to shudder. He had felt it clearly; the sensation had caught him unaware, excited him; he had thrust harder as her arms and legs came around him until finally, fiercely, they had both climaxed.

Gradually, through distracted senses, Rob felt the woman beside him move, felt her thin body stretch luxuriously and then fasten itself to his side. He absently stroked her shoulder, as outside the motel a train went rattling past, its slow moving rumble seeming to go on forever. At last Elizabeth looked at Rob and smiled with satisfaction, a smile that widened her otherwise narrow face. Then her smile turned into a yawn, which she stifled.

"Are you tired?" he asked.

She said, "A little."

"Close your eyes. Rest."

She brought his hand to her lips and kissed it. "It was better than I ever imagined," she said.

"I'm glad," he said and for some reason felt ashamed. Ashamed because he really hadn't wanted this to happen. At least not so soon, and not in some out-of-the-way motel in Jerkwater, U.S.A. When he had imagined making love with Elizabeth, he'd always pictured it like in the movies: silk sheets, soft music and candlelight, two glasses of wine sitting companionably on the table. And books. Somehow he'd always imagined Elizabeth and him surrounded by books.

Elizabeth stirred, rising up on her elbows. "What are you thinking?"

"Nothing, really," he said.

"When are you leaving Millhouse?" she asked, not looking at him. She seemed to be shying away from his answer.

"Tomorrow afternoon. I was supposed to leave today." He shrugged. "But now, well, I'll stick around until tomorrow. See if Larry shows up."

"And if he doesn't, what then?"

"Then . . . then I'll go on without him."

"Oh."

Nothing much was said after that. Elizabeth seemed content to have it that way. Soon they got dressed and went for a walk. The pond, even the midafternoon sky, was a brilliant blue. Elizabeth seemed tired but continued to walk the common, which was empty, except for a few children playing ball and sailing their boats.

The smaller boy failed to catch the ball that sailed toward him. The ball landed at Rob's feet and he picked up the sphere and tossed it back to the child.

"Here you go," Rob said.

The boy smiled, his eyebrows lifted. "Thanks!" he said, grinning, and ran back to join his buddy.

Elizabeth caught hold of Rob's hand, herself grinning, and began leading him back to the motel. She almost ran the last few steps to the door. The room was still cool from the air conditioner, even though Rob had turned it off before leaving. They began making love again, still half-dressed.

Elizabeth slept after that, and Rob sat quite still at the edge of the bed, watching her. He stared at the two tiny red marks on the side of her neck, wondering if he had caused them.

The marks seemed to disappear as the pulse in the vein of her neck quickened; a wild river of blood beat beneath pale white skin. Restlessly Elizabeth kicked at the sheets covering her body, moaned and sighed.

She was in the throes of dreaming, he guessed.

And he wondered about that too; wondered if it was possible for him to ever again become part of her dreams.

11

At the other end of town the Salingers were also wondering. It wasn't like J.D. to miss his supper. 'Twasn't like him at all.

His parents sat side by side on the porch swing, waiting.

It was a warm night. The last of the evening sun filtered through the leaves of the maple trees, and rooks called to each other across the branches.

"You think I should take a run down to the creek?" Mr. Salinger said, between puffs on his pipe.

"No, that would only embarrass the boy, Tom. Let's give him a few more minutes."

Mrs. Salinger glanced at the sky. It would be dark soon. The thought deepened her worry, but she didn't let on. J.D. was a good boy, always had been. He just probably lost track of the time, that's all. He was probably hightailing it home right this minute.

She glanced covertly at her husband. He looked tired and drawn, like someone who had experienced too much in too little time; the years of backbreaking work were engraved for all to see.

"I guess that pie is cool enough now," she said. "Would you like a piece?"

He grinned uncertainly, suddenly looking a lot younger. "Maybe so. Peach, is it?"

"Blueberry."

"My favorite," he said, getting to his feet.

A half hour later, Tom Salinger stopped at the kitchen door to light his pipe. He saw that it had grown dark outside.

His wife was at the sink, fidgeting with the dishes.

It was very quiet, the only sound that of running tap water. It was hard to believe that only a few hours earlier he had stood in the backyard in his bare feet with nothing more important on his mind than J.D.'s upcoming baseball game: Would the team win its seventh straight and go undefeated? Now, it really didn't seem to matter.

Mrs. Salinger finally said, "Why don't you go put your feet up, Tom? Watch TV."

"Not in the mood for TV," he muttered. Then he said, "I think I'll give Rudy a call. See if he'd like to play some gin rummy."

She followed his gaze to the window, then looked back at her husband. "You mean see if his son is home yet, don't you?"

"It's late, Claudine."

"J.D. knows how to take care of himself, Tom. He's a grown boy now."

"He's fourteen, for God's sake!"

"Tom, I'm just as worried—"

"I'm calling Rudy," Mr. Salinger said, determined. "And if Frankie's not home, I'm going out looking for them. I should have done it hours ago," he said, and stormed into the living room.

While he was dialing the front door burst open and J.D. stood there, grinning.

"Hi, Dad," he said. "Sorry I'm late."

Mrs. Salinger came hurrying to the kitchen door. Her hands were trembling. "J.D., where . . . where in God's name have you been?"

"I told ya, Mom. Swimming." He held up a damp bathing suit.

A few minutes later Mr. and Mrs. Salinger sat at the kitchen table watching their son eat.

The boy looked up once and smiled.

A smile filled with young sharp teeth.

12

Elizabeth Arbor awoke suddenly, just after sunset. Rob had left the room twice while she slept. Once to gas up the Jag, then again to get a bottle of vodka, a small container of orange juice, coffee, and sandwiches. He was just ransacking the bag when she awoke and peered at him over the top of the sheet.

"What time is it?" she asked.

"Almost nine o'clock."

In silence she stared out the small window to the rear of the room. Rob sipped his coffee. Soon she sat up and lit a cigarette. After a few heavy drags, she began to dress.

"I got something for us to eat," he said, sensing something was wrong. It wasn't only her silence, but rather the way she avoided looking at him.

"I'm not hungry," she said. "But thanks."

He looked at her in the soft murky light. She seemed self-conscious now. Her figure looked boyishly thin. And somehow, he couldn't quite put his finger on it, she looked different again. Perhaps it was the wrinkled skirt she still wore, the way those stripes looked to be moving even though she wasn't. He studied her image in the mirror as she straightened her hair and clothes. She looked tired, exceedingly tired.

"Are you sure you don't want to eat something?"

"Not a thing," she said and took a long drag on her freshly lit cigarette.

"How about a drink? I've got vodka . . . and some orange juice."

She looked at his reflection in the mirror. Her voice was cold when she finally spoke. "Nice of you to remember, but no thanks."

"Coffee, then?"

"Please, Rob, stop trying to force-feed me. Do I look that wanton?"

"No, you look great," he said and smiled.

She didn't smile back.

He said, "What's wrong?"

"All of it, I guess. Me." She turned to face him. "The minute I saw you today I thought, If he loves me, he'll sleep with me. But that's not necessarily true, is it?"

A silence.

"I'm ridiculous, aren't I?" she said. She gave him a long look, then shook her head and shut her eyes. "I'm sorry. I loved it. Loved sleeping with you. But now what?"

"Now, now we slow down, I guess. Get to know each other all over again."

"What does that mean?" She stared at him through a swirl of cigarette smoke.

He said, "I don't know, exactly. But—"

"I love you, damn it. I've always loved you. Don't you know that?"

Rob opened his mouth to speak, but she cut him off with a raised hand. "Please, you don't have to say anything. Not now. Too much has been said already."

Snuffing her cigarette, she collected her shoulder bag and moved to the door.

He said, "Where are you going?"

"Home."

"All right, I'll—"

"No, I'd rather walk." She turned back to face him. "You go on with what you were doing. What you have to do. Don't take this afternoon too seriously, all right? I mean, just because I take myself too seriously, it doesn't mean you have to." She hesitated, her hand on the doorknob. "You're not to blame, Rob. Really you're not. If a girl asks you to make love to her, well. . . ."

She smiled, part tender, part self-mocking, then fled the room.

After Elizabeth left, Rob broke open the bottle. His first two drinks were more orange juice than vodka. His second two drinks were more vodka than orange juice. The last three were plain vodka.

He poured another drink, his hot palm beading sweat on the cool plastic glass. The smooth vodka slipped down his gullet and mushroomed upward from his stomach into a frown that formed on his lips, and reaching his eyes made a slight salted dew.

From that moment on, the ache that had been hidden in the recesses of his mind, somewhere under fathoms of past days and nights, invaded him thoroughly.

He was still running, he realized. He was still afraid to confront his past head-on. He should have stopped Elizabeth from leaving and told her how he felt about her. How damned good—no, terrific—it was to be with her again, to feel her love, her warming presence. But something had taken hold of him, had prevented him, as always, from expressing his love.

It's me, Elizabeth. Not you.

I'm dead inside.

Outside, a woman's heels clacked slowly upon the sidewalk, and somewhere a door opened and then closed again—Rob, listening, found himself constructing an imaginary life.

It was a sweet existence, but false. Full of spring mornings and splendid sunsets, long quiet walks along the ocean and a tropical isle.

In the end all that remained were the darkening clouds of a typhoon.

Finally he laid back on the bed and closed his eyes. He fell asleep with his clothes on and sometime during the next few hours was roused by a train whistle. He lay there listening for it again, wondering if he had only been dreaming.

When he heard it again, the sound was closer, louder. He sat up and stared at the front window. There was a train coming; he could feel the building begin to tremble. He had no idea what time it was; the sky was a dusty black—the junction light flashed in the distance like an evil eye.

He could hear the train clearly now and knew it was moving at a fast speed. He saw a diffuse glow moving through the darkness. The light widened, intensified. The hot spot seemed to be heading straight for him until abruptly it swung away to his left. He rubbed his eyes and looked closer as the massive engine flashed by, and then passenger cars, all lit up inside. Faces—bodies, people huddled together talking and drinking—more cars, another face.

Oh, my God, he thought as the last face lingered before him. He could hear the train rumbling away down the tracks and yet the face hadn't moved from the window. It was still there, peering at him.

With a shock he realized that he wasn't imagining the face. Terrified, Rob stared at his mother's face. Her eyes were rolled into her head in sorrowful death, and by some cruel joke, tears like stars dotted her cheeks.

It can't be, he thought. Someone was there, staring at him—but it couldn't be his mother. *Not* his mother!

In the next instant the woman moved away from the window, the white of her dress the last thing he saw before she vanished into the night. He stumbled toward the door, pulled it open, dashed outside. The woman was moving away down the path. She turned back for an instant; he couldn't have mistaken the face. Not a second time. It *was* his mother.

He followed her, haltingly, through the underbrush and around the rear of the building, then up a small hill. On the rise he caught sight of her again. He stopped walking and stood mutely, doggedly tracking her with his eyes. Inside his head a great leaden mass of emotion stirred. Suddenly he could taste the booze welling up in his mouth, feel it writhing in his stomach.

Sick, he was going to be sick. He stooped down, his head buried in anguish. He opened his mouth but nothing came out. Only deep, choking gasps.

When he was again able to stand, he could see her clearly in the vast wooded area that stretched before him. He clambered over the embankment and looked down and spotted the woman as she headed for Nickle Road. He watched her cross the meadow and step over a low stone wall. She moved awkwardly and would be easy to catch.

He started running full out down the slight incline, through the tall grass and cattails, past white pine, birch, and poplar. Beneath his feet were moss and pine needles. He stopped for a second when he heard a car coming, its tires screeching as it skidded off Old Post Road onto Nickle Road. Then he heard a radio blaring, kids hollering and laughing, raising hell in a red Ford convertible with the top down.

In front of them, in the car's headlights, the woman stood dead still.

"Watch out!" Rob screamed and began racing toward her. The car swerved to one side, back again. He stopped, watched the car disappear over the hill, listened as the laughter, the music, died away in the distance. The woman was nowhere to be seen.

He moved slowly across the road into the thick scrub. He could see nothing now, no woman, no lights. Only the wide sweep of the cemetery and headstones. All he could do was hope against hope that he would catch up to her. Whoever she was.

As he moved deeper into the cemetery, he felt his chest tighten, and knew he was panicking.

Hurry, he told himself, *faster*. She appeared again, to his right. He froze. His fear was cold and hollow inside him now. He stared at the woman's pale form, tried to focus.

He began running toward her again, but stumbled and fell almost at once. He looked down, groped at the long tentacles of root that were wrapped around his leg. Then he was on his feet, moving blindly and unsteadily, his stare locked on the figure that moved through the darkness just beyond the trees. There, gone—there again. There was a crash of foliage ahead of him, and then silence. Had she fallen? He wasn't sure.

He looked around, and found that he was standing in perfect darkness, in the pitch-dark shadow of a tree that rose above his head into the empty moonlit night. Just ahead of him, stinking water lapped at crumbling stone.

He stood still, waiting for a sign to tell him what to do. It came—the rustling of brush to his left, as if a small animal had run through there, followed by a weird scratching sound, mournful, as though someone was dragging fingernails across a blackboard.

Rob raised his eyes and peered into the dense murk. Nothing. Just that horrible clawing sound. He moved, and something moved with him.

He turned, but too late. All he saw was a bone-white hand. Then something hard smacked across the side of his head.

Everything seemed to happen at once. Someone was on top of him now, clinging to his back, digging fingernails into his neck. In one abrupt motion, Rob reached over his shoulder, took hold of the slimy flesh and pulled, flinging the body to one side.

He turned, saw a man crouched there, eyes narrow and lips tight together. An instant later he felt a drooling mouth hit his neck, and his flesh began to crawl with blood and saliva.

A great darkness arose, drawing him breathlessly into an immense and frigid void that seemed to be sucking the life out of him.

"Say hello, Rob. Say hello to your mother," came a voice.

Rob Martin began to scream.

Jasper McCann, who was fond of reading the Bible to his sister in the moonlight, had just finished the Book of Daniel when he heard the sound. It was near midnight. A cool breeze rustled the flowers on his sister's grave and carried the strange cry above the trees, where it rose slowly and steadily into an agitated murmur, a crescendo of pain, terror, and . . . something else. "Lord protect us, sister Beth," he said. He'd come to the one place he could think of where he could find peace of mind.

For a minute he closed his eyes, wishing the sound away. The night sounds of the cemetery, the crickets and rustle of leaves in the breeze, all ceased. The horrible, agonized cry continued to rise in the air, a howl that was an outpouring of unspeakable terror.

When Jasper opened his eyes the sound was

still there, still ripping open the night. He dropped his Bible in fear, staring across the cemetery into the skeletal trees. He stumbled to his feet as the scream was suddenly cut off in midnote.

Then he heard the cracking of tree branches, and something moved through the woods. Jasper strained to see. The figure in the woods was too far to make out clearly, but whoever it was, *whatever* it was, it moved in violent rushes, first one way, then the other.

"Damn," he muttered, knowing he'd just heard the sound of the devil. Picking up his Bible, Jasper backed deeper into the gloom, then turned and began racing toward the caretaker's house. The greatest trick of the devil is to convince us he doesn't exist. Tonight, however, Jasper McCann knew otherwise.

PART FOUR

SUSPICIONS & INVESTIGATIONS (I)

And they served their idols: which were a snare unto them.
Yea, they sacrificed their sons and their daughters unto devils.
—Psalm 106

1

THE TOWN COUNCIL

An institution is the lengthened
shadow of one man.
—Emerson

The Town Council consisted of six members, all of them older men, and suddenly they realized there was trouble, big trouble—most of it having to do with Rob Martin—and that they would have to meet this Sunday morning; while everyone else in Millhouse was setting their minds to prayer, they would cluster in a shabby smoke-filled room in the rear of Jacobs Hardware and review their options.

All knew, of course, that their leader, Marshall Whitset, would have his own ideas, and that he would be calm and deliberate, confident that they had all the time they needed to do what had to be done. Whitset would be courtly, deferential, urbane—and if luck were with them the other councillors would be allowed to make suggestions, would perhaps be given an opportunity to lay out their own plans in detail. Each man thought often and poignantly about the rare times when Whitset would consent to his particular counsel.

Arnold Jacobs, a huge defiant man who owned the building in which the council met, had quarreled recently with Whitset over adding two more men to the council. Whitset had handily convinced the others just how foolish this would be. Jacobs would be the first to arrive this Sunday morning, making sure that everything was set for the meeting.

"Aren't you coming to church this morning?" his wife had asked.

"Can't. Gotta do inventory," he had said, and quietly vanished out the front door. The full heat of the early summer sun closed down on him like a curse as he crossed the gravel drive and got into his car. In the distance he could hear the sound of a train as it rolled through the junction.

Backing the car down the driveway, Jacobs began mumbling to himself, building up his courage, getting ready to confront Marshall Whitset head-on.

Thus, when Jacobs came to the junction crossing, still mumbling to himself as he waited for the freight train to go rumbling by, Peter Appleton was standing in his bedroom, fully clothed, thinking: *Every train that comes through the junction sounds like a goose. It don't whistle. It honks.* He glanced at his watch. The train was ten minutes late. And so would he be if he didn't get a move on. The others would soon be gathered at Arnold's, waiting for him.

Still, he couldn't seem to get started this morning. He'd lain awake most of the night, thinking. It was fear grabbing hold of him, that's what it was, some kind of nameless dread that turned his nights sleepless and his days to sweating.

Everything's gonna be all right, he told himself, even as he sat and reached under the bed and brought out an old beat-up Bible. So old it looked the color of dirt. Not that he was a religious man, for he was not. But this morning the fear was realer than usual, deeper inside him, and old habits were taking hold.

What would his death be like? Peter Appleton wondered, searching for an answer among the yellowing pages. With abrupt certainty, he knew that it would be different from the life he had led—and much more frightening. Maybe he'd be buried alive—conscious of movement but confined, restricted, slowly suffocating, calling out, screaming in the dark for someone, *anyone*, to help him, all the while clawing and scratching until he was picking at his own flesh, ripping and tearing it from his bones looking for a way out.

"Oh, God," he moaned and lurched to his feet. In the top drawer of his dresser he found what he was looking for. He slipped the silver crucifix into his coat pocket, but did not release Christ's metallic body.

Just in case, he thought and squeezed harder. *Just in case.*

Dr. Walker and Al Striker had no such fears. Problems came, problems went. That's what the council was for. To solve problems. They sat peacefully in a booth at the Holiday Inn, finishing their morning coffee. Neither man was married; although both men liked women, neither had ever felt the need to have one around permanently. Besides, Al Striker had once confessed, he didn't like kids, so he guessed it was just as well that he'd stayed a bachelor.

Like the other members of the council, both men had grown to manhood during the Depression. The black shadow of that time still haunted them, and solidified their friendship.

"You about ready to go?" Al Striker said.

Dr. Walker's heavy head lifted slowly, his eyes focusing on Striker's weatherbeaten face. "I guess." On the way to the register he asked, "Has everyone at the factory signed up for this month's blood drive?"

"Almost. A few holdouts." Striker reached for a toothpick.

Walker nodded. "See if you can get a hundred percent. We're running lower than usual."

A few minutes later they entered Jacobs Hardware through the back door. Everything was ready to go. Everyone was present, except for Jack Gardner, who heard the dogs howling, even in his dream. He rolled his head to one side on the pillow and his eyelids twitched in his sleep. "Stay away from me," he said clearly. "Leave me be or I'll . . ." He threw out his arm, smacking his fist against the headboard.

He opened his eyes. "Come on, goddamn it, I'm ready for ya!"

Holly Emmett looked at him from the open doorway and laughed. She was a plump but striking-looking woman in her late fifties, her face full of angelic baby-sweetness, green-eyed, rosy complexioned. About her smile, which she displayed often, there was a full, rosy quality too. At the sight of it Jack Gardner was aware of being served less by a housekeeper than by a condescending mistress.

He looked away from her. "What are you laughing at, woman? Standing over there grinning like a fool cat."

"You were dreaming about them again." She openly giggled. "You thought they were coming after you. Getting ready to eat you up."

"I never thought no such thing," he said indignantly.

"You did too. Thought those Caine dogs were coming to call you home. Thinking they were the devil himself." She remained in the doorway, shaking her head. He sat up quickly in bed.

"What time is it?" he asked.

"Eight-thirty the last time I looked."

"Eight-thirty," he shouted. "Damn it, woman, I told you to wake me at eight." He sat at the edge of the bed in his T-shirt and underwear, pulling on his socks.

"Eight, eight-thirty, what's the difference?"

Holly said. "I figured the dogs gotcha during the night and you was long gone by now." She turned and moved into the hallway giggling.

"You hush your mouth," he said angrily. He hopped to the door, pulling on his trousers, and slammed it. "Brain no bigger than a knat's ass," he shouted. "Hear that, woman?" He could hear her still laughing and carrying on in the kitchen.

He got his shirt and shoes on and then opened the window and stuck his head out. There were no clouds in the sky, just a fierce expanse of screaming blue as far as the eye could see. "Lord, I'll thank you to keep those dogs quiet from now on, and don't let them get me. Amen." He pulled his head back in and slammed the window.

In the kitchen sausage was frying on the stove. "Last of the pork," Holly said. "I'll need to do a big shopping tomorrow." Her eyes were still laughing at him.

"Where's Tony, he up yet?" Jack Gardner asked.

"Showering. He'll be right down." Holly took the biscuits out of the oven and set them in the middle of the table. "Sit down and eat while it's hot," she said.

"Can't eat, not hungry. Besides, I gotta go . . ."

"Morning, everyone." Tony Rizzo stood in the kitchen doorway yawning. "Damn, did you hear those dogs? Kept me up half the night."

Holly said, "Hear them? Heck, Jack thought they was right there in his room, didn't ya, Jack?

He was lying there screaming: 'Come on, I'm ready for you. I'm ready!' "

Tony looked at his uncle and let out a laugh that surprised even him. Holly laughed too, and Jack Gardner said, "Go on, keep it up. One of these days . . ."

"Hey, great. Biscuits and gravy," Tony cut in, winking at Holly, who was covering her mouth with the front of her apron. "Come on, Jack. Let's eat."

Jack Gardner waited for his nephew to start in on his meal before sitting down at the table. "Holly, Tony and me gotta talk somethin' private. Do you mind?"

Holly gave him a startled look, like a rabbit suddenly cornered. "Aw, no, I don't mind," she said. "I'll go into the basement and start the wash."

"You do that," Jack Gardner said, and waited for her to disappear down the basement steps before facing Tony head-on. "I got some news for ya, boy. And I don't think you're gonna like it."

"Oh, such as?" Tony said without looking up.

His uncle cleared his throat. "Such as Henderson over at the Shady Rest said he seen Elizabeth Arbor and Rob Martin duck into Rob's room yesterday. Said they spent the day there, and part of the night."

Tony looked at him, annoyance in his eyes.

"You get a real pleasure out of telling me things like that, don't you?" he said. "What makes you think it's any of my business?"

"Shoot, who you kiddin', boy? You've been in love with that girl for as long . . ."

Tony suddenly scooted back his chair away from the table. "So what? She and Rob are old friends. They have every right to spend some time together after all these years."

"Some time? I told you they were in his room half the night. Half the night," Gardner repeated dramatically.

Without saying anything, Tony went to the stove where he helped himself to coffee. Gardner snatched a sausage link from the plate and popped it into his mouth.

"That ain't all," he said, chewing.

"Ain't all what?" Tony wanted to know.

"Well, now—I'm not sure I should tell ya, seein' how this Rob Martin is still a friend of yours, and how you're gettin' mad at me for just tellin' ya what's goin' on. No, sir—I'm not at all sure . . ."

"Oh, bullshit!" Tony snapped.

"No, really," Gardner replied calmly. "Seems you care more about an outsider than you do your own kind. Damn shame. Your mother, God rest her soul, it would break her heart to see us carryin' on like we do."

"Spare me, Jack. I'm sorry I yelled at you. Besides, Rob Martin's no outsider."

"Hell he ain't. Never did belong here and you know it."

"He was born and raised here, for God's sake."

"That don't make no matter. His parents weren't. They came waltzing in here from the big city, turnin' up their noses. If it weren't for Norris Caine, well . . . anyway, Rob Martin's an outsider, sure enough. Always was, always will be. So I guess it's only right him ending up the way he did last night."

"Ending up, what do you mean?"

Jack Gardner ate another sausage link and took the time to lick the grease from his fingertips before saying, "Drunk as a skunk he was, passed out on his mother's grave. Hell, Jasper McCann said he heard the boy screaming like a crazy man, running through the bushes like his clothes were on fire. Screamin' and carryin' on . . ."

"Rob . . . did . . . what?"

"McCann right away ran and got the caretaker. By the time they got to the boy he was lying unconscious across Celia Martin's grave. I hear he whacked his head a good one on the headstone as he went down. Lost some blood."

"Where'd they take him, to the clinic?"

"Don't think so. I believe the sheriff come got him. I suspect he locked him up."

"Jesus." Tony slammed his coffee cup down on the table, and Jack Gardner drew back in his chair as the coffee splattered across the front of his shirt. Tony reached for his jacket.

"Hey, boy, where the hell you goin'? Oh, jeez, look what ya done to my shirt!"

Tony rushed from the house without looking back.

2

Rob Martin didn't know where he was, but wherever it was, he didn't like it. For one thing, it was cold; *he* was cold. For another, there seemed to be an odd smell, like meat roasting over an open pit. With his eyes still closed he licked his lips, which were dry and cracked. Then he opened one eye, just a little, felt dizzy, and closed it again.

For a while he was satisfied to just lie there and suffer. Then he began to remember. Something vague about voices, frightened voices laced with whiskey, and then the sensation of being carried and dumped into the backseat of a car. Then memories of pitch-black coal sliding down a chute into the basement, and filthy black snow and himself being alone, waiting for his parents to come home, wondering if there had been an accident, if they were all right. And being in church and not knowing who to pray to and the priest in his skirts chasing after him down a dark alley and feeling the sin of existence, his sin of existence and the father, always the Father and the Son and holy Jesus!

The air Rob breathed suddenly seemed more smoke than oxygen. Panicked, he sat bolt upright on the narrow bed and, in wonder, saw the broad outline of Sheriff Jones before him, standing, a fat green-leafed cigar stuffed into the corner of his mouth. The man appeared more ghost than real as the gray smoke curled beneath the brim of his hat, shrouding his smug features.

"Don't worry," the sheriff said. "You ain't dead."

Rob shook his head, trying to dissipate the fuzz, and saw that little blotches of blood covered the pillow, darkening its gray pillowcase. More blood shone red and brown on the floor beneath his feet and stained his shirt; he raised his hand to his forehead, and said, "What happened, what am I doing here?"

The sheriff chuckled. "You don't look so hot, my friend. You're not going to be sick, are you?"

Before Rob could reply, the sheriff had thrown open the cell door, and Rob stumbled barefooted into the hallway.

"The bathroom's in there." The sheriff pointed the way.

The room was small and stank of cheap soap and urine, and Rob held onto the sink as the taste of vodka welled up in his mouth. He cupped his hand under the faucet, turned it on and slurped. The water went halfway down and then started back up again. For a second he stood there trying not to retch. Then, still trembling, he straightened and looked at his image in the mirror.

"You going to be all right?" the sheriff hollered in from the hallway.

"Yeah, I guess so," Rob managed, his face ashen. He needed a shave. His eyes were bloodshot, and above his right eye was a nasty-looking gash that someone had matter-of-factly bandaged. Someone had also removed his shoes, socks, and jacket. They had also taken his keys, loose change, and his wristwatch.

Rob glanced around miserably. Jail. He was in jail for chrissakes. He started to move, and then stopped. Something wasn't right, he realized. Apparently he'd been arrested during the night, tossed in the slammer. And that was strange, because he was the one who'd been attacked in the cemetery last night. Using the wall for support, he asked, "How'd I get here?"

The sheriff bit down on the tip of his cigar,

muttered, "How else? I brought you."

"Why?"

"Why?" The sheriff looked at him quizzically. "Shoot, boy, you was drunk and disorderly. I don't know how it is in Miami, but here in Millhouse you can't go running around getting shit-faced and disturbing the dead. Didn't you ever hear the expression: 'May they rest in peace'?"

"Disturbing the dead? I don't know what you're talking about."

"I'm talking about smashing liquor bottles against headstones, about screaming and hollering in the night, and scaring the crap out of people. Raisin' hell, boy. That's what I'm talking about."

"Liquor bottles? I didn't smash any bottles . . ."

"No, then how'd them bottles come to be there? You were still holding one in your hand, lying unconscious across your mother's grave. Vodka, that's what you were drinking."

"But not in the cemetery," Rob insisted.

"Look, son—I know it's hard losing kinfolk. I also know how hard it is to come back to a town you ain't seen in ten years. So let's just say you got a little carried away and leave it at that. All right?" The sheriff half smiled. "Come on, I'll fix coffee." His voice trailed off as he walked down the hallway and disappeared into the main office.

Incredible, Rob thought. Absolutely a goddamned kneeslapper of a situation. Not a word about the woman at his motel window last night. About her friends, whoever they were, who'd been waiting for him in the cemetery. It was as if they had never existed. As if Rob had imagined the whole thing. In bewilderment he glanced into the cell, around its barren walls, down the hallway; the sheriff's grinning face reappeared, his lips partly open.

"Well, you comin' or what?" he asked.

As Rob entered the office, the sheriff moved to the window and let up the shades. Vicious yellow sunlight poured into the room; Rob flinched. "What . . . what time is it?" he asked.

"A little after nine."

"I spent the whole night here?"

The sheriff nodded. He poured water over instant coffee, dropped four sugar cubes into his cup. "How do you take yours?"

"Cream, no sugar. Who put the Band-Aid on my head?"

The sheriff paused. "There was only you and me here last night. So . . ."

"You didn't think taking me to the clinic was necessary?" Rob watched him closely, and saw that he was beginning to tense.

"Not really. Besides, I didn't think you'd want people to see you drunk like that. Thought you'd like to keep everything as quiet as possible. Here ya go."

Rob accepted the coffee cup, lifted it to smell the steam rising from the liquid. He tried to sound casual as he asked, "Who called you last night, told you I was in the cemetery?"

"The caretaker."

"No one else was there?"

"Jasper McCann. But he's always hanging around the cemetery. Goes there to be with his sister. Sweet young thing, she was. Died of cancer. Weren't no more than a schoolgirl when she died." He paused. "Why'd you ask about anyone else being there?"

Rob took a sip of his coffee, having come smack against a moment of truth. Dammit, had there been a woman at his window last night or not? Had he been attacked in the cemetery? Or, as the sheriff suggested, had he gotten blind drunk and imagined the whole thing? When Rob looked up the sheriff was still poised, waiting for his answer.

"No reason," Rob said. "I just thought I remembered seeing someone else there, that's all."

"Maybe you saw a ghost," the sheriff said sarcastically. Then he laughed.

"Maybe," Rob said. "Maybe so." Once again he could see those hideous faces looming out of the dark as he attempted to fight them off, darkened stains as black as coalwater on their lips, eyes rolled into their heads, flesh curiously pale.

Slowly Rob sank into the chair next to the desk. Twice before he had seen faces in the dark, faces in which the fear of life was so profound:

once just before his mother's death, the other just prior to his father's. He'd seen that look again last night, that look that comes to a person's face when things are going terribly, terribly wrong.

"Well, anyway," the sheriff said, "there wasn't any real harm done, so . . ." He opened his desk drawer, took out a manila envelope, and dropped it at Rob's elbow. "Your belongings," he said. "Your shoes and sports jacket are over there on the chair."

Rob's eyes went from one to the other, and then to the front door as Tony Rizzo's face appeared beyond the glass. Tony stepped quickly into the office.

"Morning, Counselor," the sheriff said.

"Good morning, Sheriff." Tony stood rigid, trying to keep every muscle relaxed. "Rob, you all right?"

"Yeah," Rob said quietly.

"Well, I'll be goddamned," the sheriff bellowed. "Don't tell me you two know each other?"

Tony nodded, and the sheriff began talking nonstop, barely pausing to breathe. It seemed to amuse him that Rob and Tony were friends. Hell, he'd had a friend get drunk once and watched as he fell into a river, and on and on until Tony asked, "Are you charging Rob?"

"Charging him? Hell, you do go straight at things, don't you?" the sheriff said, still smiling. He edged back around his desk. "No, I ain't charging him. I just figured it was best to have him sleep it off, that's all."

"Then he's free to go?"

The sheriff sat, abruptly formal. "Of course. His stuff's in the envelope." He shoved a form in front of Rob. "Check your things and sign here."

A few minutes later, beside Tony's green Dodge, a few doors down from the sheriff's office, Tony said, "God, you look awful."

"I feel awful," Rob echoed.

"What happened to you last night?"

"I'll tell you on the way back to the motel."

"Right. Hop in."

Rob opened the door and slid into the small front seat, his hand going to his forehead in a moment of dizziness.

"Maybe we better get you to the clinic," Tony said, starting the car. "Have them look at that."

"No, I'm all right." Rob straightened. "Go on, you got the light."

Tony eased the car through the intersection, and then down Main Street. Rob could see how nervous he was; he kept glancing in his rearview mirror and out the side window, scanning the cars and Sunday morning pedestrians, as if wondering who might be observing him.

Abruptly Rob asked, "Tony, how'd you know I was in jail?"

"What?" His mind had clearly been elsewhere. "I'm sorry, what did you say?"

"Me in jail. How'd you know?"

"Oh, my uncle told me over breakfast."

"How'd he find out?"

Tony looked quickly at him, then turned away. "Can't say. He got in late last night, so . . ."

"So," Rob persisted, "I want you to find out."

"Why?"

"Because . . ."

Once Rob started in on his story there was no stopping him. The words just came pouring out as they drove through tree-lined streets, past houses that were set behind ivied brick walls, rustic fences, and well-manicured lawns. Rob reflected, as he looked at the peaceful surroundings in the bright sunlight, that it seemed inconceivable that events such as last night's could happen.

Yet they had.

Tony turned onto Fairmont Avenue, then made a quick left and brought the car to a stop in front of the Shady Rest Motel. For a long time both men merely sat there, staring through the windshield. A few yards away Larry's steel-gray Jag sat motionless in the hot sun. MOTEL–VACANCY reflected on its hood. The motel itself, including the glass-front cubicle which served as its office, looked deserted. No traffic, no people, just a stillness that seemed unbearable.

Rob shook his head. "You don't believe me, do you?"

Tony said, "To tell you the God's truth, I don't know what to believe."

"It happened, dammit. There were at least two of them, plus the woman. They were moaning and yelping like dogs, for God's sake. I'd never seen anything like it. I . . ."

"But the sheriff said . . ."

"I don't care what he said. I was nowhere near my mother's grave when I lost consciousness. They must have dumped me there."

"But why would anyone want to do that to you?"

"I don't know," Rob said. But it suddenly seemed to him that everything, up to that moment, had to be connected—Larry's disappearance, finding the woman's body in the tree stump, the death of Ned Taylor's dog—all connected.

"That's another thing," Rob said slowly. "The sheriff never mentioned Larry Campbell. How come?"

Tony looked at him uncomprehendingly.

"I told him yesterday that Larry was missing," Rob said. "Last night he found me drunk in the cemetery—disturbing the dead, he said. Yet he never questioned me, never asked me what's going on, just smiled and said 'no harm done.'"

"Maybe he just wanted to give you a break."

Rob broke out in a nervous laugh. "Tony, the law doesn't work that way. People missing, people ripping up cemeteries, he should have at least asked me a few questions. No, something's going on."

Tony draped himself over the steering wheel. "Like what?"

"Jesus, I don't know. It's weird."

"You said the woman looked like your . . ."

"My mother, that's right. And I wasn't imagining it. I mean, I couldn't have imagined something like that. I just couldn't have."

For a second Rob felt the urge to take out his wallet, to look again at the faded snapshot he had of his mother. He wanted to wave the photo in front of Tony's incredulous face and shout, "Here, this woman, my mother. She looked like her."

But a stronger emotion took hold of him. Though he had always entirely denied even the possibility of the existence of ghosts, or of anything else supernatural, perhaps that was precisely what he had dealt with last night.

"Tony, I, ah . . ." Rob pressed his fingertips to his lips. "I'm leaving town this morning. I'll drive to the Cape and get a room for the night. I need to get some rest before interviewing Kennedy tomorrow."

Tony nodded. "Is there anything I can do?"

"Yeah." Rob looked at him. "Call Elizabeth for me when you get a chance. Tell her . . ." He broke off when he saw the look on Tony's face, a horribly pinched look that said it all. "Tony, I'm sorry, I . . ."

"Don't be sorry." He shrugged. "She's always loved you. I know that."

Rob regarded him somberly. "I didn't think I still cared for her, but . . ."

"But after yesterday, well . . ."

". . . You know about that? Did she tell you?"

"It doesn't make any difference how I found out, does it? The point is, she's in love with you. And I guess you feel the same way about her," Tony said, apparently in some pain. "So, what is it you want me to tell her?"

"Tell her . . . tell her I'm coming back, all right? As soon as I'm done with the interview, I'll be back."

Tony nodded carefully as though debating his next words. "I suppose you'll think it's resentment talking if I tell you I don't think that's such a good idea. But I'll say it anyway. Keep going, Rob. Maybe you can get Elizabeth to come to Miami. Or you could meet her somewhere else. But I wouldn't come back to Millhouse if I were you."

Rob leaned in. "Why?"

"It's just a feeling, is all. This town's got you all worked up. It's a small town, with even smaller people. There could be trouble."

Tony said this with a kind of grim contempt and then turned again to stare out the windshield.

"What else did your uncle tell you this morning?" Rob asked.

"Nothing." He turned. "Look, Rob, things are different here, now. The country's changed, and so has Millhouse. The people are closer knit. You come back here accusing people, and there's no telling what might happen."

"What about Larry?"

"Let the police handle it. If he's really missing, it's out of your hands."

Rob hesitated, but only for an instant. He opened the car door, stepped out, and then peered back into the car. "I'm afraid I can't do that, Tony. Call it reporter's instinct, madness, love, whatever. Just tell Elizabeth I'll be back."

Tony cocked his head. "All right," he said. "But you stay at my place this time, okay?"

"Okay," Rob said. "And thanks."

3

An hour later Rob was lying across his bed, still dazed by it all. The snapshot of his mother lay on the nightstand beside the bed. Although it was barely ten-thirty in the morning, he had turned on both lamps, and their harsh light spilt across his body onto the crumpled bedspread. Sitting next to the door was his suitcase, ready to go.

The phone rang.

Rob kept his eyes shut.

He felt better this way. Still, he knew that eventually he'd have to open them and face what he'd known all along—that there was no escaping his past; not the town he'd been born in, nor the people who had borne him. Especially them. Finally he had to admit that he'd never really known his mother and father. Not as individuals, without the damned labels. *Mother. Father.*

The telephone rang again.

He lifted the receiver. "Hello."

"Mr. Martin?" asked the operator.

"Yeah, it's me."

"Go ahead, Miami. Your party is on the line."

"Rob, it's Gab—what's up?"

The voice on the other end belonged to Gab Barrett, a stubborn, square-jawed, red-haired man who had become a giant in American journalism and was now the managing editor for the *Miami Herald*. A hell of a reporter in his day. A stickler for details now as managing editor. His staff was evenly divided into those who swore at him and those who swore by him.

"Gab, it's about Larry Campbell," Rob said.

"Oh?" the managing editor said. "What's he up to now? He's not giving you a hard time, is he?"

Rob took a deep breath and then jumped into the breach. Gab didn't say much until Rob got to the missing part, missing since Thursday, and that's when Gab said, "Come on, Rob, don't jerk me around. You tell Larry that I don't want any nonsense on this assignment."

"He's missing, I tell you. I looked up—and bang!—he was gone."

"Gone? Gone where?"

"That's what I'm trying to tell you. I don't know."

"Listen, Rob—you tell Larry that if he's trying to hamstring a vacation out of me, he can forget it. He's got a column to get out. I want him back in this office on schedule. You tell him that."

Rob could see that it was going to be impossible to convince Gab Barrett that Larry was really missing. Gab was like that, a man of shrewd intuition and hot streaks of impatience, never at a loss to convey his message. His credo: Never deceive people or trifle with their intelligence.

"All right, Gab," Rob said. "As soon as I see him I'll tell him."

"Good. Now are you all set for tomorrow?"

"Just about," Rob lied.

"Have you gone over your notes?"

"A hundred times," Rob lied again, and could feel Gab Barrett's credo stabbing him in the chest.

"I'll hold space for you just in case Kennedy gives you anything earthshaking. I'll expect to hear from you by five tomorrow. Oh, and listen, don't forget to quiz him on busing and school integration. It's still a hot issue. Slip Martin Luther King into the conversation—get his reaction. And for God's sake, ask him about Johnson's foreign policy. And the Bedford-Stuyvesant project. I hear the Ford and Astor Foundations are jumping aboard. You might suggest that it looks like he's trying to take over the New York party. You got all that?"

"Yeah," Rob said wearily. "I got it."

"I'm counting on you, Rob. I don't have to tell you that Kennedy hasn't given an interview since his trip to South Africa. He could be ripe to spill his guts."

Rob sighed. "I know."

"Oh, and about Larry. Tell him nice try, but no cigar."

"Right, no cigar."

A few more words and Rob hung up. It was like cutting a tie line with reality. Instinct caused him to lift the receiver again, but after a second's hesitation he dropped it into the cradle. He had once again decided not to call Elizabeth. His head was still swimming from the way they had parted. From that strange lost look she had given him.

For a moment he lay back on the bed and stared at the ceiling, trying to evoke her face, the curve of her eyelashes, the feel of her hand in his, their lips pressed together . . .

What was astonishing to Rob was the sudden, overwhelming love he felt for her. And the concern. She had looked so pale, so thin. And the strange way she—

Rob turned suddenly, caught a glimpse of a face outside his window. A woman's face, withered and framed in gray hair. He lurched forward and threw open the door.

The woman stood hunched, leaning against

her service cart. She looked to be sixty, at least, with spindly legs and chicken bones for fingers. She turned her eyes toward Rob slowly and muttered, "You checking out? No rush. You got till eleven o'clock."

There was an uncomfortable pause, and Rob asked, "Were you working here at the motel last night?"

She drew a handkerchief out of her sleeve and wiped her forehead with it, inclining her head a little. "I work mornings is all." She hesitated. "Are you checking out? The manager said . . ."

"Yes, I'm checking out," Rob answered awkwardly.

The woman tucked her handkerchief back into her sleeve. While Rob went into the room for his bag, she wheeled her cart to the door. As she came into the room, Rob picked up the snapshot of his mother and held it out. "Tell me, have you ever seen this woman before? I know the picture's faded, but . . ."

Taking the photo, the woman looked at it and then handed it back to Rob, shaking her head. "No, never seen her."

"Oh. I thought maybe she worked here."

"Not that I know of."

Rob sighed, staring at the faded image of a woman whose hair was shoulder-length and caught by a single band. She was a woman of extraordinary beauty with a broad smile and smoke-gray eyes that, at times, seemed to be measuring everything and everyone around her. A stranger, really, Rob thought. That thought smarted as much, if not more, than his now-throbbing head.

"Thanks," he said and slipped the snapshot into his jacket pocket.

A few minutes later Rob was in the Jag, his mind flying in all directions as the back tires of his car kicked up gravel along the pebbled drive. He was unaware that a pair of watery dead eyes gazed after him long after he had reached the highway, turned into the fast lane, and began heading east.

Eyes. Dead and lifeless.

They would still be there when and *if* he returned.

4

Willis Bradley, who was a part-time undertaker as well as Crestwood Lawn's caretaker, looked down at the girl's body. He didn't like embalming people, but his helper was late—well, not really late, Bradley corrected himself, since the dolt hadn't been on time once in three years. Still, someone had to get the job done and that meant he was stuck with it.

Annoyed, he reached for his bourbon bottle and took a swig, glancing sideways at the corpse. One good thing, the girl was bone-thin, couldn't weigh more than a hundred pounds, so that meant one man could do the job, sure enough.

The head needed work, though, to reduce

the swelling. He'd do that with a needle. He'd use wax and paint afterward so that no one would ever know she'd had a swollen and lumpy head. An artist, that's what he was. Except he used a corpse for his canvas.

Sometimes, looking down at a freshly done client, he'd sorta feel sad that he hadn't done more with his talent. Gone into commercial art, or something without having to deal with the dead, because there were starting to be more of them—the dead—and he was finding it rough-going. Too many people nosing around these days, asking questions.

He made a neat incision in the girl's neck and opened the carotid artery. If her spleen had been ruptured, which it was, there would be heavy amounts of blood in the lower cavity, which would have to be drawn off.

But he would find no blood, he knew. He knew from the way they brought her in that there would be no blood. No questions asked, right, fellas? Why worry about an outsider, anyway. Right, fellas?

Right, right . . .

No friends, no family, just a girl drifting through. Still, we don't want trouble. So make sure she looks good, in case a distant cousin or uncle shows up at the last minute and wonders how she'd come to die.

Another swig of liquor. He sponged her body, then clamped on the rubber tubes from the embalming machine and set the pump working. Nothing like making it all look official, right, fellas?

He glanced at the clock on the wall. Eleven A.M. and still no helper. More drunk than angry, he slipped off his green rubber apron, and stepped out the back door into the alley for a smoke. In the distance church bells rang out, calling the good folk of Millhouse to service. There were fewer of them each week, he realized. More and more were packing up and leaving town.

Don't blame ya. Don't blame ya a bit.

He was starting to shake now. Sundays always reduced him to rubble, found him most times at home, alone, dead drunk, propped up in a chair and trying to watch TV.

Not much of a life. If he wasn't preparing the dead, he was watching over them. Had been for ten years, and that suddenly seemed to him like a mighty long time to be flirting with evil.

"Sssh," he hissed aloud in a low, slurred voice and watched smoke curl beneath his nose and up around his ears. Not all of them evil, you know. But then, who's to judge? Not him, that was for sure. Hell, he couldn't even stop himself from whacking off at night or from stealing money out of the church poor box, when he was flat broke from his drinking.

They done this to ya. Them.

Oh, stop your goddamned whining. There's still time to get out, ya know.

He laughed, knowing better. Knowing that

he probably wouldn't get very far before—

He glanced around. The alley behind the building was empty, but he knew they were there, all right. Watching him.

For perhaps a minute longer he stood there, afraid to move, afraid to breathe. Then he ducked back into the building, started stitching and folding the gal's lips down to make a perfectly pleasant smile. Then he tested the cadaver's flesh, drew off the intestinal gases, and started pumping in the fluid.

In the small, out of the way room he continued to work. After all, they were paying him time and a half.

Right, fellas?

5

The unpleasant aftertaste of Rob's story stayed with Tony Rizzo for hours, like the indistinct memory of a nightmare. It was still coming over him in occasional flashes when he called Elizabeth from his office at one that afternoon. Her mother answered the phone. "Please come right over, Tony," Mrs. Arbor said. "I need to speak with you."

"Well, I'm not sure I can," Tony said, turning the pages of a brief he'd been working on.

"I realize it's Sunday," Mrs. Arbor said, and sighed heavily. "But it's important. Most important. It's . . ." Her voice trailed off.

Tony said, "Has something happened to Elizabeth?"

Mrs. Arbor answered, "That's a good description of the problem, I think. Tony, please . . ." Abruptly Tony heard a number of loud voices; they almost overwhelmed Mrs. Arbor's words. Tony realized that there were other people in the room with her.

"What's going on over there?" Tony said.

"A barbecue. Some of the men . . ." More laughter and horsing around intervened. Finally Mrs. Arbor said, "Tony, I can't talk now. Please, for Elizabeth's sake, do stop by."

Before Tony could respond the woman hung up. He looked at the receiver and then placed it gingerly on the hook. He shook his head, raising his hand to his chin, touching the stubble of whiskers. If he was going to the Arbors' he'd have to shave.

An hour later Tony found himself being escorted into the Arbors' living room by Elizabeth's mother. His face still smarted from too close a shave, too much cologne, and a pesky nick just below his jaw line.

The woman looked around apprehensively as Tony took a chair near the fireplace. The room was immaculately kept, the white doilies on the chair arms matched the white lace curtains at the windows. Though the living room was at the front of the house, its occupants could hear sounds from the backyard: voices, men's laughter, and strains of music.

Mrs. Arbor looked into the hallway, clearly checking to make sure they were alone. Beside her, red petals fell from swollen blossoms in a vase onto the polished surface of the piano. The air was filled with the heady scent of tulips past their prime.

"Well," Tony said, and suddenly felt like fleeing the room.

Mrs. Arbor turned, and as she turned she began speaking, frowning thoughtfully, eyes evasive. She told Tony how Elizabeth hadn't come home until after midnight last night, how she had hardly spoken to anyone, and how she'd awakened, screaming, in the middle of the night. So rapid was her speech that Tony hardly had time to take it all in.

"I don't understand what's going on," she concluded, a grave look on her face.

Again excessive laughter drifted into the room. In the silence that followed, Tony muttered, "The doctor said . . ."

"Blood pressure, he said. But it's more than that. It's Rob Martin is what it is," she said with certainty. "He's not in town more than three days and already Elizabeth is sick. She hardly knew who she was this morning."

The woman paused, and Tony could sense the rapidity with which her mind was working.

Making an effort to control herself, Mrs. Arbor said, "Please, Tony, you must help me. Will you?"

Tony considered this seriously.

"She'll listen to you. He'll listen to you. They're no good together, surely you can see that. Elizabeth is, well, she's . . "

"I'm what, Mother?"

Tony turned to stare into the darkness of the hallway as Elizabeth stepped forward, buttoning the front of a light summer dress. She held, crumpled under her arm, a garment of some type—another dress, perhaps—of yellow cotton, which she made a perfunctory attempt to conceal against her body.

Caught by surprise, Mrs. Arbor said, "Elizabeth, I thought you were taking a nap."

Elizabeth moved into the room, her hand lingering upon, and then abandoning, the upper button of her dress, looking at her mother longer and more reflectively. There was an unquenched sensuality in her very pale-blue eyes. And yet—as Tony looked closer—she seemed far away, as though she were unaware of anyone else being in the room with her.

"It's too hot to rest," she said. Then she said, "What were you two talking about?"

Mrs. Arbor pushed out her chin. "You know perfectly well what we were talking about."

"Yes, I suppose I do." Elizabeth looked at Tony for the first time. "Is that why you're here, Tony? Because of Rob?"

Tony cleared his throat and leaned forward, his hands cupped over his knees. "Rob left town a little while ago," he murmured, and could see the honest relief on Mrs. Arbor's face. He tried to signal to Elizabeth that there was more to his message.

"I knew it," Mrs. Arbor cried. "I knew he'd leave as soon as he . . . well, I say good riddance to the likes of him. Of all . . ."

"Mother, please, will you stop it!"

Awkwardly Tony got to his feet. He didn't want to watch mother and daughter argue.

"No, don't go. Not yet." Elizabeth turned so that her back was against him, her body touching his, and said, "Dad's having a hard time entertaining the guests all by himself, Mother. I think . . ."

"I know what you're thinking, young lady," her mother snapped. "Elizabeth, he's gone, for Pete's sake. Let him go. Yesterday was only . . ."

Elizabeth held up her hand to quiet her. "Yesterday was my business. We've been all over that. And I don't think it's polite to discuss it in front of Tony."

Mrs. Arbor sniffed in a manner that clearly conveyed her disgust. She turned away, mumbling an apology, and left the room.

Elizabeth turned. The blood rose to her face. "I'm sorry, Tony. Really."

"It's all right. You should be around when my uncle and I go at it."

She hesitated, looking deeper into his eyes. "Is he really gone?" she asked unsteadily. She stood motionless, waiting for his answer. Her long red hair, very soft and radiant, like sunlight through gauze, lay softly on her shoulders, and Tony turned away, unable to look at her.

"Rob's coming back," he said. "He wanted me to tell you that. He's coming back."

"When?" she whispered, breathless.

"I guess the day after tomorrow. He didn't make it clear."

"He told you to tell me? Why didn't he just call me himself?" When Tony didn't answer, she moved around to face him. "Tony?"

Tony sighed. "Elizabeth, there's a lot going on with Rob. I mean, a lot has happened in the last few days."

"You mean his friend being missing?" she asked, without letting his eyes go. He sat down on the couch and made room for her beside him.

Elizabeth did not move from her place near the window. The sun glared through the glass, seeming to burn her white skin, and thrusting across the floor her distorted shadow, elongated and thin, yet eloquent in its shadowy form and substance.

With intense effort, Tony tore his gaze from her, and looked at his hands. "Oh, hell, I guess you should know about last night," he said. Desire made him reach out and grip her waist, draw her down on the couch. The soft firmness of one of her breasts grazed his hand and he was enveloped in the smell of her—her body, scented soap, and the faintest trace of perfume. He felt himself erect—instantly and fully, like a schoolboy—and became horribly embarrassed.

She looked into his eyes and smiled, obviously unaware of the effect she had on him. "Does last night have anything to do with me?" she asked quietly, dropping the garment she held into her lap.

Tony made no response, just looked at her.

"Come on, what happened? Don't leave me in suspense," she teased.

For a moment Tony thought he was seeing things. Then he realized that he wasn't mistaken, that there were bloodstains on the collar of the dress she held so casually on her lap. He picked the dress up in his hands. "Elizabeth, what's this? What happened?"

She looked at him, puzzled, then glanced at the bloodstains. With a strange expression, she said, "I don't know. I . . . I was wondering that myself."

"It's your dress, isn't it?"

"Of course it's my dress."

"And you don't know how this happened?"

"I don't know, I must have . . ." Something flickered in her stare. Her face reddened.

"Did you cut yourself?"

She blinked, as though this had not occurred to her. "Oh. Oh, no," she said in a breathless voice. Then, with a shy, alluring gesture, both timid and wanton, she took the dress in her hands and said firmly, "Now stop stalling. Tell me everything Rob said. And don't leave anything out. Not a single word."

An hour later, maybe more, Tony dragged himself into his kitchen and flopped into a chair at the table. The overhead fan whirled noisily, and down the hallway the TV blared in Jack's room. Tony arched his neck, then rotated his head, trying to dislodge an ache.

Jesus, he thought. Elizabeth had looked so beautiful. So damned beautiful and yet so ill. He'd never seen her look quite like that before. Almost as though it took all of her strength just to lift her hands. And the odd expression on her face when he had told her about Rob being arrested last night—almost as if she approved of his behavior. As if . . .

"Where you been?" Jack Gardner said, appearing not from his room but from the john off the hallway.

"Elizabeth Arbor's house."

Tony's uncle looked at him strangely. "And before that?"

"The office. And before that . . . what the heck is eating you?"

"You went down to the sheriff's office to bail your friend out, didn't ya?"

"Bail him out? He wasn't arrested."

"Hell he weren't."

"Look, Jack, I've had a long . . ."

"He was arrested sure enough. He'd still be in jail if it weren't for you. I tried to warn you this mornin' how things were, but you wouldn't listen."

Tony looked at his uncle closely, and could see a nervousness beneath his craggy features. "Tell me how *what* things were?"

"Him being an outsider," Jack Gardner muttered. "You work for Caine Enterprises now. Hell, boy—you deaf as well as blind? Surely you heard . . ." He broke off, and seemed suddenly uncertain of his next words. He came farther into the room, and his face, which had been in shadow, was revealed by the full light of the kitchen. As usual he exhibited a crooked, apologetic smile.

But there was little apology in his other movements. Firmly he pointed a finger. "You ain't messin' with Rob Martin just to spite me now, are you? 'Cause if you are . . ."

Tony shook his head, exasperated. "He's a friend, Jack. He's always been a friend. And I'm going to do everything I can to help him. I owe him that."

"A friend, huh!"

"That's right. A good friend, and don't you forget it."

Jack Gardner moved toward the screen door. His walk was slow, his shoulders hunched, his long sideburns and disheveled hair making him appear an oversize monkey. "How much do you know?" he asked quietly, staring through the wire mesh.

At first Tony did not understand what he meant, but then from some recess of his mind leaped Rob's story, the goings-on in the cemetery.

When Jack Gardner looked at him there was small recognition in his eyes. "What's more important, of course, is what does *Rob* know?"

"I don't follow you," Tony said.

Jack Gardner nodded, slowly. "It's dangerous fooling around like this, boy. Stupid, too.

Your future's right here in this town. The rest of the damned country is fallin' apart. But you're safe here, 'cause we all stick together. That's important. Now what'd he tell ya?"

Tony shrugged. "Nothing much. We just talked about what happened last night, that's all."

"And?"

Before Tony could respond, the wall phone near the back door rang. Both men stared at it for a second, and then Jack swung an arm out and lifted the receiver from the hook.

"Hello. Yeah, who's this?" He turned his back on his nephew and listened. "Well, I'll be a son of a . . . when did it happen?"

Tony recognized his uncle's tone immediately—a strained calm, but urgent.

"You're kiddin'," Jack said. "Shit, I'll be right over. Hey, wait, the sheriff know yet?"

As Tony got to his feet his uncle muttered something he couldn't hear and slammed down the receiver.

"What happened?" Tony asked, trailing after his uncle, who refused to look at him. Tony reached out and took hold of his arm.

Halfway out the door Jack Gardner spun around. "It's Ned Taylor. They just found him. He's dead," he said, and tore free of Tony's grasp.

A moment later they were both hightailing it across the gravel drive, heading for the car.

6

Death. It's not really surprising in a small town, although it sometimes appears that way, so isolated and insulated are the residents that it seems as if even their most ancient and dreaded adversary is unable to get a toe through the door. But there are always deaths that defy description, that take the breath away, so peculiar are they in nature. And Ned Taylor had certainly died in the most peculiar way. Not of old age as some had predicted, nor from cancer which most people feared but never talked about, nor from suicide—Ned Taylor certainly was capable of such an act, losing his wife the way he had, in a car accident he'd caused while sitting drunk behind the wheel of his Ford pickup—nor from ulcers or from a heart attack or getting run over by the Marlow brothers, who used the dirt road beside his farm as a drag strip.

No, none of these deaths would have surprised anyone, especially those who knew Ned Taylor best. But what had happened to Ned was, well, downright weird.

The men were already gathered in Ned's back forty by the time Tony pulled his green Dodge to a stop at the edge of the isolated dirt road and got out. The police photographer, deputies, sheriff, county coroner—they were all there, milling around.

A Norman Rockwell painting, Tony mused as he followed his uncle up the slope of hill. Men standing in quiet contemplation, hands hitched in their belts, hats tossed back on their heads, the old barn and two-story farmhouse off to the right, and as far as the eye could see, acres of cropland waiting to be harvested.

No one turned to acknowledge Tony and his uncle as they approached. Everyone was too busy staring at Ned's tractor. The engine was still running, the baler still champing, but the machine did not move.

As Tony and Jack reached the group, the sheriff shook his head, then turned to Marshall Whitset—the Ugly One—and said, "He must have gotten down from the tractor, leaving the engine turning, and used his hand to free that limb. The baler must have grabbed him and chopped him up."

Tony looked closer and could see that Ned Taylor had made two bales. There was a little of him left over that the machine didn't know what to do with, so it sort of threw the bits aside, a hand here, an arm there.

"Damned strange, if you ask me," Deputy Salino said. Tony noticed that a large part of his neck was wrapped in white gauze.

The sheriff popped a piece of straw into his mouth. "How's that?"

"The man's been farming his whole life. He knows better than to do a damn fool thing like that."

A few neighboring farmers stood off to the side, nodding in agreement. These men had spent all their lives on the same land that had supported their fathers and grandfathers and unknown generations before that. One of them, Eric Knopf, looked especially distraught.

Tony eased beside the sheriff and asked, "When did it happen?"

The sheriff turned. "I reckon about an hour ago."

"I've never known Ned to work on Sundays," Tony said, and could feel his uncle's eyes boring into the back of his neck.

"Neither have I," said Knopf, and spit speculatively.

Men were starting to talk among themselves now, while the line of cars on the road was doubling. The women had started to arrive and were leaning from car windows, shouting and waving to friends.

A real Sunday picnic, Tony thought miserably.

"You got any beer with you?" one of the gals shouted, and the sheriff turned to stare off into the sun as a group of kids made their way across the field. People were coming from all directions now, some gaping, others laughing uproariously.

Finally Knopf hollered to the sheriff, "How long you gonna leave him like that?"

The sheriff said, "Long as it takes to get a clear picture of what happened!"

Knopf waved an angry hand. "What about all these people?"

Deputy Salino started functioning. The kids he warned off with a yell. The others he pushed back, and then he headed to the dirt road where he started dispersing the traffic.

The sheriff's other deputy, young enough to be the sheriff's son, knelt beside one of the bales. "His head's in here, I think," he said with an unusual calm.

"Jesus," said Tony; beside him the sheriff remained silent as the photographer knelt beside the bale and snapped a picture.

The deputy looked up. "Should we take the bale apart?"

The sheriff looked at him with distaste. "Why, you thinking of selling souvenirs?"

"Maybe," the kid said, smoothing his mustache.

When Tony next glanced around he noticed that his uncle had shouldered Marshall Whitset off to the side, where they stood talking. Jack looked excited and disturbed, but Whitset just shook his head calmly and kicked dirt from his right shoe.

Tony was surprised to find Whitset there at all. As head of the Town Council, he usually stayed as far out of people's reach as possible. When Jack Gardner saw Tony staring his way, he quit talking. Whitset nodded to Tony, then turned back to gaze at the tractor, which suddenly sputtered, then coughed, then went dead.

The silence which followed was almost deafening.

"Looks like it's gonna be a long, hot summer," Salino said in the silence, rejoining the younger deputy, who was still fascinated with guessing what parts of Ned Taylor were in which bale.

The sheriff said, "Hope not. I've gained too much weight for one of those." Then he turned to face Tony. "Did your friend get off all right this morning?"

"Rob? Oh, yeah. Left town a while ago," Tony said.

With an exaggerated gesture the sheriff jabbed at his teeth with the piece of straw, screwing up his mouth, making a sucking sound. "His friend ever turn up?"

Tony shook his head. "Not that I know of."

"Well," the sheriff said, "he's damned lucky you dropped in this morning, 'cause he'd probably still be in jail."

A police van suddenly appeared off the

main road. All eyes followed its progress as it bumped and ground its way into the field.

"I thought you said there were no charges against him," Tony said.

The sheriff said, "There was until you showed up. But seeing how your uncle's on the Town Council, I figured, well . . ."

"How'd you know he was leaving town this morning?" Tony asked.

"I'm the law around here. It's my job to know." The sheriff half smiled, then looked at his two deputies. "Pete, check the gas tank on the tractor, let me know if it's empty or the damn thing just quit on its own."

As Salino climbed aboard the tractor the sheriff took out a note pad and jotted down the time. "Well, if you'll excuse me, Counselor, I got work to do."

"Sure, go ahead."

The sheriff stepped away, first saying to Tony, "Tell your friend that if he's thinking of coming back to town, he should think again. 'Cause the next time he gets in trouble in my town, his ass belongs to me."

Still half smiling, the sheriff moved away toward the van.

An hour later most of the onlookers had gone, but the sheriff and his team were still milling about; measurements and blood samples were taken, footprints were cast. Tony thought it odd that the sheriff should go to such lengths over what appeared to be an accident.

Tony leaned against the fender of his car and waited. Two more members of the Town Council had shown up: an obviously bored Dr. Walker, dressed in a plaid jacket, and Arnold Jacobs, who seemed annoyed and not at all in a mood to deal with Ned Taylor's new split personality.

Displaying exaggerated gestures and a mixed bag of expressions, they convened near the fence, Marshall Whitset holding court right there in the open. From time to time Jack would glance Tony's way, then stick his nose back into the conversation.

Tony watched as the two bales were loaded into the police van. The sheriff shouted, "Watch it, for chrissakes," as Salino let one of the bales fall to the ground.

A loud, hacking cough came from the right, and Tony glanced around, saw young Kenny Long sitting on the tailgate of his pickup, bringing up phlegm.

Tony walked over to him, waited for him to straighten and reach for another beer from his cooler.

"Hi, Kenny. How's it going?"

The boy shrugged. "Too fucking hot," he said, and Tony could tell by his slurred voice that he was drunk.

"Mind if I join you?"

"Sure, Mr. Rizzo. Help yourself." His complexion was white, bone-white, accented by the deep purple shadows under his eyes. He raised his hand to the cooler and then let it drop to his knee.

Tony sat on the tailgate beside him. "You're hitting the stuff pretty heavy, aren't you?" he asked gently.

"Ain't even started yet," he said, and drank, the beer spilling from his mouth onto his denim shirt.

"What's the matter, Willis Bradley not treating you right?"

"Hell," Kenny laughed, and drank again. "I ain't no undertaker, I told him that. I'm a driver, is all. But he keeps asking me to work on those bodies. No, sir—I sure and hell ain't gonna work on no more bodies. No, sir . . ."

Tony leaned forward, concerned. "He's just trying to find work for you, that's all. He means well."

"Yeah, I guess." Kenny sighed, and his chest seemed to collapse. "Still, like I told him . . . the girl, she's . . . oh, hell, I didn't want to embalm her or anyone else no more. But he said she needs a decent funeral . . . and that's my job. Some job . . . Jesus, I ain't never seen anyone look like that. Never . . ."

Tony looked at him strangely. "Has someone died that I don't know about?" he asked.

". . . Brought her in last night, they did. A girl. Head swollen, must have been in water or something. They found her just inside the cemetery . . ." He looked up suddenly and seemed to realize, perhaps for the first time, what he was saying. He looked dejectedly at his beer bottle.

Tony regarded him somberly. "Was she from around here? Millhouse?"

"No, look, she . . . Mr. Rizzo, I don't want no trouble. I shouldn'ta been shooting off my mouth. I'm just supposed to deliver a message to Mr. Whitset over there, that's all."

"I understand," Tony said. "But the girl, who was she, do you know?"

"Stranger, I think. I'm not sure."

"Didn't Bradley tell you who she was, where she came from?"

"Willis don't tell me nothing," Kenny said.

He put his hand to his eyes and Tony saw that he was crying.

"Kenny?"

He wiped away the tears but would not look at Tony. Instead he reached for his hat, slapped it against his knee, then stood. "I'm drunk, is all. Please, I don't want trouble," he said. "No one's supposed to know."

He clutched at Tony's arm, his eyes glazed with fear, forehead beaded with sweat.

Solemnly Tony rose, unbuttoned his jacket, and leaned against the side of the truck, considering Kenny's words.

"Okay, Kenny," he said at last. "You can trust me. I won't say a word. But I want you to do me a favor."

"Yeah, like what?"

"I want more information on this girl," Tony said.

Kenny drew back. "No, I can't do that. If they find out . . ."

"Who's they?"

"Willis, I meant."

"Bullshit. You said *they*." Tony nodded toward the councilmen. "You mean them?"

Kenny turned to glance into the field. Whitset was staring their way now, with frowning eyes.

"I gotta go," he said.

"Call me tomorrow at my office. You know the number. Will you do that?"

"I'll see ya . . ."

"Tomorrow, okay?" Tony said, and watched as Kenny stumbled into the field. Was this girl the one Rob Martin had spoken of? Who was she?

As Tony walked back to his car he noticed that dark clouds had moved in from the south, covering the sun and casting a gray cloak over the landscape. Yet the heat persisted, as did Rob's story about finding a girl's body in a tree trunk.

"What was Rob's description?" Tony asked himself, then remembered. She was like an Angel of Death. The only difference: She had a swollen head.

The thought hung on for the next hour, like the grease smell outside Sue's Cafe. Not even the radio could banish it. Finally Jack Gardner returned to the car. He seemed tired, yet unaccustomedly calm. In utter quiet, they drove home.

7

Nights are grievously long in Millhouse, made even longer by the absolute stillness that comes with the dark. Some say that the people's thoughts create the stillness. That the people of Millhouse know how to settle down and meditate after a long day. Others say it's because most people in Millhouse retire early, a habit inherited from generations when farming was the only industry. And then others, well—they don't say anything at all. They just know better than to be caught out in Millhouse after dark.

He brought the fresh vial of blood to his blackened lips and drank. He had chosen to drink alone tonight. The others were to remain locked in, until he could decide what his next course of action might be.

Solemnly, stately, he finished the last of the blood in the vial, then reached for another and, drinking slowly, drained it as well. Still, he was not satisfied. An incurable longing filled him, born from a desire that had been with him for some time now.

The desire for flesh.

Womanly flesh, soft and sweetly scented.

The thought made him erect, and he flung the next vial against the wall, causing bloody flowers to bloom on the ancient yellowing wallpaper.

He rose to his feet, inflamed, knowing that he could not stave off his desire any longer. The taste and touch of flesh, its engrossing texture, were spiritual nourishment to him.

He needed it, and nothing could take its place. Upon flesh his thoughts would become known. His life would be gloriously extended, beyond the reaches of any mortal. He would become Godlike.

All killing is sacrificial, and all sacrifice is eating.

Killing is eating.

Slowly he stepped out of his soft velvet slippers.

The cold flooring against his bare feet made him swoon.

Eat; this is my body.

Smiling, he slipped into the shadows. Moments later he saw the moonlight. Still smiling, he began his attack.

Mrs. Arbor heard a noise upstairs. Had she imagined it? She wasn't sure. The TV was off. Elizabeth and Mr. Arbor had both gone to bed early.

She put down her knitting, listened for a moment. No, she hadn't imagined it, because there it was again. An odd sound she couldn't quite identify.

She rose to her feet to investigate.

In the hallway she looked around. The sound, whatever it was, appeared to be coming from Elizabeth's room.

What is she doing up there?

She switched on the hall light, then went upstairs quietly, past her own bedroom, pausing a moment there to gaze at the door. If the noise had disturbed her husband he would have already been up, asking questions. She moved on to Elizabeth's room.

At the door she listened. There was silence suddenly. Then there was one heavy thud on the floor, as if someone had fallen . . .

In his room, in bed, Joe Arbor awoke when he heard the noise. A loud thud, as if someone had thrown open a shutter, causing it to bang against the house. He sat up, gazed around the darkness of his room. He could see a spill of light beneath his door. Then he heard his wife say, "Elizabeth? Elizabeth, are you all right?"

Quickly he rose from bed.

His wife turned to stare at him as he entered the hallway. "What is it?" he asked, seeing the strange look on her face.

"I don't know. I heard a noise and . . ."

"Is Elizabeth all right?" Joe Arbor raced forward, his bare feet making heavy smacking sounds against the pegboard floor.

"I don't know," Mrs. Arbor cried. "Her door is locked."

Joe Arbor tried the knob. It didn't move. "Elizabeth? Elizabeth, you all right?" He banged on the door. "Elizabeth!"

From inside the room came an ear-shattering cry.

"Elizabeth?" With sudden desperation Joe Arbor flung his body against the door. It refused to give. "Oh, Jesus," he whined.

"The key," Mrs. Arbor said. "It's in my jewelry box, I think." She moved swiftly down the hallway.

Mr. Arbor put his ear to the door and listened, heard the sound of movement. "Elizabeth, please, open the door," he cried. The sound vanished as Mrs. Arbor came rushing back with a small ring of keys and handed it to her husband.

He tried one key but it did not fit. He stabbed at the lock with a second key; it was blocked. He glanced nervously at his wife, then back to the door. The third key fit and, with a fierce thrust, Mr. Arbor entered the room.

Elizabeth was lying prone, naked and quite still, across the bed; her thin shoulders glistened in the light from a single candle on the table opposite the opened window. Her mouth was wide open and her eyes closed. Her face was smeared hideously with red makeup.

Mrs. Arbor reached for the light switch, and her husband said, "No, don't!"

As she came farther into the room, she saw he was drawing in deep, shuddering breaths and his chest heaved and subsided painfully. "Why, what is it, what's happened?"

She moved past her husband and glanced down. And Lucille Arbor began to scream.

8

The girl Marianne had no mother or father to wail over her. No husband or boyfriend to kick down her door at the last moment to save her. She had been abandoned by the world months ago, and only the old black man living below her heard the sound, but he figured that if she wanted to screw around, that was her business.

That's the way things were in the few streets that made up the area of Millhouse called the Kitchen. Around the corner from the Greyhound bus depot, it was home for the less fortunate: the drifters, the disabled, people just plain down on their luck.

The black man, Mosley Green, just rolled

over and went to sleep. In the automobile graveyard across the road the crippled junkman's dog rushed toward the fence, and began to bark furiously. His howling rose and swam for a couple of minutes against the flat distance of the sky like the commotion of a pack of angry wolves, uncertain in flight; then just quit.

In the stillness the girl could feel his hot tongue licking the sweat from her breasts and between her legs. Each time he drew blood, she would shudder.

"Again," she breathed in a deep lustful voice. The hard face came again to her throat, which was aglow with sweat. His breath was hot, and when she reached out and took hold of him he began to tremble.

"Oh, yes," she moaned, her naked body rising up from the mattress. "More," she wailed. "Harder . . ."

Her finger went to her opening then into it. Teeth bit, drew blood, then a hot licking tongue smeared it across her neck.

Finally, with a shuddering climax, she sank back onto the bed and closed her eyes. She felt his tongue again, one last time, traveling down the length of her body.

Then she passed into a deep sleep filled with the odd sensation of being submerged in water.

Thus came Monday, raining.

SUSPICIONS AND INVESTIGATIONS (II)

1

THE SECOND HOMECOMING

Hyannis Port to New Bedford, New Bedford to Providence, then east to the Connecticut border: Route 171 through Woodstock valley . . . ten hours after leaving Robert Kennedy's summer home, Rob was sitting in a small cafe stalling for time. He was exhausted, though he had made more stops than usual—mainly for water, which the Jag seemed to guzzle insatiably.

As the towns drifted by, he thought and drove, and drove and thought, until his mind was humming with the engine. The country isn't right, it seemed to be saying. Neither are its leaders.

What had most struck Rob about Kennedy was how ill at ease he seemed, and the difficulty he had in talking; his voice often trailing off, his sentences were grammatically incomplete. Instead of finding a man filled with confidence, Rob had found a man lost and grappling with the times.

The unrest seemed to Rob to be all around him. Everywhere he looked, as he drove, there was a disturbing sense of alienation. Men and women shouted protests in front of a supermarket in Providence. "Down with rising food prices!" they yelled. Down the road, another demonstration, this one protesting the upcoming launching of the Pargo nuclear submarine at Groton in September.

The newspaper headlines were no better. "*Colleges Warned to Curb Drug Use*: The latest poll taken indicates that forty percent of all college students use some sort of drugs." "*Firearms a Menace to Society*: Deranged boy shoots six people to death before taking his own life." "*Race Riot in Chicago.*" "*Heat Wave Sweeps Nation*: 69 deaths attributed to the heat."

Bewildered, Rob glanced down at his food, thinking of his own predicament. The more he thought about it, the more unbelievable his speculations became. Was Larry Campbell dead? Had someone killed him? Did those same people try to kill him in the cemetery? If so, why? And even if Larry hadn't been killed, why had he disappeared? And who was the woman

Rob had seen outside his motel window? Somehow Rob could only touch the fringe of reason, could only guess, in fierce flurries of speculation, what was happening. Yet his gut told him that whatever that something was . . . was strange and evil.

Millhouse, when he arrived, was as still and dark as a grave. The rain had let up some time ago, but deep puddles filled the streets.

Like a stick drifting in a slow current Rob headed up Fairmont Avenue toward the railroad tracks, and turned right, off the paving into a puddle-pocked dirt road, which was edged by new foliage in the deep, brilliant green of July. The tall oak and elm trees were still dripping, shaking off the rain's burden.

As Rob rounded the first curve, he realized he wasn't all that sure where Tony Rizzo lived. All the houses in this part of town looked the same, and Rob hadn't seen the house in ten years. He hadn't seen it much before that, either. Tony had always preferred to come to Rob's house. "Less formal," he used to say.

Rob glanced nervously through the windshield. Locust Hill Road was turning out to be longer than he remembered, the houses farther apart.

Then Rob saw it, sitting back among trees with a sweeping lawn. He eased the car up the drive and shut off the engine. His shoes disappeared into a puddle as he stepped from the car.

"Dammit," he muttered and moved away to the door of the white Victorian house.

He pushed the bell and waited. When he got no answer, he knocked. Still no one came to the door. He glanced at his watch. It was a little past nine P.M.

Remembering Tony's instructions, Rob retraced his steps. "If no one is home when you arrive," Tony had said, "use the key hidden in the flowerpot under the front porch." Just as he reached the edge of the steps the door behind him opened.

"Yeah, whataya want?" came a voice.

Rob turned to stare into Jack Gardner's watery gray eyes. He was wearing only a pair of dirty-brown trousers; his feet and chest were bare.

"Hello, Jack," Rob said. "Is Tony here?"

"He's out," the man said irritably. "Won't be back until late."

Rob shrugged. "Well, he told me . . ."

"What?" the man said. "What did he tell you? That you could stay here? Well, you can't. This is my house, too. He shouldn't have said that without asking me first."

His eyes studied Rob in subtle yet unmistakable amusement. Or was it contempt?

Rob nodded. "All right, Jack. But can I at least come in for a while, wait for him?"

The man's face was suddenly impassive, his thin mouth straight. "I suppose you're expecting me to change my mind, is that it?" Casually he flicked the next sentence. "Mind telling me how you got that gash on your head?"

Rob was caught off guard. "It's none of your business," he stammered through his anger.

Jack Gardner nodded without surprise, and continued in the same casual tone. "My guess is that somebody rapped you a good one."

"Guess away."

"Shoot, boy, you're still a wise ass. You always was."

At that moment Tony's green Dodge pulled into the drive, the hot beams of its headlights casting heavy shadows across the old man's face. He squinted into the light, stepping forward.

"Shit," he muttered and spit off the side of the porch. "You listen, boy," he said, turning to Rob. "A day, two at most, I want you out of here. You got that?" Without waiting for Tony to get out of the car, he stormed into the house.

2

The knock on the door caused Rob to turn with a start.

"Can I come in?" Tony said, and Rob said, "Sure."

Tony came into the room with a fresh set of towels and a blanket. "I'm sorry the room's in such a mess," he said. "Holly was supposed to straighten it. Guess she forgot." He paused. "You're bleeding."

"What?"

"Your forehead. It's bleeding."

Rob glanced in the small mirror over the dresser. "Damn thing keeps opening up."

"You don't look so good," Tony said, unable to disguise his concern. "You should have had that looked at."

"I should have done a lot of things." Rob took his handkerchief and pressed it to his forehead. In the mirror he could see Tony staring at him. He looked self-conscious and ill at ease. Rob said, "It's a little hot for a blanket, isn't it?"

Tony glanced absently at the blanket in his hands, then tossed it and the towels onto the chair beside the door. "I guess," he said. It was obvious that he had more pressing things on his mind.

"Uncle Jack giving you a hard time about me staying here?" Rob asked. Tony made no response, so Rob said, "Maybe he's right. Maybe I should . . ."

Tony pushed the door closed. "Sit down," he said. "Let's talk."

"About what?"

He sat on the edge of the bed. Breaking loose his tie, he said, "About the girl's body you found in the tree stump." Then he said, "A lot happened while you were away. And it's all fucking weird if you ask me. First of all, Ned Taylor is dead."

Rob looked up. "You're kidding."

"No, a baler chopped him up yesterday. Damndest thing I've ever seen. Parts of him were everywhere. But what's even stranger is the way his death was handled. I've never seen the sheriff so interested in investigating a death before."

"What was there to investigate? It was an accident, wasn't it?"

"That's just it. It had to be an accident, right? So then why bother taking footprint castings and blood samples? And half the Town Council showed up, including Whitset. Why?"

Puzzled, Rob said, "But the girl's body, you said."

"I'm getting to that. While I was at Ned Taylor's farm I ran into Kenny Long. He works with Willis Bradley, the caretaker for Crestwood Lawn. He told me they brought in a girl the night before last. Found her dead in the cemetery. When I asked him who she was, he panicked. No one is supposed to know, he said. He told me he never saw anything like it. That her head . . ."

Rob was like a fish caught at the end of a line. He knew instantly what Tony would say next, and he was at once overcome with astonishment. "I knew it," he exclaimed. "I knew I wasn't imagining it . . ."

Tony held up his hand to silence him. Stealthy footsteps shuffled across the landing and descended the staircase.

"Jack, is that you?" Tony called out.

The clandestine sound moved away in the direction of the kitchen. After a moment the back door slammed shut. Tony quickly walked to the window and looked out. He nodded. "It was Jack. There he is now."

"Where's he going?"

"Who knows." Tony turned. "He's been acting strange for days. Everyone has. The Town Council, the sheriff, Kenny Long . . . I asked him to call me today but he never did. So I did some checking on my own. Sure enough, a girl was buried this morning, in an unmarked grave."

"Jesus," Rob breathed. "So there really is something going on."

"Here, take a look at this." Tony took a newspaper clipping from his jacket pocket. "It's from last week's paper."

Rob unfolded it and read: "*The Ghoulish Vandals.* Clarksville, CT—Police will keep a round-the-clock vigil at St. Agnes's Cemetery because of the desecration . . ." Rob looked up. "It says here that the same thing happened ten years ago to the day."

"Ten years ago—July third. Five days after you left town. Five days before you came back."

"And?"

"I don't know. A coincidence?"

"No. Hell, no. I don't believe in coincidences." Rob's mind was reeling now, throbbing with possibilities. He looked again at the clipping and then back to Tony. "What do you make of it?" he asked.

Tony stuck a cigarette into his mouth and

extracted a lighter from his pocket. He clicked forth a flame. "I don't know," he said, tossing the lighter on the dresser.

"Hold on, Tony. You don't go through all this trouble without having a hunch."

"I tell you, I don't know," he said irritably. "Look, I hear things but that doesn't mean . . ."

"What things?"

"Things," Tony muttered, "like . . . like dead people who aren't really dead."

Rob laughed, a grating, nervous laugh. "What, you mean ghosts?"

"I'm only telling you what I heard," Tony said defensively. "Right after you left town years ago things started to happen. Nobody would talk about it. But sometimes I'd overhear things.

"Norris Caine was mentioned, and . . ."

3

Rob could not take it all in, not at first.

But as Tony went on talking he could see the woman's face again, hovering outside his motel window, her eyes grievous and tearful, her skin as pale and ghostly as a late-winter sky.

He said, "But what has Norris Caine to do with me?"

"Jesus, Rob—all I know is that some people think Norris Caine is still around."

"That's impossible. We went to his funeral. We saw his body. Everyone did."

"I know, I know," Tony muttered, annoyed, nervous, pacing back and forth as if his moving would help the situation. "But the way Julia

Caine was buried, don't you think that was a bit strange?"

"Of course. But the Caines were always strange. Right?"

"I guess . . ."

"Oh, hell, none of this makes sense," Rob said in disgust. "None of it."

"I'm only trying to help."

"I know that, and I'm grateful." Rob hesitated, the newspaper clipping sticking to his sweaty fingers. "Mind if I keep this?" he said.

"Sure. What are you thinking of doing?"

"I don't know. Maybe Larry Campbell is somewhere goofing off. Or maybe he's . . . I don't know. I'll just have to start doing some nosing around of my own."

Tony looked at him somberly. "You better be careful, Rob. The sheriff was none too friendly the last time we talked. I don't think he liked you very much."

"That's his problem."

"I'm serious, Rob. This can be a dangerous town when it wants to be. You can't trust anyone. Especially the sheriff."

"So, okay. I stand warned."

Characteristically Tony fingered his lean jaw for a moment. Then he said, "It's late and you must be beat. I'll, ah—I'll let you get some sleep. If you need anything, just give a yell."

"I will, and thanks again for your help."

At the door Tony said, "Oh, before I forget. Don't pay any attention to our housekeeper.

You'll undoubtedly collide with her in the morning, and if I know Holly she'll say the wrong thing and . . ."

"Tony?"

"Yeah?"

"Did you ever find out how your uncle knew I was thrown in jail Saturday night?"

Tony hesitated. "No. No, I didn't."

"Oh," Rob said. A moment later, after Tony had left the room, he lay back on the bed and closed his eyes.

4

The old man made his way through the alley, his work boots disappearing into puddles as he glanced around nervously. He could feel the night grow in intensity, and wasn't sure it was safe—even for him—to be blundering around in the dark.

For some reason he couldn't find the door.

Distracted, he put on his glasses. The world grew less fuzzy, but more frightening. He jumped over the next puddle and stopped beside a metal door. Glancing over his shoulder, he knocked.

An eye gazed at him through the peephole, and then the door opened.

They were all there, waiting for him.

5

The shadow loomed for a moment, and then swayed vaguely down upon him. He felt it was going to suffocate him, a darkness of obscene human flesh, head bloated and swollen, eyes nearly popped, avalanching over him, drowning him.

Rob opened his eyes and sat up in bed.

He couldn't go to sleep without images drifting into his mind. Vague images, yet very much alive and moving toward him. He glanced at the luminous hands of the alarm clock; it was 2:15 A.M. Jack Gardner had slipped into the house over an hour ago, and now all was silent.

Earlier, Rob had showered, then spent the evening typing the Kennedy interview. It stank, he finally realized, and wound up throwing the first draft away. The second draft was no better.

Elizabeth kept entering his mind. He thought about calling her, but knew he was not prepared to deal with her. Strange, he thought. Somehow he never seemed up to the task. In commitment there is *responsibility*. Is that what it was? Fear that he would somehow be responsible for her. He'd always loved her, he knew that now. Loved to be with her. But he just could not bring himself to the realization that he was worthy of her, or that he was the one to make her happy.

Elizabeth, I love you . . .

I . . .

With a long sigh, Rob dropped his head to the pillow. The sky, what little of it he could see through the window, seemed very far away. Alight with stars above a heavy isolated darkness, it waited. For what, he knew not.

Soon his eyes closed.

After a time he heard somebody go past his door. Whoever it was paused outside and gently turned the knob.

Was he dreaming it?

He wasn't sure.

Too exhausted to investigate, Rob kept his eyes closed, and soon drifted into a deep, all-encompassing sleep.

6

The man must have been there for a long time, because his image took shape by degrees in Rob's mind as he slowly ascended to wakefulness. He stood hunched, his back to the bed, searching through Rob's clothes that were strewn across the chair.

Rob's eyelids fluttered for a moment, as his gaze traveled across the room. The day, gray in the morning, was now hot and overcast. Before Rob could move, the man spun around to face him.

"Get up," Jack Gardner said without preamble. "The sheriff's downstairs. He wants to see you."

"What?" Rob said, staring at the world through drooping eyelids as heavy as tree trunks.

"You deaf? I said . . ."

"The sheriff, I know. What's he want with me?"

Jack Gardner smiled. "I reckon that's between you and him."

Rob sat up in bed. "Where's Tony?"

"Gone to his office. But he can't help ya none." His smile turned ugly as he added, "No, sir. Not this time, he can't. Now get dressed."

Forty minutes later, perhaps more, Rob found himself walking through the backwoods of Millhouse. The sheriff shuffled along ahead of him like an angry bear, pushing brush and tree limbs aside, raising hell when one of the limbs snagged his white silk shirt. It was cooler in the woods, but not much, and the mixture of heat and moisture had created a light veil of fog which rolled upward from the ground.

The climb grew steeper, and as they backtracked around a fortress of rock heading toward an isolated clearing, Rob saw an obviously impatient Salino, dressed in street clothes, waiting for them with three other men.

Salino met them at the clearing's edge and said, "The coroner's been here for a while. He's been wondering where you were."

"What'd he think, that I was off somewhere having a quickie?" the sheriff grumbled. He stopped to remove his hat and wiped sweat from the headband with his handkerchief. "Shoot, this damned heat is killing me."

Salino eyed Rob suspiciously. "He know yet?" he asked.

"Know what?" Rob said, and turned to confront the sheriff.

"In due time, son. All in . . ."

"You've been telling me that for the last half hour, since we met at Tony's. Now what's going on?"

"You'll just have to see." The sheriff glanced at the clearing, waved his hat toward the men, then began walking. "Come on," he said.

Single file now, the sheriff hollering a playful greeting in front, they moved on into the clearing. With a grunt of exhaustion, he stopped beside what looked to be a pile of discarded blankets.

"Did you have a look yet, Thomas?" the sheriff asked one of the three men, who were wearing gray, light-brown, and dark-blue suits; all wore ties. One of the men, the thinnest, stepped forward, and took his time about it. He wasn't in a hurry. Nobody seemed to be in a hurry on this scorching July day, except Rob.

"Yeah, I had a look," the man said, the sudden harsh sunlight highlighting his emaciated face. Fog drifted lazily over his shoes.

"And?" the sheriff said.

"And . . . it's hard to say. He was floating in water, his lungs are edematous. But there's usually a large quantity of foam protruding from the victim's mouth and nostrils. None here, though. We'll just have to wait for the autopsy."

The sheriff nodded, sucking on his teeth at the same time. Then he said, "Pete," and, tossing his hand out, gestured toward the pile of blankets at his feet.

Salino turned his head away when he removed the first blanket, and there rose the sudden smell of decaying, rancid meat, and the horrible miasma that seems to surround a decomposing animal.

"Damn," Salino said, barely able to continue. As he pulled the second blanket away, there appeared feet and legs, swollen and blue. Reflex caused Rob to take a step backward.

"Easy, son," the sheriff said.

Rob tried turning his head away, but some morbid urge kept his gaze fixed on the sight. Hesitantly Salino lifted the last blanket, and Rob found himself staring down at a grayish-blue corpse, long dead, the fingers of its right hand half eaten away by rats.

"Oh, Jesus," Rob breathed, and could feel his knees giving way.

The sheriff reached out to steady him. "A couple of kids found him," he said. "They poked around at him for a while before they realized what they'd found. It is Larry Campbell, isn't it?"

Trying to catch his breath, Rob hardly recognized Larry. His long hair had been cut short and was caked with mud. His mustache was gone, his upper lip gashed and bruised, and the side of his face and neck were covered with purple puncture marks. "Yeah, it's him," Rob finally managed, and then realized he was going to be sick.

As Rob vomited a few steps away, the sheriff gave instructions. The three men disappeared into the trees. Salino sat dejectedly on a rock, a cigarette trembling between his lips. Himself still shaking, Rob straightened. The sheriff ambled up beside him.

"I have to have your friend taken to the coroner's office for an autopsy," he said. "That all right with you?"

"I guess." Rob wiped sweat from his face.

"Does he have any family?"

"No, none that I know of."

"No parents?"

"His father was killed in the war. His mother is . . . I don't know . . . I think he told me she died . . ."

The sheriff turned suddenly and hollered, "Hey, Doc, get away from there!"

Over the sheriff's broad shoulders Rob saw an old man kneeling beside Larry Campbell's body. He let go of the blanket, and then rose slowly to his feet, his white hair combed straight back, his rough, uneven features impassive.

"What the hell you doin' here, anyways?" The sheriff took a step forward, but before he could take another, the old man turned and, with a slow but purposeful gait, disappeared into the woods.

"Who was that?" Rob asked, looking after him.

"Old Doc Tanner. He lives just the other side of that hill." The sheriff turned to face Salino. "What are you thinking about for chrissakes. Didn't you see him comin'?"

"No," Salino said flatly, staring off into the sun.

"Well, pay attention from now on." Without looking at Rob, he added, "Let's go, you and I got some talking to do."

7

They took Standford Road, and Hilltop Avenue into town. The houses along the way were old. Many had been abandoned, others burnt out, leaving only fireplaces and chimneys looming in the rubble. A once-thriving community looked all but forgotten.

"You all right?" the sheriff asked.

Rob nodded, still unable to comprehend that Larry Campbell was actually dead.

"You feel yourself getting sick again, put your head down."

Rob took a breath of conditioned air, then opened his mouth and tried to breathe even deeper as his hand massaged the side of his forehead.

They drove eastward.

The sky turned brighter, battered by the sun.

They drove eastward, eastward, past the football field and Caine Park.

Jesus said: "In the world ye shall have tribulations: but be of good cheer; I have overcome the world."

Remembering that, Rob felt a little better. But not for long.

"Okay, so why'd you lie to me?" the sheriff abruptly asked, and turned onto Fairmont Avenue.

"Lie . . . what are you talking about?" Furious, Rob faced the sheriff, staring him down.

The man appraised Rob for a second, then said, "Your description of Larry Campbell. You said he had a mustache. You also told me he had long hair. Ain't that what you said?"

Rob leaned forward slightly, confused. "He . . . he must have shaven off the mustache when he got his hair cut."

"Huh," the sheriff grunted. "Got his hair cut. Now how'd you know he did that?"

"Because his hair was long the last time we were together. He always wore it long."

"And you drove up from Miami together, you said. Took you two days . . ."

"That's right."

"Did you have drugs with you?" The sheriff carefully eased the car around Millhouse Square and entered onto Main Street.

Rob hesitated, not sure what his answer

should be. Damned if he did mention the drugs, and probably damned if he didn't.

Sheriff Jones sighed heavily, easing up on the accelerator. "I'm trying very hard to understand what's happened here," he said. " 'Cause it just doesn't make any sense. You see, when I first went through Campbell's clothes this morning, I found a motel key. He checked into the Wallace Inn in Peabody late Thursday night. I know, 'cause I went over there before picking you up. You know where Peabody is?"

"Yeah," Rob said gloomily. "Next town over."

"That's right. I went through his room, and do you know what I found?"

"Drugs," Rob halfheartedly confessed.

The sheriff stopped the car suddenly, shut off the ignition, and jammed his foot down hard on the emergency brake. "That's right, drugs. And a shotgun," he said, and turned to face Rob squarely. "Now let's you and me go inside and see if we can get this thing sorted out."

Without saying another word, he swung himself out of the car and hooked his thumb in his belt. Rob stepped from the car shakily, glancing at the door to the police station.

"That's right, you take a good look at it," the sheriff said. " 'Cause if you don't start telling me the goddamn truth, you're just liable to be calling it home."

Across the street, Kenny Long sat behind the wheel of his dusty pickup and watched the sheriff following the stranger into the station. He'd heard there had been another death, and thought that maybe this might be a good time to tell the sheriff what he knew.

Beside him his wife sat quietly, breast-feeding their baby. Her face was frozen in the impassive ashen mold of sorrow, the helplessness of her situation.

"Hungry today," she muttered, switching the baby to her other breast.

"I know, I know," he said. "Christ, you gotta keep reminding me all the time."

"No, Kenny, I only meant . . ."

"I know what you meant, so just shut the fuck up." Tears welled in his eyes.

The baby was his youngest. And God knew Kenny loved him. Loved his wife too. But he couldn't go on no more, knowing what he knew, seeing how things were starting to get out of hand.

But hc never could hold onto a job. No way. Except, of course, for working with Willis Bradley. And that was only because he knew too much for them to mess with him. Still, something had to be done.

But that's the way things were in Millhouse, weren't they? Keep your mouth shut and you were taken care of. A job, maybe. Or perhaps, if you were lucky, you got the mortgage paid on your house. Even those living in the Kitchen, like himself, were taken care of. An air conditioner when the summer got too hot, a new TV.

Most folks got something, but not everyone. No, not everyone.

Kenny looked up when the baby started crying.

"Ssssh," his wife said. "Hush, now . . ."

She was still a young woman but looked years older than her true age. It was his fault. All his fault.

He gazed again at the police station, made up his mind, and was reaching for the door handle when Al Jacobs's bulky frame blocked the door. Al Striker stood behind him. Both men stooped as they talked.

"Hello, Kenny," Jacobs said. "Ma'am, how's the young one doing?"

"He's fine," she said, rocking him.

"Good, good," Jacobs said. Then he said, "Did you get the clothes we sent over?"

"We did. Thank you."

"No thanks necessary, ma'am. After all, that's what good neighboring is all about."

Al Striker suddenly moved closer. "Kenny, you got a minute? Marshall Whitset wants to see you."

Kenny looked at his hands on the steering wheel. Without turning to face the men, he asked, "Why, is something wrong?"

Jacobs said, "Not at all. He just wants to talk to you."

The baby started crying again, and Kenny drew a breath. "I'll stop by later, if that's all right."

Al Striker leaned an elbow on the window ledge. "It really needs to be now, Kenny. The missus will be all right." He took a step back and opened the door.

Kenny hesitated, sweat coating his face, then slid from the truck.

This can be a dangerous town when it wants to be, Tony had said. *You can't trust anyone. Especially the sheriff.*

The remark kept running through Rob's mind as he told his story. When he got to a part he thought was a no-no, he skipped over it. The air conditioner rumbled noisily in the corner. The sheriff sat back in his chair and looked interested when Rob mentioned the girl's body he'd found in the tree stump. He was about to tell Jones that he thought this was the same girl Willis Bradley buried yesterday in an unmarked grave when the "no-no" sign flashed and he jumped ahead.

A Coke and two trips to the bathroom later, the sheriff said, "You say they were waiting for you. You think this woman deliberately lured you into the cemetery?"

"That's right. There were at least two of them, besides her. They . . ." Ron's voice broke.

"Go on. It's . . . quite a story," the sheriff said, taking out a cheap cigar and unwrapping it.

"Look, you asked me to tell you the truth."

"All right, calm down." Cigar in his mouth, the sheriff lit it. "This woman who was outside your window, what'd she look like?"

Rob hesitated, then stalled more by waving away smoke. "I don't know," he lied.

"You don't know?" the sheriff boomed. "Well now, goddamn, some broad sticks her face in your motel window, but you don't know what she looks like. No matter, you hightail it after her. Into a cemetery, no less. At twelve o'clock at night. Why'd you go after her?"

"I don't know. I . . ."

"You were drunk."

"Maybe . . ."

"No maybes about it. You were shit-faced. Okay, so maybe you didn't see her face. Maybe you just got horny all of a sudden. That it?"

Rob said nothing.

Sheriff Jones suddenly lurched forward in his chair and pointed a warning finger across the desk. "Okay, now you listen good, goddamn it—'cause I'm gonna tell *you* a story. Friday night my deputy got his friggin' neck ripped open . . . by your Larry Campbell. That's right. We caught him beside a warehouse eating Ned Taylor's dog. He took off running but we eventually caught up with him. Before Salino could get out of the car your friend started chewing on his neck like it was a piece of steak or something. I never seen anything like it. Now if drugs were involved and you knew about those drugs, that makes you an accessory. Now what the hell was wrong with him?"

"I don't know," Rob muttered, hanging tough.

"Did you know he was holed up at the Wallace Inn?"

"No!"

"How about the shotgun? You know about that? And don't lie to me, because one way or the other I'm gonna find out. And when I do I'm gonna nail somebody's ass. Nail it good."

Rob thought: he's only interested in one thing—finding out how he can involve me in Larry Campbell's death. He said, "Look, I'm not answering any more questions without . . ."

"Without your lawyer friend present," the sheriff filled in succinctly.

"Precisely."

"Kind of touchy all of a sudden, ain't you? For someone who's maybe had a friend killed."

"When and if you prove that, I'll be glad to cooperate. Right now I seem to fall under the category of suspect. So . . ."

Sheriff Jones smiled and got to his feet. Each time he stood, Rob realized all over again just how big a man Jones really was. Casually he blew cigar smoke and went to the window. "All right," he said. "But things are different here than in Miami. I think you're gonna find that out. And when you do . . ."

Rob waited for him to continue. When he didn't, he said, "We through?"

"Yeah, we're through."

Slowly, without uttering another word, Rob got to his feet. He had no way of knowing that the worst part of his stay in Millhouse was just beginning.

8

The news came to Tony Rizzo as two successive shocks. Larry Campbell's death shook him, badly. Word of Elizabeth's latest collapse was even worse.

"Is there anything I can do?" he asked, adjusting the telephone at his ear. Around him the office steamed with heat.

"Nothing," Mrs. Arbor sobbed. "Except . . ."

Before she could finish the thought, Joe Arbor came on the line. "Tony, you tell that son of a bitch to stay away from my daughter. You hear me? You tell him if I catch him around my daughter . . ."

"Joe, Rob Martin didn't get back to town until late last night. Came right to my house. And as far as I know, he never left it."

"Bullshit," was the reply. "He was right there in Elizabeth's room last night. Used the porch roof to get to her window. We found the screen pulled off."

"What time was that?"

"What difference does that make? Dammit, you tell that . . ."

Suddenly Tony heard a noise, as if the receiver on the other end had fallen to the floor. Mrs. Arbor soon returned to the line. "Tony?"

"Yes, I'm here."

"Tony, please, we don't want any trouble. Elizabeth is very sick. My husband and I are upset. You can understand that. Tell Rob Martin that my daughter doesn't want to see him anymore. Please, Tony, tell him that." With a whimper, she hung up.

It was just after two P.M. when Tony lowered the receiver into its cradle, closed down the office for the day, and headed for the street. Joe Arbor's angry words followed Tony into the car; words that were unusual for him. If ever there was a peace-loving man, it was Joe Arbor.

As Tony drove he noticed that Millhouse looked dusty again, ocher and drab, despite yesterday's rain. Even the trees appeared exhausted. People had given up the streets, and most of the stores had drawn down their shades and awnings to ward off the sun's stubborn glare.

"It's the damned heat," Tony mumbled to himself. Another 100° day, or more. This made how many? Ten in a row, eleven? He had lost count, but knew it was some kind of record.

The sounds of window fans, air conditioners, kids splashing about in wading pools, drifted into the car as he turned onto Locust Hill Road.

When he pulled into his driveway he saw Rob's gray Jag parked beneath the shade tree; his uncle's car was gone. The house, when he entered it, was semidark. Someone, Holly, he guessed, had drawn the shades.

He listened, and heard a light tapping sound coming from above. He stared at the staircase with an anxiousness which was surprising to him. He found himself imagining things; things that hadn't entered his mind since he was a boy, when his father would play tricks on him, like hanging white tissue paper from the ceiling in his room at night. And making weird sounds from the closet.

For a moment he heard his father's voice, toneless and flat: *The only thing you gotta fear in the dark is yourself. Your mind, boy, will kill you quicker than anything.*

Still the odd, unfamiliar tapping sound persisted.

Tony moved up the stairs, forcing himself to

take each step. The upstairs was even darker, and reaching the top landing he flicked on the hall light. He moved to Rob's door, listened. The sound, he now realized, was Rob's typewriter.

Lightly he rapped on the door.

A cautious voice said, "Who is it?"

"Rob, it's Tony . . ."

A few minutes later they sat in the kitchen, drinking beer. The fan whirled noisily above them, its blades slicing the dead air.

"The sheriff took me to the station for questioning," Rob said. "I told him all I knew, all that's happened to me, but I don't think he believed me. You're right. He's not to be trusted."

Tony wiped foam from his chin. "You told him about Willis Bradley burying that girl?"

"No, I figured that was for us to know and him to find out."

Tony gave him what was meant to be a coolly audacious look, then lifted the beer bottle to his lips and drank. The silence which followed stood like a sieve between them, through which words came, but none of the emotions.

"How did Larry Campbell die?" asked Tony reluctantly.

"They don't know yet. But I can tell you it wasn't in a normal way."

"Where'd they take his body?"

"To the coroner's office in Peabody. They're going to perform an autopsy. I called my paper and told them what happened. They say Larry's got a brother living in Atlanta. They're tracking him down now. I gave them this number; I hope you don't mind."

"Mind? Hell, no, I don't mind," Tony said with false bravado. Then he got up, took another beer from the refrigerator, and, holding the door open, cooled himself.

In the silence, Rob said, "While I was at the station the sheriff told me a pretty weird story of his own."

"Oh?" Tony turned to face him.

"He claims Larry killed Ned Taylor's dog. Said he caught him behind a warehouse, eating the damn thing."

Tony stared at him. "You're joking."

"I wish I were. He said when they tried to arrest him, he attacked Salino and nearly tore his throat out."

"Do you think it was the drugs?"

Rob shook his head miserably. "I don't think so. Sure, Larry could act odd when he was stoned. He might run off, holler, smash a window, but not do something like this. Either the sheriff is lying, or . . ."

They stared at each other, their thoughts running along the same track. It was Tony who finally said, "The Norris Caine story. Can it be true?"

Rob got to his feet, went to the screen door, and peered out. "Maybe," he said. "But that still doesn't explain Larry's behavior, does it?"

"Unless," Tony said, thinking, "unless . . . well, I'm not really sure how to put this. Unless whoever killed him caused him to act that way."

And then he explained: Rob listened puzzled to Tony's account of what he had heard about Norris Caine.

"Are you saying that the man's some sort of a ghoul or something?" Rob asked incredulously.

"I don't know. I only know that three people are dead. I remember people dying in similarly strange ways some years back. All along Standford Road. Now no one lives up there. Except for the Salingers and . . ."

"The Arbors," Rob finished.

"And . . ." Tony hesitated, a thin layer of sweat beading his forehead. "Look, I didn't want to bring this up. Not after what you've been through. But . . . Elizabeth is sick again."

"Sick? You mean her blood pressure?"

"I think it's more than that. Right after you left town on Sunday, she collapsed again. She had another relapse last night."

"Oh, Jesus . . ."

"Her parents called me today at the office. They think her illness is your fault. They said you went over to her house last night and . . ."

"I did what?"

Tony shrugged. "I'm only telling you what Joe Arbor told me." He paused. "Did you? Go over there last night?"

Rob looked away, incapable of speech, incapable of any clear thought other than to acknowledge the uneasiness he now felt.

"Look, Rob, if you did go over there . . ."

"No. The answer is no." He glanced around sharply. "Tony, I gotta see her. Talk to her."

"I don't see how that's possible. Joe made it pretty clear . . ."

"I don't care," Rob shrilled, his voice dry and brittle. From across the room, Tony stared at him. "Please, Tony—I must see her. I *must.*"

It wasn't until later—after Holly had made an appearance, fixed dinner, and quickly fled the house—that Rob came out with his idea.

"Well?" he asked.

For a second, Tony stood by the table. Rob wondered if he was thinking of saying no. Tony waited an instant longer. Then: "All right," he said. "Let's do it."

9

At a certain point Standford Road made a ninety-degree curve and you could leave it, cut across a vacant field, and reach it again near Elizabeth's house. Rob had done just that: parked the Jag, walked purposefully among rubble, bricks, rusted bedsprings, the remnants of a basement foundation, until he came to the west side of the field covered with tall dry weeds. He stood behind one of the large elms and waited.

The sun had already left the sky, and although it was not quite dark, everything appeared to be cast in heavy black shadows. Elizabeth's house, gothically eccentric with wooden semicircular porch, was dark, except for the softly lighted living-room window.

It was ten minutes before nine when Rob heard the telephone ring inside the house. Heart thumping with lunatic intensity, he watched as Mrs. Arbor moved past the window to answer the telephone. He knew that Mr. Arbor was working the second shift—four to twelve—at the factory. He also knew that Tony had to be damned convincing if he was to get Elizabeth's mother to leave the house.

With her back to the window, Mrs. Arbor listened, and Rob began calculating, trying to figure out the conversation as it ensued. After a few moments, the woman nodded, said something else, and hung up.

Suddenly the woman was scurrying about; she disappeared for a moment, then returned to the living room. After a brief pause to look around, she moved out of sight again and the front porch light went on. When she appeared at the door, she was wearing a light raincoat and carrying her purse.

Soon Tony's car appeared. Mrs. Arbor stood on the front porch. She looked back over her shoulder once, then moved onto the sidewalk, heading for the car.

Rob waited, holding his breath in the hot, dense July night until Tony drove off. There were no clouds, no stars, no moon. The house loomed black before him, except for the glow of the living room and porch lights.

He moved toward the lights. The TV was on,

yet the living room was empty. Somehow he had imagined Elizabeth would be sitting there. At first, it was a relief to see she was not. But the feeling was short-lived, for the empty room suddenly filled him with foreboding.

He raised his hand to the door and knocked, heard something move behind him, and turned. Nothing. Only the vacant field from whence he had sprung, its deep intensity of solitude absorbing him into itself.

Forcing himself around, he reached for the doorknob and turned it. Again relief, and then alarm, upon discovering that Mrs. Arbor had left the door unlocked. He moved into the living room and glanced around. The Arbors were conservative people, one couch, two side chairs, a piano—everything neat. He shut off the TV.

"Elizabeth?" he called out. His voice echoed. "Elizabeth, it's Rob."

Everything remained quiet. Around him the house yawned. Creaked. Then creaked again, and Rob suddenly realized he was hearing footsteps. Quiet footsteps, but there nonetheless. Above his head. He moved to the staircase.

"Elizabeth?" He waited, expecting to see her come to the head of the stairs. When she did not, he started his climb.

Stupid, he told himself. Don't do this. Don't go up there. What if Mr. Arbor comes home unexpectedly, or Tony can't stall Mrs. Arbor long enough?

Still he climbed, ignoring his own warnings. The upstairs was dark and as he looked around, he saw a light, dim and elusive, beneath one of the bedroom doors. He stepped forward, listened.

Then, without knocking, he opened the door. The room wavered before his gaze, colors came and went, blending with the gloom that threatened to overpower all.

Empty. No Elizabeth, only a white summer dress thrown casually over the green quilt bedspread. A small table lamp burned on the table beside the window, casting an odd, thinly veiled, pale-orange light that barely made it to the door. A pair of velvet slippers were tucked beneath the table's chair.

Eyes riveted on the table, Rob hesitantly moved forward. Notepaper was scattered about the table's smooth mahogany surface, as if by some miracle God had breathed life into the dead air, causing a wind to scatter them about.

He lifted one of the papers and read:

> Dear Rob:
>
> So much has happened since you've been away. I'm afraid to fall asleep at night for fear . . .

The note ended abruptly, a harsh ink line extending from the letter *r* down to the middle of the paper, as if Elizabeth had suddenly lost control of her hand.

Rob read the note again, then glanced from

the window into the gloomy night. Across the way the field looked a solid mess of blackness, a few trees managing to distinguish themselves.

It was only then he realized that the window was open, with no screen to keep out the bugs. And that the lamp he stood beside was under attack. He watched as first a moth, then a fly, battered itself against the light bulb, then against the lamp shade. In a frenzy, both began looking for a way of escape.

The buzzing of the fly grew louder. Now there were two of them, then three, all furiously smashing against the lamp shade. Rob dropped the notepaper to the floor when he heard another sound. Louder and more frightening. Someone was moving around below.

"Elizabeth?" he called out, and then felt that he might have made a mistake. As the footsteps stopped, he realized that they could not be Elizabeth's. They were too heavy, too quick, to be hers.

In a single, continuous movement he stepped through the door and dashed along the hallway. At the head of the stairs he stopped cold. A shadow quickly passed below him and disappeared.

Mr. Arbor? he wondered.

Mrs. Arbor?

Or was he imagining things?

"Hello?" he called out. The house was silent.

Trembling, he started down the stairs. No

words this time, because whoever it was, no matter, would not be interested in his cover story.

Reaching the bottom step he paused, then remained utterly still, staring at a glimmer of mahogany here, a sudden flicker of silver there, and felt something like panic. Now was the moment, he thought. If he did not move now, he would never move. Now was the moment . . . now. *Oh, God, now*!

At last, rushing forward, he bounded for the door.

10

The fever had been growing in her all day, and just before dark it burst into a full-fledged fire, its greedy flames scurrying beneath her flesh in a dozen different directions. She had called in sick, told Sue Woodard that she wasn't feeling well, and spent the day in bed. But now, with night upon her, she felt thrilled with burning desire and drunk with the berserkness of its cause.

The stairs creaked and groaned as she took the last of them two at a time. She hoped she hadn't roused the Negro living below her. At the door she paused to look back; the man who followed after her still seemed unsure of himself, and then she smiled and slipped the key into its lock.

She had unfastened the top buttons of her dress by the time he stepped hesitantly into the room. She could feel her excitement travel upward to her breasts, and when he looked at her in the dim light she began to tremble.

"I'm a love child," she said, giggling. "Do you know what that is?"

The man nodded. "You hang out in Woodstock."

Greg Harrison he said his name was, and he had been standing alone outside the Greyhound bus depot when she spotted him. He had a two-hour wait for the next bus to New York, so . . .

"That's right," she said. "I love Woodstock. Have you ever been there?"

The man put down his suitcase and closed the door. "No, no, I haven't." When he turned around to face her he saw that she had removed her dress. She wore only a slender pair of black panties, and as she threw her shoulders back and expanded her chest, he could feel himself grow hard.

"I was just there recently, with friends."

"You live here in Millhouse?"

"I do now," she said. "I work in a little cafe on Main Street." She smiled. "You don't even know my name, do you?"

He shook his head in bewilderment.

"Marianne. But my friends call me Mary,

like in Jesus, Mary and . . . Greg, I like your name. It's strong. Greg Harrison," she breathed. "It sounds like you should be a movie star or something."

"Do you do this sort of thing often?" he asked.

"What, invite people to my room?" She licked her lips with her soft pink tongue.

"Yes," he said.

She laughed. "We're the love generation, haven't you heard?"

She studied him carefully—graying hair, lonely eyes, lightweight business suit, pleasant aroma of his cologne. She reached out and took his hand.

Soon he felt her warm, soft flesh against his as he crawled naked into her bed. She pushed her breasts toward him, and he gladly squeezed with both hands, then placed his mouth over one of the nipples. She closed her eyes and moaned. And kept on moaning, each lustful cry growing louder with each new position, each new thrust, until finally she screamed with orgasm.

She lay still after that, her eyes closed, her body stretched out in the blackness. He could barely make out her features. So damn young, he thought. And felt ashamed. Yet, in some strange way, he felt peaceful.

Soon he let himself relax, but did not close his eyes for fear of falling asleep. His gaze moved slowly about the room, as he listened to her soft breathing.

Above and around him shadows shifted, and then he heard—or thought he heard—the sound of movement near the open window, like the rustling of feathers. He sat up and immediately felt the difference in temperature, as if a cold breeze had entered the room. Then came the odor: a bittersweet scent which reminded him of the smell of the dead.

He listened. The brief flutter was followed quickly by a loud, dull thud. He strained but could see nothing in the darkness. Still, he had the uneasy feeling that someone had entered the room.

"Marianne," he said, and groped for her beside him. He started when he felt how cold her flesh had become. "Marianne?" he almost cried.

He drew his hand away as there was another sound of movement, closer to the bed. He tried to rise but felt his shoulder gripped by something hard, metallic, like fishhooks cutting into his flesh.

He screamed, once, then smelled an animal stench in his nostrils and felt teeth sink into his neck. Beating his arms wildly about his head, he managed to stumble forward. The girl suddenly rose up out of the dark with teeth bared and lunged at him from the opposite direction. He fell to the floor, stunned.

The first spurt of blood shot onto the bed, the second gush went into his eyes as he arched his shoulders and flung his head back. A man's face appeared, briefly, before going to his neck, the force of the blow driving him again to the floor.

He found himself on his knees, beside the bed. He was wet. Blood streamed into his mouth. The girl stood above him, drooling, and he heard cries and shrieks of orgiastic pleasure, and a sucking sound. First one was on him, then the other, and then, losing consciousness, he heard no more. The Drink had begun.

11

After long minutes in which everything happened in slow motion, and every step he took seemed isolated, time was racing again and his heart and mind with it.

Where the hell am I? Rob wondered.

He had begun to tremble so hard that his teeth were chattering. Some part of him was still standing in Elizabeth's house, utterly helpless, trying to figure out where she was, and who had been there. Another part of him pushed tree limbs aside, looking for a path, a sign as to where he was.

The vacant field seemed to have grown in width and depth, as a theater changes when the play begins, filled suddenly by an unexplained meaning. As he stumbled through it he realized that somehow he must have gotten turned around. Where a house once stood, now only a gaping basement remained.

"Jesus," Rob breathed, staring into a dark and fathomless crevice. One more step and he would have gone over the edge. Slowly he backed away, turned. Off to the right he could barely make out Elizabeth's house, the glowing bedroom window the only sign of life in an otherwise gloomy setting.

I should have turned left, not right, he thought, and realized he was near Hilltop Avenue, clear across the other side of the field.

He glanced north. Yes, that way.

He started to move, and then stopped. Twenty yards away, no more, a chimney loomed out of the rubble. A shadow moved and skipped across its surface. The shadow looked manlike, yet . . .

Like a flash, it fell away behind the bricks, leaving the chimney's surface colorless and flat. Rob's gaze intensified. No sound, only a whisper of a breeze that rose, making shadows where none had been, as tree branches started to sway. And then suddenly, from behind the chimney, there came the wild shrieking cry of an animal.

Rob stood frozen in terror, staring at the giant bricks. The cry kept rising, a horribly elongated blood-curdling yelp, filling the night air in all directions, until finally it popped like a punctured balloon.

Then all was silent, until the sound of crackling twigs and plundering footsteps arose. Rob dropped to one knee as a young boy stepped into the open. He held a cat in his hands. He looked at it, mumbling to himself. Then he tore the animal's body open, and brought it to his mouth. Rob's jaw slackened, and his lower lip quivered in disgust.

Again and again the boy rotated the cat in his hands, greedily tearing at its innards. He became furious at times, like a child who hadn't been given enough to eat. He cursed at the cat, pounded it with his fist, until finally he cast the carcass aside, and stood for a moment wiping blood from his hands and mouth with a handkerchief. Then, as if in a drunken stupor, he moved away into the darkness.

Rob rose unsteadily to his feet, staring after the boy. Sweat dripped into his eyes and he closed them, shaking his head in bewilderment.

Off in the distance he heard a woman's voice, light and airy, "J.D., you out there?"

A voice answered back, "Yeah, Mom. I'm just putting my bike away."

Slowly Rob opened his eyes. His heart hammered within his chest.

As he lurched forward, he knew—oh, Christ, yes—he knew without doubt where he was.

12

The man said, "I've been waiting for you."

Still trembling, the keys to the Jag rattling in his hand, Rob spun away from the car to stare into Doc Tanner's gaunt face. Tanner stood beside the road, under a large elm, and his dark-brown suit blended perfectly, making him appear almost invisible. Only his white hair and piercing green eyes came forth in the gloom.

"I was . . ." Rob's voice broke.

"I know where you were. I have to talk to you." The man shuffled into the light. "But not here. Not here," he muttered, his hand going furtively to his chest, and Rob saw that he had taken hold of a gold crucifix, which hung heavy and awkward outside his tan shirt.

"Talk about what?" Rob asked. Tanner's eyes kept darting around, and he seemed barely able to keep himself still, shuffling his feet from side to side.

"Not here, I said." He looked deep into Rob's eyes for the first time. "If you've got someplace special to go, then tell me. I appreciate frankness."

"No, no place," Rob said.

"My house is just the other side of that hill. Will that be all right?"

Rob hesitated, staring at the fingers kneading the crucifix, the urgent eyes, the mouth severe in repose. "All right," he said. "Get in."

A few minutes later, Rob followed Tanner up the narrow walkway, prepared for almost anything. Here not a breath of air moved a blade of grass; there was scarcely a sound—the blackbirds were silent, the crickets not yet roused to their nightly chirping. Nearby was a quiet pond. Two boats were out, and Rob heard laughter shrill from one of them.

"Damn kids never know when they're well off." Doc Tanner was having trouble fitting the key into the lock. "I don't like kids—never have. They're too unpredictable."

The door opened suddenly, and Rob wondered as he followed the man inside if he had seen and heard precisely what Rob had seen and heard only minutes before. Was it J.D. Salinger they were about to discuss?

"Let's go in the kitchen," Doc Tanner said. He turned lights on as he went, in the living room, hallway, and then the kitchen.

As Rob stepped inside, he noticed that the back door was protected by a police bar, something he thought people used only in big cities. The room smelled of old coffee grounds, stale pipe tobacco, must, and mold.

"Can I get you something to drink?" The man seemed more relaxed as he ambled to the cabinet beside the sink. Water dripped from the tap, beating tattoos against stainless steel.

"A Coke?" Rob asked tentatively.

"I said drink. Wine, beer . . ."

"A beer would be fine." Rob watched him take an envelope from the cabinet, then moved to the refrigerator. "Those kids shouldn't be out after dark. It isn't safe." With the envelope stuck under his arm, Tanner took two beers from the refrigerator and handed one to Rob.

"Thanks."

The kitchen table where they sat was small, and the men's legs collided as Rob stretched out. The man didn't seem to notice.

"You remember me, I guess?" Doc Tanner said. "From when you were a boy."

Rob sort of smiled. Was the man serious? Each of his gestures, his movements, brought a rush of memory: the *flick-flick* of the old guy's trousers as he came into the waiting room and told Rob that his mother would be all right; the smell of his pipe tobacco when he would stop by the house, *Rob, age seven*—"The boy's got measles." All the old emotions welled up—the good, the bad . . .

"Of course I remember you," Rob said.

"I wasn't so sure you had. When you looked at me today, I thought . . ."

"I wasn't thinking too clearly today."

"None of us are," Tanner mumbled, his eyes downcast, worrying at one corner of the manila envelope. "I'm sorry about your friend. Really sorry."

"Thanks."

"How old was he?"

Rob noticed that his heart had begun to race again, but he steadied himself. "Larry was twenty-four."

The man's hand groped for the crucifix around his neck. "Does the sheriff know how he died?"

"No, they're going to do an autopsy," Rob said.

Tanner's face took on, briefly, a puzzled look. Then he snorted, "An autopsy, huh. I like that. And you? What do you think caused his death?"

Rob drew a deep breath before answering, and noticed—for the first time—a shotgun propped against the side of the refrigerator. On the floor, beside the butt of the weapon, was a bottle of wine, a brandy bottle, and a stack of tattered books topped by a disheveled Bible.

"Are my questions making you nervous?" came a flat voice, and Rob turned and saw Tanner staring at him. It was a rather frightening gaze. Bottomless.

"No, I was just . . ."

"Looking for signs that I'm crazy," he stated. "Well, I'm not crazy. I'm seventy-two years old, my wife died four years ago, and I live alone. Every winter I vacation alone, go nowhere in particular, and come back alone. I have no pets, no hobbies, and I'm not looking for sympathy. However, people around here seem to think I'm nuts."

"What makes you think that?"

"Hell, I overhear things, catch the looks. And I'm sure when you hear what I have to say, you'll think the same thing." The man nodded gravely. "In fact, I'm sure of it."

That was the moment, at least Rob would later swear it was, when he felt something go cold inside him. Perhaps it was the look of the man: the ashen skin, the reddened eyelids, the trembling lips that served as an ominous warning not to go on with the conversation. Still, somehow compelled, Rob said, "Why don't you just say what's on your mind, and let me be the judge?"

The old man considered.

"All right," he said at last. "I think I know how your friend died. What killed him."

Rob stared in amazement. "Okay, then," he said, hesitantly, making an effort at control. "If you know, tell me."

The old man's watery eyes looked away for a moment, then returned to meet Rob's gaze. "I think," he said, "that he was killed by vampires."

13

When Doc Tanner finished his story, he paused. His face was white, as if an unseen chill had permanently iced his cheeks, leaving only tiny blotches of dried red skin to flake on his forehead. Sometime before, he had prepared to light his pipe. And he sat now with the lighter in one hand, pipe in the other, still as a mannequin, staring at Rob. Rob was staring at the Bible. He turned suddenly, took out a cigarette, and the old man flicked his lighter to life and held it out. As Rob inhaled deeply, Tanner uncapped the brandy bottle, filled his glass, and downed its contents in one swift gulp. Around them the house settled, creaking.

"You're serious about all this, aren't you?" Rob said finally.

"Deadly serious," Tanner said, wiping a trickle of brandy from his lips. "You know anything about vampires?"

"If you mean have I personally studied them, the answer is no."

"You see those books on the floor? I've read them all." He said this with a touch of anger, as if to challenge anyone who questioned his faculties. Crinkled lines webbed out from the corners of his eyes for a moment, then his gaze came to light on Rob's face. "Most of the authors believe that vampirism is founded on superstitions which grew with the advent of Christianity. The church, you see, is to blame. 'Drink this in remembrance that Christ's blood was shed for thee, and be thankful.' "

He massaged his chin, fully embarked upon a lecture. "Some believed that the soul lived within the blood, that it was the source of life. One book deals with cannibalism as a cause. Man is a carnivorous animal and hungers for meat. The succulent fleshy bloodred steak, the delicate slim slices of beef," he said, with a brittle chuckle that resounded in the small room.

Rob nervously crushed his cigarette out in the ashtray.

"But there are others who offer a simpler explanation," the old man went on, once again pouring brandy into his glass, which resembled an old jelly jar. "Suicide, for one. Or excommunication, or those who die an untimely death, an unhappy death or an unavenged death. Another book mentions lycanthropy. Do you know what that is?"

As he lifted the glass to his lips, Rob said, "It's a disease, isn't it?"

Tanner paused in midaction. "A form of mental illness, yes." Then he swallowed. "The victim imagines himself to be a wolf." He looked deep into the empty glass. "The victim usually suffers loss of speech, runs around on all fours, growling and eating raw meat."

Rob shook his head. "No offense, but I just can't relate to all this. I mean, we're actually sitting here discussing werewolves, for God's sake."

"Vampires," Doc Tanner corrected.

"Right." Rob could see the boy, J.D. Salinger, his eyes frantic, his mouth salivating, as he tore open the cat's body. "I take it from the crucifix you're wearing," he stammered, "that you're Catholic. How can you even consider such things?"

The old man slammed his open palm to the table. "Because if I accept God as Good, I must also accept the existence of Evil."

"Evil, as in?"

"As in vampires. Don't shake your head. I tell you Norris Caine is still with us." The old man was suddenly on his feet. "And he has others with him."

"What proof do you have?"

"Proof? You saw your friend's body, those puncture marks on his neck. And I don't need an autopsy to tell me his body was drained of blood."

"The coroner was there. He didn't seem to know . . ."

"He does what the sheriff tells him to do. If what I'm saying is true, do you think they'll admit it? Anyway, if it's proof you want, read this." He opened the manila envelope and took out a small book. "It's all in there. Read it."

The book was an old ledger, its black pebble-grained cover worn at the edges. As Rob opened it, one of the yellowing pages fell to the table. Inserting it back into the ledger, he began to read.

> Aug. 9—The salesman from Chicago was my first death. And his death, of course, was necessary in order that there would be no turning back. I committed myself by the killing of this man. I felt no pain at having killed him. No remorse. Nor sorrow. He was a fat cat who needed to die. That was all. And then, after I had killed this man, I drank of his blood.
>
> I was a beginner then and did not know the proper way to drink. I flung his body over a garbage can and let his blood drip into a discarded pie tin. When the tin had filled with a fair portion of the man's blood, I drank. Later, while sitting on my bed, I thought: This is either the beginning

or the end of my life. But even then, in that moment, I knew the truth. It was merely the beginning of things.

And then I screamed, muffling the sound with my pillow.

I realized later that my scream was a scream of passion, of pure pleasure at what I had done. At what I had accomplished both that day, and what I dreamed of accomplishing in the future. I also realized that I had known all along that I was going to kill him, even before I had actually done so, that I had been waiting for just the right moment to dedicate myself. Waiting for years.

Each step we take from childhood on, we build up information. A small incident here, an image there. Sometimes it's the sudden scent of perfume inhaled as a woman draws near. An aunt, perhaps, or a cousin. I had such a cousin. She lived in a big house in Boston, and once a year my mother and I would take the train to her house . . .

Nov. 7—Lust Murder. The sexual act is completed with body, after Drink.
Necrophagy. Parts of a corpse are eaten.
Necrostuprum. Body-stealing.

Jan. 4—His name is John Erdman. He is a beautiful man, and claims to know the secret of life. He knows what I've been up to. He has offered to prepare me for life after death. When I mentioned this to Julia, she became frightened. Prayer is what matters to her. But she will learn, and, eventually, she will succumb.

Feb. 12—Boston is perfect for the Drink. It is filled with so many people who are homeless, without friends, without relatives to question their untimely deaths. A dark place wherein darker places exist, the hidden little courtyards, the recessed doorways, the many alleys that wind and twist away into the soft gloom of night.

Who would believe an old wino when he cries: "But he bit me!" Or a prostitute or businessman who'd rather stay on at the local bar near his office than go home to an empty apartment. Boston is full of such stories that no one really believes . . .

And the parks. So many different parks to choose from. And so many people to blame for the deaths. "The Negro did it. I seen him. Did it with a knife." Or maybe it was that white trash junkie that's been hanging around. The war between the haves and have-nots. They blame each other, yet they cannot see past their prejudices to understand that they are all victims. They are all part of the Drink.

Mar. 2—Invest your sons in war; it is good business. It is all blood-letting of sorts. Beneath the flag waving, behind the pretty speeches lurks the same message: Take, eat; this is my body.

Mar. 20—She came to me again last night, to my bed. A delicate woman, lovely. John was furious with me. He says I must remain pure if I am to go on. I believe he is jealous. When the time is right, I shall be forced to kill him. He knows me too well, all the problems that make up the length and breadth of my existence. He knows how I hunger for a woman's flesh. He says it will not sustain me. I smile, and say: We will see, we will see.

Rob read quickly now, turning page after page, until he came to the last entry.

Apr. 9—I will pursue my course now without a backward glance. Somehow I know the end of this life draws near. I must be ready when the end does come. I must prepare my coffin.

Unaware that he was doing it, Rob glanced up.

"Norris Caine wrote those words," Doc Tanner said, and his eyes seemed full of sudden purpose. "Now do you believe me?"

"How did you get hold of this?" Rob asked.

"I used to play chess with a young man who worked as his secretary. The boy came to me one night. He told me what he had seen and heard. He'd found the ledger by accident, and he was frightened. He left town the night he gave it to me. I've not heard from him since."

"Does anyone else know about this?"

"There must be others in town who know. But I believe they're working for Norris Caine. To protect him."

"Oh, Jesus . . . I don't know . . ." Rob shook his head miserably. "A madman, yes. But a vampire . . ." The very word stuck in his throat, made him feel—what? Not silly, because people had died. And in very strange ways. Incredulous, perhaps. Even weary with the notion that such things could actually exist.

"It's important that you, of all people, believe me." Doc Tanner stood in the shadows now, his eyes glassy, a lock of his white hair falling limp across his perspiring forehead.

"Why? Why me?"

"Because I believe you are involved in all this. That your coming back to Millhouse has reopened the book."

Rob stared at him for a full ten seconds after his disturbing suggestion, waiting for some indication that he was joking. When none was forthcoming, he said, "I don't understand. What are you talking about?"

The old man lowered his head. "I don't understand it myself. I've only heard rumors . . . about your mother and father. Somehow they have been linked with Norris Caine."

As Rob sat there, his glance fell on the

ledger, which he had left open. At first it was as though he were observing a foreign language, which drew all his concentration to the exclusion of all else around him. Then, with a kind of gummy thickness, fear swept over him, and the words became a horror the mere sight of which filled him with revulsion. The ledger he now knew contained the record of hundreds of helpless victims through whose rotting limbs crawled worms, blood sucking and evil, worms that reached out. . . . His mother's face appeared, horribly distorted, pressed to glass, peering at him, always peering with those vacant eyes, body defiled and buried.

Hot shame and disgust rose from the roots of his manhood into his stomach and chest. He pushed away from the table, stood bolt upright; the chair went crashing to the floor.

Doc Tanner came rushing toward him, panicked at what he saw.

"No," Rob screamed. "I don't want to hear any more!"

"Sue Woodard. Talk to Sue Woodard," the old man shouted as Rob stumbled into the living room. The old man followed him, into the hallway, out into the humid, hot night.

"Listen to me. Take this. Wear it at all times." He forced the gold crucifix into Rob's hand.

With a violent shove, Rob pushed him aside, spun around. A moment later he had the car's headlights on, but the engine wouldn't start. The old man's face appeared in the beams of light. He was saying something Rob couldn't understand; something he didn't want to understand.

The engine suddenly came alive, and as the tires spun around in the drive, the old man pounded on the window, hissing, screaming, "Sue Woodard. Ask Sue Woodard!"

Rob fled into the night, the roar of the engine drowning out the old man's words, the road's curve erasing his sagging image from the rearview mirror.

Now only blackness remained.

Only . . .

. . . blackness. That, and the gold crucifix that lay on the seat beside him.

PART FIVE

IN SEARCH OF A HIDING PLACE

It's actually a game of hide-and-seek, isn't it? After all, the wisdom of God is to conceal a thing, while the shame of man is to find it out.

—Anonymous

1

The nights and days that followed left Rob feeling isolated, frightened of his own thoughts, too confused to unscramble all that had happened to him—all that was about to happen to him.

"Elizabeth was taken to the clinic for observation," Tony said one morning. "They're keeping her there for a few days, for tests." Rob nodded blankly, then muttered that he needed to be alone and closed his door. As he paced tears of helplessness welled in his eyes, and all the shadows over his life—his parents' possible involvement with Norris Caine the darkest of all—were placed on hold. The room grew smaller and messier. Each day was heralded by a slight rap on his door.

"Breakfast," Holly would say, but Rob would not eat, could not eat. Nor would he talk to anyone, except for a brief phone call, which he took in Tony's room. It was Gab Barrett from the *Miami Herald*. Larry's body was to be flown to Atlanta, as per his brother's instructions. The *Herald* was seeing to all the arrangements.

Cause of death: a drug overdose.

And Rob began to tremble inwardly.

"Rob, I know this really isn't the right time, but . . ." Barrett paused, as in the background Rob could hear the city room going full steam.

"Yeah, Gab?"

"The Kennedy interview you sent us. Frankly speaking, it isn't very good. There are too many loose ends. Would you mind . . ."

No, Rob didn't care if a staff writer rewrote his article. He only needed a week or two off, that was all. Just a little time to sort things out. Gab, veteran that he was, understood and hung up.

"I tried getting in touch with Kenny Long today," Tony said deep into the third night. "But he's gone. Packed up his wife and kids and left town."

"Doc Tanner was right," Rob muttered and stared out into the moonless night. Below him were the dark shadows of the backyard, a deep well of blackness between the wall that cut the backyard off from the surrounding area. There was a vague outline of a shed, from whose window a small shaft of light spilled. Rob had seen Jack Gardner enter the shed earlier, heard a buzz saw turned on, but all was quiet now, and Rob wondered what he was up to.

"Doc Tanner?" Tony had moved up beside him. "When did you see him?"

Rob hesitated. He still hadn't told Tony of their encounter. He said, "Is he reliable, Tony? I mean, I hardly recognized him. Jesus, he's gotten so old . . ."

Tony's answer was less than direct. "He had a falling out with the clinic some years back. He still has a few patients, but not many. He drinks a little now, and spends most of his time alone."

"But do you think he's a reliable source?"

"Source?"

"Oh, Jesus, Tony—can you count on him telling you the truth? Or is he . . ." Rob broke off.

"If you're asking me is he a raving loony, I don't think so. Although some people believe he's senile."

"And you? What do you believe?"

Tony hesitated. "My personal opinion, he's one of the sanest people I know. A bit eccentric, perhaps. Why?"

Abruptly the sound of a buzz saw echoed up from the backyard. Distracted, Tony moved closer to the window and looked down. "He's been at it now for almost three hours . . ."

"Tony?"

"Yeah?"

"Did you ever get the letter I sent you? The one saying I might stop by Millhouse around the seventh of this month?"

Tony kept his back to the room, away from Rob, his gaze still parting the darkness below. The sound of the buzz saw grew quiet again. "No, I didn't get any letter." Then he turned. "You sent a letter?"

Rob stared at him. "I guess it got lost."

"Yeah, I guess it did," Tony said quickly. Then he added, "By the way, I went to the clinic again today, but they still aren't letting Elizabeth have visitors."

Rob turned now, the very mention of her name filling him with embarrassment. Some fucking hero, he thought. Come riding in on your Jag charger and what happens? He said, "Do you think it's anything serious?"

"Nah, the nurse said Elizabeth nearly socked her in the jaw yesterday. Sounds to me like she's her old self."

"Then why are they keeping her in isolation?"

"Excitement, I guess. You know Elizabeth. She can get pretty worked up when she wants to."

Rob sighed, and Tony said, "Have you made a decision?"

"About what?"

A moth smacked against the window screen heavily, saggingly, then passed.

"About Larry," Tony said. "Do you think someone caused his death, or do you believe he died from a drug overdose like the sheriff said?"

Rob made no answer.

"Look, Rob, I know you're taking Larry's death pretty hard." He shrugged. "That's why I've kept my distance. But . . ."

"It shocked me, yeah. But that's only part of it."

"And the other part?"

"I don't know. There's just so much I don't understand."

"Like what?"

"Like who was in Elizabeth's house the other night?" The hint of a smile glimmered on Tony's face. It stopped Rob for an instant, then he went on. "I know, you already told me, Mrs. Walker stopped by to pick up preserves. So when I called out, why didn't she answer?"

"Maybe she'd already gone out the back door."

"To where?"

There was tense silence.

"Look, I'm trying desperately, for once in my life, to face facts," Rob said. "That's why I wanted you to talk to Elizabeth. Maybe she has an explanation. And what about that girl? Why keep her death a secret? And why would Kenny Long suddenly leave town, unless . . ."

"Unless what?"

"Unless he was pressured to do so. First Ned Taylor's dog gets killed. Then Ned Taylor himself. Someone tries to finish me off in the cemetery. Larry turns up dead. And . . . I never mentioned this, but the other morning, when Jack came to wake me up, I caught him going through my clothes . . ."

"Wait a minute, hold on. Are you saying Jack's part of all this?"

Rob thought for a moment. "Maybe not just him, but the whole Town Council. Maybe they got a problem on their hands and don't know how to get rid of it."

Tony turned, annoyed. "No, I don't think so."

"Why?"

"Well, for one thing, Peter Appleton is a good solid Christian. He wouldn't get involved in anything underhanded. Neither would Dr. Walker."

"Maybe they don't know."

"Rob, listen to me. Doc Tanner probably told you something wild about the Town Council. They're part of the reason he left the clinic. He doesn't like any of them. Including my uncle."

"Then you're saying his information may be false."

Tony looked at him sharply. "What information? Look, if it's got anything to do with my uncle I want to know."

Rob hesitated, clearly caught in a predicament. Say the wrong thing and Tony would surely confront his uncle. Don't say enough, and Tony would think Rob was crazy. Could he trust Tony in the first place?

They stood there for some minutes, Rob trying to unblur his mind and put it in some sort of perspective. It wasn't easy.

"Okay," Tony finally said, moving away to the door. "Suit yourself. But I'm telling you you're all wrong where Jack is concerned. Granted, he doesn't like you. But in his own way he's a solid Christian too. You remember that."

Before Rob could respond, Tony was gone. As the door closed the raw sound of the buzz saw rose again, higher and faster than before, as if its teeth had grown sharper. Seconds grew to minutes, and Rob could feel his grip on reality lessening, his strength ebbing away, leaving him with only one thought: Either Tony was lying about not receiving his letter, or Jack Gardner had intercepted the letter and known all along that he was coming back to Millhouse.

Abruptly, Doc Tanner's gaunt and frightened face drifted up out of the gloom. *It's important that you believe me*, he pleaded. *Your mother and father are linked with Norris Caine. Talk to Sue Woodard. Ask her.*

2

The next day's headline of the Peabody *Sentinel* read: "*Mass Violence Marks Crime Picture in America.*"

Rob folded the newspaper in half and read how on Thursday, the fourteenth of July, eight student nurses had been brutally slain in their two-story dormitory in Chicago. The article hastened to draw a parallel between those murders and the ones detailed in *In Cold Blood*, the new Truman Capote novel in which he chronicled the slaughtering of the Clutter family in western Kansas in November of 1959.

Rules are breaking down in these United States, the article intoned. Icons are crumbling.

Beliefs in the family, organized religion, liberal social orthodoxy, the American dream, all falling apart. Proof positive was the latest film showing in town: *Who's Afraid of Virginia Woolf?*

Who's afraid of Virginia Woolf? Rob mused.

"I am," he sighed and put the paper aside. As another day slipped into night, he climbed into bed and drifted into a disturbing, swirling, void of blackness that left him with the uneasy feeling that what he was falling into was his own unmarked grave.

3

On Monday, July 18, Rob was awakened by a hurried banging upon his door. It was barely light in the room, but when he opened his eyes he could see the doorknob begin to turn. He felt light-headed and frightened.

"Who is it? Who's there?"

"It's Holly, Mr. Martin. You've got a phone call."

He got up, pulled on a robe, and opened the door barefooted. Holly Emmett wore a red apron, and her face was full of concern.

"My office?"

"No, it's Tony. He says it's important."

Quickly Rob moved down the stairs and picked up the phone. "Hello?"

Tony was speaking with someone on the other end in a harsh whisper that came across as hissing. After a second, he said, "Rob, it's Tony. I think you'd better get down to the sheriff's office right away."

"What time is it?"

"Eight o'clock. You'd better hurry."

"Why, what's up?"

Tony hesitated. "I'd rather you saw for yourself."

"All right. I'll be right there."

Rob hung up and quickly retraced his steps upstairs. The room, as he entered it, was still cast in a dim light. He got dressed hurriedly, and could not help thinking of Doc Tanner. If the old man's speculations weren't speculations at all, but rather a firm grasp of the truth, then . . . Rob's gaze slipped away to the dresser, where the mirror, the white china jug, and the gold crucifix were blurred points of light in the grayness.

He saw clearly the choice being offered him, and, as speculation was replaced by belief, he took the crucifix and put it into his jacket pocket. As he returned to the downstairs hallway, Holly was standing there with a pot and dish towel in her hand.

"Is everything all right?" she asked.

"I don't know. Tony didn't say."

She frowned. "I bet it's something to do with Jack. He didn't come home again last night. He hasn't slept in this house since . . ." She broke off.

"I know, and I'm sorry. A few more days and I'll be leaving."

"No, please, I didn't mean anything by it. It's just, well . . ." She sighed. "Jack never was any good around strangers. You know how he is. And, well, he's really a kind man. You should know that."

"I'll keep that in mind," Rob said, harsher than he had intended. As he climbed into the Jag, he could see Holly's face peering at him through the window. When she realized she'd been seen, she quickly let the curtain fall back into place.

4

As Rob rounded Millhouse Square, he could see that a crowd had already gathered in front of the sheriff's office. Like a ricocheting bullet, word had apparently spread, and now in the suffocating heat townspeople mingled with outsiders. A flock of technicians unrolled spools of cable, set up cameras, and made chalk marks on the sidewalk.

A state trooper appeared suddenly from the building, waved off reporters, and walked to his car. A police van pulled into view from the opposite direction. The street was jammed now with vehicles, and the trooper shouted at people to back it up.

When Rob got out of his car, the trooper

glanced his way, then was distracted by a woman who seemed frantic to speak to him. Waving her arms and pointing, she pulled him onto the sidewalk.

Rob could see Tony standing in front of Betty Walker's ice cream parlor talking with Marshall Whitset. When Rob moved closer, Whitset said something to Tony, who turned and started walking toward Rob.

"What's going on?" Rob asked.

Tony looked at him for a full ten seconds, beads of sweat covering his face. "They've got a girl inside. Marianne, she works at Sue Woodard's cafe."

"I know, I met her when I first got to town."

"Jesus, Rob, you should see her. I mean, God . . . she killed a man. They found his body in her apartment this morning. She . . . she hacked him to death or something. I mean . . ."

"Take it easy. Calm down."

"When they were bringing her into the station she said—listen to this—she screamed, 'He made me do it. The vampire . . .' "

Perhaps it was Tony's unexpected use of the word *vampire*; perhaps it was something more personal. Impulsively Rob groped at the crucifix in his pocket. "Are you sure?" he said.

"Of course I'm sure. I wasn't standing ten feet away from her."

"Anyone else hear her?"

"No, I was just going across to Betty's for a newspaper. The street was deserted."

"Have you told anybody yet? What you heard?"

"Hell, no. You think I'd repeat something as crazy as that?"

Rob couldn't help glancing at Whitset, whose bulky frame filled Betty Walker's doorway. Sure enough, he was spying, expressionless.

"Well, don't," Rob said. "Not until we know what we're dealing with."

Tony stared at him, his eyes full of distress and grief. "Why, do you think there's a connection?"

"Let's just wait and see." But Rob already knew the answer, already knew that Tony had been dead-on when he said: *Doc Tanner is the sanest man I know.*

People were filling the streets now, and Rob inched forward, trying to get closer to the station door without calling attention to himself. Faces loomed from out of the crowd. Conversation came and went in snatches.

". . . That's one way to do it, by God. Trip and fall into your own goddamn baler. Ned never did have any sense . . ." The man with long unkempt hair and whiskers stopped talking to peer at Rob as he passed.

Tony said, "Listen, I'll wait for you here."

Rob nodded, moved through a knot of women in head scarves, children tugging at their skirts.

"No Christian upbringing, that's the trouble," the youngest of the women said. "If . . ." She yanked the little girl's arm up. "MaryLou, if you don't stop pulling on me, I'll . . ."

"I'm hungry," the child whined.

"Hush up!"

As Rob moved forward, he saw an occasional familiar face: Ronny Hubbert stood off to the side, leaning on his truck and eating an apple. Recognition flared in his eyes momentarily, but then he turned and started talking to his wife, who had grown rounder and fuller with the years.

Peter Appleton stood with his back to Rob, excitedly talking to a calm Al Striker. The closer Rob got to the station, the tighter the crowd became; faces blended, words mixed.

"Damned if they didn't launch Gemini 10 this morning, right on schedule . . . Poor Gloria, I don't know why she doesn't . . . Darned funny business, the killing that's going on these days. I just read of a case up near Two Rivers where a man and his wife . . ."

Rob never heard the rest. He'd had another thought. It was something Doc Tanner had said. That Norris Caine had others with him. Was Marianne one of them? And the woman at his motel window, was she . . .

Reaching the front of the station, Rob glanced around. A young reporter standing beside him shouted to a friend, "Bring the camera. I think they're getting ready to bring her out."

Coming toward them now, the state trooper

pushed people aside. "What's the girl's name?" one of the reporters shouted to the trooper. Another shouted, "How old is she?"

Rob stood mute, his mind on other matters. His reporter's instinct was diminished by the feeling that he was closer to the truth than he wanted to be.

Your mother and father are involved with Norris Caine. They are . . .

The phrase, in variations, with all its implications, kept turning over in his mind, twisting his face in uncertainty. A hand reached out, pushed him back, slamming him into the reporter next to him.

"Hey, we're reporters," the guy complained.

"I don't give a crap who you are. Keep the doorway clear." Slowly, very slowly, the trooper moved to the door and stood with his back to it, as if daring anyone to enter.

"Pig," the reporter muttered under his breath. The station door opened, and Rob could feel hands pulling him out of the way. He was pushed aside and spun around. The crowd jammed up around him. As he regained his balance, voices started shouting questions. He could see a figure taking shape in front of him.

"Why'd you kill him?" someone shouted.

Eyes, green, sunken, and bloodshot, scanned the crowd. Hair hung disheveled over her shoulders, and her lips were dry and cracked.

"Here, you'll need this." A crucifix was held out.

The girl spat at the face in front of her.

Rob jerked away, brought his hand to his cheek, and quickly wiped the spit off. He stared into the girl's face, into an expression filled with a viciousness and revulsion he rarely saw. Her mouth was open; she gasped in animal wheezes.

"You can't look at it, can you?" he whispered, and before he could lift the crucifix again, Sheriff Jones stepped between them.

"All right, out of the way," he said, and took hold of her arm.

Rob pressed closer. "I'm a reporter. I have a right . . ."

"Not in this town, you ain't."

Now, standing in front of the restrained but threatening sheriff, Rob was aware of other men watching him. They had moved closer, forming a circle around the girl, and began moving her through the crowd.

"She's nothin' but filthy scum," a woman shouted, the exasperation in her voice as sharp as the lines in her face. "Damn hippie, why don't you stay where you belong?"

People were straining, trying to get a closer look. The girl glanced back over her shoulder, her eyes meeting Rob's. Then, her gaze losing its intensity, she bowed her head, letting herself be led to the patrol car.

"Go back where you belong. Go back . . ." The crowd, as if caught in the grip of some perverse energy, began chanting and banging the side of the car as she climbed into the backseat. Sheriff Jones moved in beside her and closed the door.

Rob found himself in the middle of an angry mob, trying to get closer. The girl dropped her head back and her eyes were rolled into her head. On her neck, just below her right ear, were two reddish-looking puncture marks.

Oh, Jesus, Rob thought, pushing himself forward, trying to get a better look. Larry had had those same marks, and . . . Elizabeth. He flung his arms out. Someone mistook the gesture, grabbed hold of him, and yanked. Cameras flashed, and the girl suddenly lurched toward the window, her fingernails extended, giving up all human appearance, mouthing obscenities at the photographers.

People shouted back at her. A bottle flew past Rob and crashed into the street. Jones shoved the girl back into her seat as the patrol car was started up.

Only one person stood absolutely still in the mayhem. Rob looked at him. His face was hidden in the shadow of his hat brim. You wouldn't guess his connection with the wild happening except for the obvious bloodstains on his shirt and the way his young fingers probed at the corner of his mouth.

When the boy, J.D. Salinger, saw Rob staring at him, he turned quickly and walked away.

* * *

Driving to the clinic, Rob became aware of a tan Chevy following him. He pretended not to notice, but when he got to the corner of Elm and Beach streets, he ran the light and at the next street made a quick turn, then turned again into the alley and stopped.

He watched as after a moment the tan Chevy drove by. After waiting a second or two longer, he eased the Jag out of the alley.

When Rob entered the room he found Elizabeth asleep. He hadn't come through the clinic's main entrance. Going into the emergency waiting room, he found no nurse. Only a mother carrying on over her son's broken arm. Elizabeth's room was on the same floor, two swinging doors and a small corridor away.

He inched closer to the bed and looked down. Elizabeth's face looked peaceful in sleep. Lying still, with red hair flowing over her pillow, she seemed undisturbed by the goings on outside the clinic. Her drapes were drawn shut. Only a hazy light prevailed.

Gently, he brushed hair aside and gazed at her neck. A flesh-colored Band-Aid clung there. He hesitated, wondering, afraid to move. A sudden noise in the hallway turned him around, and he watched an empty gurney being wheeled past the door.

"Rob?" came a voice.

When he turned back Elizabeth's intense

pale-green eyes were there to greet him. She smiled and held out her arms. "Oh, God, it's so good to see you," she breathed.

Her embrace was warm, and as he held her, he could feel her trembling, a strange kind of shiver that seemed to go on forever.

"I never thought I'd see you again," she said at last. "How did you get in here? They're not—"

He placed his hand to her lips. "Ssssh," he said, still looking at her, his hand moving aside strands of loose hair. "Are you all right? I've been worried about you." His words weren't as casual as he'd intended.

She forced a laugh. "It's nothing, really. I keep having these fainting spells. Dr. Walker doesn't seem concerned, so . . ." She hesitated. "Why are you looking at me like that? Do I look that awful?"

"No, you look beautiful." Rob had to clear his throat against a sudden dryness. "Your neck, has something happened to it?"

Elizabeth's hand went mechanically to the Band-Aid. "Oh, it's some sort of a rash. Dr. Walker put two different ointments on it, but it still itches like crazy."

In a low voice, Rob said, "Mind if I have a look?"

"Why?" she asked.

Somehow Rob couldn't find the words and, overwhelmed by it all, his sudden fatigue, Larry's death, the girl Marianne, he lowered his head.

"Hey, don't look so damned crestfallen," Elizabeth said. "If looking at my rash is going to get you turned on, then look." She tore the Band-Aid from her neck and tossed it on the metal table beside her bed.

Rob slowly lifted his head, saw a small red blotch and nothing more. No puncture marks, and yet . . . he looked closer. Was he imagining the two enlarged darker areas under the rash? In the dim light of the room it was hard to tell.

"So, what do you see?" Elizabeth quipped. "Your future?"

Rob half smiled. "I hope so, Liz."

She smiled. "Liz? Do you know how long it's been since you've called me that?"

"Too long, I guess."

"Yeah, too long." She placed her mouth to his, ran her tongue over his lips. "It's been horrible these past few days without you," she said. She stared softly into his eyes, reaching out to touch his face with her fingertip.

He started to reply, but found that he could not speak, remembering the note he'd found in her room, the handwriting tense and disjointed. He shook his head slowly in a sudden spasm of anxiety.

"What's the matter, Rob?" she asked.

"I . . . I missed you too," he said. Then he said, "Have you been having trouble sleeping?"

She looked at him in amazement. "How'd you know that?"

Rob stared at her with quiet determination.

"Have you? Are you afraid to fall asleep at night?"

"Oh, I keep having this damn silly nightmare. That someone is in my room."

"Someone?"

"I don't know who it is, really. A man, I think. It's silly."

"Yeah." Rob slowly took out the crucifix. "I brought this for you. I want you to wear it."

Elizabeth took the crucifix and her eyes, though they seemed to be studying it, moved away slightly. "A crucifix. But I'm not . . ."

"Religious, I know. But I want you to wear it. All right? For me. It's important. Don't take it off, not for any reason."

"It's beautiful."

"Here, let me." He could feel himself trembling as he fastened it around her neck.

When he next looked at her, he saw there were tears in her eyes, and she bent down quickly, pressing her lips with startling tenderness against his hand and murmuring, "Oh, God, I'm so glad you came back for me. So glad."

It was hard to believe, but never until that moment had Rob understood fully the love she felt for him. If he had been aware, he had, in his stubbornness, so totally blocked it from his mind that it now crashed upon him with the force of an avalanche.

"Elizabeth?" he said in a hushed, constricted voice.

"Yes."

"The other night, I . . . I went to your house. No one was home, but . . ."

Before Rob could go on, Elizabeth jerked away from him, her eyes fixed on the door in feverish agitation.

"What's going on in here?" The voice was shrill and brittle, and when Rob turned he saw the doorway filled with a woman, the likes of which he had rarely seen. Tall, impassive, features as pointed as steel spikes. Only her eyes revealed her hostile vitality.

"Oh, nurse, this is a friend . . ."

"How did you get in here?" The woman moved swiftly into the room. "Who are you? What are you doing here?"

Rob rose to his feet. "Remember, don't take the crucifix off," he said to Elizabeth. To the nurse he said nothing. A moment later he was hurrying down the hallway, past the front desk, feeling a strange sense of haste, as if he were pursued.

As he walked into the parking lot he looked at Elizabeth's window, feeling sure that she would be there; he was not mistaken. He did not dare to pause, for he heard the clattering of male interns behind him; but he felt in that brief parting glance more hope than he had in days.

5

THE SHERIFF

It was midafternoon by the time the sheriff got back to his office. The state police had treated him like a rube, and to make matters worse, they were taking the case away from him. "After all, Sheriff, the girl's from New Haven, the guy from New York. It's a state matter."

"State matter, my ass!" he growled now, flinging his hat down on the desk.

Deputy Salino looked at him. "Something weird is going on, Conley. You know that, don't you?"

"No shit, Sherlock. Listen, you get back over to the girl's apartment. Go over it again before they seal it off."

"But we ain't supposed . . ."

"Now, goddamn it. If you find anything unusual, bring it back."

As Salino hightailed it out the door the telephone rang. "Sheriff's office. Sheriff Jones speaking."

Thomas Rey identified himself, then: "It's the weirdest damn thing I've ever seen. I think you better come on over."

"Where are you, Thomas?" asked Jones.

"At the morgue in Peabody with Larson."

"Whataya got?"

"I'd rather not talk about it over the phone."

"Okay, I'll be right over."

The morgue in Peabody wasn't much of a morgue. One room with four slab drawers, usually empty of bodies. No windows, one door, and a chemical smell that could curl your hair.

Jones stared down at the body on the stainless-steel table that formed a rectangle island in an otherwise empty room. The tag attached to the corpse's toe read: Greg Harrison.

"The wounds," Thomas Rey said, drawing the sheet back, "are not knife wounds. Hell, no. They're not flat like a blade nor are they anywhere deep enough." His stubby fingers moved deftly over the ashen flesh of the corpse, outlining each gash. "Hard to say what caused them, but definitely not a knife. Teeth, maybe."

Jones's eyes rolled in his head. "That's just great. You're telling me the girl bit him to death?"

"There's more," Rey said.

As if on cue, Larry Larson, who had been short of words up till now, raised the head of the corpse and turned it to one side. "See these marks along the neck?" he said.

"Yeah, I see them."

"Well, they weren't made by the same object as the wounds on the shoulder and along his arm. They're wider and deeper, and the penetration is different . . ."

Rey put in, "Like two objects, used by two different people."

Sheriff Jones removed his hat, letting out a long sigh. "Tell me straight, Thomas. What are we dealing with here?"

Thomas Rey shrugged. "Don't know. But I still haven't told you the shocker. You remember how I told you that the Campbell fella lost a lot of blood before dying? Well, this poor son of a bitch lost it all. There ain't a drop left in him. Not a drop."

"Oh, Jesus." Jones shook his head wearily. "Mean anything?"

"Well, hell—we had a dog killed a week or so ago. Old Doc Tanner told me the same thing. That the damn dog was bled dry."

The three men stood around Greg Harrison's body, silent, distracted, lost in thought.

Finally Jones said, "Can you keep this quiet?"

Thomas Rey looked at Larson, then turned back to face the sheriff. "I'm not sure, Conley. With the Campbell fella it was different. We all agreed that blaming his death on drugs was the best out. I mean, we really couldn't pin it down, so . . ."

"So?" The sheriff was starting to get edgy.

"So we labeled it a drug overdose. But with this fella here, it's different. We have the state boys to answer to."

"Can you stall them, then?" Jones asked.

"I guess. For a little while. Why, you on to something?"

"Maybe," the sheriff said.

Thomas Rey sighed. "I tell you, Conley, I've never seen anything like this. A body completely drained of blood . . ."

"Another thing," Larson said, his voice lifting a notch higher. "Look here." He pointed to one of the puncture marks on the corpse's neck. "The wounds keep opening and closing. Look, see for yourself."

Jones peered closely at the mark. He stiffened, staring for a long time. Then it happened, the puncture wound yawned, opening out like a flower. Then it closed down again.

They all looked at each other.

"It's as if," Larson said, "he's still alive . . ."

* * *

When the sheriff returned to his house it was already dark. Deep shadows clung to the floor, walls, and ceiling of his living room. He did not turn on the light. He knew his way by heart. He flicked on the TV, drew a beer from the refrigerator, and flopped down on the couch. He never bothered to turn up the sound on the TV.

He sat in silence, his hand unconsciously straying along the surface of his revolver as if preparing himself. When he saw the shadow move across his kitchen floor he did not react, just kept one eye on the television set.

The shadow changed to a thicker substance now, a hulk of flesh, wrapped in a cheap searsucker suit. The big man did not say anything, but rather stood in the doorway, staring.

Jones smiled sardonically. "Well, Marshall, shall we talk?"

There was a long silence and then lips finally quivered into life. "Why not, Conley? It's been long overdue." With that, Marshall Whitset smiled.

6

Surrounded by deep shadows, Rob sat on the couch in the living room and waited. A light rain tapped annoyingly on the roof, streaked the windows; sunlight had been replaced by moonglow, and still no one showed themselves at the house. It was as if the Rizzo family, by a mere wave of the great magician Merlin's cloak, had vanished from the earth.

He had called Tony's office several times that day but never got an answer. Twice he had stopped by, only to find the office closed. He'd spent time in the cemetery, staring down at his parents' graves, then searching the area where he thought he'd been attacked. He reexamined the tree stump where he had discovered the girl's body. No body there now, but a piece of greenish material, as if torn from a dress, had been snagged by the stump. At last, exhausted, he returned to the house, expecting to find Tony there. If not Tony, at least Holly preparing dinner, or Jack sulking in the shed out back. None had been the case.

And now, as the rain thickened and beat harder, Rob felt the sickening helplessness of being shut in, as he imagined the most forlorn mental patient felt in the confines of a strait jacket.

At another time, in another frame of mind, he would have known what to do. But now he was confused and scared. Wearily, he reached out to turn on the lamp, but stopped his arm midswing, letting it fall instead to the armrest.

Sue, I have to talk to you, he had said.

Sue Woodard had stared at him as if she were looking at a ghost. Around them dishes and coffee cups rattled. I'm busy, she said. Please, Rob . . .

But I have to talk to you. It's about . . .

Please, not now.

When then? Tell me when.

Tonight, at my house, she said in a low voice. Around nine.

Rob's eyes moved in the darkness as he glanced at his watch. Unreadable, but he knew it was already past nine. Yet he could not bring himself to get up from the couch. He sat there with his legs on the coffee table and his feet dangling over the edge, his will lost in the shadow that started below the table and fanned outward toward the door.

He studied the shadow for a moment. Then a slackened wire in his mind jerked tight. He sat up straight on the couch. Listen! Somebody's out on the porch. Do you hear? Listen!

The beating of rain on the roof slowed.

Tap, tap, tap, tap . . .

You're crazy, he told himself.

Listen! he insisted inwardly. He rose to his feet. There *was* somebody walking around out there.

Silence.

The footsteps neither progressed nor receded, but merely stopped. He heard a faint shuffling sound and could picture someone standing behind the front door, waiting, listening . . .

He held his breath.

"Mr. Martin?" came a voice from behind him, and he spun around and nearly knocked over the lamp. He reached out and took hold of the shade. A woman stood before him in the kitchen doorway, a faceless woman whose form seemed misshapen.

"Who are you, what do you want?"

"I'm Nancy Emmett," the woman said, without moving.

Straightening the lamp, Rob flicked it on. Nancy Emmett, no more than thirty, with narrow eyes and lips, stared at him. He could see that beneath her raincoat she was pregnant.

"I'm sorry, did I frighten you?" she said.

"It's all right. I was just sitting here."

Her gaze drifted across the room. "My sister asked me to come," she said, her voice soft, with a soothing rhythm. "My husband's standing outside. Do you mind?" She made a vague gesture toward the front door.

"Oh, no. Not at all."

In the quiet, she moved to the door and opened it. "Fred, Mr. Martin is here."

"Oh," said a voice. "I'll wait in the car, then. Don't be long."

"I won't." She watched as apparently someone made his way down the front steps. "I was going to leave you a note, but . . ."

"A note?" Rob wondered.

Her eyes quickly moved to take in the room; she preferred not to look at him directly. She started to unbutton her coat and then stopped.

"Holly is ill," she said. "I'm afraid she'll be confined to bed for a few days."

Rob murmured, "I'm sorry. Is it anything serious?"

"The flu, we think. She was going to tell you that Tony was unexpectedly called away on business. He said he'll call you as soon as he has a free moment."

Her words came easily, so very easily, as if rehearsed. Rob could feel the noose getting tighter, the lies more brazen.

"Oh," he nodded. "Where'd he go?"

"Boston," said the seemingly innocent carrier of messages. "Holly was worried about you being here all alone." She looked at him now, for the first time. Her eyes, soft and hazel, seemed devoid of expression. "If there's anything I can do . . ."

"No," Rob said, and anger rose up within him. He could feel his lips and eyes grow cold. Very well, then, he thought. I'll go it alone. But you're not getting rid of me that easily. His voice was strained, softly shrill: "I don't need anything. You just tell Holly I hope she gets better real soon. Okay?"

The woman looked at him with curious indifference. "Are you sure? I'm free tomorrow . . ."

"I didn't hear a car pull up." Rob moved to the window and peered out. "Your husband said he'd wait for you in the car. I don't see any."

"We were visiting with the Collins family. They live a few houses down."

Rob turned. "And you walked? In the rain?"

"We took the back footpath. It's covered with trees."

"And Holly gave you the key?"

"I've always had a key to this house."

"Give it to me," Rob demanded, and watched as the woman feigned confusion. "I said, I want the key."

She seemed for a moment unsure, pausing and turning to the front door with a sudden and faint look of alarm. Then, going into her purse, she took out a small key ring with two keys and handed it to him.

"Good," Rob said, enjoying her discomfort, wishing all her nameless sins to turn against her. "Now you tell whoever sent you that I'll still be here tomorrow. And that I'd appreciate them not sending anyone to spy on me. Is that clear?"

The woman nodded, moving away to the door and opening it. She looked back briefly. "You're making a dreadful mistake," she said.

"Right," Rob said, feeling sure of himself. Yet the woman's words still clung to the room, haunted him, long after she had closed the door. And then, from atop Mountainview Road, came the sound of Julia Caine's dogs. Howling.

7

Sue Woodard placed her empty bourbon glass down on the dresser and kicked off her heels. Then she took off her dress, panties, and bra, and stood naked before the mirror, looking at herself. She hated what she saw. She was forty-seven, but in the harsh glow of the lamp she thought she looked much older. She stared at her milky-white skin, her sunken eyes, the excess weight that clung to her hips and thighs.

Her breasts felt swollen and appeared to sag more than usual. She took them in her hands, squeezed each nipple, trying to tease them back to life.

She remembered—oh, dear God, how she

remembered—the looks Rob Martin used to give her. How he would hang around the cafe, willing to do odd jobs. But she had been younger, then. Prettier.

Fuck it! she thought.

The bourbon bottle shook in her hand as she poured herself another drink. Most times the booze helped her to forget her troubles.

But not tonight.

Not tonight.

Still naked, she sat at the edge of the bed and lifted her glass. Liquor spilt from the corner of her mouth as she drank. She could hear the Caine dogs howling in the distance. The whole town probably could. She paid them no mind.

On fire. That's what she wanted to be for Rob Martin. On fire. Shame welled up in her, yet she could not pull herself together. She knew what was happening. Why Rob was coming to see her. Yet somehow it didn't seem to matter. Nothing mattered.

She placed a hand on her thigh, stroked. Fatigue and alcohol slowed her movements, but nothing could diminish her building desire. The red negligee, she thought. And high heels. He'd like that.

As she was putting on the negligee Rob came to the front door. The dogs had stopped their racket, and the deep lush sound of night rose against a starless sky. She received him expectantly, and for a brief moment he seemed just as eager to be with her. Then he started in with the questions, avoiding her gaze, moving away from her.

"I don't know what you're talking about." Sue stood near the end of the couch, looking down at him.

"Norris Caine. He's still alive, isn't he?"

Sue spoke louder; her voice trembled. "Rob, honey, that's ridiculous. This Marianne thing has got you upset. Come on, have a drink. Please, hon." She reached out and ran her fingers through his hair.

He carefully took hold of her hand. "Sue, don't."

Her look of satisfaction disappeared as she said, "What's the matter? You used to like me. Don't you like me anymore?"

"Of course I do, but . . ."

"Then stop asking me questions. Okay?"

Rob could feel his chest growing tighter. "My mother," he said, looking at Sue directly. "You and she were good friends. You spent a lot of time together, so tell me straight. Was she ever involved with Norris Caine?"

Sue pursed her lips and stared at him, rocking back on her heels. With a sudden gesture of concealment, she gripped the front of her negligee and pulled it closed. "Okay," she said after a few moments of thought. "I'll tell you, but first give old Sue a little kiss." She smiled, but Rob heard the uncertainty in her voice.

With a motion that startled him, she

reached out and took hold of his face. Her bourbon-soaked lips went to his mouth, her tongue inside it. As they kissed she started to lower her body against his.

Then her wet tongue slipped into his ear, and she whispered, "Tell me what you want me to do, Rob. I'll do anything for you, you know that."

"Sue, no . . ."

She released him, and dropped to her knees in front of him. The corners of her mouth twitched in a suggestive smile as she slid her hand between his legs. "Would you like me to do this for you? Use the words, Rob. Tell me what to do."

Rising, she began to straddle him. Rob tried to pull away but she kept coming, trapping him. Her negligee was open to reveal large and swollen breasts, the nipples erect. She groped for his crotch, trying to undo his zipper.

"Fuck me," she moaned. "Stick it in me, Rob. Stick it in me."

He took hold of her and forced her away. "You're drunk, Sue. Now stop it!" He could see the tension in her face as it grew redder, and he made an effort to lower his voice. "I'm sorry, Sue. Really, I am."

Sue had gradually eased away, and now she stared at him with a trace of anger. "Sorry, hell. You fucking men are all the same. A bunch of friggin' losers."

Whether it was what she said, or perhaps

the sarcastic lilt to her voice, Rob was himself brought to anger. "I came here because I thought you were a friend. Because I thought you could help me. Not because I was looking to screw you."

"Did you, now. Well, well, well . . ." She turned and picked up her glass, swallowing its contents in one gulp. "Jesus, do you know what it's like living in this God-forsaken town year after year?" she said, her hand reaching for a cigarette. "The loneliness, the goddamn endless wait for night to be over. When I saw you the other night, standing there, it all came back to me. The dreams, the desires, flooded over me. I couldn't sleep for days after that. I just kept thinking, dreaming about what it would be like to be your age again. To have someone like you take me away." She looked at him, the unlit cigarette dangling from her fingertips. "Can you understand that?"

"Yeah, I guess I can . . ."

"Guess. You guess? Let me tell you something . . . ten years ago I could have wrapped you around my little pinky. I saw the hunger in your eyes every time you looked at me. If this was ten years ago, would you be telling me no? Would you?"

"I thought I made it clear why I wanted to see you."

"Clear, huh. What's the matter, you suddenly get cold feet? Or is your problem higher up, like between your legs, maybe?"

"All right, Sue. Forget it." He got to his feet.

With almost every word underscored with emphasis, she said, "All right, hell. You want the truth, I'll give you the truth. Your mother and Norris Caine were lovers. That's right, *lovers*," she hissed.

Rob laughed, ragged and harsh. "What?"

"Look at you, you're so fucking naive. He was banging the pants off her, and your father, dumb rube that he was, found out about it. Not being able to face the fact that he could no longer satisfy your mother—not the way Norris Caine could—your father killed him. Shot him in the head while he slept," she screamed. "Your father killed Norris Caine!"

Rob looked at her in disbelief. "You're drunk. You don't know what you're saying," he cried.

"He killed him," she laughed, an hysterical laugh, nodding her head in a short, positive spasm. "Suicide, everyone said. They didn't want the publicity. Didn't want the damn thing dragged out. Because . . . oh, Jesus, they knew Norris was still around, that he . . ." She stopped to take in a ragged breath to dissipate the adrenaline surge.

Rob's heart was pounding like a jack hammer, bursting in his chest, causing a wild sickening sensation he'd never experienced before.

"Norris came back to get your mother," Sue cried. "I'm not drunk, no—he came back." Tears coursed down her cheeks, and her body started to sag. "Oh, Jesus, help us . . . I've seen her, your mother. Long after she died. Both of them . . . they killed your father. His death was no accident . . . no, they . . ."

Rob turned. A second later he was dashing down Sue Woodard's front steps. As he stumbled forward, Sue pressed her face to the screen door, yelled, "Rob, honey, come back. Please, come back!"

8

Rob felt as if he were falling through time and space. He drove, foot slammed to the gas pedal, each curve becoming more dangerous. His thoughts were crowded with people from his boyhood; he had never before consciously realized how much of him was made up by other people, their voices, their appearances, directing him, impeding him—attempting to control him.

Suddenly Rob swung the Jag to the right, pulling it out of a skid. A sixteen-wheeler blew its horn as he sped past. He was drifting over the white line again. Slow down, he told himself. Yet his foot stayed glued to the pedal.

He had gone back to the house, into Jack's shed, and taken a flashlight, two shovels, and a pickax. Metal smashed against metal in the backseat as he swung the car around the next curve. Ahead of him the road narrowed, the harsh glow of his headlights highlighting the front gate to the cemetery.

Turning onto Nickle Road he eased up on the gas pedal, glancing at the caretaker's house as he passed. He caught a glimpse of the building's rustic facade, the curtainless windows behind which a small orange light shone. No matter.

Without allowing himself to think about it further, he drove another hundred yards and stopped the car beside the knoll Tony and he had used to observe Julia Caine's funeral.

He shut off the engine, killed the lights. A soft breeze touched his face as he took tools and flashlight from the backseat. Hesitantly he closed the car's door. The low-riding clouds shifted in the wind, causing the moonglow to expand and retract. A light rain tapped on the car's roof.

Rob paused a moment longer, then moved into the bushes, found the opening, and slid between the broken slats of the fence. He quickly turned and followed the fence, ducking when a car turned onto Old Post Road.

A police car, he realized, and crouched still lower. *Oh, Jesus*, he thought. *What if they see the Jag*? But the patrol car continued on its way and disappeared past the railroad tracks.

He got to his feet, fixed his eyes on the darkest and safest spot to cross the cemetery without being seen, and began moving toward it. And as he moved he became aware of what he was *actually* doing. Still he moved on, past tombstones, into the thick growth of trees, ignoring the confusion and pain in his troubled heart.

It wasn't much of a headstone; a simple slab of polished red granite which read: CELIA MARTIN, followed by the inscription: SHE LOVED LIFE, and the dates. No flowers, just grass that had turned to weeds.

Rob knelt in silence for a moment, thinking, remembering how things used to be. The warmth of her hands, the sly little smile whenever she would catch him doing something awful, like drawing monsters on his bedroom wall, or kicking the cat, or . . .

Slowly he pulled up the weeds, tears welling in his eyes. *Please, Mom, be here. Please* . . . Each word brought a fresh rush of memory, and then the realization that he was stalling. The best thing, he told himself, was not to think at all. It was only getting in his way. Slowly he stood and removed his jacket.

The pickax went into the ground easily enough. After loosening a fair amount of topsoil, he began digging. He threw the dirt to the left side of the grave, making a mound between himself and the caretaker's house, working harder as the hole deepened.

He paused now and then to catch his breath, and to wipe the sweat from his eyes. The moonlight was constant now; the rain had all but stopped. He wouldn't use the flashlight unless he had to.

He kept digging.

He stopped only once more, when he got a terrible cramp in his gut. The horrible jolt nearly doubled him over, then subsided as quickly as it had come.

An hour later, he drove the shovel into something hard, causing the handle to slam into his chest. He groped for his jacket, took out the flashlight, and aimed its beam down.

The light caught bits of the metal grave liner. He brushed dirt aside to make sure, then climbed out of the grave and got the pickax. He lowered it into the grave, hooking the claw underneath the liner. The thin metal liner came up easily, but made a racket when he dragged it up over the edge.

He quickly turned off the flashlight and waited. The caretaker's door remained closed. Satisfied, he got down into the grave again, knelt on his mother's coffin, looking for the latch. With both hands he pushed away dirt, felt metal. Then felt nausea rising into his throat. The latch was undone.

"Oh, Christ," he moaned. "Please, God, no!" he wailed, banging his fist against the coffin lid, as if to destroy it. He climbed out of the grave, propped the flashlight so that it shone down into the hole, and then lowered the pickax again.

Once the steel claw hooked beneath the lid, he yanked, sending the lid of the coffin flying open.

And everything stopped.

As from beneath his trembling body pebbles dropped into the hole, and he watched them bounce hollowly inside his mother's empty coffin.

9

Elizabeth's eyes suddenly shot open in the darkness. At once the bone-white hand withdrew itself from her neck. The heat in the room was intense, but Elizabeth, sprawled out under a blanket, shivered and clutched the blanket tighter.

"What are you doing?" she cried.

The nurse's face came into sharp focus as she said, "I'm afraid you're not allowed to sleep with that on."

Elizabeth's hand went to the crucifix around her neck. "It's just a crucifix," she stammered.

"Hospital regulations," the woman said,

determined. She moved closer, carrying a chemical smell that seemed to rise from the thin hand she held out. "I'm sorry," she said. "But accidents have happened because of the wearing of jewelry."

Elizabeth hesitated, looked closer at the woman, and realized she'd never seen her before. Yet somehow she looked familiar. "Where's Nurse Luden?" she asked.

"It's her night off," the woman said. Though she spoke directly, her eyes seemed averted.

Elizabeth's gaze fell away to the open doorway. The hallway beyond was cast in gloomy shadows, and not a sound could be heard. Not even the nocturnal muttering of nurses, nor the rattling of trays, only an odd silence. She said, "Has something happened to the lights?"

"Why do you ask?"

"The hallway looks so dark."

"We always keep it that way at night. You probably haven't noticed." She stared down at Elizabeth, her hand still extended. "Would you like me to keep that for you until morning?"

"No," Elizabeth said. "I'll just keep it here beside my bed."

The woman's hand slowly withdrew. "All right, then. Sleep well."

"Thank you."

Elizabeth hesitantly removed the crucifix from around her neck and laid it on the nightstand beside her bed. She stared at it for a while, and then felt her eyelids grow heavy. She closed her eyes and soon found herself walking through a dark tunnel. From the opposite end the lone figure of a man began moving toward her.

"Do I scare you?" a voice said, as if from a great distance.

"No," she said softly. Too softly, as if she hadn't spoken at all.

"You don't have to be scared. It doesn't have to be that way, between us."

Elizabeth fought to open her eyes, but something heavy seemed to be pressed to them. She stopped walking and stared at the figure as it approached. It was the same man she had seen so many times before, the same animal eyes that had contributed so much to his appearance. Harsh and uncompromising, yet erotically pleasing. His thin black lips parted, and he smiled.

"Do you think I'm attractive?" he said, his eyes riveted to hers.

Elizabeth could not speak. She was struggling to come up out of her dream. She was still in her room, she knew, because she could see the crucifix still lying on the table beside her arm. Slowly she reached out for it.

In the tunnel, the man took hold of her arm. "Do you?" he asked, his eyes growing wider, an accusing tone underlining his words.

"Yes, yes," she murmured, unable to stop herself from saying it.

"It means everything to me," he said, his

voice returning to its usual smoothness. He moved closer, and as he did, she quickly drew away. "No, don't. I wouldn't hurt you. It doesn't have to be like that."

"But I can't . . . there's . . . someone else," she breathed. The words sounded strange to her. She couldn't understand why she was saying them.

"But you dream about me. Not him. About you and me. Together. Isn't that true?" he said, his eyes never leaving hers, his hand moving away long strands of hair from the side of her neck. "You are inviting me to come closer. You are anxious to remove your clothes. To stand naked before me while I drink," he went on in a soft monotone. "Yes, you can feel it now, can't you? The desire, the longing, your body trembling with excitement . . ."

Elizabeth shuddered. The sensation rose, scorching, whirling, opening her up like a flower in the sudden heat of the night. Slowly she began to undo her nightgown.

"Yes," she whispered. "Oh, yes, drink . . ." she moaned.

And then he laughed. A wicked laugh that continued to ring hollowly in her ears as he lowered his mouth to the succulent white flesh of her throat and drank.

10

Mrs. Salinger's voice was harsh even in a whisper, and J.D. recoiled as if being pursued by demons. "Come back here this instant," she hissed. "Your father's asleep. Do you want me to wake him and tell him what you've been up to?"

"But, Mom, I didn't do anything bad."

"It's evil, what you've done. Maybe you don't understand that. But it's filthy and evil."

"I didn't . . ."

"Stop it," she said, and slapped him hard. "Stop pretending. You killed that bird. I saw you. I saw you!" She paused, and for a moment a sobbing spasm shook her body.

The young boy stood there, anger suddenly

gripping his features. "I did not," he said. Then he said, "And . . . and don't slap me no more. Not ever again."

Mrs. Salinger's voice was no longer a whisper but rose higher, shriller, as she said, "Where have you been going every night? Tell me."

"Oh, Mom, nowhere . . ."

She shook her head. "What's happening to you? You never lied to me before. Why are you acting like this?" Her face was streaked with tears, and she had begun to shiver uncontrollably. "Your Bible, where is it?" she asked.

Her son drew back, turned away. She yanked him around. "You burned it, didn't you? Yes, that's what you were burning the other night. Newspapers, you said, but the next morning I checked." She reached into her pocket and took out charred pages. "Your Bible. Oh, dear Christ, may He forgive you."

"Christ!" J.D. cried, his voice toneless, barely above a whisper.

"Yes!" she screamed and dug her fingernails into his arm. "Tomorrow, first thing, you and I are going to church. And we will pray. I will pray that all is forgiven. You will be cleansed, you'll be yourself again," she said in an odd, sibilant hiss.

The boy yanked his arm free of her grasp; then he stumbled backward and dropped to the floor, vomiting over the carpet, battering the floor blindly with his fists and choking. "No," he screamed. "No, no . . ."

As his mother stood frozen, watching him, J.D.'s father came rushing into the room, his eyes glazed at what he saw. He yelled something that no one seemed to understand. Then he yanked the boy to his feet and guided him into the bathroom, where he began wiping vomit from his son's chin and cheeks.

"Pray," Mrs. Salinger muttered, tears spilling from her eyes. "I will pray for us all."

11

Millhouse was dark, except for a few streetlamps, and even they cast barely more light than a pale-orange wash that was quickly eaten up by shadows. Rob too felt eaten up, demolished by the discovery of his mother's empty grave. He wanted to scream but would not.

Slowly he eased up on the gas pedal as he approached Millhouse Square. Everything was quiet around him. Even the purring of the Jag's engine seemed to fade away. A moment of prolonged emptiness followed, as if Rob's heart had stopped beating, as if the town itself had died.

Then, very gradually, the stillness, the emptiness, seemed to come alive. It came alive with the sudden movement of whiteness beside one of the trees. Rob looked closer. There, again! he thought, and watched a brief flash of whiteness move through Sullivan Park.

He stopped the car on the curve of the square, rolled his window down. Exhaust fumes rose before his eyes like steam; he shut off the car and got out, his eyes trying to part the darkness. The form moved away from him, disappeared for a moment.

As he walked across the street, he could see nothing but the dark outline of trees, the statue of Thomas Sullivan standing forlornly in the center of the park. Whoever, whatever, it was had moved behind the statue. As he moved closer and started around the cast-iron figure, he saw the whiteness again. But now there was substance to it, and form.

A woman was sitting there in a white robe, head buried between her legs, arms up over her head as though for protection. Though Rob had not fully grasped who it was, some deep-seated dread began to build within him.

Slowly the woman lifted her face and turned toward him. His heart froze, his eyes fixed on the skin that was bleached white, quivering lips, eyes sunken and red . . .

"Oh, dear God," he moaned and reached out.

With a horrible shudder he drew Elizabeth into his arms.

Doc Tanner sat staring at the closed door, his fingers wrapped tightly around his brandy glass. It was a few moments before he could shake the interruption from his mind.

He tried to focus on the thought he had had, just before Rob Martin had brought the Arbor girl into his house. He reached for a book, started shuffling through pages. He stopped to look at a photograph of a group of initiates preparing a cannibals' feast in Fiji. On the next page was a picture of *Baital*, an Indian variety of vampire, as described in Sir Richard Burton's *Tales of Hindu Devilry*.

The winged creature hovered menacingly in the air, its sharp teeth and claws reaching for its victim's throat. Tanner sighed heavily, turned the page.

In the next room, Rob stood gazing down at Elizabeth as she slept. She had appeared so drained and weakened when he had found her that he was relieved to see her resting so well. He himself felt exhausted. His arms and shoulders ached from all the shoveling he had done; his legs threatened to give out. Wearily, he turned and, with one eye still on Elizabeth, slipped quietly from the room.

The old man's eyes lifted slowly from the book.

"What are you feeling now?" he asked Rob.

"Are you ready to talk about vampires?"

Rob took a moment before he replied. "Yes," he said. And the old man nodded.

12

Dawn. Gray and humid; Millhouse getting ready for a new day. The sun broke with a sudden intensity above the trees, casting heavy shadows down upon the town.

Somewhere below oak flooring, in the dark confines of cement, a bleached-white hand drew closed the lid of a coffin. A moment's pause, then the vampire lowered her head and began to lose consciousness. A transformation was taking place. Sound, light, and shape drifted from her senses, making her shiver.

For a brief instant, there was some echo of resistance in her, some shrill voice of protest in dim tones. Then it ceased and she smiled, knowing it would not be long before she saw her son again.

Soon, she thought. And then she stiffened. She could sense the sun's dead yellow eye forcing its way through the cracks in the flooring above. In her reverie she had miscalculated. She thrashed about in the coffin for a second, head spinning, her fingernails digging into the fresh wood. Then, with a violent lurch, she flung herself facedown, panting and whining like a dog.

For the moment, at least, she would have to be content with howling.

Rob Martin looked up. He'd heard an odd, distant mournful sound.

He rose to his feet and quickly went to the window, surprised to see it had grown light outside. Mist clung to the ground, shrouding Doc Tanner's narrow grass-choked walkway. Rhododendrons stood tall, twisted and entwined with lilac bushes, and bound together with tendrils of ivy. No hand had checked their progress, and to a casual observer the house looked all but forgotten.

Abruptly the sound stopped. Behind Rob a chair creaked, and he turned. Doc Tanner's eyes went to his and then back to the two men who sat opposite him at the table.

It had been a night of indecision and confusion. Of phone calls, always with the same thought in mind: Who to trust? It was obvious that they could not go it alone. Finally, Ronny Hubbert and Eric Knopf were called and summoned to the house.

Now, as the three men sat in silence, Rob wondered if it had been the right decision.

"I don't like it," Hubbert said, breaking the silence. "And I'm still not convinced."

Doc Tanner was a little vexed. He rose to his feet, deep lines furrowing his brow. "Your skepticism is understandable. But we have no further proof than what we have already offered."

"And if they aren't vampires, what then?" Hubbert asked. "We could all end up on trial for murder."

Knopf said, "I'm afraid he's right, John. I say we go to the sheriff. Let him handle this."

"We're not sure he can be trusted."

"I don't see where we have a choice."

"And if he's protecting Norris Caine, what then? There've been a lot of strange disappearances and unexplained deaths around Millhouse. Who would be in a better position to cover up what happens than Jones? You both remember what happened on Standford Road a few years back."

Hubbert stared at Tanner with amused contempt, a look reserved for idiots. "And you're telling us you believe it was vampires. Is that it?"

"I'm sure of it." Doc Tanner suddenly reached for the back of the chair to steady himself.

Rob stepped beside him. "Are you all right?"

"Tired, is all."

Hubbert slid forward in his chair. "Look, I've lived in Millhouse my whole life. I ain't blind. Ain't dumb, neither. People die, turn up missing, I get curious. But till now, there's always been a reasonable explanation."

Doc Tanner looked at him sharply. "What reasonable explanation was there for Ned Taylor's death? You were both friends of Ned's, that's why I called you. You know damn well that someone threw him into that baler."

Hubbert settled back in his chair. His expression hardened. "Why? Why would anyone want to hurt Ned?"

"Because they killed his dog. He probably started to go after them himself."

Knopf tented his fingers in front of his mouth. "Sheriff claims that Larry Campbell killed Ned's dog, John. You telling us he's lying?"

"No, because Campbell probably did," Tanner said, averting his eyes from Rob's. "But I'm not sure Ned knew that. All he knew was that the dog was bled dry. A few years back it was some of his cattle."

"We all lose cattle now and again," Knopf said. He stroked his fair beard and looked at Rob. "Do you really believe your friend was killed by vampires?"

"Yes," Rob said, his voice thin and shrill.

Hubbert arched his brows in scorn. "Are you denying that Campbell was on drugs? That he was a junkie?"

Rob felt angered by Hubbert's remark. He also felt helpless and demeaned. "Sure, he was using drugs," he said. "But Norris Caine counted on that to throw us off the track. You read his diary. 'So many people to blame for the deaths.' He even specifically mentions white trash junkies in one of the entries."

Doc Tanner had been struck by Rob's words, and he said, "It is clear that our Mr. Caine is presenting us with a choice."

Knopf said, "Which is?"

"The choice between the evil of reality and the evil of the unknown. Reality, however disturbing, is easier to accept. It's in front of us, therefore we needn't look further."

"So what are you telling me?" Hubbert said. "That I'm lazy or something because I don't see things as you do?"

"Not at all. If all men saw reality in the same light it would be disastrous. But if you see a man fall down a set of stairs with a whiskey bottle in his hand, and I tell you he's drunk, you'd have no trouble believing me. If, however, I told you a ghost pushed him down the stairs, would you believe me?"

"Not if I saw the whiskey bottle, I wouldn't."

"That's precisely Rob's point. The Caines have always used the obvious to manipulate the people of Millhouse. The '29 Depression, World War Two. Now Norris uses these troubled times . . . drugs, the younger generation . . . protect me, he says, and I'll protect you."

"But if what you say is true," Knopf muttered, "and we agree to help you, we'd be badly outnumbered. The Town Council must know, some of the men at the factory . . ."

"That's why it's important for us to act quickly. Today."

"All right," Hubbert said, his eyes seeking and restless, and fluttering in thick black lashes. "Let's say Eric and I agree. How do we get into the Caine house? There's still dogs guarding the place."

"Promazine," Doc Tanner replied. "We lace meat with promazine and toss it over the fence. That should hold them for a while."

"And if it doesn't?"

"Well, then . . . Rob and I had better be prepared to run."

Hubbert stiffened. "You and Rob? What about us?"

Rob looked at him, recognizing that confused stare. He had seen it many times in Millhouse, but usually not on people like Hubbert. "We'll need someone to keep an eye on the house while we go in," Rob said. "We want you to park your truck near the front gate, let the air out of the tires, and pretend you're fixing it. That way you'll have a clear view of the road and the house."

"And me?" Eric Knopf asked.

"You stay here with the girl," Doc Tanner filled in. "She'll need someone. And I want to be certain we have a safe place to return to should anything go wrong."

Hubbert shook his head. "No, sir. Before putting my ass in a sling, I want to see with my own eyes. I want in that house."

Rob said, "An outside backup is more important. If something goes wrong in there, we'll need help."

"My son," Hubbert said. "I'll have him do it. He can use the small van. It'll be quicker and easier that way."

Doc Tanner moved slowly around the table, carefully considering each suggestion. He said, "I believe the fewer people involved at this point the better."

Hubbert lifted his massive shoulders and turned. "Listen, Doc, I still think all this is a bunch of horseshit. But if it turns out that it ain't, I want someone outside that's gonna be of some use. My son's old enough and strong enough to whip anyone in this room. That includes me."

Rob turned, thinking as he did. "We really could use an extra man," he said to Tanner, who was still shaking his head.

"That's no good. We'd have to tell him what's going on, and . . ."

"Bullshit," Hubbert boomed. "He'll do what I tell him, no questions asked."

All eyes went to Doc Tanner. Outside, the sun rose higher, driving harsh splashes of sunlight into the room. Slowly Tanner unbuttoned his gray vest, his eyes wandering to the wall clock. It was a few minutes past seven.

"If you're determined to go in with us," Tanner said, "then I believe your son is our best choice."

Knopf looked away to the closed door. Already the strain was presenting itself, furrowing his brow, pinching the skin around his eyes and mouth. "The girl?" he asked. "Does she have any idea what all this is about?" He turned to face Rob.

"I don't think so," Rob said. "She was delirious last night when I found her."

Knopf and Hubbert exchanged glances.

Tanner dropped wearily into his chair. "I think it best we tell her as little as possible. She has had direct contact with one of them. If she realizes this, there's no telling what her reaction will be."

"If she's had contact with a vampire, how come she's not one of them?" Hubbert stared directly across the table into Doc Tanner's eyes. His confusion had once again been replaced by disbelief, his voice almost mocking.

The old man gradually eased forward in his chair. "Not everyone bitten becomes a vampire," he said, trying to get beyond Hubbert's incredulity. "If the victim is drained too deeply, he or she dies. It is a gradual process of blood letting, of romancing the spirit, of breaking down the willpower. Stealing the very soul of a person, if you will."

Knopf sighed heavily. "And you believe that's what happened to that gal working at Sue's place?"

"Yes, and from what Rob told me last night, the Salinger boy as well."

"You're kidding," Hubbert said, aghast. "J.D.?"

Rob drew closer to the table. "I saw him tearing apart and eating a cat the other night."

"Jesus H. Christ . . . How many others you figure there are?"

Doc Tanner removed his glasses, pressed fingers into his eyes. "It's hard to say. But we have to be prepared for the worst."

"The worst? What can be worse than coming face-to-face with a vampire?"

"Coming face-to-face with ten of them," Doc Tanner said. Everyone began to laugh, until they saw the serious look on the old man's face. Hubbert was the last to stop chuckling, the harsh sound of his voice dying in the sudden silence.

13

Something was about to happen, Tom Salinger could tell. He glanced nervously at his wife, who sat rigid on the hard wooden bench beside him, her hands twisting her handkerchief, her eyes riveted on the small, dimly lit hallway leading to Father Ryan's private chamber. The smell of burnt candle wax and flowers past their prime drifted in from the chapel off to the side. A small shaft of morning sunlight streamed in through the stained-glass window.

"He's been with J.D. for almost an hour," Mr. Salinger said. "I wonder what they're doing in there?"

Mrs. Salinger bowed her head, her gray hair only partly concealed by her veil, which was of the lightest transparent silk. She regarded her hands with increased melancholy. "I'm frightened, Tom," she murmured. "I'm really scared."

"Everything will be all right." He slipped a comforting arm around his wife's shoulder. "Father Ryan is a good man. He baptized J.D. He'll know how to help him."

"You speak as a Catholic," she said. "But . . ."

She stopped speaking when she heard a loud shrieking cry coming from Father Ryan's chamber. An almost unbearable sound that rose higher, until it became lost in the sudden crash of furniture.

Mr. Salinger rose and dashed toward the hallway. His wife screamed something he could not understand, clinging to his arm, trying to hold him back. The door to the room stood ajar. Father Ryan was standing in the middle of the floor. Slouched in one corner was J.D., half-naked, his face ravaged by an unnatural look of old age, a letter opener like a knife in his outstretched hand. From behind the desk smoke and flames rose out of a trash basket.

"*You*!" J.D. screamed as his father entered the room. "You're as fucking stupid as he is!" Mr. Salinger saw the priest take a step back, away from the boy's vehement snarl.

"In the name of Jesus," Father Ryan muttered weakly, his eyes brimming with tears. "Renounce this evil . . ."

"Shut up, you miserable shit!" As his father moved closer, J.D. raised the letter opener. "Stay away or I'll stick you like I did him."

"Put it down!" his father yelled.

The priest, regaining his composure, started toward the boy. "Repent, save yourself . . ."

J.D. laughed, a hideous crackling sound that interrupted the priest's words. "No power anywhere can stop him. He's stronger than death. No one is stronger!"

In a flash the fire jumped up, a living red weed that took hold of the lace curtains at the window, running along the window ledge, and across the floor and walls.

As Tom Salinger attempted to rush forward, Father Ryan grabbed hold of his arm. "No, don't," the priest shouted. The small room began darkening with smoke.

"J.D.!" Mrs. Salinger screamed; everyone was shouting and screaming as quickly lashing tongues of flames reached out for J.D.'s flesh. He laughed and stepped deeper into the inferno. Then he dropped to his knees and began to babble incoherently.

With a sudden lurch, Salinger broke free of the priest's grasp. He looked, and saw his son reaching out for help, and he moved toward him, pushing into the flames.

A strong hand groped, took hold of J.D., and began dragging him toward the door. Everyone drew back into the hallway, as the fire triumphantly claimed the room.

The fire continued to burn long after J.D. and his father were admitted to Peabody General. Father and son. One would make it. One would not.

14

"We must drive a nail into the center of the forehead," Tanner said. "Between the eyes, just above the bridge of the nose." Hesitantly he lifted one of the large metal nails from the table and held it up.

"What about the traditional stake through the heart?" Hubbert asked, and Knopf wiped sweat from his brow.

Rob leaned back against the kitchen counter, still trying to catch his breath. He had done exactly as Tanner had instructed. He had gone back to the Rizzo house, packed his clothes, and left a note on the kitchen table saying he'd left town. He took Fairmont Avenue out of town, then backtracked, and without being seen had parked his car in Doc Tanner's garage.

"We mustn't be taken in by what we see in movies," the old man said. "The heart is not an easy organ to locate. It is the forehead we must go for, the brain."

Then, as if his fears had frozen into some awful reality, Hubbert said, "But it's daylight, for chrissakes. You telling me that if we don't get it right, there's a chance we could be attacked by one of them?"

"I have no way of telling," the old man confessed. "Legend has it that they cannot rise during daylight. But I wouldn't count on that."

"That's great, that's really great." Hubbert pushed back from the table and got to his feet.

Tanner continued. "First we must stuff the mouth with a cloth soaked in gasoline. Then set it afire. As soon as this is done, we drive the nail in. There must be no hesitation. Is that clear?"

"Why the cloth in the mouth?" Knopf asked, having gone as ghostly white as Hubbert.

"This will prevent the spirit from leaving the body. As the nail strikes the brain, there will be a release. Most likely a scream. We mustn't allow the spirit to leave the body."

"So what if it does?" Hubbert stared at the doctor, clenching and unclenching his large fists. It was a moment before the doctor realized that he had been asked a direct question.

"Spirit is real," the old man finally murmured, his voice oddly smooth and lulling. "In fact, spirit is the basis of all reality. Evil spirit in particular is personal, and it is intelligent. In a sense it is not *of* this material world, but it is *in* this material world. We must be very careful." He pointed to the crucifixes lying on the table. "Therefore, we will each wear one of these. And carry a vial of holy water."

Hubbert moved back to the table. "And what will they be doing while we're stuffing rags in their mouths?"

"Nothing, I hope. Their sleep is a deep one. It is after the nail enters the skull that we have to be prepared."

For a moment there was silence, and then Rob said, "It's nine o'clock. We're wasting time." He heard a tightness in his own voice that was close to fear. He tried to control it. "We should be going."

The doctor hunched his body forward. His face looked sunken, the eyes deeply socketed. "We must rest first," he said. "At least two hours. That will give Ronny a chance to get his son in place. And also to nose around town. I'll be interested to hear what the mood is."

Hubbert sneered. "If what you say is true, it'll be business as usual."

"Still, get what information you can. And don't underestimate anyone. And now, if you don't mind, Rob and I will rest. You should be back here by eleven."

Nodding, Hubbert left. Knopf moved into the living room and turned on the TV. In the hallway Doc Tanner took hold of Rob's arm and said, "They don't know that one of them might be your mother. I see no reason to tell them, do you?"

"No," Rob murmured. And then Elizabeth went through his mind.

The way she clung to him last night. She had been violated; the marks on her neck kept opening and closing, as if crying out; her flesh had a mind of its own, driven by the dreadful purity of evil. All of this Rob saw and felt in a flash. And in the next second he backed toward the doorway, turned, and stepped into the bedroom and closed the door.

Elizabeth stirred under the blanket, her hand outstretched and clinging to the headboard. She was not awake, but not quite asleep either. She seemed aware of Rob's presence in the room.

He stared down at her, the gentle reflected light filtering in through the windows highlighting her already soft features. He felt strangely distant from her, yet he wanted desperately to close the gap.

He lay down beside her as gently as he could. Elizabeth moved closer to him, and he gladly let the warmth of her body flow into him and closed his eyes.

He floated now, as if in a vacuum.

Both floated.

Beyond any reaches of evil.

15

At a quarter past nine, the sheriff pulled his car into Tony Rizzo's drive and shut off the engine. Jack Gardner was seated beside him, his callused fingers nervously tugging on his overalls.

Annoyed, the sheriff stared around, his eyes making a quick sweep of the front porch, then the side of the house where the driveway widened into a space large enough to park three cars. All three slots were empty.

"I don't see his car," the sheriff said.

Jack Gardner looked at the house for a moment, his gray eyes squinting into the sunlight. "Maybe he and the girl hightailed it out of town."

The sheriff shook his head. "Not likely. Let's take a look."

The house was dark and quiet. Jack Gardner poked his head into the living room, then glanced upstairs. "I'll go up and check."

"No," the sheriff said. "It's obvious he isn't here."

"Then where is he?" Gardner moved away and glanced out the window. "He must be with the girl. Where would he take her?"

"That's really not my problem, is it?"

"Whitset said . . ."

"I don't give a fuck what Whitset said," the sheriff boomed. "Now you sons of bitches ain't telling me the truth, are you? No, sir."

"What are you talking about?"

"I'm talking about that bullshit story Whitset handed me last night. Expecting me to believe that the boy killed his friend."

"I was here, I tell you. I overheard him telling someone on the telephone that he killed him over that girl, Marianne."

"And then he and Marianne killed that fella over at the Peabody morgue. Is that what you're telling me?"

Jack Gardner said, "He must have."

"Bullshit," the sheriff said, and began to come toward him. "You can see me all right, can't you, Jack? You can hear me? People make mistakes. They do things they're sorry for later. Now the Town Council has fucked up, hasn't it? You're all in shit way up over your heads. Now that's really the truth, isn't it?"

As if shell-shocked, Gardner turned, trying to get away from the sheriff. Then he looked back at him, having stepped toward the kitchen. "I don't know what you're talking about."

"You know."

Gardner made a gesture of exasperation. "Don't pressure me, Conley. I ain't done nothin'. None of us have. It's Rob Martin that's rippin' the town apart. It's him."

"Is that why you're carrying that gun, Jack?"

"What gun?"

The sheriff moved suddenly, grabbed Gardner's arm. "Give it to me."

Jack Gardner stiffened and slowly pulled a small revolver out of his pocket—it appeared to be a toy pistol in his oversize hand. "I always carry this," he muttered.

"Not anymore, you don't." The sheriff took the revolver, went to the front door, and looked out at Locus Hill Road. "You've all been lying to me, Jack," he said. "Now I've always leaned your way. You know that. Even when I shouldn't have. But I ain't leaning no more."

He turned back to Gardner.

"You tell Whitset that," he said. "You tell him and the others that I'm gonna find out the truth this time."

Gardner lowered his head, muttered, "It's gonna cost you your job, Conley."

The sheriff smirked. "Never was much of a job anyway. Not much of a town, either, when you come right down to it. So you tell the council that, all right, Jack? You also tell them that if anything happens to Elizabeth Arbor or Rob Martin, well . . ."

With a last glance at the revolver in his hand, the sheriff turned and left the house.

"We've looked everywhere," Deputy Pete Salino said to Joe Arbor. "She's disappeared." For a moment everything seemed utterly unreal —this man who was his friend, standing pale before him; while his wife sat trembling in a corner, clinging to Elizabeth's bloodstained dress. He sighed. "You say you just found the dress this morning?"

Joe Arbor nodded. "That's right."

Distractedly Salino sipped at the coffee, his eyes fixed on a bright patch of sunlight on the kitchen counter. "Then she didn't wear the dress to the clinic. Is that right?"

"No," Mrs. Arbor murmured, and Salino turned to look at her, feeling a deep sense of strangeness. Behind her, through the window, he could still see billows of smoke that he knew were coming from St. Andrews Church. That too had been a strange happening, and no one— not even Father Ryan—seemed willing to talk about it.

Slowly, mechanically, Salino raised his hand to his neck, which was throbbing. His wound, despite the stitches, kept opening, and a slimy green pus kept seeping through the bandage. And with it, a sour stench. He kept seeing Larry Campbell's body. And he wondered, What the hell is happening to us? All of us?

"Don't worry, Joe," he heard himself saying. "We'll find her. She probably just got tired of being cooped up in the clinic. Went for a walk or something. We'll find her."

Joe Arbor nodded again. There was nothing else to say. Mrs. Arbor said, "Those stories. They're true, aren't they, Joe? All these years and they're finally coming true."

In tears, she went running from the room.

16

Rob Martin awoke suddenly. The room was dim and unfamiliar. There was a faint voice in his ears. He lay still, eyes open, and the voice began to clarify.

"It's time," Doc Tanner said, his face a mere shadow, backlit by the sun's rays streaming in from the hallway. Rob propped himself up on his elbows; Elizabeth was still lying beside him. She stirred as Tanner stepped back into the hall and closed the door, and she smiled weakly when she saw Rob.

"Hi," he said.

"Hi," she whispered.

"How are you feeling?"

"Confused." She sat up and glanced around the room. Her hand went out mechanically and drew the blanket up to her body. She appeared to be shivering, and her eyes seemed unable to adjust. "Where . . ."

"You're in Doc Tanner's house." He took her hand and held it; they gazed into each other's eyes.

"Something terrible is happening, isn't it?" she said softly.

"Yes."

"He came to me again last night. That man. He was there in my room. I ran. I . . ."

"I know." He reached out and brushed a wisp of hair away from her eyes.

"Who is he, Rob?" she asked.

He shook his head, unable to answer.

"Is the whole town going crazy?" she said. "Or just me?"

"Things will work out, I promise," he whispered. "You'll be safe here." Elizabeth responded instantly, pressing herself against him. He held her for a moment and then drew back. "I have to leave the house for a while. Eric Knopf will be staying here while I'm gone."

Elizabeth had no reaction. She didn't even ask why Knopf needed to stay with her.

"I should be back in a few hours," he said. "It's something I must do."

She nodded, and he slowly rose, leaning over to gently kiss her pale cheek.

"Rob?"

"Yes?"

"Will we be together when this is all over?" She stared up at him, her expression puzzled and childlike.

"Yes," he uttered, struck with her beauty, even in her weakened condition. "Rest now," he said. "Promise me you'll rest."

Elizabeth forced herself to settle back despite her impulse to take hold of Rob. As he moved to the door her mind whirled with unwanted memories. Yet she did not move, did not call out.

Her eyes closed moments after he had left the room. Unwillingly, she was being drawn back into another realm of existence, and she thought: *Please, God, don't let me dream.*

17

It was eleven-thirty when Rob Martin and Ronny Hubbert climbed into the backseat of Tanner's black Pontiac, each wearing a crucifix he had given them, each carrying a vial of holy water. No one said anything as the old man drove off, heading west, making sure to keep to the back roads. The smell of gasoline wafted up from the gas can in Hubbert's hands as Tanner swung the car around a series of sharp curves and then started back across the east side of the mountain.

Soon the upper part of the Caine house appeared, its top spires jetting into a sac of clear blue sky like angry spears, signifying the mood of the family who had occupied the house for more than seventy-five years.

Hubbert leaned forward in his seat. "The caretaker's road is just up ahead," he said.

Tanner nodded, and Rob could feel his gut tighten as they turned onto a narrow dirt lane, obviously little used. Deep, overgrown foliage pressed the road on both sides; overhead, the trees seemed locked together.

"Can we make it through here?" Rob asked.

Tanner muttered, "I think so."

The car bumped slowly over potholes for a few hundred yards and foliage began brushing the sides of the car; still there was no sign of the back gate. Rob peered over Tanner's shoulder, trying to see beyond the heavy brush. Fear. That was his chief sensation. He was certain that gradually he would lose the ability to go through with his self-appointed task.

"Look," Hubbert said, and pointed to the massive steel fence hidden under thick vines and bushes. The fence disappeared and, about forty yards away, broke through the shrubbery again.

Around the next bend the gate appeared, flanked by two brick pillars. Everything grew quiet as Tanner stepped on the brake and shut off the engine. All peered down a sharp incline of drive which disappeared from view shortly beyond the pillars.

"Do you think the dogs know we're back here?" Hubbert said in a hushed voice.

"You can count on it," Tanner said. He hesitated a moment, then picked up a small package of meat and got out of the car. Hubbert waited until Rob got out, and then handed him the gas can and a workman's sack containing two hammers and a dozen large nails. The sack also held a Bible, a flashlight, more vials of holy water, and several invocations Tanner had scribbled on pieces of paper.

Rob took the gas can and sack and glanced up. Around him the woods rose, solidly, with coarse high grass and dead trees; it was hot and silent and heavy with the smell of plants baking in the sun.

"Jesus," Hubbert shrilled and slammed the car door.

Tanner tensed. "What happened?"

"Goddamn thorn got me." He was rubbing his arm against his side.

"Well," Tanner said. "If the dogs didn't know we were here, they do now."

A moment later there was no doubt. They appeared suddenly, their massive legs carrying them forward; three animals large enough to be seen from a distance but only against the hot white stones of the gravel drive.

Tanner quickly tossed the meat over the fence, and then withdrew to the back of the car where he crouched down beside Rob. Hubbert squatted beside them.

At first the dogs were more sound than

actual presence, yelping with murderous excitement. Rob rose from his crouch upon seeing their maddened red eyes. He stepped back as the lead dog smashed against the fence, its teeth snapping at the air. Saliva dripped from its fangs as it lunged.

Then things got quiet. Rob heard yelps and moans of appeasement, and the soft sound of meat being torn apart. He watched as each dog, having gone its separate way, succumbed to the promazine with which Tanner had laced the meat.

As Rob jimmied open the rear window of the Caine house, Hubbert nudged Tanner. The old man turned away and closed his eyes. High color spread up from his throat, suffusing his face. Slowly he made the sign of the cross. Hubbert bowed his head.

"God be with us," Tanner said. "And forgive us our sins and those of our forefathers. Do not punish us for our offenses. But deliver us from evil. Be our tower of strength in the face of our enemy. Let your power reign with us, O God, forever and ever. Amen."

Rob stared silently at the old man for a moment, slowly made the sign of the cross, then hoisted himself into the open window and jumped into the room.

Hubbert was next, and he hesitated briefly before entering. For Tanner it was an effort, and he huffed audibly as the men helped him through the window, his chest heaving, not with excitement but from exertion.

"Are you all right?" Rob asked, seeing Hubbert's doubtful expression.

Trembling, the old man removed the crucifix from around his neck. His reply was simple and direct. "Behold the Cross of the Lord. It is my strength and my salvation."

Quickly he withdrew to the door, his thin frame washed in bleached pastels of diffused light. As Hubbert moved toward him, Rob felt the room around them tighten, as if the walls were desperately clutching their past, as if the present was about to fall away, leaving them in a pale golden slumber from which they would never wake.

Rob forced himself to move through a room of unmitigated grandeur; a room formal and elegant, sensuous, a trifle haughty—pomp reined in by exquisite taste. Yet there was the distinct feeling of isolation and decay. Of death in hibernation.

Single file, they moved into the hallway. To Rob the house seemed unusually dark. Until Tanner had led him past the living room, he was sure they would not be able to find their way without the use of the flashlight. He stopped momentarily to glance beyond the huge archway and saw the faint outline of furniture hidden beneath dust covers, a back staircase, and a warren of tiny alcoves. Everything seemed to float before his eyes like a still from an unfinished film.

He started when Tanner took hold of his arm.

"The basement," the old man whispered.

Together they moved forward, and Rob felt a tremor of fear and disgust as Tanner opened the kitchen door at the end of the hallway.

Animal carcasses, slaughtered, some beheaded, lay on the kitchen counter. Blood dripped from the counter's surface onto the green and white tile floor. A dog, its eyes glazed and frozen, stared at them from its impaled position on the kitchen wall.

And then, from below the house, there came the malevolent feeling of evil.

18

Most Unclean Spirit," Tanner said shrilly, holding up his cross. "Invading Spirits. Everyone of you! In the name of Our Lord Jesus Christ: Be uprooted and expelled from our midst!"

From below there seemed to come a distant cry. Beneath their feet the floor began to shake. Hubbert cried out.

"Stay put," Doc Tanner ordered, and quickly went to the basement door and listened. "Yes," he said. "I'm sure they're down there."

Rob moved closer to the counter. "The blood is still fresh," he said. He backed away with a shudder.

Hastily the old man removed the sack from Hubbert's shoulder, took out a hammer, and handed it to Rob. Then he removed the flashlight. "Remember," he said. "We must not hesitate."

Hubbert stood mute, his large shoulders hunched, his mouth twisted in confusion. "But we must be certain," he said, his voice tight with fear.

"You will soon have all the proof you need," Tanner said.

One by one, they looked at each other.

"Let's go," Tanner said.

Slowly, purposefully, they entered the basement and started down the narrow staircase into the dense gloom below.

19

A half mile away, Sheriff Conley Jones drove his police car. His right hand rested between his legs. Sunk down in himself, buried in his thoughts like a mole in the earth, he eased the car around Millhouse Square. Around him all colors were fused into the brightness of the day. Yet all life and activity along Main Street seemed dormant, as if the people of Millhouse were asleep or hidden. Even the dogs were nowhere to be seen. Only a solitary cat licked and preened itself in the shadow of Betty Walker's awning.

The police radio broke the silence. "Yeah?" said the sheriff, answering.

Deputy Collins said, "Father Ryan still ain't saying much."

"That right?" the sheriff answered again. He stopped the patrol car in front of the station and shut off the engine. "Stay with him. I'll be over in a few minutes."

"Gotcha," Collins said, and went off the air.

Annoyed, the sheriff entered the station, turned on the air conditioner, and sat behind his desk. He dragged a beer from the cooler. It was a hot day. The beer was cold.

He'd finished just about half the bottle when Deputy Salino stepped quietly out from the back room. He had that "look" the sheriff had come to know so well lately—his eyes heavy-lidded and almost closed, his head tilted to one side, hands hanging by his sides as if he were in some sort of a trance.

"You find out anything from the Arbors?" the sheriff asked. His voice sounded like nails scraping the inside of a bait bucket. He cleared his throat.

When Salino made no reply, the sheriff looked at him closer, and saw that his face was abstracted and bloodless.

"Well, did ya?" the sheriff said.

Slowly Salino's lips began to move, but there was no audible sound. Then he shifted his stance, turned in a half circle, first toward the window, then in the direction of the back room. When he spoke, at last, he spoke in scraps of words and sentences. ". . . there's something . . . evil . . . I feel . . ."

But his voice sank to a whisper and died away completely. His face wore a look of fear. His lips were working furiously, but nothing came out.

"For chrissakes, what did Joe Arbor tell you?"

Salino's face suddenly mirrored confusion and anger. He drew back and with a low hiss of breath, cried, "We're . . . all gonna die. *Christ . . . Christ . . . Christ . . .*" White foam began spilling from the corners of his mouth.

The sheriff lurched from his chair, and felt an icy sensation enter his own fingers and hand as he took hold of Salino's arm. He let go fast.

"Help me!" Salino moaned, staggering back against the wall. His hand shot to his neck, clawed at the bandage: green pus covered his fingers. The look of strained rage on his face was replaced by a look of crushed, broken helplessness.

His moan rose higher, changed to a growling, then increased in volume. *"Help meeee!"* Suddenly his eyes rolled up in his head, and he stood still for a second, before collapsing in a heap on the floor.

Jack Gardner stood in his own kitchen, reading the note again, just to be sure. Overhead the fan rotated noisily, and for a moment he let the cool air caress his face. The note was from

Rob Martin, that much was certain. "Sure enough," he muttered. Then he got a new fifth of whiskey from the pantry and sat down. The whiskey went down hot and soft and raw, all at the same time. And he began to feel better.

There was no suspicion in his mind that the note was a lie. For him, at least, the biggest problem facing the Town Council had left town.

He took a second and third drink. Then he picked up the telephone and dialed.

After giving Marshall Whitset the news, he said, "Now all we have to do is take care of the sheriff."

Whitset hesitated on the other end, and Gardner pressed the receiver tighter to his ear. When Whitset's voice next came over the line it seemed to be drifting off. "Are you sure . . . sheriff . . . Maybe we . . ." The emotion in Whitset's voice was peculiar, different from anything he'd encountered before.

"Wait a minute now," Gardner said, growing alarmed. "I tell you we have to get rid of him. He means to cause us trouble . . ."

Then Gardner paused, because he felt a twinge of simultaneous annoyance and caution; he imagined he could see Whitset's coldly staring, rapidly blinking eyes. No, not Whitset's eyes—but those of someone standing still behind him. He turned suddenly, and came face-o-face with Tony Rizzo. He was standing in the doorway, stiffly, suitcase at his side. Though Gardner couldn't have said for sure how he knew it, he knew that his nephew had changed. That he had had direct contact with them.

Christ! Gardner thought, momentarily frightened.

Then, without saying a word, he lowered the receiver into its cradle.

20

The sudden stillness of the basement startled Rob, in fact for an instant terrified him, until he realized that it was only that Tanner and Hubbert had stopped moving, and ahead of him they stood frozen.

There was absolute quiet.

Tanner had raised his trembling right hand, leveled the flashlight, and was carefully searching the surrounding area, the pale-yellow beam of light skipping over the walls of the basement. The stark loneliness of gray crumbling brick soon revealed itself, its rough surface steeped in suffering and veiled in a lacework of webs, as if someone had brought in a cobweb machine, the kind that spins webs for horror films.

But Rob knew it wasn't a film he was in. This was real, it was actually happening, and just for a moment the thought nearly sent him fleeing up the stairs into the daylight beyond.

"There," Tanner said. "Over there."

Rob watched as Hubbert and Tanner moved to the far corner of the room, where five coffins, their lids closed, rested upon cement slabs. He had desperately hoped to find the basement empty; but standing there, looking at the coffins, he could feel all hope die.

A moment later, Tanner lifted the first lid.

Hubbert reached out for the wall to steady himself, and then laughed. A grating laugh that died in his throat. "Empty," he said with a violent release of breath. "It's empty!"

Rob moved closer, hooked his fingers beneath the next coffin lid. Something stopped him from opening it.

"Go on, open it," Hubbert said, his voice filled with a new confidence. For him it had suddenly become easy. "You want me to do it?"

Rob would have said something to cancel Hubbert's cockiness, but nothing came to him. It was as if his mind had stopped dead. For an instant he had a vision of ghosts everywhere, all looking at him in the darkness, filling the room, coming closer, groaning, clutching their hands to his throat. The lid wobbled in his hand as he opened it.

When Rob looked down, slowly, he saw his mother lying there, perfectly still and spotlighted by Tanner's flashlight, her face bloodless gray, her heavy eyelids drawn shut. She wore a flower-print dress with faded shoes, her hair brushed straight down over her shoulders. Rob reached out toward the wall to steady himself—exactly as Hubbert had reached out only moments ago.

"Leave now," Tanner said, and for decency's sake, or kindness's sake, he turned Rob away, trying to lead him to the stairs.

Rob shook his head, and he knew there were tears on his cheeks. "Let's do what has to be done." But even as he spoke, he could feel the pulsing in his temples, the sudden increase of pain in his head, then blending, shrieking panic—and suddenly he was violently ashamed, disgusted beyond words.

"Please, let's do it quickly," he pleaded, already moving forward. Tanner hovered over the coffin for a moment, then parted her lips and gently inserted the piece of cloth doused in gasoline into her mouth. Rob placed the nail dead-center of her forehead.

Now Tanner stepped forward with a lighted match. Hubbert looked at him in bewilderment, as if he half expected someone to jump from a hiding place and holler, *surprise!*

Rob swallowed, trying to shake his desperation. As he raised the hammer, the grittiness of reproach seized his mind. "God forgive us," he muttered, "for what we are about to do."

Tanner leaned in and lit the rag. For a moment only a tiny blue flame appeared, running this way and that, almost appearing to go out. Then, startlingly, the rag erupted into flames.

"Now," Tanner said, and Rob brought the hammer down, striking the nail squarely. The look of complete and utter rage on his mother's face as her eyes flew open, bloodshot and fiery, would haunt him for the rest of his life. Her hand shot up, grabbed hold of Tanner's jacket. Tanner stumbled back, trying to free himself.

Rob brought the hammer down again, driving the nail deeper into her skull. Blood spurted from the puncture, splattering Hubbert's shirt as he ripped her hand off Tanner, only to wind up snagged himself. He gasped and pulled away, eyes watering in the smoke from the gag.

Rob raised the hammer again but could not bring it down. He felt light-headed, his thoughts tumbling one over the other, his illusions of evil turning into substance and enveloping him.

Regaining his balance, Tanner raised his crucifix above the coffin, shouted, "I enjoin you under penalty, Ancient Serpent! In the name of Our Creator! In the name of Him who has power to send you into Hell! Depart from this place! Now!"

Rob watched as his mother's body rose and fell, convulsing in its box. Through the yellow haze of smoke, amid the confusion and panic, he saw his mother's mouth open, her long teeth protruding through the rag.

"God the Father commands you!" Tanner

shouted. "God the Son commands you! Get out!" Tanner leaned over the coffin, holding the crucifix close to her forehead.

She drew back, screamed silently, her eyes darting from side to side as her spirit looked for a way to escape her body. Her hands and arms thrust at her tormentors, then fell back. Her body grew still, save for her left leg, which twitched a few more times, then stopped.

Still Rob imagined he could hear her screams, but very dimly now, almost lost to the ear. Behind the dying flames he could see the light going out in her eyes as her skin blackened.

Then her torment broke; her tortured face seemed to be replaced by another, a face Rob knew, a face he needed to see. His mother's true face. It was as if the spirit of the woman he had known had returned—had been set free.

The men drew back.

Dimly Rob heard Tanner say, "Let us handle the rest."

Rob glanced down at his hands, covered with his mother's blood. Then he stumbled backward, groped for the banister, felt himself climbing upward, yet at the same time he felt as though he were sinking.

Around him the house screamed: *Murderer*!

He stumbled into the kitchen, using the walls for support. Then he stood there, staring, seeing only the faint outline of his own shadow as it started to sag. Lower. Closer to the floor.

* * *

It was just before two when Tanner and Hubbert finally emerged from the basement. It had been the longest, most painful hour of Rob's life.

Without speaking, Hubbert crossed to the back door, opened it, and stepped onto the porch. There he threw his head back, and gulped in the dead lifeless air as though it were pure oxygen. Tanner stood beside Rob, his face and neck covered with large globs of sweat, his eyes still trying to adjust from the darkness below.

"There were two more," he said, his voice a mere whisper. "Both were men."

Light fell in tinted, dusty beams through the doorway onto Tanner's face and over the countertop. When Tanner moved, his blood-soaked shirt turned a brilliant red, and Rob gave a little start and looked into his eyes.

"Were either of the men Norris Caine?" he asked.

Tanner shook his head. "They must have moved him and his sister to another location," he said.

His words hung for a moment over the two men like a curse that would not be denied. Each knew what the other was thinking, yet neither spoke. Slowly, trancelike, not making a sound, Tanner moved to the door.

Perdurable evil, Rob thought, and followed the old man into the sunlight. Off to the side, next to the porch, Hubbert was urinating. Rob blinked hard, trying to catch his bearings. Before him the walkway stretched out, following the spiked iron fence, past the caretaker's cottage, and curving around to the gate beyond.

Off to the side, on Mountainview Road, was Hubbert's van. His son stood perfectly still, staring. Hubbert gave a slight wave of his hand, and the boy immediately bent and began pumping air back into the tire.

Together, the three men started up the walkway. Though he was perspiring, Rob felt chilled. He glanced about uneasily as he plodded forward; the vacant eyelike windows of the caretaker's house seemed to come alive as he passed.

And he paused, wondering if they shouldn't have checked the rest of the house. The cottage. As if reading his mind, Tanner glanced back and said, "Norris Caine isn't here. I would know if he was."

Reluctantly Rob moved on. He followed the path as it tunneled through the trees, and as he walked he felt a sudden jolt of terror. It was more than fear. He stopped in his tracks.

"Tanner."

Tanner turned to follow Rob's gaze and saw, to his left, the low-slung body of a dog as it moved through the bushes, circling around, heading them off before they could reach the back gate. Both men stood motionless as the animal stepped into the open, saliva dripping from its slack jaws.

Ahead of them, Hubbert crouched to pick up the crowbar he'd used earlier to bust the lock on the gate. The dog kept its back to him, its eyes riveted on the two men. And then it started coming, its movement sudden and full of fury. Tanner stumbled back. The dog sprang into the air, hurling itself on Tanner as he turned to run.

Before Rob could respond, he heard Hubbert cry out: "Watch out behind you!" As he turned, a second dog attacked, its jaws tearing into the flesh of his leg. He fell to his knees, rolled over, and grabbed the dog's neck, trying to hold it back.

Hubbert was beside Tanner now, swinging wildly with the crowbar, connecting with the dog's head. But the animal hung on, until Hubbert, in desperation, stabbed the crowbar into the animal's back.

Rob heard the first dog's horrified wail as he smashed his fist into his attacker's face. The dog fell back, stunned. Rob tried to get to his feet but could not. The dog lunged at him again. Hubbert circled around, trying to catch it from behind.

Then Hubbert lifted the crowbar and brought it down. The dog gave a moan of agony as he brought the bar down again, and again, and again, until there was only the sound of Hubbert's voice, weeping like a child.

Mercifully, the third dog had never appeared.

21

Night, black as pitch, crept in. And with it, the long, dark corridor of the Peabody morgue turned still as a grave, and almost as airless. Along the edges of the ceiling, shadows gathered into darkness, smoky and impenetrable; in the morgue itself there was only the strange, murky glow of the night light, more yellow than white, a light that seemed to be of its own making.

Bob Oswell, the janitor, paused in the act of picking up an infinitesimal piece of gauze from the tile floor, and stood listening.

"Okay, stop your clowning around," he called out. Oswell was a small, thin man, his face racked with lines of age and too much booze, but in that moment his voice boomed, as if his gut were telling him something his brain couldn't comprehend. His gut was telling him that someone was moving around just beyond the doorway. His brain was saying: *Don't be ridiculous*!

Yet he had heard footsteps, hadn't he?

"Who's back there?" he shouted, and felt like a real dummy. "I said . . ." He stopped, because dummy or not—there they were again. Footsteps. Quicker this time. And with purpose.

He wished, suddenly, that he hadn't taken that fifth drink. Hadn't waited so long to get the place cleaned up. He never did like working nights, especially when there was someone laid out.

He had, earlier, ages ago it seemed, lamented Greg Harrison's death. Lamented the fact that the poor bastard had gotten involved with the likes of a woman who lived in Millhouse's "Kitchen." He had done that once himself, and nearly gotten killed. He was younger then, a hellraiser, and only went to Millhouse now when the missus wanted to see her sister.

That's what Bob Oswell was thinking of—his sister-in-law, Gretchen—when the darkness ahead of him parted. The naked man with the black hair and vacant blue eyes came at him so fast he hadn't time to react.

As teeth tore into his neck, he realized—*Oh, Christ! Oh, dear sweet Jesus!*—that he was going to die.

22

The darkness of Deputy Salino's hospital room was broken only by the pale moonlight that came though his window, seeming to cast his face a ghostly white.

He had opened his eyes once, gazed around the room in slow, uncomprehending horror, and then closed them again. The sheriff had half expected him to speak, but he hadn't.

An hour later the sheriff was still staring with intensity into Salino's face. His heavy eyelids were closed, his breathing short and labored. Then his stony face relaxed. The nurse moved beside his bed, where she paused. She, too, had turned a ghostly white.

The doctor was there, saying something the sheriff didn't want to hear, couldn't accept. But when it was repeated again, well . . .

The sheriff got to his feet, watched as they pulled the sheet up over Salino's face. Beside the bed, on the nightstand, stood a silver drinking pitcher. As the sheriff gazed into its smooth metal surface, he saw reflected there his own image. An image that swirled with color, a specter of red, aflamed like a demon.

And he knew, without a doubt, that he would be next to die.

23

The moon turned, spilling its murky amber light over the town. Thick clouds gathered above the horizon line. From the bedroom window Rob could see the storm approaching, almost feel it—a thick gummy sensation that made him glance again at the old man who lay still in his bed, his body twisted with pain and filled with his own self-prescribed medication.

Please, God—help us, Rob thought, and felt a grim, determined loathing grip his innards. Norris Caine had tricked them. He had used Rob's mother and the others as bait. While he himself had fled.

The thought burned in Rob's mind.

Shuddering, he drew a deep breath, feeling pain dart through his leg, and then turned with a start when Doc Tanner suddenly cried out in his sleep. Quickly he took the cold compress and placed it to the old man's forehead. Behind him, the door to the bedroom opened, and Elizabeth came into the room.

She stood for a moment in half shadows, staring down at Tanner as though witnessing her own suffering and pain.

"Is he any better?" she asked.

Rob shook his head. "He's still burning with fever. I think . . ." He broke off when he saw Elizabeth rock back on her heels, and for a moment felt fear again. He cleared his throat with difficulty. "How are you feeling?" he asked.

Without speaking, she turned her head a little to look out the window. She stood there as though suspended in time, and somehow he joined her in a strange deep empathy, deeper than any he'd ever known before.

"He's still out there, isn't he?" she murmured.

And Rob could feel himself hopelessly drawn to the pull of evil that called to him from just beyond the walls of Tanner's house.

A lurking evil.

Cold and calculating.

"We mustn't give up," he said, feeling Tanner's body heat burning through the cloth. Dipping it into the ice bucket, he pressed it again to the old man's forehead.

"Norris Caine never leave us alone," Elizabeth said solemnly. "We belong to him now."

Rob looked at her, unable to respond. Slowly, with head bowed, she began to leave the room.

"Elizabeth?" Rob called out.

Her head came up abruptly; she gave him a long look, searching. Then she raised her hand to her neck. "This is him," she said. "I can feel him. He is here, has been, will be, until the end."

Before Rob could speak she turned and left the room, the door closing behind her with a dull thud.

24

The sheriff got out of his patrol car without bothering to roll up the windows and began walking across the gravel drive toward his house. Overhead, clouds blotted the moon. The street behind him was deserted. All was quiet. He did not hear the footsteps behind him as he passed between the hedges, only a breath of sound, no louder than a sigh.

He felt whatever it was, felt it around his neck, a sharp thin wire, maybe—a cord—and then he felt it tighten, saw his hand go for his revolver as if it weren't his own, reach out, fall short.

He fell forward between the shrubbery. Not

from a blow, but something. He couldn't utter anything, breath gone. Then the pain came, a horrible excruciating pain that traveled the length of his body. He managed to cry out, once; his voice came out as a gurgle of blood.

Still he tried to get to his feet. Again something pushed him down onto his knees, where his head rolled to one side, out of control.

At the last moment, tongue protruding, eyes popping, he thought he saw Whitset's face staring at him through the darkness, a malevolent face, half smiling—or was it Striker's? The face appeared and then was washed away by a seizure of color, a cruelty of red, as if his own blood were flooding his eyes.

Then, no color, and no pain either. Only darkness.

25

Eric Knopf had left Tanner's house some time ago, a frightened man, muttering to himself, his hand wrapped tightly around his crucifix. Hubbert had also gone, only to return around midnight with news of Salino's death.

Tanner was sitting up in bed now, his thin frame propped against the headboard, his body twisted with discomfort.

"Do you think his death is part of all this?" Hubbert asked.

The old man looked away out the window to the treetops of the woods and saw them swaying. Distractedly he said, "The sheriff claims Rob's friend was the one who attacked Salino.

Obviously . . . obviously he had contact with one of them and infected Salino."

Hubbert moved with agitation about the room. "We damn well better not wait any longer. Let's call in the State Police if we have to."

"And tell them what?" Tanner said. "By now the council has probably covered its tracks. We'd end up sounding like a bunch of lunatics."

"We have to do something," Hubbert objected. "The whole town is wondering where Elizabeth Arbor is. We can't hide her out here much longer, not without putting ourselves in danger."

"Tonight," Rob said, his eyes going anxiously to Tanner. "Norris Caine has to be out there somewhere."

Tanner lifted himself higher in the bed, grimacing with pain as he did. "No. Only a fool would try taking one of them at night. You and Ronny must wait till morning. Then . . ."

"Then what?" Hubbert exploded. "How are we going to find him? He could be hiding anywhere. He could have left town, for that matter."

Tanner looked at him shrewdly. "You flatter us, my friend. This is *his* town. He would not abandon it because of us. No, he is still in Millhouse."

Irritably Hubbert snapped, "But where?"

For a moment Tanner hesitated. Large oily beads of sweat covered his forehead, which he wiped away with his handkerchief. "We must think as he would think," he said at last. "He would choose a place where he could sleep under constant surveillance."

Hubbert moved closer to the bed. "The factory," he said. "There's plenty of empty rooms there."

"I don't think so," Tanner said. "I'm sure that not all the men working at the factory are aware of what's going on. Caine wouldn't risk being discovered. Besides, he is accustomed to luxury."

Rob joined Hubbert beside the bed. "The caretaker's house at the cemetery," he said. "Willis Bradley must be part of all this, or else why would Kenny Long leave town so suddenly?"

Tanner blinked his eyes against the unshielded glare of the light, a single bulb which protruded from the unshaded lamp beside the bed. "Bradley knows, that much is certain," he said. "But he's a heavy drinker. I don't think Caine would place himself in such an unpredictable circumstance."

"Jesus!" Hubbert threw up his hands in exasperation. "Let's be honest, he could be anywhere."

There was silence for a moment. Then:

"Someone's house," Tanner muttered.

"What?"

"He would most likely choose someone's house. A person he could trust. Someone who has total knowledge of what he is, the evil involved."

Rob looked to Hubbert, and then back to Tanner. "One of the councilmen?"

Merely by mentioning the group, Rob created a new wave of emotion. A slow deliberate caution crept in. "Perhaps," Tanner said, sniffing the air as though it were a sample to be tested. "But would any of them be so brazen as to actually involve their families with such a man? Let their wives and children be exposed?"

Hubbert said, "Doc Walker and Al Striker aren't married."

Tanner immediately ruled out Doctor Walker as having too much to lose should anything go wrong. "But Al Striker," he said. "Well, that's a possibility."

"I don't think so," Hubbert said, somewhat disdainfully. "He practically lives at the factory. Besides, he hasn't got the stomach for it. He's a wimp when you get right down to it."

"We're all wimps when it comes to Norris Caine," Rob said, and realized too late that he had said the wrong thing.

Hubbert glared at him, his neck and face reddening. "Goddamn it, you brought this evil down on us. Now you stand here calling us names. I'm scared, okay? I've got a wife and kids and I'm scared. I'm not ashamed to admit it, neither."

"Hold on, Ronny." Tanner tried lifting his

legs over the side of the bed. "All Rob meant was . . ."

"I know what he meant. And he's right. Don't you think I know what we're dealing with here?"

Rob sighed. "I didn't mean anything by it. I'm sorry."

"Sorry, shit." Hubbert moved to the door. At the last minute he turned back, saying, "I ain't never run out on nobody. But this is different. We can't win. Even if we found Caine we'd be beaten, and you know it. There's probably twenty more just like him out there. It's no use, I tell you. No use at all."

Tanner rose shakily to his feet, clinging to the headboard for support. "Then we will find them," he shrieked, his entire body trembling. "And destroy them. It's God's will."

Hubbert laughed, a ragged, raspy sound that seemed to die in his throat. "God's will? Look around you, Doc. God is dead, haven't you heard?"

"No," Tanner moaned, slamming his fist down on the headboard. "That's what Caine wants us to believe. Your disbelief is his salvation! Only faith will save us."

Hubbert's face was suddenly impassive, his thin mouth straight. "Yeah, well—I can think of other ways of saving myself." Defeated, he flicked the next sentence at Rob. "I suggest you start doing the same."

He opened the door.

"Ronny, wait!" Tanner cried out, and then collapsed into Rob's arms. Rob eased him back into the bed. Hubbert was gone. All that remained was the empty doorway, and beyond it the imagined image of Norris Caine.

26

No one had to tell Rob that the people of Millhouse had locked all their doors and windows this humid July night. As he lay there on the couch, he could feel them, hidden away, watching, waiting—hoping that it was their neighbor's house Caine would visit, and not their own. He found it hard to believe that for years practically everyone in town could know that the town was possessed with evil, and yet do nothing about it.

A subconscious decision, Rob guessed. He could imagine their thinking—as long as I'm all right, as long as my family and friends continue to prosper, and aren't directly involved with the evil, then what does it matter if others are sacrificed? A cruel thought, unfair, perhaps. But then these were cruel times, the nation's people divided, each person desperately trying to guarantee his future.

Wearily Rob rolled over on his side and closed his eyes. He could hear the loud ticking of the antique clock on the mantel. A steady tic-toc that began to lull him. When the clock chimed three times on the hour, he was still half-awake.

He thought he heard Elizabeth moving around in her room, and started to go to her. But he had no words to comfort her, and so lay where he was.

He never heard the clock strike four. He was dreaming. It was a slow-moving dream, nothing disturbing. He was sitting on the front porch of his old house on Elm Street. He watched as his mother stepped out from behind the screen door, her face freshly scrubbed, her light-green summer dress lifted slightly by a breeze, her eyes startlingly alive, her smile widening as she moved toward him.

He could not tell later how long it took for his mother to materialize from behind the door, but it seemed like an eternity, and when at last she was there, her arms reaching out for him, he smiled.

A warm sensation shuddered through his body as she drew him near. Slowly he went into her arms, still smiling.

And then he felt it. A sharp pain as her teeth sank into his neck.

"No!" he screamed, seeing his own blood smeared across her face. With a fierce lunge, she came at him again. Then he heard someone else screaming. The sound roared into his ears, darted through his brain. He sat bolt upright on the couch and glanced around the room. Someone had turned off the hall light.

Fear leaped into his gut as he stumbled to his feet. As he reached for the table lamp he heard Tanner call out.

"In God's name—" Tanner began, but never finished.

Rob hit the light switch; the room remained dark. He heard another horrible shriek and ran toward the sound without thought. There was not even a gleam of light in the hallway. His eyes ached for vision with a fierce, spiritual need.

Trembling, his mind unable to pursue a single line of reasoning, he flung open the door to Tanner's room. The bed was empty. The lace curtains gleamed in the moonlight. Suddenly a black shadow flashed across the lace, frantic, like some epileptic horror of absolute evil.

Rob turned, aware now of two sources of terror. The image he had seen, and the interior of his mind where the image was received.

Oh, God, no . . .

He stood before Elizabeth's door. He could not remember moving, nor what sound he had heard that had taken him across the hall . . . but here he was, his hand already pushing open the door. What followed took only seconds.

Doc Tanner came stumbling toward him out of the darkness. Tanner screamed wordlessly, his body twisting like a puppet whose controller, strings tangled in his fingers, had gone raving mad . . . Suddenly he stopped, looked at Rob with his mouth agape, then fell facedown on the floor.

From beyond the open window, Elizabeth cried out, once. Her shrill voice clung to the still night air for a moment, despair and fear underlining her words.

"Help me. Rob, please help me . . ."

Rob barely had time to see the immense shadow loom and sway down upon him. The figure filled the entire room with its massive shoulders and swollen head. Before he could move, the shadow avalanched over him, heavy and obscene. He threw out his arms but whoever, whatever, it was drove him back against the wall.

Waves of nausea and horror swept him, filled his body, until at last the living darkness pressed its blood-soaked hands over his eyes . . .

Then came the flames.

A fire that grew redder and more frightening than any hell.

27

Willis Bradley had smoked his last cigarette. His booze was all gone. He stood at the window, puzzled and disturbed and half-drunk, staring out at the grounds of the the cemetery. When they'd brought the Salinger boy in an hour ago, he had expected it. It confirmed the line of his reasoning . . . *Reality is if they don't get what they want, you're dead.*

His eyes skittered from one tombstone to the next, each shrouded in a low bank of fog. *Reality is who will turn up dead next?*

He threw the stub of his cigarette down and wandered over to the dresser. It was a cubby-hole of a room, the constant damp chill of its brick walls oppressive. He stopped to stare at his reflection in the mirror.

The sun will be up soon, he thought.

He raised his hand, ran it over the stubble of his face. "Reality is . . ." he began, then stopped. He stood quite still, his arm extended, his lips quivering against his open palm. In the utter quiet he felt himself falling into hysteria. He began to laugh and moan, his body sinking helplessly to the floor.

"Reality is . . . the glory of night," said a voice.

Willis Bradley turned with a start, stared at the man who filled the doorway. His face was expressionless. Slowly Bradley got to his feet.

The two men stared at each other over the lamp.

At last the man smiled, the first gleams of sunlight highlighting his shoulders. "Dawn," he said. "What a bitch . . . what a sweet fat bitch."

28

Even in sleep there had been pain . . . a skull-crushing pressure around the eyes, the forehead, the temples. A weariness too deep to appease with sleep. A body ache born of despair . . . of futile battles with a foe hellbent to baffle you . . . mock you . . . destroy you . . .

Being awake was worse. Rob raced into consciousness with a scream. His body shot forward in bed, his eyes and mouth opened into chasms of urgency. His arms flailed, then became purposeful as he beat at the human body who leaned over him, restraining him.

The man, an older man, stood there and let himself be hit. There was something in his face that suggested he didn't care how many times Rob's fists pummeled him, or where the blows fell. There was even a suggestion that he welcomed the attack, felt it as some strange sort of relief. He didn't fight back, and for that reason, after a particularly vicious blow to the man's chest was received stoically, Rob stopped.

"Okay, then," the man said gravely as Rob fell back on his sweat-dampened pillow. "Okay, then," he uttered again, soothingly.

"Mr. Salinger," Rob managed weakly, only then recognizing the face that had aged fully a generation since Rob had seen him on the street only days before.

Another nod as Salinger's face sagged still deeper, the deep folds seeming to fall into themselves and create new, deeper folds of tired age. Across his arms and part of his neck his flesh had been burnt away, and the covering bandages were filthy and sagging.

"Doc's house is gone," Salinger said, dropping into a nearby rocker.

"Doc's house," Rob repeated, trying to connect with what those words meant.

Salinger rocked gently and the floor creaked. Creak . . . creak into the silence as Rob tried to think. "Doc Tanner's house," the man resumed in a minute, "and Doc too. Gone. The fire was—"

"Fire?" Rob said urgently, sitting up again. Only now was he remembering his last moments of consciousness. Fire. Screams, some of them his own. "The fire took the house and—"

"And the Doc," nodded Salinger. His chair creaked again.

The news knotted Rob's gut. A spasm of remorse, then sorrow, took hold of him.

"And—" Rob's voice broke. He could not say it at first, and then suddenly he could. "Elizabeth?" It came out like a plaintive cry. He was seeing the face, feeling the warmth of her body. Elizabeth. "Was she . . ."

The man's brows knitted into one thick straight line. "Elizabeth?" he repeated.

"Elizabeth Arbor."

"Oh, the Arbor girl." Creak . . . creak. He continued. "The fire . . . it was a real hot hell-hole. I saw Doc's body on fire. I saw you. You were out cold on the floor by the window. I didn't see any girl. No."

Rob's eyes began to chase a loudly buzzing fly around the room. Faded flowering wallpaper hung as a backdrop to the performing insect. White patterned drapes. A bookcase with a few dark old books inside. A white vase holding artificial flowers. A huge Bible on the bedside table. Both men stared at the Bible for a while.

"Am I at your house?" Rob wondered after a while.

"Yeah, I brought you here. I didn't think you'd want to go to the clinic." Salinger laughed harshly.

"Why wouldn't I want to go to the clinic?" Rob asked.

"Because of them. They run the clinic, don't they?"

"Who are 'they'?"

He gave Rob a long look. "Well, now, that's an interesting question, isn't it?" he muttered, making the rocker creak. "I guess we here in Millhouse have never really looked too closely at that particular question, eh?"

"No," Rob agreed hesitantly.

"Not that we haven't felt their presence. The unseen host sort of thing. The boss the ghetto workers slave for. You know what I mean . . . they call him 'the man.' You don't always know who 'the man is though, do you? It can seem to be one person and then again you can be all wrong. I guess. Yeah, I guess." Creak . . . creak . . .

Rob said, "Who did you think the man was?"

"Well, now," Salinger said heavily, "I guess we all thought it was Norris Caine. Mr. Norris, I was told to call him once. I was delivering some furniture to 'Mr. Norris' then. But then again at the plant it was 'Mr. Caine.' And it was Mr. Caine who everybody said kept the town up. Made sure everybody ate, everybody who wanted one had a job."

"Nice man, right?" Rob murmured, thinking his sarcasm was contained.

"No, you're right, he was a real son of a bitch," Salinger said as though Rob had been the first to put the label on Caine. "You know, he ran people out of town if they weren't 'cooperators.' He burned houses. Sometimes the people were still in 'em. But you didn't say anything. Not if you intended to go on living in Millhouse. And eating. And working."

"So then Norris Caine *was* the man."

"No, I guess not."

"Why?" Rob dragged himself to a more upright seated position. The pain in his body centralized in his shoulders. His head continued to throb. "Why wasn't Norris Caine the man?"

"Because . . . can't you feel the evil? Norris Caine is dead and it's all still happening. The evil isn't dead. It's worse than it ever was. The cattle that died over the years . . . you remember the cattle? Then it was a few people . . . now . . ." Tears rolled down the man's face, but he took no notice of them, made no attempt to dry them as he went on. "My son, J.D., died last night because of that evil. I don't guess you knew."

"I'm sorry," Rob said through dry-caked lips.

"Yeah, I know. J.D. and the Doc and all the others. And you can feel something building up. You even know where you shouldn't be fooling around. The Town Council . . . the clinic . . . I wonder now over the years just how many pints and quarts and gallons of my blood did I give to those people anyway?"

Salinger stopped rocking in his chair now, his face frozen in the impassive ashen mold of guilt and sorrow, the shock of what he, the father, had done, as if the horror of it were almost engraved in his forehead, wrinkling from the sudden downcast eyes.

Cautiously Rob asked, "Why did you think they wanted it? The blood, I mean."

Salinger's eyes came up slowly. "At first, I thought it was for our own blood bank. The town's. Then word leaked out . . . some of the men who worked there . . . there was never any real blood supply available. No matter how fast it went in, that's how fast it came out. Now what do you think about that?"

"I . . . ah . . ." Rob's mind raced. He was trying to calculate how much of his knowledge he dared entrust to this shell-shocked man.

"Now what do you think about that?" Salinger repeated, rocking backward and forward again. Almost dreamily, he muttered, "I wish Norris Caine were alive. If he were alive, I'd know the bastard was 'the man.' If he were alive, I'd know who to blame for the evil. I still wouldn't know what it was all about, though. Isn't that something?"

Rob watched him. "Why is that?"

"Because I never wanted to know, that's why. We in Millhouse are divided into two groups. Those that want to know and them that don't. The ones who wanted to know, those were the ones who wanted to be big shots. Didn't care if they lost their souls."

"So then the rest of you—"

"We're as bad as the big shots," Salinger

interrupted. "Maybe worse. What we are is cowards. You know, I never stopped to think you can lose your soul just as easy by being a coward as a big shot. One of them monkeys with their eyes and their ears and their mouths covered. I never thought about that."

"But if Norris Caine were alive . . ." murmured Rob, testing the water.

"If he were alive, then I'd know he killed my son. Then I'd kill him," said the man calmly. He had apparently finished his days as a coward.

Rob's eyes went to the clock, an oaken one, clacking monotonously over the desk in the corner. It said a few minutes past five o'clock.

"Is that the right time?" he asked.

"You've been out all day," came a voice.

Rob's head suddenly spun dangerously. Still he swung his feet over the side of the bed and stood, hanging onto the bedpost. "I have to get dressed," he said simply, stating the need of his whole existence at that moment. "I have to get out of here."

Salinger uttered no protest, no suggestion that Rob should stay in bed. Instead he asked, "Where you going? Out of town?"

Rob tore the sweat-soaked shirt from his body and almost fell. He grabbed onto the bedpost again and reached for the clean shirt Salinger handed over. It was a largish white cotton short-sleeved shirt.

"No, I guess I'm staying on for a while," he murmured.

"Oh," nodded Salinger. And as Rob's eyes held his, he sensed a question. "What is it you want to know?"

"Just where is the Town Council these days?" Rob muttered, feeling some vitality work into his body.

"Something's stirring at Tony Rizzo's house," Salinger said. "I drove this town over this morning, coming home. Seemed like I was seeing the whole place with new eyes. Seeing myself with new eyes. All I kept asking myself was Why?" The tears ran smoothly down. "Why did I let Norris Caine put food on my table? There were those who didn't, you know. There were those who picked up and left town. And then there were others. Well, I told you about those burned-up houses . . ." The man's voice died away.

"You say you wish Norris Caine were alive," Rob said, zipping his pants. He stood there on his own balance, hanging onto neither post nor bed.

"Yes. Well . . ."

"And if he were alive, you said you'd like to kill him . . ."

The man started to say yes again, but didn't. There was something in Rob's eyes that took his voice away. The two men looked at each other for a long time.

Something was stirring at Tony Rizzo's house. Rob, too, had driven the town over.

Beside him, silent, long-jawed, sat Salinger. He wasn't as old as Doc had been, but seemed older. Calmer, too, as though he had lost all ability to feel fear. As though he had lost all there was to lose.

"Not many cars on the road," Rob said.

"It's one of those afternoons," Salinger said as if Rob should know what he meant by "one of those afternoons."

By this time it was after six-thirty. Rob glanced nervously through the windshield. Overhead the sun had dropped a notch lower in the sky, and he knew they were entering that stretch of time that would soon yield to twilight.

He slowed the car. Tony's house was no more than two hundred yards ahead and to the right. It was shielded by a clump of trees, a curve of the road. After thinking about it, Rob pulled onto the last intervening side road, drove alongside a field, then braked to a stop and removed the key to the ignition. Salinger was already getting out of the car, not waiting for an explanation. Rob offered none. Instead he reached into the backseat, removed the sack containing hammer, cloth, nails. Salinger picked up the container of gasoline before Rob could take it. Both men turned without a word and headed through the field.

"Late in the day," Salinger grunted when Tony's house appeared over the squat hill that was the last barrier between themselves and the house.

"Yeah, I know," Rob returned, wiping away the sweat that had already built on his forehead.

"Maybe tomorrow . . ."

"Who in the hell knows if there'll ever be another tomorrow," Rob said tersely.

"Look," said Salinger. "I got nothing to lose. I was thinking that you—"

"I got nothing to lose either."

"Okay, then."

The men approached the house cautiously, but only silence greeted them. There was not a car, not a sign of the activity that Rob had observed less than an hour ago.

Rob prowled around the back and found the back entrance and windows sealed securely.

"Hell, they've been nailed shut," Salinger said, peering through into the dark kitchen.

Without a word, Rob took out the hammer and sent it flying against the base of the window. Glass flew. The sound was anything but muted.

"Goddamn you, Norris Caine, I'm coming to get your ass," he muttered through clenched teeth and struck a second blow. More glass went scattering across the grass. Three more swings of the hammer and Salinger was able to open the window, cutting his thumb severely in his efforts. Blood dripped. Neither man reacted.

Rob said, "I'm going through first. Here, let's stand that beer case on its side, then . . ."

An instant later, they stood together in the back hallway, listening.

"It sounds quiet . . ." Salinger strained to

hear some half-imagined sound. Ahead of him Rob paused, then quickly turned and took hold of the door leading to the basement.

"Wait!" Salinger cried, spinning around to face the kitchen. "Somebody's in there. Do you hear? Listen."

"I don't hear anything."

"Listen!" Salinger insisted. Eyes locked on the entryway, he slipped his hand in his pocket and produced a small gun.

"Hold on," Rob said, moving beside him.

"Sons of bitches," Salinger muttered. "I'll kill every last one of them before they get me." Waving the gun in the air he yelled out, "Whoever you are, I've got a gun! I'll blow your fucking head off if you try anything funny."

Rob took hold of him. "Calm down," he ordered, forcing Salinger around to face him. The man's eyes were wide. "You can't lose control on me. Not now."

Salinger appeared to be listening, but not to Rob. "There's someone in there, I tell you." He jerked his arm free, started for the kitchen.

"We're wasting precious time." As Rob approached the doorway, he could see the light in the kitchen had grown dimmer; the sun had dropped lower in the sky.

Salinger had already moved into the room and stood near the counter, gun raised, ready to fire. Abruptly he turned, and as he turned, he hollered: "Watch out!"

Rob jumped aside as Salinger, his nerves

completely shot, pointed the gun toward the closet door. Both men froze, watched the door slowly open. Rob would not remember later which came first. The sudden stink of death, or the shriek that erupted from Salinger's throat as Jack Gardner fell from the closet, his skin white, his body dead weight as it crashed facedown on the floor.

"Jesus," Salinger breathed. "*Jesus . . .*"

Rob hesitated, then knelt beside the body, making sure that Jack Gardner was dead. There were no outward signs of violence, no marks on his neck. Rob's mind raced. Heart attack? he wondered. If so, then why leave his body in the closet? Unless . . . unless they were planning to come back for him. Or—his next thought stopped him cold—or they left him to join Caine after the sun went down.

"They've killed one of their own," Salinger muttered, moving closer.

"Yeah. But why?" Rob stood, unable to put it all together.

"He probably crossed them," Salinger said, his voice calmer now.

"After all these years?"

Both men stood silent for a moment. Then Salinger said, "We all have a breaking point."

Rob's eyes had already traveled back to the basement door. It seemed like any other door, no secrets hidden behind it, no evil. Just an ordinary goddamn door whose brass knob gleamed in the soft light; a door he had passed fifty times in the last few days as he went from living room to kitchen, and then back again. He pictured Tony Rizzo now, sitting in the living room. Both of them talking. As boys, as adults, the world around them normal and safe.

"Do you think Caine's down there?" Salinger asked.

Rob hesitated. "There's only one way to find out."

Moving slowly, they entered the hallway.

29

Deputy Jimmy Collins should have known something was wrong weeks ago. He certainly should have viewed Ned Taylor's death with more than a curious eye for the macabre. But he was a rookie, after all, only a year on the job. To him, death was still more of a fascination than a disturbance.

But the sight of Sheriff Jones hanging from a rope tied to the lowest beam of his living-room ceiling, his eyes open and bulging, his tongue blue and protruding—that sight sent Collins into the bathroom where he vomited.

After pulling himself together, he returned to the living room and reread the note he had found. It was the sheriff's handwriting. "Salino's death was my fault. I cannot live with the guilt."

Now, as Jimmy removed the rope from around the sheriff's thick neck and lowered his body onto the couch, he knew something was terribly wrong in Millhouse.

All day the streets had been empty. Only Ronny Hubbert and his son had moved in and out of their house, loading their two vans with belongings. Mrs. Hubbert and her youngest son crouched more than sat in the front seat of the smallest van and watched. Eric Knopf had appeared briefly to talk with Hubbert. He too had his family in the car.

After a brief exchange, the two men shook hands, slapped each other fervently on the shoulders. Then both car and vans drove off together.

Jimmy Collins hesitated now, too shaken to move, to call for assistance. But who was left to call? Salino was gone. The sheriff was gone. He was the only one left.

The sheriff was staring at him. Slowly Jimmy reached over and closed the glassy eyes. Then he sat there, unable to move. The room, when he next looked up, was nearly dark. Twilight had fallen on Millhouse. And with the changing of light, Jimmy had the odd sensation that he would never again see the light of day.

Shuddering, he broke down and wept.

30

The basement steps fell away into the darkness below. And Rob thought: *Caine is down there. Oh, yes.*

He was experiencing that same sensation of hibernating evil he'd experienced in the Caine house only yesterday. A cold, chilling sensation that rose on the musty air and rode there, filling his nostrils, causing his mind's eye to focus too hard on the unknown. On the possibility of his own death.

Ah, poor boy. Is that it?

"What?" Rob said sharply, wheeling around.

"I said, we'll need a flashlight." Salinger

hovered behind him, peering over his shoulder.

"We don't have time. Let's just keep going." Rob grasped the handle of the gasoline can tighter as beneath his feet the stairs creaked, and he glanced under the staircase and saw only a stack of old newspapers. Rapidly he descended to the bottom, willing the crucifix he wore around his neck to pass some of its power into him.

At the bottom of the steps, Salinger, stopping heavily behind him, took hold of his arm. Without speaking, he nodded toward the small narrow window. Only a thin ray of light filtered through.

"We'll have to hurry," Rob said, and Salinger nodded.

Deep shadows had already claimed most of the basement. Rob stepped forward without further hesitation, and Salinger followed, gripping the handle of the hammer.

When they reached the center of the room, both men paused and glanced at each other in bewilderment. Rob saw a steady stream of sweat running down the side of Salinger's face, as constant as a river, and everything in him went cold.

The basement was empty.

Salinger lowered his hammer, the tension partially leaving his face. "They're not here," he said. The words came out almost as a devout wish.

"They must be here," Rob insisted. "Because I can feel them."

Quickly he scanned the room again. Nothing behind the furnace. Nothing against the farthest wall. Except . . . he looked closer now, and realized he was staring at a door. He moved forward; Salinger went with him.

The large slab of wood, now that he examined it, was less than two feet wide and ran from floor to ceiling. It appeared to be a covering for a closet, nothing more. Dried mortar had oozed between the stonework around it. Rob felt its surface, then tapped. It returned a hollow sound.

"It's sure as hell a door," Salinger grunted from behind him.

Yes, Rob thought. But where was the knob? He glanced to the side and saw the spine of a hinge. Then he saw another: two hinges.

"The hammer," he whispered. "Give me the hammer."

"Hurry," Salinger said, glancing again toward the window. "For chrissakes, hurry."

Rob inserted the claw of the hammer between the door and the bricks, and pulled. The door resisted, then loosened, then with a screech of hinges opened.

A gleam of light shone through the crack, then a glimmer of metal. As the door swung farther open, two coffins were revealed, resting side by side beneath the low slung roof of a small chamber. The room released a rancid odor, vile and nauseating.

"Oh, God," came a whimper. The voice belonged to Salinger, who stood stark still, trembling, near hysteria. His whole body resonated a fine tremor, but his hands were pathetic fluttering things, more like wild birds than hands, obviously beyond his control.

Rob unslung the sack from his shoulder, took out a second hammer, and handed it to Salinger. It was a lighter hammer than the one he held, its claws sharp as knives. Perhaps, Rob thought, grasping at the hope, its touch would drag Salinger back to sensibility, or at least quiet those pathetic fluttering hands.

Salinger pushed the hammer away. "I can't," he whispered.

"You've got to," Rob insisted. "For your son. For Doc and the others. I can't—I can't do it alone."

Salinger looked at him, his head shaking slowly. Rob could see that he was crying and that the tears ran down his face and dripped from his chin. He seemed oblivious to Rob, to everything but the two coffins.

"One of them is 'the man,'" Rob said, not letting himself speculate on who the other might be. "The one who rules your life. End it, Tom. Now." Rob took hold of his arm and found that Salinger had almost quit shaking. Still, he tried to pull away.

"No," Rob said. "You have to stay, you have

to help me!" He waited, knowing that everything depended on Salinger now. How much time? he wondered. He glanced to the window. Nearly dark.

Suddenly, almost pulling Rob over, Salinger wrenched the hammer from his hand. "Let's do it," he said, and broke into an hysterical laugh. It was a sound ragged with hatred and disdain. He held no respect now for his quarry, and that, Rob thought, was the key to salvation.

31

Together they moved into the small, airless chamber, its confines narrow and crowded with Jack Gardner's tools. Salinger threw open the lid of the nearest coffin. Julia Caine's face appeared —a withered flower, but her cheeks were still flushed, her lips a ruby red.

Salinger stood over her, cursing softly, while Rob moved to the next coffin, fearing the worst. Fearing that he would find Elizabeth in that coffin. *Elizabeth*, and not Norris Caine.

Ahead of him the casket seemed to float upward, rise, imponderable and potent, suspended like some titantic symbol, vast and black and evil.

Hands trembling, he reached out. The lid of the coffin rose easily.

"Tom!" he exclaimed, his voice shattered with a mixture of relief and fear. "It's him!"

Salinger came around and they stood together staring down at a face neither had seen for a decade, but one both remembered. A still handsome face, high cheekbones flushed with color, blackened thin lips moist and still bearing even in sleep a triumphant smirk. Hands resting on his chest, his rings came forth like flames of fire, his long fingers locked into each other—as if in mocking prayer.

"The son of a . . ." Salinger began, but never finished. Instead he took a cloth and poured gasoline over it. As he stuffed the rag into Caine's mouth, he said, "Burn forever in hell, you bastard!"

Rob thought he saw a change in Caine's still countenance. He hastily placed the nail center of his forehead, raised the hammer. There could be no doubt. Caine's blackened lips had flexed downward. Salinger quickly lit the rag.

Flames erupted at once. So did Norris Caine.

"Watch out!" Salinger cried.

Caine's eyes and arms and mouth all opened out in one furious thrust. As he began to rise, Rob brought the hammer down. The nail went two inches deep into his forehead and Norris Caine screamed.

"*Nooooo*! You can't do this!" he wailed, the

rag in his mouth already bitten half away.

Rob brought the hammer down again, crushing his skull, too frightened and out of control to hit the nail cleanly.

As he brought the hammer down once more he heard a blast of gunfire. And then another and saw Salinger standing there pulling the trigger on his hand gun as he pointed it directly into Caine's face.

A raw expulsion of breath wheezed through the vampire's throat, his head snapped back. Yet he refused to relent, kept coming. And suddenly it was not a nameless, sightless fear that held Rob enthralled, but the fear of his own death.

It was the clarity of that fear that held him, and then released him. Filled with blind panic, he groped for the pickax propped against the wall.

As Caine lunged, Rob lifted the ax over his head and brought it down hard. Caine screeched, some wild and unintelligible babble of frustration. His hands went to the ax, pulled.

Salinger fired off two more rounds, the bullets shattering Caine's cheekbone and jaw.

Smells now, horrid, putrifying, began to release themselves from his body as he tried in desperation to remove the ax from his chest. Suddenly the color left his face, his lips tightened. His eyes closed and then opened as he sagged to his knees inside the coffin. At the same instant, blood began trickling from the corners of his mouth, running down his chin.

Yet his eyes still glared, revealing his contempt for his two adversaries. His mouth, still half-stuffed with the burning rag, opened, spewing forth not words but ideas.

Whatever is killed becomes the father. Idiots! I am your father! Drink, eat, the world as food feeds on itself. As I shall feed on you. On you!

As Salinger pulled the trigger again, Rob ripped the crucifix from his neck and held it out.

Caine rose up, groaning in agony. Then, with a convulsive scream, began to expand his chest.

"I will kill youuuuu—"

His scream rose and both men watched as his chest opened like the dried peel of old fruit, but the ax held. As he twisted, his breath came in erratic gasps, then deep-throated moans, until at last he fell on his back, his eyes closed and his face contorted.

Then all movement stopped.

Except for his tongue which slipped from between his lips. Like a dog in heat, he licked himself. Licked at the blood covering his face. A hideous rotating of extended flesh and tissue that grew slower, and slower, until . . .

All that remained was a basilisk mask, frozen in horror.

32

"Is she in there?" Rob cried out from the farthest bedroom.

"No," Salinger replied, his voice still shaken.

Julia Caine had succumbed to death quickly, almost as if she had welcomed it, and now the only thing on Rob's mind was to find Elizabeth. He rushed back into the downstairs hallway. Salinger was just starting up the stairs. The last rays of twilight filtered into the house through the front windows.

"There could be others up there," Rob said. "We've got to be careful."

"That's why I've got these." Salinger held

up several dowels from a chair, each of their ends splintered into a fine point. "The next son of a bitch comes at me is gonna be as dead as those two downstairs."

"Let's go," Rob said.

When they reached the second-floor landing Rob clutched the claw hammer tightly and swallowed. Salinger stood next to him, staring down at the dark red stains on the carpet.

"Something's been going on up here," he whispered.

And Rob could feel his desperation expanding, feel all hope die as the hallway suddenly shrank into darkness. Night had come, totally and completely. Panicked, he looked toward the first bedroom door. Then his eyes traveled farther down the hallway.

He saw Tony Rizzo before Salinger did. He did not know where he came from, but Tony was there, his features emerging from the soft gloom, his body shrouded in the same black suit Norris Caine had been wearing. He was walking toward them, slowly.

Salinger turned abruptly, saw him coming.

Both men stood still at his advance, a somber figure, looking neither right nor left, but coming straight at them.

"Tony, is that you?" Rob called out, still not sure he was seeing clearly.

Tony stopped twenty feet away from them, no more, staring at them in silence. Then, "Go back," he said. "We don't want any more trouble. Leave now, while you are still able."

Rob watched as Tony's lips started to part, his teeth becoming visible. *Oh, dear God, no . . . no, not you.* Rob could feel the whole of his existence disappearing. Everything that he ever believed in dying right before his eyes. "Please, Tony," he called out. "Let me help you. We're friends . . ."

"Elizabeth is mine now," Tony said. "Leave us in peace."

Rob could feel Salinger beside him, his muscles tightening, expanding, as he readied himself.

What followed took only seconds. There was a quick flash of movement as Tony sprang forward. The light wood in Salinger's hand gleamed as he rushed past Rob to greet him.

"No!" Rob screamed, trying to stop him. Too late.

In one swift movement Salinger drove the stake into Tony's heart, twisted. Tony's onrushing roar became a wild bellow, then turned to a gurgle; a torrent of red appeared across his shirt, a brightly flowing curtain melting across his chest.

Without removing the stake, Salinger rose on his toes and drove it in deeper. Impaled, Tony screamed. Then he dropped to his knees. Convulsive heaves wracked his body, the veins in his neck bulging, arms flailing as he toppled over on his side, the blood gushing from the wound.

Dimly Rob heard Salinger say, "You check

in that room. I'll check in here." Still Rob did not move. Instead he knelt beside the man who had been his friend, listened to his shallow breathing. Slowly Tony lifted his head and then dropped it backward. His eyes were like the empty windows of an abandoned house as he searched for Rob's face, found it and focused on it.

"Tony," Rob said, gently squeezing the hand that tried to squeeze back. "You and I were always—" He swallowed and could not continue.

Tony—yes, it was the old Tony lying there now. The cold dead something had vanished from his eyes.

"What is it?" Rob asked, sensing that he was trying to speak; something hovered about his lips. Was it a name . . . Elizabeth?

Too late for words; Tony's face had suddenly turned a blue-white pallor, his mouth hung slack like a gaping wound. Too late for anything, as a final gasp escaped from between his lips. Then the atmosphere in the hallway was unutterably silent, a void in which nothing stirred.

A large hand descended on Rob's shoulder.

"Go on," Salinger said. "He wouldn't be needing you now. He's at peace."

33

The room, as Rob entered it, was bathed in moonglow. The window was open, the lace curtains lifted on a slight summer's breeze. Patterns floated against the walls, dissolved into darkness on the oakwood floor. Here and there an object drew a point of moonlight and gave off a gleam of illumination. Thus, a single gleaming floorboard drew attention to itself and a plain glass ashtray crystallized into beauty. Beyond these tokens of the night, the room was further touched with something intangible. An atmosphere that was almost visible, something composed of deep dark silence.

In the chair opposite the desk Elizabeth sat.

So quietly, so simply.

She was looking down at the floor, not at Rob. Her face was unreadable, a part of the shadows. The curtains moved gently behind her.

She said nothing. Waited.

She was wearing a delicate-patterned summer dress, a dark green scarf around her neck. Her hands lay limp in her lap, as if she had been drained of all energy, all life.

The next move is mine, Rob thought. But now that the moment had come, he was reluctant to act. Better just to watch her, to become a part of her waiting, to feel his own breath come in the slow waves that lifted and lowered her breast.

Through the walls there came the sound of Salinger blundering around in the next room. The curtains billowed once more, and then returned to their sedate vertical folds. Rob's hand closed tightly around the hammer. He had imagined so many ways of their meeting again, and yet none like this.

None like this . . .

At last she moved, her head rising with the strangeness and aura of another world. The look she gave him was small, lancing; of only a fraction of a moment, yet in that moment their eyes met. So cold, so calm.

Without warning, she stood and began walking toward him. Like a tired, long-traveled spirit, she came, walking—no, almost gliding around the bed, her feet seeming to scarcely touch the floorboards. Rob watched with transfixed gaze, straining to see every nuance on the pale face that drifted in and out of shadows.

Then, as if from a great distance, he heard her voice. Lush and soothing, it flowed over him like a surging tide.

"Rob . . . Rob . . . is that you? Is it really you . . ."

He let a few stunned, torn seconds pass. Let her come closer, her arms outstretched. Her lips moist and warm in the dark.

And then she was upon him. . . .

As she put her arms around him, weeping, dissolving into him, her lips pressing firmly against his, he could suddenly feel himself let go. He held her then, kissed her as desperately as she was kissing him, felt his tears blend with hers.

She stroked his hair, ran her slender fingers across his shoulders, his chest as though she could hardly believe he was there, as though she hungered for him more deeply than anyone could possibly hunger for another person . . .

"Liz?" Rob whispered, trying to draw back just enough to look deeply into her eyes.

Instead she pressed closer, kissing his eyes, his cheeks, the hair around his temples, the side of his throat . . .

He felt she was asking something of him, something she wanted him to give, rather than take from him. Some part of him that, once given, would join them forever.

"Yes," he heard himself whisper and could feel himself giving what she asked, committing himself. "It's all over, Liz. We're together now," he said, feeling the part of him that had been so long cold—that part of him that had frozen when he saw them carry his mother away so long ago—feeling that part of him thaw. He clung still closer to her, sensing that she was all right, would be all right, and it was that knowledge that had made him whole. He held her, and he felt her trembling, and cradled her, rocked her.

"You better leave now," Salinger said from behind them. He stood staring at Elizabeth as if viewing a ghost.

"She's all right," Rob said. "All right." He looked at Elizabeth with the bemused gaze of one who sees a loved one long missing and feared dead now miraculously returned to the living world.

Salinger nodded. "I saw headlights on the back road. They might be heading this way. Take my car. Don't stop for anything. Anyone. Just keep going."

"What about you?" Rob asked. But he could see Salinger's mind had already swung all the way into oblivion.

"I still have things to do," he muttered. His words had the effect of closing a book. "Now go on," he said. "Hurry."

34

They left the house moments later. But not before Rob had made Salinger promise to give Tony a decent burial. It was a furtive, almost desperate request, born out of guilt that usually grips a survivor after a disaster. The discussion took no more than seconds, out of Elizabeth's hearing—still, Rob knew that eventually he would have to tell her of Tony's demise—and Salinger listened intently.

In the end, Salinger agreed to do the best he could. He was standing in the driveway under the large elm when the car pulled away from the house. His hand came up in a small gentle wave of good-bye, and then fell limply at his side.

For Rob, the gesture said it all, lingered in his mind. It had been almost fatherly, as though deprived of his son, Salinger had shifted that paternal tie to Rob. *You go on now,* he could hear the man saying. *You go on. And God be with you . . .*

The road leading out of Millhouse was dark. No houses now, only a road that snaked upward over Nickle Mountain. At the crest of the hill Rob pulled the car off to the side and stopped. Elizabeth looked at him.

"Why are we stopping?" she wondered, her breath coming a bit harder as she saw the expression on Rob's face.

"Look behind you," he said, and opened the car door. As he stood there in the cool heady atmosphere of the ancient mountain, he could see flames rising in the night. Tremulous and golden, they rose from the house of Caine.

Perhaps, Rob thought, trying to understand what must have been in Tom Salinger's mind when he struck the first match, fire might bring purification, might neutralize the evil that had been. He tried to imagine Salinger going from room to room, lighting curtains, using chairs as kindling wood. In his mind's eye, he could see coffins burning, the body of Tony Rizzo . . . yes, perhaps . . .

"It was best," Rob said to Elizabeth who had come to stand at his side, her arm around him, her head on his shoulder.

They stood together watching the flames become visible in more and more windows, burn brighter, until a shower of sparks and smoke filled the Millhouse sky like a moving towering shroud.

"Time to go," Rob murmured, sensing how calm Elizabeth had become, how calm they both were, as though the brooding past had lifted from their shoulders and been blown away by the cold breeze of Nickle Mountain.

Rob helped Elizabeth back into the car and climbed in after her. A moment later they began descending the mountain, heading east, the fire behind them still raging, silent as it warmed.

EPILOGUE

However 1966 history is recorded, it will not be as a reasonable or peaceful year. There were shocking incidents of mass murder in every corner of the world: Thousands were killed in bloody outbreaks in Nigeria; tens of thousands were slaughtered following the downfall of President Sukarno in Indonesia; in the United States, in a two-week period of July and August, eight student nurses were slain by an intruder in Chicago, and an honor student at the University of Texas shot forty-six persons, killing sixteen.

Elsewhere, in a small town in Ohio, a young girl and four of her student friends were arrested for using farm animals as sacrifices in bizarre occult rituals. When questioned, she screamed: "We are 'the Chosen Ones!' UFOs, recent cattle mutilations, are the work of the devil. 'The Vampire' is organizing covens throughout the U.S. to supply himself with blood he needs for sustenance."

For Rob, the consequences of his excursion into his past continued as a sort of macabre fantasy, something not unlike a child's nightmare that would not go away as neatly as Tom Salinger had burned away two square miles of Millhouse.

For memory is impervious to matches, and only time has a way of fading it, if we are lucky, of smoothing the sharp edges, until finally it can no longer lay claim to one's future.

At the crest of Marriott Dunes near Hollywood Beach in Florida, Rob looked out over the sand to where Elizabeth stood by the sea. The sunlight highlighted the long red strands of hair that played gently on the winter's breeze, tangling it in a fine mesh across her face. Her slender body looked rejuvenated and full of peaceful calm. Sweeping the hair from her eyes, she started to walk slowly toward him.

Behind her, the deep blue-green water rolled lazily onto the beach in soft, rounded crests of white-capped waves. Gulls called out, the sky was vast and peaceful and benign.

Journeys end in lovers' meeting, Rob thought, and in so thinking, so hoping, he bounded up and began jogging toward her. She saw him coming and smiled. Then she was running too, her arms outstretched, as they always were, for him.